PENGUIN BOOKS

The Code Girls

Daisy Styles grew up in Lancashire, surrounded by family and a community of strong women. She loved to listen to their stories of life in the cotton mill, in the home, at the pub, on the dance floor, in the local church, or just what happened to them on the bus going into town. It was from these women, particularly her vibrant mother and Irish grandmother, that Daisy learnt the art of storytelling.

The landscape of north Norfolk captivated Daisy's imagination. With its sweeping skies and vast, empty beaches it is the perfect backdrop for a saga, a space big enough and wild enough to stage a drama about women working in code-breaking during the Second World War.

By the same author

The Bomb Girls

The Code Girls

DAISY STYLES

PENGUIN BOOKS

PENGUIN BOOKS

UK | USA | Canada | Ireland | Australia
India | New Zealand | South Africa

Penguin Books is part of the Penguin Random House group of companies
whose addresses can be found at global.penguinrandomhouse.com.

First published 2016
001

Copyright © Daisy Styles, 2016

The moral right of the author has been asserted

Set in 12.5/14.75 pt Garamond MT Std
Typeset by Jouve (UK), Milton Keynes
Printed in Great Britain by Clays Ltd, St Ives plc

A CIP catalogue record for this book is available from the British Library

ISBN: 978–1–405–92436–8

For my sweet boys, Patrick and Oscar Tarling,
'Peeps' and 'Cherub' in Vancouver.
Love, Dodo!

PART ONE

1941

1. Ava

'Friday dinner time,' thought Ava, as she tucked her long, dark hair under her cook's hat and checked her reflection in the small, cracked mirror hanging on the canteen wall. Even smeared with grease, the glass revealed the irrepressible sparkle in Ava's dark blue eyes. She beamed her characteristic wide-open smile, which revealed her small, white teeth and a charming dimple in her left cheek. She was taller than most of her girlfriends, long-legged and shapely with a full bust, softly curving hips and a willowy, twenty-inch waist. Ava was fortunate; her strong frame and athletic build were down to hard work and plenty of walking in all weathers on the wild Lancashire moors.

With her voluminous hair neatly tucked under her cotton hat, Ava wrote the day's menu in white chalk on the canteen noticeboard; two years ago, Friday's menu would always have been fish, cod and haddock freshly delivered from Fleetwood market. Ava had quickly learnt how to skin and fillet fish, but that was before the outbreak of war and the start of food rationing. Nowadays, it was impossible to buy enough fish to feed a family, never mind two hundred mill workers. As rationing got tougher and tougher, Ava had tried variations: parsnip fritters, corn-beef fritters, fake sausage fritters – mince (very little) mixed with oatmeal and herbs made a tasty fritter. But on a Friday, the workers, predominantly Catholics, didn't eat meat; it was a day of abstinence. The best and most popular alternative to fish

3

was Ava's delicious 'scallops', fresh local spuds washed, peeled and thickly sliced then dipped in a thick, creamy, yellow batter made from dried eggs combined with milk and water. Deeply fried in a vat of fat, Ava served the golden-brown scallops with mushy peas or butter beans and pickled red cabbage. It made her laugh when customers asked for chips as well.

'You'll sink like a brick with all them spuds inside you!' she teased.

'You've got to have chips on a Friday, cock,' one of her customers said with a wink. 'It's a bugger we can't 'ave fish like in't th'owd days, but your scallops are bloody beltin'! Give us another, wil't?'

Ava smiled as she dropped a few more of her scallops on his plate; she loved these people and she loved her strong, tight-knit, hard-working community. Half the people queuing up for their dinner lived within a block of Ava, in identical red-brick terraced houses, stacked back to back, row upon row, and reaching up to the foothills of the moors which dominated the landscape of the mill town. Everybody knew everybody else's business; it couldn't be otherwise when outdoor privies were shared and women gathered at the wash house to swap gossip and smoke cigarettes while they did their weekly wash. Then they'd hang it out on washing lines threaded across the network of backstreets, where children played under the wet sheets that flapped like ships' sails in the breeze. The neighbours' over-familiar questions about her future had recently become both an irritant and an embarrassment to Ava.

'So when are you going to get yourself conscripted, our Ava? All't lasses in't town have gone off to do their bit for't war, but you're still here. Can you not stand thowt o' leaving us, like?' neighbours and relatives alike teased.

Ava had self-consciously assured them she was definitely leaving; there was no choice: female conscription was obligatory for women between the ages of eighteen and thirty. Women were being deployed all over the country, and most of Ava's friends had already gone – some to munitions factories in Yorkshire and Wales; others had signed up to work as land girls in Scotland – but Ava had held back. She felt guilty, of course; would people think she was trying to duck out of war work, that she was unpatriotic? She was, in fact, fiercely patriotic and passionately believed in committing one hundred per cent to the war effort, but she was determined to do something big, something bold, something that would push her to the limit in her sacrifice for king and country. Three months after female conscription had been authorized by the government, Ava was well aware that she had to do something soon, otherwise the Labour Exchange would be on her tail and find war work for her.

'Ava! Check on them apple pies, lovie!' Audrey, the canteen boss, yelled, as the workers settled down on long wooden benches that ran alongside scrubbed wooden tables to eat their meal.

Ava dashed over to the huge oven, where her pies were browning nicely. She was looking forward to seeing what the customers' reactions would be when they tucked into their puddings. She'd added a surprise ingredient. Last night, she'd ridden Shamrock across the moors to her favourite spot, where wild winberries grew in abundance. Leaving the mare to crop clumps of tough grass, Ava had collected a large amount of the small, fruity berries, and she'd mixed them with baking apples, then covered the mix with a thick pastry crust. As she inspected the pies, she could see rich purple juice seeping through the edges. They would taste delicious served with custard, but she'd have to warn Audrey to cut thin slices if every worker was to have their fair share of her pudding.

Ava loved the Lancashire moors, especially at this time of the year, late spring, when the days were long and the nights were warm. Once work was finished and tea was cleared away at home, she'd change into a pair of baggy tweed trousers and head for the hills. Just a short walk up an old cobbled lane lined with oak and ash trees and Ava was on the moors, where, most evenings, she rode an old cob mare that belonged to a local farmer. He'd asked her if she'd like to take care of his horse Shamrock, who needed exercising now that his daughter had left home. Ava wasn't an experienced rider, but she was certainly not going to turn down the offer. Luckily, Shamrock was willing and patient with Ava, who took many a tumble as she learnt the hard way how to make the mare walk, trot, canter and how to keep her seat over the bumpy moorland terrain. Ava and Shamrock developed a trusting, companionable relationship, both of them enjoying their rides over the rolling moors, with only the skylarks and curlews for company.

It was while she'd been up at the farm the previous evening, tacking up Shamrock in readiness for a ride out, that she'd caught sight of the local newspaper, which had been left lying around by the farmer in the tack room.

WOMEN WORKING IN COMMUNICATION CENTRES

Ava laid down Shamrock's reins and hurried over to read the article.

As the war rolls on, more and more women are required to fill the spaces left by men who have gone to fight on the front line. Conscripted women are needed for training in communications, decoding, Morse, tracking, signalling, administration, interception and mapping intelligence in military-command control centres. Training Centres offering intense six-month training are opening across the country to provide women, potential code girls, with the necessary skills for this vital war work.

Ava's deep blue eyes blazed with excitement. With her heart beating double time and her pulse pounding, she let the paper drop into her lap and gazed out over the open stable door at the arching blue sky.

'*This* is what I've been waiting for,' she said out loud. 'I could be a code girl!'

The first spare moment she had, she dashed into the Labour Exchange in the high street and marched boldly up to the desk.

'I want to be a code girl!' she had announced, with a proud ring in her voice.

The woman behind the desk raised her eyebrows.

'Code girl?' she asked.

'I want to work in communications,' Ava explained. 'Please can I sign up?'

'What's your present employment?' the woman asked.

'Canteen cook.'

There was no doubting the shock on the woman's face.

'Canteen cook!' she exclaimed.

Ava nodded.

'At Dove Mill. I'm second in charge,' she added with a proud smile.

'Cooking isn't exactly the right kind of background for a communications trainee,' the woman retorted. 'They'll be looking for more academic lasses, them with a bit of schooling behind them.'

Ava's eyes flashed with indignation.

'Women are doing jobs nobody ever expected them to be doing all over England right now – why shouldn't I?'

The woman nodded.

'I'm not going to argue with that,' she replied, handing Ava an application form and a pen. 'Fill this in. When it comes to "present employment", you must state your current job.'

'But –' Ava protested.

'You can add that you want to train in communications because you feel you have an aptitude for it,' the woman quickly explained.

Smiling happily, Ava filled in the form, writing 'Canteen Cook' as her profession but adding in big bold capitals that she wanted to switch to communications:

'I want to be a code girl, as I believe it's far more beneficial to my king and country than me cooking in the Dove Mill canteen in Bolton.'

'That should do it,' she said, as she returned the completed form to the woman at the desk.

'Don't build your hopes up, lovie,' the woman advised. 'Be prepared to knuckle down and do anything that's required.'

'I'll knuckle down to anything,' Ava said with a winning smile.

The woman watched Ava walk away. She was a stunning girl, but good looks didn't always pay dividends. With a war on, people got what they were given and did as they were told.

'I've enlisted as a code girl,' Ava proudly told her boss the next day.

Audrey looked up from the mound of pastry she was mixing and burst out laughing.

8

'And what's a code girl when she's at home?'

Standing by the massive industrial oven, stirring a mince-and-onion stew bulked up with root vegetables such as swede, parsnips and turnips, Ava reiterated what she'd read in the paper.

'It could be anything from operations, tracking, signals, administration, interception, decoding, Morse – even working in military-command control centres,' she said with a bit of a swagger.

'Sounds too much like bloody spying to me!' Audrey joked. 'Here, roll that lot out,' she added, pushing half the pastry across the table to Ava. 'Roll it thin, mind. We've two hundred hungry mouths to feed; a little must go a long way.'

As the two women at either end of the table rolled and cut pastry to fit into huge tin trays, Audrey continued, 'How are you going to cope with all that brainy stuff?'

'I'll learn,' Ava said with conviction. 'I really want to improve myself.'

'Well, good luck to you, lass, but I bet they turn you down,' Audrey said, as she poured the cooled mince-and-onion mix into the trays, now lined with pastry. 'It's not like you went to grammar school and got a good education.' Audrey slapped a pastry crust on top of the filling and neatly nipped in the edges. 'Them stuck-up communications toffs will be looking for brains, certificates and qualifications – none of which you've got, Ava, love!'

Ava smiled confidently.

'Don't worry, Audrey – I'll be a good code girl; it's exactly the war work I've been looking for.'

A fortnight later, Ava was packing her small, cheap suitcase, helped by her mother, who was carefully folding her few dresses before laying them on top of Ava's freshly ironed blouses and new tweed skirt.

'Do you think you've got enough frocks?' Mrs Downham asked.

'They'll do for now,' Ava replied, wrapping her two pairs of battered shoes, which her mother had polished till they shone, in the newspaper.

'I wish I could have bought you a warm twin set,' her mother said wistfully.

'Mam!' Ava cried. 'Stop worrying; it's a communications centre, not a fashion school.'

Seeing the tears welling up in her mother's eyes, Ava took hold of her hands.

'I'll write every week,' she promised.

Her mother nodded sadly.

'I wish you weren't going so far away. Norfolk's the other side of the country, miles away from here.'

'I have to go where the government sends me,' Ava pointed out. 'You should be thrilled it's only Norfolk; I could be in Scotland felling trees like Marjorie Todd from round the corner!'

Her mother gave a bleak smile.

'I always knew this town wasn't big enough for you,' she said, as she stroked her daughter's long, dark hair. 'You were made for better things.'

'Mam, this isn't about daydreams, this is my contribution to beating Hitler,' Ava said with a laugh, and kissed her mother's cheek.

Before leaving, Ava had to say goodbye to Shamrock, something she'd been dreading doing since the moment she'd signed up. The old mare's excited whinny did nothing to lift Ava's spirits.

'Hey, sweetheart,' she said softly.

Shamrock nudged her softly in the chest.

'I haven't forgotten,' Ava murmured, as she produced the mandatory carrot, expected on every visit.

As Shamrock contentedly crunched on it, Ava gulped back the tears that were threatening to overwhelm her.

'I don't know how to say this, sweetheart,' she said. 'You see, I've got to leave you.'

Oblivious to the changes that were about to unfold, Shamrock snickered, then nuzzled Ava's arm. Even though Ava had found a nice, local lass to replace her, she still felt guilty about leaving Shamrock. How could you explain to a dumb animal that your life was about to change for ever. Ava thought about the thousands upon thousands of young men who had joined up in September 1939, when Prime Minister Clement Atlee had announced that England was at war with Germany. How many lives had been shattered by their departure? How many homes had been broken, and families wrecked, by the loss of a loved one who never came home?

Sighing, Ava bent to kiss Shamrock's soft, velvety muzzle. Her sacrifice amounted to nothing compared to that of the soldiers, sailors and pilots who were risking their lives fighting the enemy in planes, ships and on land, in armoured tanks. Two years in, and the war was not going well; Britain was ill-prepared and ill-equipped when compared to the organized might of the Third Reich. The evacuation of Dunkirk in May 1940 had shown the true grit of the British. They'd launched thousands of boats into the North Sea on the hazardous mission to rescue soldiers from the Normandy beaches, but the losses on that fateful day had cut deep, as did the continual bombing of Britain's major cities. The nation, no longer gripped with the irrefutable belief that it would win the war, began to fear the worst: an invasion.

'Which is why we all have to do our bit,' Ava said, swiping away sentimental tears with the back of her hand. 'I'll miss you, sweetheart,' she whispered, and kissed Shamrock for the last time. Turning, she briskly walked away, leaving the old mare neighing shrilly behind her.

Ava's last day at home was fraught with emotion. Her little sister kept bursting into tears, and if her mum packed her case once, she packed it twenty times. Their last meal together was eaten in an awkward silence, with none of the usual family banter and easy teasing. It was a relief when tea was over and Ava could busy herself with washing-up while her parents gathered round the big Bakelite radio, where the news reader announced in a grim voice that Operation Barbarossa was underway, the Germans were marching on Russia.

'Bloody 'ell,' said Ava's dad, as he puffed hard on a Woodbine. 'There'll be no stopping the buggers now!'

'The Russians are bound to put up a fight, they're not going to take it lying down,' Mrs Downham insisted.

'Aye, but what guns and weapons have they got against the Huns?' Mr Downham pointed out. 'It could end up a bloodbath for the Bolshies.'

'Thank God it's the summer – at least they won't be fighting in five feet of snow,' Mrs Downham murmured.

Ava boiled up some milk and made cocoa for them all, then sat as usual by the coal fire, with her parents on either side of her.

'We'll miss you, our lass,' her dad said softly.

Ava took hold of their hands.

'I'll miss you, too.'

She would miss them for sure, but – she thought rather guiltily – there was a wonderful new world waiting for her in Norfolk.

The next morning, Ava settled her suitcase in the netted luggage rack of the compartment she was travelling in, then leant out of the open window to smile at her family, who stood on the platform with heavy, sorrowful faces.

'Write!' her mum sobbed, dabbing away her tears with a hankie.

'Don't forget me!' yelled her little sister.

'Take care of yourself, lass,' her dad cried, as the heavy steam train pulled out of the station.

'I love you!' Ava shouted, through a belching cloud of black smoke.

As the platform receded, Ava sat back in her seat and sighed. The goodbyes were over; her adventure was beginning! Having never travelled further south than Rhyl, Ava was wide-eyed as she peered out of the window at the ever-changing countryside. The wild northern moors gave way to the Peak District, with its tidy grey stone farmhouses nestled neatly between green fields, where sheep grazed.

'What wouldn't I give for one of them woolly lambs roasted with potatoes, Yorkshire pud, mint sauce and gravy,' said a young lad in a soldier's uniform on the opposite side of the carriage.

'That's never going to happen,' said an older soldier, who was sitting next to him, puffing hard on a cigarette. 'Them animals will be made into mince and spread thin across half the county. I can't remember when I last had a solid piece of meat put in front of me,' he added, and took a greaseproof parcel out of his overcoat pocket.

'Fancy a beef-paste buttie, sweetheart?' he asked with a wink.

'In exchange for one of my carrot buns,' Ava replied, opening a small tin she'd packed with home-made buns.

'That'll be a rare treat,' said the soldier. He bit into the bun and nearly swallowed it whole.

'You, too,' Ava said, proffering the tin to all the soldiers in the carriage.

By the time it had done the rounds, there was only one bun left, but the soldiers each gave Ava something in return for her kindness: half an orange, a piece of chocolate, a soggy sandwich, a cigarette and cold tea from a bottle.

The cheery soldiers got off at Peterborough, where Ava changed lines. On the slow train to Norwich, her heart began to pound with excitement. She had to keep reminding herself that this was war work, her sacrifice to save the country from fascism. The only problem was, it felt more like a great adventure rather than a painful sacrifice, and she was having trouble keeping the smile off her face. A third and final train took her to Wells-next-the-Sea on the north Norfolk coast. As Ava walked along the platform, she felt the sea air blowing breezily around her and tasted sea salt on her lips. Her stomach flipped with nerves as she joined a few girls standing outside the station.

'Are you going to Walsingham Communication Centre,' a cheery, red-headed, young woman asked.

Ava nodded.

'Join the queue, we're waiting for a lift.'

The lift turned out to be a rickety old jeep.

'Hop in, ladies. I'm Peter, gamekeeper-cum-gardener from Walsingham Hall.'

As he piled their luggage on the roof, the new code girls

squeezed in tightly beside each other. Instead of sitting side by side, they sat on benches facing each other, and when Peter cranked the gears and the jeep bounced forward they all fell towards each other, almost into each other's' laps.

'Hold on tight!' he warned, too late.

Though the sun had set, the light lingered in the eastern sky. Peering through the window, Ava could see the towns-people had dutifully pulled down their black-out blinds. Peter drove to the hall without any headlights to guide the way.

'How do you know where you're going?' laughed one of the girls.

'Instinct,' Peter replied, without taking his eyes off the twisting road for a second.

Ten minutes later, Peter took a sharp left turn and swung into a drive flanked by elaborate metal gates gilded with an elaborate coat of arms.

'That's the hall,' Peter said, dropping down a gear to make his way up the drive, which threaded through a deer park. Even in the half-light, Ava could see fallow deer grazing under ancient oak and horse-chestnut trees. They rattled over a cattle grid, then, with a swoop, Peter came to a halt in front of Walsingham Hall. Ava caught her breath. She'd expected a big place that could accommodate a lot of people, but she hadn't expected *this*.

'It's beautiful,' she breathed, as she stepped out of the jeep and gazed up at the majestic building that towered before her.

'One of the finest stately homes in the country,' Peter said proudly. 'Just wait till you see it in the daylight. It's a sight to behold.'

As the girls tumbled out of the jeep, Peter called out, 'Make your way indoors. I'll follow with your luggage.'

With their feet crunching on the gravel drive, the trainees pushed open the heavy front door and entered the elegant marble hall, which was decorated with ancestral portraits hung in huge, ornate gold frames.

'Nobody mentioned we'd be billeted in Buckingham Palace!' giggled one of the girls.

Her laughter faded as a grim-faced woman dressed from head to toe in black approached.

'Your accommodation is in the south wing,' she said, in a voice that bristled with contempt. 'Follow me.' Then she quickly moved off, as if she wanted no association with any of the newcomers.

'Who's she?' Ava whispered to Peter, who was staggering along with as many cases as he could carry.

'Timms, the housekeeper,' he gasped, under the strain of his heavy load. 'She doesn't like you,' he added with a wink.

'She's made that perfectly obvious,' Ava replied.

The makeshift dormitories in the south wing had been built in what must have been a series of connecting drawing rooms, all with high ceilings decorated with swirling stucco plasterwork and floor-to-ceiling windows draped in blackout blinds.

'In there,' barked Timms, before turning her stiff-as-a-ramrod back on the trainees and walking away, disapproval evident in every step she took.

'She's a regular bundle of laughs!' tittered the cheery red-headed girl.

'Don't worry, you won't be seeing much of her,' Peter assured them with a chuckle.

'Thank God for that,' thought Ava.

The yawning girls selected their bunk beds, then made their way along the dark, bewildering corridors to the bathroom, which had a line of sinks running along one wall and a line of lavatories running along the opposite wall.

'Oooh!' exclaimed an impressed trainee as she switched on a tap. 'Hot and cold water – more than we get at home.'

'Thank goodness!' joked another trainee, as she dashed into the nearest cubicle. 'One minute longer and I would have wet myself!'

Ava cleaned her teeth, washed her face, then dabbed her skin with a few blobs of Ponds Cold Cream, a parting gift from Audrey. As she settled herself in a bottom bunk, Ava pulled a blanket and a scratchy, starched single sheet over her body, then looked nervously up as the woman on the top bunk bounced around, causing the bed springs to sag and twang over Ava's face.

'Will I ever get to sleep?' she wondered, as a few girls started to snore. A few even sniffed, as if they were crying.

Ava eventually slipped into a deep, exhausted sleep, and the smile that had been on her face all day remained there through the night. It was the smile of a girl who just couldn't wait to see what tomorrow would bring.

2. Ruby

Ruby didn't know which was worse, being below stairs with Mrs Timms looming about with a face like concrete, or serving supper to the irritable Walsingham family, who'd been literally kicked upstairs to the first-floor suites in order to free up the whole of the ground floor for the communication trainees and their tutors.

Small but shapely with a long, jet-black bob and almond-shaped dark brown eyes, twenty-year-old Ruby enhanced her looks by colouring her full, pouty lips with bright red lipstick, a colour much favoured by her favourite film star, Jane Russell. Ruby had grown up on the Walsingham estate. Her family lived and worked there and after leaving school at the age of fourteen she'd followed in their footsteps and been taken on as a maid. There was very little about the Walsinghams that Ruby and her family didn't know.

She knew Lady Diana had a drink problem; Ruby removed the empty bottles of sherry and brandy from her ladyship's sitting room every morning. She knew Edward, heir to the Walsingham title, and who had so far avoided joining up, enjoyed shooting parties and driving round the countryside in an expensive open-top sports car. Ruby knew Lord Walsingham had a mistress in London and Lady Walsingham had a more local admirer, on the Sandringham estate; she also knew that Lady Annabelle, the Walsingham's youngest daughter and a genuinely nice person, was generally disliked by her family.

Unlike Timms, Ruby did not believe that the Walsinghams were related to God; they were simply her employers. She would serve and feed them, empty their chamber pots and light their fires, but she didn't revere them like the old servants, most of whom had recently been packed off by Brigadier Charles Rydal when Walsingham Hall was requisitioned by the government for vital war work.

'The house is full of common girls,' raged Lady Diana, lifting her glass in order for Ruby to top it up.

'Don't you think you've had enough?' her elegant mother, Lady Caroline, remarked. 'You've been drinking since lunch time.'

'I need it after what I've just witnessed,' Diana said, as she poured half a glass of claret down her throat. 'They're wandering around the house like they own the place.'

'They do!' her brother, Edward, snapped. 'Since the government have taken it upon themselves to steal our home, those commoners have more ownership of it than we do.'

'I can't believe you let them do it, Papa!' Diana cried, and turned to her father, who was glaring at the soup that Ruby had placed before him.

'What in God's name is this, Ruby?' he asked.

Ruby sighed inwardly; she had known when she saw the tureen of grey soup that it would not go down well.

'Potato and parsnip, sir.'

'Isn't that what you feed pigs?' Edward sneered, letting the soup on his spoon plop messily back into his bowl.

Ruby felt like saying, Haven't you heard of rationing? Half the nation is hungry! You should consider yourself bloody lucky to have something to eat – and somebody to serve it to you, too! Instead, out of force of habit, she muttered apologetically, 'Sorry, sir.'

As she removed the untouched soup and replaced it with some stringy lamb, sprouts and roast potatoes, Diana, now well on the way to being drunk, grumbled on.

'When can we reclaim our home, Papa?'

'When the war is over,' he replied, as he set to on his meat, which was mercifully improved by Ruby's rich gravy.

'But the house will be in ruins by then,' his daughter moaned.

'If we lose the war, it won't even belong to us. Hitler might relieve the king of his Sandringham estate and hand Walsingham over to some "deserving" Gestapo general. We could be out on the street,' Edward spitefully pointed out.

Diana's pretty but sulky face paled.

'Just when I thought things couldn't get much worse,' she fumed.

'Things will get much worse, darling,' her father boomed from the head of the table. 'We're losing this war. For two years we've made no real progress, unlike the Germans, who are successfully claiming most of Europe. The Luftwaffe are far superior to our RAF, their naval fleet is stronger, their army better prepared. We Brits are failing badly.'

'You do surprise me,' Edward sniggered.

Lady Caroline looked at her son with cool disdain,

'It's a pity you studied at Cambridge and not Sandringham; you should be fighting on the front line like all the Walsingham sons before you.'

'Oh, God! Not that again,' Edward groaned, as he pushed back his chair and lit up a cigarette.

'Mummy's quite right,' Diana chipped in. 'Your Cambridge chums are a bunch of intellectual snobs who spend their time just talking about the war. I simply don't know how you all get away with it.'

'There are alternative ways of fighting a war other than running at the enemy with a bayonet,' Edward retorted, and blew a cloud of smoke into the air.

His lordship slammed down his silver knife and fork with a resounding clatter.

'Oh, pray do tell me what these "alternative ways" might be?' he demanded.

Ruby shifted slightly on her feet. Although she was used to being an 'invisible' servant, she nevertheless wondered, as she had many times before, why the aristocracy assumed that servants had no ears, and no feelings. Their lord and ladyships could say whatever they liked in front of Ruby, or any other servant, for that matter, but if she so much as breathed a word of tonight's conversation she would be fired on the spot.

Edward turned to his father.

'Alternatives such as translating, planning, communication, subterfuge, radar mapping, to mention a few,' snapped Edward.

'That's not what *real* men do,' Diana scoffed. 'Anyway,' she added with a nasty smile. 'Half of your Cambridge chums are queers!' She rocked unsteadily, with drunken laughter.

Edward rose and pushed back his chair so violently it fell to the floor.

'I've had enough!' he said, and walked out of the room, leaving Ruby to pick up the chair and set it back in its correct place.

'Shall I serve dessert, madam?' she asked Lady Walsingham, who wearily shook her head.

'Leave it, Ruby, we'll serve ourselves.'

Ruby lifted a large tray piled high with plates and cutlery. 'Will that be all, Your Ladyship?'

Lady Caroline nodded, but Diana called out, 'Bring coffee soon.'

As Ruby negotiated the winding, dark back staircase that led to the kitchen, she considered what an enormous amount of hard work this new arrangement was going to entail. Previously, the family had been served meals in the magnificent dining room overlooking the formal gardens, which at this time of the year were fragrant with standard roses, lilies and carnations. Now transformed to a utilitarian canteen for the code girls, the dining room was only a flight of stairs up from the kitchen, but with the family relegated to the first floor, their meals had to be carried up and down the precipitous back stairway three times a day.

'Mostly by soddin' *me*!' Ruby grumbled to herself, staggering under the weight of the wobbling tray.

The brigadier in charge of the new communications centre was on a tight budget, sacrifices had to be made; he had told the staff this on his arrival. Within days, he had fired the old servants, retainers who'd worked below stairs under the iron rule of Timms, the housekeeper, and Dodds, the family butler, for decades. He had ruthlessly streamlined the kitchen staff down to leave only Ruby, Dodds and Timms. If he'd had his own way, he would have fired Timms and Dodds, too, but both had lifetime tenure at the hall, a privileged position they blatantly exploited.

The housekeeper was sitting in the scullery when Ruby came in with the heavy tray.

'You'd better set to and wash those things up,' she snapped.

'You could help. I've got to take coffee up,' Ruby snapped back.

'I won't lift a hand to help,' Timms seethed. 'Not after what that brigadier did to me and my staff.'

'He couldn't afford to keep on servants who weren't up to the job,' Ruby reminded her.

Timms's eyes flashed in anger.

'How dare you say my staff were inadequate.'

'They were sitting it out to their retirement, I knew it, you knew it and the brigadier knew it, too,' Ruby pointed out.

'He's made his cuts,' Timms retorted, a twist of a smile on her thin face. 'Now all he's left with is *you*!'

Ruby couldn't argue with that. As she set an old coffee pot to bubble on the Aga, she recalled the brigadier's words.

'I appreciate you can't single-handedly produce food for all of us, Ruby, and I realize that you'll get no or little help from Dodds and Timms,' he'd added, with a knowing smile, 'but I promise I'll recruit new staff just as soon as I can.'

Ruby had stared at him in surprise. He was a stern-looking man in his late thirties with a military bearing and a clipped voice, but when he smiled his whole face softened and his large brown eyes lit up. Unfortunately, the smile came and went as quickly as a light going on and off.

'Until then,' the brigadier continued brusquely, 'we'll just have to grin and bear it.'

Knowing that there would have been discontent upstairs, Timms slyly asked, 'Did his lordship enjoy his supper?'

Ruby shrugged and turned away; she wasn't going to give the housekeeper anything to gloat about. Behind Ruby's back, Timms smiled; she was proud of her links with the Walsingham family, whom she'd provided with delicious cuisine for decades. She'd employed the best cook in the county, supervising the menus herself, buying in top-quality goods and using the finest produce, a lot of it from the estate. Cheese, cream, milk, locally reared meat, game shot on the estate: venison, duck, pheasant, wood pigeon, hare; vegetables plucked straight from the earth, fresh fish daily and exotic fruits grown in the greenhouse. It had been a time of plenty, and the Walsinghams' table had vied with that of the king's at Sandringham. Now all that largesse was a thing of the past, the Great Hall was in ruins, trashed by commoners and usurpers. Unable to accept the radical changes and deal with the demands of food rationing, Timms's cook had upped and left. Ruby wished with all her heart that Timms had moved with her, but the old bat, well aware of her rights of tenure, stayed on; it gave her a sadistic pleasure to not lift a finger while poor Ruby ran herself ragged.

Grabbing the coffee pot from the Aga, Ruby poured the steaming contents into an Edwardian silver coffee pot and placed it on a tray, alongside delicate china cups and saucers, sugar and cream. Heaving the loaded tray, she walked past Timms and made her way up the back staircase again, wondering what time she'd get to bed after clearing the supper, preparing breakfast for the trainees and sending out a grocery order for the following day's supper.

'One thing's for sure,' she said to herself as she puffed and panted up the stairs, 'I can't carry on like this – I'll be dead in a week!'

3. Walsingham Hall

Ava woke up with a start; the bed springs overhead twanged and bent as the hefty girl in the top bunk lowered herself to the ground and yawned loudly.

'Wakey wakey!' she called, and hurried off to the bathroom.

Ava hung back. Left alone, she listened to the new sounds around her: footsteps hurrying down echoing corridors, girls calling excitedly to one another and, from outside, riotous birdsong. She pulled the black-out blind by the bed, which flipped up to reveal rolling parkland and the stunning façade of Walsingham Hall. It had seemed large and majestic last night but spread before her now, brimming with sunshine, its golden brickwork and classical columns glowed with a luminous light that hurt her eyes. Flights of steps ran to the right and left of the elaborately carved front door, leading on to a circular gravel drive. Ava imagined horse-drawn carriages bearing ladies in crinolines and gentlemen in black suits and stove-pipe hats arriving for weekend parties a century ago. Spellbound, she stared at the Greek-style carved pillars that ran along the front of the house, each embellished with carvings of ancient gods.

'It's the most beautiful place I've ever seen,' Ava murmured.

Rolling over on to her tummy, she leant on her elbows so she could watch the deer grazing under the ancient oaks which flanked the curve of the long drive, which ended at a huge ornamental gate which, she remembered from last night, bore the Walsingham coat of arms.

Ava felt like she was on a film set, and that, at any moment, Laurence Olivier was going to swoop up in a Bentley with Vivien Leigh beside him.

The sound of a bell ringing made her jump out of bed and reach for one of her dresses, which she'd hung up before she went to sleep. Looking at them now in the lovely morning light made her heart sink; they were so limp and tired – and her shoes! She picked them up then dropped them back on to the floor: for all her mother's hard polishing, they still looked worn and tatty. She wondered how the other trainees would be dressed? Surely not all of them would be well off enough to afford a whole new wardrobe? There must be other girls from poor backgrounds like her own. Determined not to be cast down on such a glorious summer morning, Ava shrugged and hurried to the bathroom, where she cheered up when she examined her reflection in the mirror over the sink. Her long, rich-brown hair glowed with health, her blue eyes were big and bright, there was a flush of excitement on her high cheekbones and her teeth showed white and straight under her curved, smiling lips. Feeling nervous and thrilled at the same time, Ava ran down the winding corridors and joined the other girls in the old library, where a tall, military-looking man and a short, slim frowning woman were standing in front of the huge marble fireplace, both holding clipboards.

'Good morning, ladies – or should I say, welcome, code girls. I'm Brigadier Charles Rydal and this is my senior, Miss Cox.' The woman beside him smiled thinly. 'Before we have breakfast we need to run down the list of trainees to make sure you've all arrived safely.'

'You're the first to arrive. Some more new conscripts will join us later,' Miss Cox explained. 'Please respond when I call your names, then you're free to go into breakfast.'

Ava stood and waited as Miss Cox briskly worked her way down the list until only one girl remained in the now almost empty library: Ava.

'Where should I go?' she asked.

The brigadier checked the list. 'And you are . . . ?'

'Ava Downham.'

The brigadier frowned, still scanning his list. 'Your name doesn't appear to be here –'

Miss Cox interrupted him. 'She's downstairs, remember, sir?'

When the brigadier didn't immediately respond, she bossily reminded him, 'She's the girl from Bolton who's the canteen cook.'

'Ah, yes, now I recall.'

'You're upstairs – you should be downstairs,' Miss Cox explained.

Still thinking she was supposed to join other trainees, Ava asked, 'Can you direct me to the downstairs classrooms, please?'

Miss Cox sharply put her right.

'There are no classrooms below stairs, just the kitchen – you're the new cook.'

If she'd been hit with a sledge hammer, Ava couldn't have been more winded. Her mind raced, she couldn't believe she was hearing right.

'I think there's been a mistake.'

'I don't think so,' said Miss Cox sharply

'I signed up to train in communications,' Ava spluttered. 'To be a code girl!'

'You might have signed up for one thing, but you've finished up with quite another,' Miss Cox answered briskly.

Seeing Ava's eyes begin to fill up, the brigadier added in a kind but firm voice, 'We have a crisis; we have no cook and almost thirty people to feed. I'm sorry to disappoint, but needs must.'

Panic washed over Ava; they *must* have got it wrong. Steadying herself, she took a deep breath to calm her raging thoughts.

'I'm happy to do my duty, sir, but I did state on my conscription form that I was keen to work in communications. I know that's where my strengths lie.' She paused to look from the brigadier to Miss Cox. 'Are you sure there hasn't been a mistake?'

The brigadier shook his head. 'There's been no mistake, Miss Downham.' Before she could even open her mouth to protest he added firmly, 'Sorry, we all have to make sacrifices – there's a war on. Feeding vital war workers is just as important as learning communication skills.'

Again, Ava caught her breath. Although she was devastated, she knew that if she overstepped the mark and refused to accept his orders, he would have to take action. Bowing her head to hide the scalding tears that were beginning to roll down her cheeks, Ava dumbly nodded.

'Dodds will show you the way,' said Miss Cox.

Ava followed the butler below stairs; she couldn't believe that the subterranean labyrinth of dark, winding passages was to be her world henceforth. The mill canteen where she'd worked had large windows that opened wide and gave on to views of rolling moors; this kitchen, which seemed to sprawl from one gloomy room to another, had no windows. Water flowed into slop sinks, the only oven was a huge old

Aga and, worst of all, the tall, resentful-looking woman in black from the previous evening was staring at Ava as if she was a piece of dirt.

'And who are you?' Timms asked.

Angered by her rudeness, Ava attempted to walk past, but the woman blocked her path.

'Answer me!' the woman cried.

She was sick of being bossed about but Ava made a supreme effort to be polite to the arrogant woman standing before her.

'I'm the new cook,' she said.

Timms's eyes raked over Ava, taking in her poor clothes and old shoes.

'Are you indeed?' she murmured. 'And what experience do you bring to Walsingham Hall?'

'I've worked in a mill canteen for nearly five years, cooking for over two hundred workers,' Ava answered, with a more than confident tone to her voice.

'Canteen food!' scoffed Timms.

Ava had had enough now. It was one thing to be ordered to do kitchen work by the brigadier, but to be insulted, on top of that, by a total stranger, who hadn't even the manners to introduce herself, was seriously out of order. The tension in the room was broken by the appearance of a pretty young woman with black hair and lively, dark eyes who rushed into the kitchen bearing a loaded tray, which she plonked down in order to shake Ava vigorously by the hand.

'Welcome, welcome!' she cried. 'I'm Ruby, the maid,' she said with a wide smile.

Seeing the attractive girl making an effort to get between her and the dragon of a woman in black, Ava responded with words which nearly choked her. 'I'm Ava . . . the new cook.'

Ruby sagged with relief. 'Thank God for that!'

Timms scowled at the girls, who were smiling at each other.

'Well, this should be interesting, two girls cooking for thirty. Let's see how you manage that,' she said viciously.

Unable to hold her tongue a minute longer, Ava retorted, 'We'll manage just fine as long as you stay out of my kitchen!'

As a scowling Timms walked away with her head held high, Ruby covered her mouth to hide her laughter.

'I never thought I'd hear anybody tell Timms to bugger off.'

Ava was far from amused, though. After two altercations in rapid succession, she felt sick to her stomach. Slumping into an old Windsor chair, she sat with her head in her hands.

'Oh, God,' she wailed. 'I want to go home.'

Ruby put a comforting arm around her shoulder. 'Fancy a cuppa?'

Ava nodded and blinked back the tears; thank God she'd found an ally.

Ava's first few days below stairs were a baptism of fire, as she familiarized herself with a kitchen and domestic apartments that were simply 'out of the Ark!' as she put it.

Ruby gave her a tour of the maze-like passages, flinging open doors to numerous rooms. Ava shook her head in disbelief.

'How many rooms are there, and what are they all for?' she cried.

Ruby grinned at Ava's stunned face.

'They all have a purpose,' she said, and chanted out the function of each room. 'Washing, drying, ironing, sewing, prepping, storing, baking, chilling and freezing; rooms for linen, china, boots, shoes, silver, dogs, guns, servants, flower arranging and gardening.'

In the massive walk-in pantry, which had a huge, granite slab for cold storage, Ava incredulously examined the bottles, jars and tins which lined the shelves, which were as deep and numerous as a small library.

'I've never seen half of this stuff before!'

In the larder further down the corridor hung two dead hares and a couple of pigeons, all of which smelt high and meaty.

'Where did they come from?' Ava shuddered and grimaced at the congealed blood on the stone larder floor that had dripped from the game.

'Townie!' teased Ruby. 'They're from the Walsingham estate. Peter, the gardener, drops off any surplus kill whenever he can.'

'Ugh! But they're all bloody,' cried Ava, squeamishly.

'I've been disembowelling rabbits and plucking pheasants since I was a kid, used to get twopence for every carcass.'

'Good, you can be the pheasant plucker – I'll stick with the cooking!' Ava declared.

'The Walsinghams appreciate the odd game pie or brace of pheasants,' Ruby informed her. 'Believe me, there's nothing easier than shoving some buttered pheasants in the low oven of the Aga – they cook themselves and the RAF officers can't get enough of them,' she added with a wink.

Ava stopped dead in her tracks. '*What* RAF officers?'

Ruby tipped her head in the direction of the officers' billet. 'In the west wing.'

Ava shook her head again in disbelief. 'Nobody mentioned any RAF officers to me!'

31

Ruby shrugged as she replied, 'Don't worry, they come and go.'

'Exactly how many come and go?' Ava persisted.

'Depends,' Ruby said, and counted up on her fingers. 'Last month there were about six here on short-term leave; they're no trouble,' she assured startled Ava. 'They usually arrive after a bombing raid, hungry as lions, sleep round the clock, then return to duty back on the base.' She giggled and added. 'I quite enjoy serving supper to good-looking RAF officers!'

Ava continued her questioning. 'Where's the airfield?'

'About five miles away, at the far end of the estate – between two turnip fields!' Ruby replied.

Ava felt weak at the thought of how many mouths they had to feed. Where on earth would all the food come from?

'Maybe that old bat Timms is right.' She sighed heavily. 'Maybe we won't manage.'

Ruby frowned and shook her dark hair. 'This is our war work, Ava,' she declared fiercely. 'We might not be learning Morse and breaking codes –'

'If only!' Ava groaned.

'But we're feeding brave lads who risk their lives every day and every night for their country, and we're doing our best for the code girls, too,' Ruby insisted. 'We might be stuck skivvying below stairs, but it's our bit to beat Hitler and win this damned bloody war!' she finished, with a burst of passion.

Ava smiled at Ruby. Although she was small and slender, she had the heart of a warrior.

'You're right, lass,' she replied. 'Time for less moaning and more action.'

Ruby grinned. 'That's right. 'Keep calm and cook!'

*

Ruby's phenomenal efficiency facilitated Ava's entry to the world of 'downstairs'; she knew where every pot, pan, tureen, bread knife, glass, napkin, plate and ladle was kept. And she understood the weird, idiosyncratic workings of the ancient Aga, which had to be constantly fed with seasoned logs.

'It's a contrary bugger of a thing,' Ruby joked as she stoked it. 'But it works.'

She knew how to clear the kitchen flue and the slop sink waste pipe, how many buckets of coal had to be carted up to the first-floor sitting room every morning, what time her ladyship might want coffee served; in a blink, she could put her hand on a bag of starch, a tin of furniture polish, a packet of caustic soda, a potato peeler, a meat cleaver, a rolling pin, a pudding bowl or a soufflé dish. She could even predict what veg Peter would deliver every morning.

'How can you possibly know that?' Ava laughed as Peter walked in with exactly what Ruby had foretold.

'Salad, carrots, new potatoes, peas and the last of the asparagus,' Ruby chanted. 'It's simple, it's that time of the year. It doesn't take much, it's just knowing what the different seasons bring! Mind you, a lot of the estate produce goes to the local shops and markets. We can't hog it all, even though we have a hall full of hungry workers.'

'Just thank God for what we can get,' Ava said, as she shelled peas into a basin. ''Cos there's precious little fresh veg you can buy with ration coupons!'

Everybody living at the hall handed over their ration books to Ava, who prepared menus based on what she could buy with the combined points. Well used to planning menus using only rationed goods, Ava more or less cooked the same food for the trainees as she had for the mill workers.

Corn-beef fritters, shepherd's pie, cottage pie, parsnip soup, split-pea soup, cheesey baked potatoes, nourishing stews made from any left-over meat, with a bit of added Oxo or Marmite, curried carrots, Spam hash, cheese and potato dumplings, Lord Woolton pie, and numerous variations of pasties based on whatever Peter the gardener delivered to the hall.

Ruby, who was used to a more luxurious style of pre-war cooking, when every dish turned out by the cook swam in cream, sherry, brandy and butter, was impressed by Ava's ability to improvise plain but wholesome meals from very little.

'You have to make not much go a long way,' Ava explained. 'It's possible to feed a big plate meat pie to a dozen people if you cut it carefully and fill up the rest of the plate with chips and gravy.'

'Lord and Lady Walsingham are not going to appreciate plate meat pie, chips and gravy,' Ruby giggled.

Ava burst out laughing. 'Daft buggers! They don't know what they're missing.'

4. Maudie

'*Haben Sie wandte sich die Brötchen, Maudie, meine liebe?*'

'Yes, Papa. I've taken the bread out of the oven,' Maudie replied.

'And the cinnamon swirls?' her mother called from the shop, where she was laying warm rye bread in the shop window.

'Of course, Mumia.'

Maudie smiled to herself; she loved these early mornings in the bakery with her parents, chatting in German or Polish, or sometimes Yiddish, as they checked everything was in order before the bakery opened and the customers poured in. They didn't just come for the fine produce the Fazakerly family provided on a daily basis, they came for a gossip or a bit of sympathy, or sometimes just to have a good moan. This was the stuff of life to Maudie; a caring, sharing community where each neighbour looked out for the other. Growing up in London's East End, Maudie had witnessed the Mosley rallies, angry, shouting Blackshirts striding through her streets, claiming that fascism was an ideal belief. Like the rest of her heavily populated Jewish community, she had nothing but contempt for Mosley's men, and for the bourgeoisie, too, for that matter. Maudie had imbibed socialism with her mother's milk, and grew up with her father's passionate belief that all men were equal.

'Women, too, Papa!' Maudie often reminded him.

Maudie had arrived in England with her parents, seeking refuge from the growing terrors of the Nazis' anti-Semitic attacks, which were sweeping across Germany in the early thirties. Now twenty and a grown woman, Maudie was tall and slender with narrow hips and long legs. She had a mass of auburn curls, penetrating, intelligent, green eyes, a scattering of freckles across her pert nose and a wide, generous mouth. Her parents were proud of their clever, independently minded, beautiful daughter, though they constantly regretted that they couldn't afford to put her through university.

'A girl like you could be a lawyer, a doctor even,' her father often said.

'Oh, Papa, stop it!' Maudie would laugh at the tragic expression on his face. 'I don't care about university; I'm free to learn what I want. There are books in the library. I can educate myself while I help you and Mumia in the shop.'

Mr Fazakerley nodded and chuckled.

'The shop would close down without you. They used to come for our food but now they come to admire your looks, *liebling*.'

Mrs Fazakerley tutted loudly. 'Stop turning the girl's head, she knows how beautiful she is,' she said, and threw Maudie a look of pure love.

'My legs are too long, my mouth's too big and my eyes are the colour of lime leaves – I don't call that beautiful.'

Seeing the hurt look in her mother's eyes, Maudie put her arms around her shoulders and kissed her on both cheeks. 'But I'm glad you think so, Mumia.'

Mr Fazakerley was right; Maudie attracted customers because of her looks, her wit and her astonishing talent for baking. Since she was a child, she had loved working in the bakery alongside her parents, but it was as she grew up and started experimenting with new recipes that her creativity really took off. Maudie's cinnamon swirls, soft teacakes,

German fruit tarts, seeded Polish bread and Jewish flatbread, as well as the more traditional English cakes, pies and pastries she made, were never on the shop shelves long. Rationing certainly limited the variety of goods they could produce in the bakery, but that didn't stop Maudie trying out new recipes, which, though frugal in ingredients, were rich with inspired additions like spices, herbs, nuts and dried fruits.

The value of hard work had been instilled into Maudie by her parents, who remained grateful to Britain for opening its doors to them when they were in need. Like her parents, Maudie loved England with a passion; when female conscription was announced, she willingly volunteered, thrilled that her small effort might be part of a much bigger effort to defeat Hitler, the man who had driven her parents out of their homeland.

She knew her parents were dreading her going, she knew that leaving them and the family business would be a big wrench, but she also knew her parents wanted more for their prodigiously clever only child. It was time for Maudie to stretch her wings and fly. As she tapped the underside of a batch of fennel buns to see if they were cooked through, she realized she was nervous about telling her parents her latest news.

'Mrs Stein was saying her Lucy isn't settling down to work as well as she had hoped,' her mother said, as she laid rows of iced buns underneath the glass-topped counter.

'Not surprising, moving up to Yorkshire to build planes – the girl's always been timid,' her father replied from the bakery, where he was stacking hot cheese rolls.

Maudie took a deep breath; this was an appropriate moment to break her news. Without looking up from the tray of cinnamon rolls she was now glazing, she said brightly, 'You know the course I told you about?'

'In Norfolk?' her parents said in chorus.

'That's the one – they've accepted me.'

Maudie's mother stopped what she was doing. '*Liebling!*' she gasped.

Mr Fazakerley abandoned the cheese rolls. Maudie could see he was upset, but he kept a brave face as he asked, 'When do you go, my dear?'

'I've got to report right away, Papa.'

A slow, proud smile spread across his face as he replied, 'Then we must prepare you for your journey, *Schätzle!*'

Over the next few days, Maudie's parents went into overdrive. In between baking and serving customers, they helped their daughter sort out all the things they thought she would need. In the end, there was so much stuff laid out on Maudie's bed that her father had to go out and borrow a bigger suitcase from one of his customers.

'I'm sure I won't need so much,' Maudie protested. 'I'm studying communications, not going on holiday.'

'It will be cold in Norfolk, and foggy, too, it's damp so close to the sea – you will need warm clothes and boots!' her mother cried.

After hours of washing, ironing, polishing and starching, Maudie's case was finally packed. She'd even managed to squeeze her favourite books, written by Karl Marx and Sigmund Freud, in among her clothes.

'There'll be no time for reading, not with all the studying you'll be doing,' her mother said, removing the books. Maudie promptly put them back in the case.

'I'm going nowhere without my bibles,' she joked.

The customers were keen to hear Maudie's plans.

'A communications training centre in Norfolk,' her

mother said, with a proud ring in her voice. 'No more cooking and baking for my *liebling*.'

'We shall miss you very much.'

'You've always been a clever girl.'

'Time to use that brain of yours.'

'Oh, but the tragedy of having no more cinnamon custard tarts and fennel bread,' one old lady sighed.

'I'll be back to visit and bake for you soon, I promise,' Maudie said, hugging the old woman, who she'd known since she was a child

'God bless and take care of you, child,' the woman replied, wiping a tear from her rheumy eyes.

The worse thing of all was saying goodbye to her parents. They insisted on accompanying her across war-torn London. Rubble, sewage and shattered timber were strewn across their paths.

'God help us all,' Mrs Fazakerly murmured, as she stepped over a table that had been blasted out of a bombed block of flats.

They all tried to keep a lid on their emotions, talking about the weather, the price of the train ticket, asking Maudie if she had enough food for the journey.

'I could feed the entire train,' Maudie laughed, holding up the food hamper that her mother and father had sacrificed their food rations to pack with their daughter's favourite treats, including gingerbread biscuits in the shape of little cottages, the first things Maudie had ever made in the bakery. She'd been so small she'd had to stand on a stool to reach the table.

When the train thundered into King's Cross station, her father set about finding an empty carriage with no men in it who might trouble her. He tucked her up in her seat as if she was still the precious child they'd brought out of Germany, terrified at every step of the way that they'd be stopped and separated. When Maudie saw her father's hands trembling, she took hold of them and kissed them gently.

'Papa, I'll be fine. Please don't worry about me.'

A great plume of black smoke belched out of the engine and the train lurched forward.

'Get out quickly,' Maudie laughed. 'Or you'll be coming to Norfolk with me!'

Back on the platform, her father put a hand around his wife's shaking shoulders.

'I love you, my *liebling*,' sobbed heartbroken Mrs Fazakerly.

'Take care, my dear,' her father called, as the train pulled away.

Black smoke obliterated them from Maudie's view. She wiped tears from her eyes, reached into her hamper and drew out a nutty gingerbread biscuit; how fortunate she was to have such loving and devoted parents.

'I'll never let them down,' she murmured, as the train gathered speed and headed east towards the sea and King's Lynn.

Luckily for Maudie, she had no idea how her destiny was being decided; otherwise, she might have alighted from the train at the first stop. As the train bearing Maudie headed out of King's Cross station, overworked Ava was begging the brigadier for extra help.

'Ruby and I work an eighteen-hour day, sir, ordering, preparing, cooking food for everybody in this house – and you know we get no help from either Timms or Dobbs.'

The brigadier would have liked nothing more than to escort the resentful Timms from the building, but his hands were tied by the fact that she had permanent tenure at the hall. He couldn't share his thoughts with the overworked girl standing before him, her dark hair tumbling around her pale, tired face. Feeling guilty, he said, 'I promise I will do my utmost to find you another cook.'

Ava swallowed hard; if this was her war effort, she had to grin and bear it. At least she wasn't on the front line, being bombed by German artillery. Raising a weak smile, she answered, politely enough, 'Thank you, sir, we're at breaking point below stairs.'

When she arrived back in the kitchen, Ruby informed her that Timms had 'accidentally' dropped salt into the rice pudding, which Ava had used the whole day's quota of milk in making.

Ava tasted the salty rice and grimaced. 'We'd better knock up stewed apples and dried-milk custard to replace this muck,' she said.

Ruby heaved the vast pan off the Aga. 'Shall I give it to Peter to feed to the pigs?'

Ava vehemently shook her head. 'Drain it. We'll mix the rice with some mince and onions and make meatballs tomorrow,' she said.

Ruby leant forward to give her a quick peck on the cheek. 'Thanks for not letting Timms grind you down,' she said with a grin.

'She does grind me down,' Ava confessed, 'but I'll be damned if I'll show it!'

Upstairs, the brigadier was genuinely concerned.

'What in God's name can we do?' he said to Miss Cox. 'The staff below stairs are falling apart.'

Miss Cox raised her heavily made-up eyebrows to the

elaborately carved plaster ceiling, where intertwined cherubs kissed each other.

'I'd like to do something about it,' the brigadier continued, 'but where are we going to find a trained cook out here in the wilds of north Norfolk?'

Miss Cox cast an eye down the list of trainees due to arrive that day.

'I think help might be at hand, sir,' she said with a slow smile.

Maudie, alighting from the jeep wasn't quite sure how she felt about being billeted in a stately home with a drive the length of Buckingham Palace.

'Bit over the top,' she muttered, as she and the newcomers followed Peter, who was hauling their luggage into the south wing.

'Bloody gorgeous,' said the ecstatic girl beside her. 'Really posh!'

Maudie rolled her eyes. This wasn't a great start; she would honestly have preferred to stay in a Nissen hut rather than be surrounded by the baroque gilded statues standing on plinths in gloomy alcoves.

'Is that a naked woman next to a man showing his willie?' the same giggling girl tittered, as she pointed to a series of classical paintings depicting the Rape of Lucretia that ran along the length of the main hall.

'Well, it's not a banana!' her friend said, and the two of them broke out into shrieks of raucous laughter.

Desperate to get her companions' eyes off the classical rape scene on the walls high over their heads, Maudie quickened her pace.

'Better get a move on,' she said. 'We need to bag our beds.'

'You're right there; I'm Sheila, by the way. In'tit exciting?' she gushed.

'I hope so,' Maudie answered flatly.

The six new code girls were welcomed by Miss Cox, who swiftly ticked their names on her clip chart.

'All present and correct,' she said.

As the girls turned to go, Miss Cox drew Maudie aside. 'Could I have a word, please?'

Surprised, Maudie asked anxiously, 'Is there a problem?'

'We have a slight problem on our hands,' Miss Cox started.

One minute later, Maudie was reeling with shock.

'A *cook*!' she gasped.

Miss Cox's tone took on a sharper note. 'Those are your orders, young lady.'

'There's been a mistake!' Maudie cried. 'May I please see the officer in charge?'

Miss Cox turned away quickly.

'Very well, follow me,' she snapped.

Some moments later, the brigadier sighed as he listened to Maudie; no matter how strong her argument was, she would get exactly the same answer he had only recently given to Ava.

'I quite understand your disappointment, Miss Fazarkerley, but the best way you could help your country right now is to join the staff below stairs, because if the cook doesn't get help very soon she might well blow Walsingham Hall and everybody in it to kingdom come.'

Maudie's green eyes opened wide and she replied with a hint of a smile, 'This is a woman I have *got* to meet!'

5. Upstairs

Lady Diana, who could hardly stand up straight, on account of the bottle of black-market Bollinger she'd downed only an hour ago, was making her rather unsteady way to the hammock strung between two old elm trees on the family's private lawn, where, in previous summers, they'd held fetes, garden parties and high teas. She blamed her bore of a brother, Edward, for her excesses; he and his loathsome Cambridge friend had made lunch unbearable with their talk of war and government policies. Christ! She had felt a migraine coming on as their long-winded conversation drifted from Rommel and Goebbels to Churchill and Attlee. Would they ever return to the joy of trivial conversation? Famed for her style and beauty rather than her brainpower, Lady Diana withered in the company of intellectuals, and on this particular occasion she'd buried her boredom in an excess of alcohol.

Hiccupping slightly, she wound her wobbly way through the rose garden, around the ornamental lake, past the tennis courts and the outdoor swimming pool, to the private lawn, where she all but collapsed into the hammock. It didn't have quite the desired effect. For a start, it made her feel sick as it swung back and forth in the baking heat. and the nearby racket of a cranking engine simply wouldn't go away. Heaving herself up, she scowled and peered over the hedge to see what was making the noise. Her bad mood heightened when she saw it was an army truck with over a dozen excited young women on board.

'Bugger!' she groaned. 'More trainees!'

Diana watched the truck pull up at the front door of the hall and saw the giggling girls disembark, calling goodbyes to the soldiers in the cab. These commoners were treating *her* beautiful home as if it was Butlins holiday camp! They ate in her ancestral dining room, slept in rooms designed for lords and ladies, walked barefoot across their deer park, all the while lowering the tone with their common ways, loud laughter and endless chatter. The worst thing of all was the thought that this wretched lot of trainees would be replaced by another wretched lot in six months' time; women in cheap shoes carrying cheap suitcases would come and go like a bad smell twice a year until the bloody war was over.

'I want to die!' Diana wailed, as she flung herself out of the hammock and staggered through the grounds and back indoors, up the sweeping staircase to the first-floor suites which the ghastly brigadier had deemed suitable for the Walsingham family.

In the ornate drawing room, a third of the size of the one they'd previously occupied on the ground floor, she found her younger sister, Lady Annabelle, curled up on the rose-coloured sofa, reading a book.

'Oh, it's you!' she sneered in disgust.

Well used to her sister, Annabelle had no problem ignoring Diana, who in any case lit into her straight away. Weaving her way unsteadily across the room to the drinks tray, where she poured herself a stiff brandy, Diana drawled, 'S'pose you like those common little tarts downstairs?'

Annabelle sighed. She knew exactly what was coming, but out of habit she prevaricated. 'I've not actually met any of them yet.'

Diana threw herself into a large plush armchair and

surveyed her sister as if she was a piece of meat in a butcher's shop.

'Some might say you're pretty in a dull, English rose sort of way,' she started. 'Blonde hair, blue eyes – ruined by those god-awful spectacles you wear – overweight, too: you need to drop at least a stone.'

Annabelle closed her book and got up. She'd been here too many times not to know that this conversation was going nowhere good. Doling out humiliation was Diana's forte; she'd spent years lacerating her younger sister with cruel, barbed comments, but as the years rolled by Annabelle had learnt how to deal with it. She just walked away.

'Yes, off you go,' Diana scoffed as Annabelle headed for the drawing-room door. 'No doubt the bores downstairs will relish an earnest chat about the bloody worthiness of female conscription.'

Annabelle paused in the doorway. 'Even you can't dodge conscription, Diana.'

Diana's cheeks flushed with anger. 'Don't kid yourself! I can pull rank just like that,' she said, snapping her perfectly manicured fingers. 'You won't catch me filling shells or dragging bloody cart horses over muddy fields.'

'You might have no choice,' Annabelle said, and slammed the door hard behind her. Annabelle smiled to herself as she skipped downstairs. 'I think I won that round!' she said gleefully to herself.

Sometimes, Annabelle genuinely wondered if she'd been swapped in the Portland maternity hospital where she was born for somebody else's child. Lady Caroline often referred to her youngest child as 'a mistake'; in truth, Annabelle knew she was an unmitigated disaster. She didn't look like any of her family. As a child, desperate to find somebody to relate to, Annabelle had examined all of her ancestors' portraits hanging in the Great Hall and had come to the conclusion that she vaguely resembled a grand but slightly dumpy Lady Walsingham who had lived in the eighteenth century. It was cold comfort to think she was a throwback to the time of Queen Anne.

For a naturally gregarious girl, Annabelle had had a lonely childhood, with few friends to play with, except when she was at school, where she had been popular. At home, though, there was little to do apart from ride her pony along the beach or cycle through the woods to the family's summer house, set in the sand dunes facing the North Sea. Here, one happy summer, she had set up a little library and a desk, where she sat, gazing out to sea as she wrote her secret diary, which she hid under a floorboard. She cooked sausages and eggs on a Primus stove and made hot chocolate and tea. Alone, but perfectly content and relaxed, she would happily have holed up there all through the summer, but her brother, Edward, discovered her hideaway and kicked her and her belongings on to the beach, then padlocked the summer house so she couldn't use it again.

As Annabelle passed a large gilded mirror on the landing, she stopped to examine herself. Diana was right: she was a bit of an undistinguished English rose, and a bit on the plump side, but her pale blue eyes were pretty and she liked the way her fair hair curled softly around her heart-shaped face. Standing tall, she peered this way and that to check out her body. She was tall, with strong, athletic arms and legs, a full bust and curvy hips. She could easily drop a stone, as Diana had so bitchily suggested, but Annabelle made no secret of her love of good food and her passion for cooking. Her family frowned on it; women of her class did not lower themselves to cook, that was the job of the hired staff. Annabelle didn't give two hoots about protocol! Why couldn't she cook a meal, make a cake, bake bread? She'd cooked every weekend at boarding school, making teatime treats for her friends and fry-ups on Sunday mornings; she'd always cooked at her friends' houses, begging them to allow her the freedom of their kitchens, where she was in her element, putting together a Sunday roast or a great big creamy meringue. Why was she denied the pleasure of her own kitchen? The answer that came back was always the same: 'It's not the Walsingham way.'

The fact that she had no interest in or enthusiasm for clothes, fashion, balls, being a deb, grand houses, hunting, cocktail parties and seeking out an eligible husband incensed her family and further alienated Annabelle from them. The happiest years of her life so far had been at Cheltenham Ladies' College, where she had excelled at maths, statistics and physics. Annabelle had wanted nothing more than to study maths at university, but her father had declared that her expensive education had so far left her radicalized, political and far too independent for a woman of her class, and he wasn't going to shell out another penny on her.

'So what am I going to do?' Annabelle had asked. 'Waste away my life, waiting for some chinless wonder to propose to me – is that what you want?'

'I'd certainly like somebody to take you off my hands,' his lordship had retorted. 'Though what man in his right mind would want a rebellious young woman like you?'

Her mother had introduced her to endless wealthy young men, who'd shown no interest in the plain, bespectacled younger Walsingham daughter. When Lady Caroline's ghastly 'Get Together' evenings loomed, either in London or Norfolk, Annabelle went out of her way to make herself as frumpy and unattractive as possible. She would frizz up her hair or purposely cut her fringe too short; she would apply her make-up badly, smothering her cheeks with rouge so she looked like she was running a fever. She purposely wore clothes that emphasized her wide hips and podgy tummy. The overall look was deeply unattractive and caused any potential beau to fall by the wayside, which was exactly what Annabelle hoped for. If she ever had a relationship with a man, it would be a man of her choosing; she wasn't prepared to be paraded in the marriage marketplace just to appease her family.

When female conscription was announced by Ernest Bevan, Minister for Labour in the Churchill government, Annabelle was the only Walsingham daughter who was excited; her angry sister refused to enlist, but Annabelle, desperate to get away from her family and serve her country, was prepared to do anything! Her mother had insisted that she couldn't do common war work, like herding cows or filling shells with cordite; that would ruin the family name.

'Who cares?' Annabelle had asked. 'It doesn't matter what I do as long as it's something that will bring this awful war to an end.'

Diana had rolled her eyes at Annabelle's passionate patriotic outburst. 'Spare us the drama,' she'd mocked.

'A nice little job in the War Office would be more suitable,' Lady Caroline suggested. 'You never know, you might meet an eligible young man there. Wouldn't that be perfect?'

This time, it was Annabelle's turn to roll her eyes. Would her mother ever see her as anything other than marriage material? Restless and fuming with impatience, Annabelle had remained at home, waiting for the 'right job' to show up, quite unlike her dilettante brother and sister, who seemed to be drifting through the war as if it wasn't really happening.

Walking down the ornately carved wooden staircase that gave on to the Great Hall, Annabelle slowed her steps when she heard a male voice ringing out from down below. Crouching behind the shadowy balustrade, Annabelle peeped out and saw a group of trainees listening to a military-looking chap in a tweed suit. Leaning forward, she strained her ears to catch what he was saying.

'Welcome. I'm Brigadier Charles Rydal and, standing next to me, is your senior tutor, Miss Cox.'

Annabelle peered out further and saw a smart middle-aged woman, who then took over from the brigadier.

'The government urgently needs trained women to work in administration, messaging, signalling, information, encoding, decoding and transmitting.'

'We'll turn you out in six months' time, ready to do vital war work,' the brigadier added.

'You'll find your timetables and dorm assignments pinned up on the bulletin board. Our operational rooms are in the south wing. You'll meet your fellow trainees over supper, which is served at six thirty, prompt,' Miss Cox added.

Smelling fragrant cherry tobacco smoke drifting up the stairwell, Annabelle stood up and looked down at Brigadier Charles Rydal, who was puffing thoughtfully on his pipe. Hearing the stairs creak, he quickly looked up and saw a pretty, fair-haired girl gazing down on him.

'Can I help?' he called out.

Annabelle didn't reply. She slipped back into the shadows and so failed to see the brigadier addressing a pale-faced Maudie, who was still in a state of deep shock. Instead,

Annabelle skipped back up the stairs, smiling to herself; for sure Charles Rydal could help. This was *exactly* the work that she wanted to do; *exactly* what she'd been waiting for. It was a pity that the training took place in her own home, but that wasn't going to stop Annabelle from formulating a bold escape plan.

As she slipped into her bedroom on the first floor, Ava was setting tables in the elegant dining room, which had been transformed into a large canteen with Formica-topped tables and metal chairs. Stern portraits of long-dead Walsinghams glared down at Ava as she laid out cutlery for supper.

'The new occupants should have you lot rolling in your graves!' Ava muttered irreverently.

She'd overheard the brigadier's welcome to the latest recruits, and she'd had to force herself to stop being envious; she knew that cooking below stairs was her war work, at least for the time being, and she was determined to do it well, but every so often she couldn't help but yearn to swop her cook's black dress and pinafore for a tweed skirt and twinset, an outfit much favoured by the eager trainees. A hand gripping her arm made Ava jump sky-high.

'Ow!' she yelped.

'Sorry, Ava,' spluttered a red-faced Ruby. 'You'll never guess what Timms has done now.'

'What?'

'Come and see for yourself!'

Ava hurried after Ruby, who was now dashing breathlessly downstairs to the kitchen, where acrid smoke and the smell of burnt meat made them both gag.

'God almighty!' cried Ava, as she dragged the burning pan off the Aga. 'I left this simmering only ten minutes ago – what happened?'

'Don't look at me!' Ruby retorted indignantly. 'It's that old cow Timms, she must have put the pan on the hotplate while I was in the laundry room. By the time I smelt burning, it was too late.

'It's ruined!' Ava fumed.

'We can't turn our backs on the old bitch for a second!'

Swearing furiously under her breath, Ruby caught sight of Timms watching her. The housekeeper's expression was evidence of her vindictive delight.

'Don't say anything,' Ava hissed under her breath. 'Don't give her any more reason to gloat.'

The two girls held her gaze and Timms turned and left the room. Only once they were alone did Ava let out a loud groan, 'What the hell are we going to serve for supper now?'

'With a bit of luck, only the bottom will be burnt,' a bold voice rang out.

Ava and Ruby looked up in surprise; standing in the kitchen door, wearing a cook's uniform, was a tall, young woman with blazing auburn hair.

'We can make shepherd's pie with the good bits,' she said. 'I'm Maudie – c'mon, I'll help you peel some spuds!'

Ava and Ruby instinctively took to Maudie. Over the next few days, it became clear that she would shoulder the burden of working downstairs with humour and determination. There were, however, a few awkward moments when Maudie felt like she was in the way. Ava and Ruby had been working in tandem for weeks now and had their own routine. It was all new to Maudie. Sensing her discomfort, Ava had a quiet word with the self-conscious newcomer.

'I know we rush about like headless chickens,' she said one day as she poured tea for them both. 'With only two of us down here, we've got used to hitting the ground running every morning, which must make life difficult for you, when you don't know what's coming next.'

Maudie smiled shyly. 'It is a bit like that,' she confessed. 'It's hard to know where things are, this place is a Victorian warren. I got lost somewhere between the sewing room and the pantry the other day!' she admitted with a laugh.

Ava laughed, too. 'I was just the same. If it weren't for Ruby, I'd never have made my way around the place! Look, lovie, we're all in this together. Whenever you don't know something, just ask.'

Looking relieved, Maudie poured them both a second cup of tea. 'Thanks, Ava. I'll do just that!'

After a few weeks of getting to know her surroundings, both upstairs and downstairs, Maudie visibly relaxed and, as she became more comfortable in the company of her new friends, she entertained them by irreverently mimicking people she'd met in the hall.

'Who's this?' she said, and struck a tense, formal pose and said in a clipped voice, 'I'm trying to hide it, but I'm secretly in love with Brigadier Charles Rydal!'

'Miss Cox!' shrieked Ruby, wiping tears of laughter from her eyes.

'And this?' Maudie challenged, flinging back her shoulders and striding like a man across the flagged kitchen floor, booming, 'That's all I can find at this time o'te year, missus, sprouts, carrots and a lobster from yon marshes!'

'Peter!' howled Ava, as she rocked with laughter.

'Do Timms. Please do Timms,' Ruby begged.

Maudie thought for a few seconds, then drew herself up to her full height, pinched in her mouth and nose, scowled and peered around the kitchen before saying in a high, whining voice, 'I wouldn't lift a finger to help any of you shameful hussies. I work for her ladyship, and I'll work only for her ladyship till the day I die!'

The kitchen rang with shrieks of laughter, cut short by the appearance of Timms.

'What's so funny?' she snapped.

Ava, Maudie and Ruby, covered their mouths to smother their giggles.

'We've just been chopping onions for supper,' Ruby lied. 'It's brought us out in floods of tears.'

The three new friends couldn't have looked more different: dark-haired, blue-eyed Ava, with her direct, straight-talking, honest manner; green-eyed, clever Maudie, with her flaming auburn hair and strong political views; and small, slim, dark-eyed Ruby.

Her new friends' opinions often took Ruby aback. 'We women are Churchill's secret army,' Maudie said one day as they were rolling pastry for a dozen stringy-mince-and-onion pies. 'We're not allowed to fight with guns, but we can drive buses, work on the land, assemble planes and fill bombs. We're a force to be reckoned with,' she finished proudly.

The longer they worked together, the more Maudie's politics challenged the status quo that Ruby had previously accepted

'Why should we accept a master-and-slave society?' Maudie asked one day, as she mopped the flagstone floor. 'All men are born equal,' she said, repeating her father's favourite quote. 'And women, too, I always tell him!'

Ava looked up from scrubbing the slop sink with Vim. 'If

this sodding war proves anything, it's that class – middle, lower or upper – isn't worth that!' She snapped her fingers together with a loud click.

Ruby could feel a creeping sensation under her skin when Ava and Maudie spoke out so boldly; their words affected her so much, goosebumps appeared on her arms. Although she came from from a long line of Walsingham servants, she liked what Ava and Maudie had to say about equality. Added to which, the war was forging new ideas. Society was changing, established roles were being challenged by the millions of women who were now stepping into dead or absent men's shoes. Ruby realized she'd never been happier in her life. Below stairs had become a whole new world full of laughter and teasing, combined with endless hours of talk and discussion as they prepared one meal after another, day after day, seven days a week.

'You two should be running the government. You could put Winston Churchill out of a job!' Ruby laughed. She loved the chemistry that flowed between Ava and Maudie.

'I thought, thanks to female conscription, I had a job right here,' Maudie half joked.

'You have,' chuckled Ruby. 'It's just not the job you applied for!'

'I fancied myself as a code-breaker, yet here I am, stretching out ration coupons to feed trainees.' Maudie sighed.

'Well, as you know, I had no such expectations,' Ruby said bluntly.

Feeling embarrassed, Maudie and Ava exchanged a guilty look.

'Sorry, Ruby, no disrespect,' Ava apologized. 'It's not like we're moaning –'

'Oh, we are!' Maudie cried.

'But we've got to bite the bullet,' Ava quickly added. 'The brigadier was desperate for cooks, and we ticked the box.'

'Thank God!' Ruby laughed. 'Otherwise, it'd be me and Timms battling it out to the bitter end.'

'Well, seeing as I'm stuck down here in the bowels of the kitchen with just you two for company,' Maudie said with a cheeky wink, 'I suggest we use our versatile female brains to work out a more streamlined way of working.'

Ava threw up her arms in frustration. 'There is *so much* to do!' she cried.

'Exactly!' Maudie exclaimed. 'Which is why we've got to save on time and energy.'

Ruby frowned as she asked, 'How can we change things? People have to eat.'

Picking up a notepad and pencil, Maudie grinned at her friends. 'Sit,' she said, nodding towards the large, scrubbed kitchen table.

Pushing aside a basket of shallots and tomatoes Peter had dropped off earlier, Ava and Ruby obediently sat down on either side of Maudie, who started to write in her notebook.

'Four meals a day for twenty-five girls, two staff, the gentry upstairs and however many RAF officers might turn up,' she muttered, as she scribbled.

'We cook for just over thirty most days, and there's never anything left over,' Ava said.

'Breakfast's not such a problem since we went self-service,' Ruby remarked.

'It's dinner and supper that are the problem,' Ava groaned. 'There's just not enough time between clearing one meal and starting another.'

Maudie, who'd been drawing doodles of bread and cakes in the margins of her notebook, said, 'We could do a self-service tea, just like breakfast. Fresh seeded rolls with fish- or meat-paste spreads – that wouldn't gobble up the ration coupons.'

Ava smiled and nodded.

'Show of hands, ladies!'

All three shot their right hand up into the air.

Maudie turned a page of her notebook. 'On to lunches and suppers.'

'Soup and a main, or main and a pud, for lunch,' Ava said.

'Same for supper, but failing on account of never having enough time,' Ruby added.

'So we should go for a single-course supper,' Maudie suggested. 'Macaroni cheese, Spam fritters, veggie pasties – stodgy stuff that fills everybody up.'

'One course would make life so much easier,' Ava agreed.

Fired up now, Maudie urged her friends on. 'Come on, comrades, let's work out some daily menus based on our ration coupons and whatever we get free from the estate.'

'The estate deliveries are a bit hit and miss, depending on the time of the year,' Ruby pointed out. 'There's always plenty of veg and milk and fruit in the summer; we get some eggs, but not a lot, occasionally cheese. There's rabbit and pigeon all year round, sometimes herrings and crab from local fishermen. We're lucky compared to others.'

Ava and Maudie nodded in agreement.

'We're luckier than most,' Maudie echoed.

'But we've got plenty of mouths to feed, four times a day, from now till the end of the war.'

'Let's make a start,' Maudie said, pen poised once more. 'Monday?'

'Shepherd's pie with loads of root veg and Oxo stock, stewed fruit and custard for lunch; cheese-and-potato bake for supper,' Ava promptly replied.

'Tuesday?' Maudie regarded a thoughtful-looking Ava.

'Potato hash, rice pudding. Beans on toast for supper.'

'Wednesday?'

'Split-pea soup, mince-and-onion pie,' Ruby chimed in. 'And macaroni cheese for supper.'

'May I make a suggestion for Thursday?' Maudie asked.

Ava and Ruby nodded.

'Cheese-and-tomato flan and apple strudel for lunch; Spam salad for supper.'

Ruby smiled and licked her lips.

'How do you make apple strudel?'

'I'll show you,' Maudie promised. 'Friday?'

'*Fish!*' they all chorused.

'Fish cake and mash for main, and any veg that we can stick in a soup,' laughed Ruby.

'Fish paste on toast for supper,' Ava concluded.

'Saturday?' Maudie asked.

'Lord Woolton pie and apple fritters for lunch.' Ava paused. 'Can't do beans on toast again.' She groaned, as she tried to think of something quick and easy for Saturday's supper.

'I could do spicy paprika sausage in tomato sauce?' Maudie suggested.

'Done! What will we put in the sausage, though?' Ava asked.

'A few old socks!' Maudie teased.

'Sunday?' Ruby called out.

'We could do a mock roast with mince and spam and plenty of fresh herbs, and a fruit pie and custard,' Ava said.

'Supper?' Maudie asked.

Ruby grimaced. 'I'm feeling sick, thinking about all this food!'

'Come on, it's the last item on the weekly menu,' Maudie urged.

'Sunday supper?' Ava replied. 'Assorted sandwiches and fake chocolate cake.'

Maudie dropped her pencil on to the table. 'Done!'

'Are we going to follow this week in and week out?' Ruby asked.

'Yes, but we can vary it with seasonal vegetables and whatever Peter delivers,' Ava replied, as she lit up a Woodbine and inhaled deeply.

'What about the gentry upstairs?' Ruby asked anxiously.

'What about them?' Maudie exclaimed.

'They're not going to like apple fritters and potato hash.' Ruby giggled nervously. 'They're used to finer things.'

'Oh, come on!' Maudie cried. 'They can't have preferential treatment. We've all got to make sacrifices'

'No chance,' Ava added. 'I had a run-in with her ladyship after Timms promised her all kinds of luxuries: salmon mousse, beef Wellington, caviar, and God knows what! When I reminded her ladyship we were on rationed goods, she said the estate would provide, at which point I had to tell her that most of the produce from the estate was requisitioned for those with greater needs than hers. She certainly wasn't happy about it, but she'll have to lump it!'

Maudie gave a wicked smile. 'We should lock Timms in the wine cellar and throw away the key!' she joked.

'Talking of the wine cellar, the Walsinghams expect to be served wine at lunch and supper,' Ruby told her friends.

'A fine hock with beans on toast!' mocked Maudie.

'We've got more than enough to do,' Ava retorted, as she stubbed out her cigarette. 'It's Dodds's job to go running up and down the back stairs with bottles of booze, not ours.'

'The rate Lady Diana's knocking it back, the cellar will be empty before long,' Ruby remarked.

Maudie threw up her hands as she cried, 'What those wretched people drink is not our problem!'

With a purposeful smile, Ava pushed back her chair. 'If we're going to start on our new menus, I'd better ring in the grocery order.'

'What's Tuesday?' Ruby asked, nodding towards Maudie's open notebook.

'Potato hash and rice pudding!' Maudie replied.

'I'll soak the rice and start peeling the spuds,' Ruby volunteered.

'And I'll go and check what veg and milk Peter's left in the back pantry,' said Maudie.

Before the girls hurried away, they smiled at each other. They had agreed on a daily plan which *had* to work if they were to feed thirty hungry mouths and survive the rigours of wartime rationing.

6. Bella Wells

Annabelle took deep breaths as she made her way down the grand staircase that led into the Great Hall, from which rooms ran off to the left and right; the airy ground floor had been Annabelle's home until a few months ago, so she was intrigued by the changes that had taken place. The requisitioned areas had a distinct boarding-school air about them. She'd noticed the changes in the dining room before. The spacious drawing room appeared cramped; it was cluttered with battered old sofas and armchairs, there were newspapers strewn around the room and overflowing ashtrays left out on table-tops and the fire hadn't been lit. The room had the institutional smell of cold tea, cabbage and cigarette smoke but, for all that, Annabelle, unlike her sister, Diana, liked the changes. Hearing the sound of laughter and female voices, Annabelle hurried down the corridor to the secretary's office.

'Excuse me, could you point me in the direction of the brigadier's office, please?' she asked when she got there.

'Is it urgent? He's busy,' the heavily made-up secretary replied, as she hammered the keys of her Remington typewriter.

'Er . . .' Annabelle dithered.

Her indecision caused the secretary to stop typing and scan the young woman standing tensely before her.

'Come back later,' she said, grabbed a sheaf of papers and rose from the desk.

Annabelle stayed where she was. She wasn't going to put off this meeting one minute longer. Pretending to be looking out of the window, she waited till the secretary's footsteps had faded away, then hurried on down the corridor, looking for the brigadier's name on the doors she passed by. The smell of cherry tobacco led her to his office. The door was half open. She tapped on it softly and waited.

'Come in.'

Anabelle stepped into the office. 'May I have a moment of your time?' she asked.

The brigadier looked up and his face registered surprise. What could Lady Annabelle Walsingham want of him?

'Certainly,' he said, indicating a chair.

Terrified that the secretary would walk in and order her out, Annabelle quickly launched into her pre-rehearsed piece.

'I'd like to train in communications,' she blurted out. 'I achieved top marks in my Higher School Certificate in Maths, Statistics and Physics at Cheltenham Ladies' College.' She blushed as she said this. The brigadier was sure to think she was showing off, but she had to impress him with her qualifications if she was to get him to take her seriously. 'I'm sure I have an aptitude for communications and I really want to do my bit for the war effort,' she added earnestly.

The brigadier looked at the girl in front of him. With her softly curling blonde hair and charming dimple, she had a sweetness and intensity that touched him. If she was telling the truth about her qualifications, she was without doubt better qualified to do the course than most of the girls already enrolled. But . . . there was one big but.

'Are your parents aware of your intentions, Lady Annabelle?' he asked.

She cringed; she hated the sound of her title on his lips; it set her apart from the ordinary and everything she hoped to achieve.

'They really aren't in a position to stop me, in any case. Female conscription is obligatory,' she replied, and defiantly stuck out her little chin.

'You're quite right.'

'Would you consider my request, sir?' she asked.

'I would have to see evidence of your examination results, plus I'd need a reference and a doctor's report,' he replied. 'If all of those are in order, I would have no reason to turn you down.'

Annabelle couldn't stop herself smiling. He noticed her fine, even teeth and, again, the delightful dimple in her right cheek.

'Thank you, sir. I shall attend to your requests right away.' As she rose from her chair, she said, rather awkwardly, 'I would prefer to keep my real identity from the other trainees.'

The brigadier's thick brown eyebrows shot up.

'I think it would be uncomfortable for both them and for me if they knew I was the daughter of Lord and Lady Walsingham. It's best that I'm just one of the crowd,' she finished.

'As you wish,' he replied.

As Annabelle left the room, closing the door softly behind her, the brigadier couldn't help but admire her composed determination. Smiling to himself, he stuffed the stem of his pipe back into his mouth and returned to the papers piled up on his desk.

Annabelle virtually skipped back upstairs. She was determined not to hang about, waiting for 'the right moment' to break the news, because she knew there never would be one. She could easily get copies of her examination results, and she was certain of getting a glowing reference from her old headmistress at Cheltenham Ladies' College. She'd always been a favourite of hers. She'd book an appointment for a check-up with her doctor in Fakenham immediately. Nothing was going to hold her back; nothing was going to keep her banged up with her poisonous family a minute longer than necessary.

Annabelle checked the rooms upstairs. Only her mother was in, writing letters at her desk. The rest of the family were due back for lunch; she'd have to wait till then. Restless and impatient, Annabelle took herself for a walk around the garden, where she found Peter, busy digging up new potatoes and young carrots.

'Digging for victory?' she asked, quoting a popular government slogan.

Peter smiled fondly at her. Always the same, young Miss Annabelle, open and easy-going, treating everybody as an equal. When she was a little girl, she'd loved to grub about in the garden alongside him.

'Grab a spade and get stuck in!' he laughed.

As they dug in companionable ease, Annabelle asked about the arrangements below stairs.

'Ruby's got two new cooks, young girls,' Peter told her.

'Good luck to them,' said Annabelle. 'They'll have their work cut out, that's for sure.'

When she'd finished digging her trench, Annabelle volunteered to drop off the vegetables at the hall. She carried the heavy crate into the back pantry, where she bumped into a tall, slim auburn-haired woman.

'How do you do?' Annabelle said politely.

Maudie returned the greeting and relieved Annabelle of the crate. 'Thanks for the veg,' she added, with a smile that lit up her tired green eyes.

Feeling sorry for the attractive young woman, Annabelle added, 'Peter tells me there are new cooks below stairs.'

Maudie nodded and swiped a lock of curly hair from her eyes. 'I'm the latest cook to arrive, Ava was the first,' she answered.

'And you've got Ruby and Timms?' Annabelle asked.

Maudie raised her eyebrows in surprise. 'Mmmmm, I wouldn't say we've got Timms,' she replied, with a smile that revealed her even white teeth. 'She tends to avoid us.'

Annabelle didn't need any further explanation; she knew that, after rubbing shoulders with the upper classes for over forty years, Timms assumed she was one of them, too.

'Maybe you're better off running your kitchen without the old guard,' Annabelle said cautiously.

Maudie nodded in agreement. 'For sure. We've got a good routine going, but it's still a route march.'

Annabelle couldn't stop herself from saying, 'I think you're all amazing!'

'We try our best,' Maudie said with a quick smile. 'Thanks again.' She carried the loaded crate down the long, dark corridor to the kitchen.

Annabelle hurried back to her room, where she washed her hands and face, combed her hair then studied her reflection in the mirror. Her eyes were bright and steely; determined.

'Time to drop the bombshell!'

Between vegetable soup and grilled kidneys, a treat of a dish – Ruby had sourced the kidneys from the local butcher in Wells – but which everybody ate without any comment or obvious appreciation, Annabelle made her announcement.

'You're *what*?' her mother gasped.

'You heard me, Mama. I'm joining the code girls downstairs. The brigadier's agreed, he said a healthy young woman of my age is obliged to do war work – it's the patriotic thing to do.' She knew she shouldn't stoke the fire, but she couldn't resist having a poke at her idle sister.

'Do you really have to do your so-called "war work" right under our noses?' Diana seethed. 'By agreeing to join those girls, you're conceding that the government was right to requisition our home.'

'It's not the only stately home in the land that's been requisitioned for war purposes,' Annabelle retorted. 'Anyway, I intend to change my name so they won't connect me with this family.'

'You're a bloody little traitor!' Diana raged, as she poured a big glug of white wine into her glass.

'It's not so bad an idea,' Edward said with a sneer of a smile. 'Annabelle could be our little go-between downstairs. She could sneak back here with all the gossip and keep us entertained with tales of common life,' he mocked.

Annabelle glared at her self-seeking brother. 'I don't think so,' she answered coldly.

Diana turned to her father. 'Papa, tell the stupid girl she's got to stop this nonsense.'

His lordship shrugged and looked dispassionately at his younger daughter. She had always been an enigma to him.

'I'm afraid I can't do that, Diana, for the reasons your sister has so succinctly pointed out. I rather wish that her training was elsewhere, then I wouldn't have to suffer the humiliation, but if she goes under a false name, nobody need know but us and the servants.'

'Have you a new name in mind?' her mother, from the other end of the table, asked in icy tones.

Annabelle nodded. 'Bella Wells.'

Lady Diana flopped back in her chair. 'Christ! It sounds like an ice-cream!'

'My new identity must be kept strictly confidential,' Bella insisted.

Lady Walsingham threw up her hands and cried out in disgust, 'I'd rather die than reveal to any of my acquaintances how low you've stooped.'

Edward turned to Diana and said with malicious humour, 'Better be careful, sis. If the worthy brigadier discovers there's an elder Walsingham daughter dodging conscription, you could be in *big* trouble.'

'You can talk!' Diana snapped. 'What's your bit for the war effort? Discussing the pros and cons of Hitler and Goebbels over brandy and cigars?'

Aware of an argument brewing, Annabelle quickly rose from the table. 'One more thing, Papa,' she said. 'Please would you instruct Dodds and Timms of my change of circumstances? I wouldn't want them to be embarrassed if they bump into me with the trainees.'

'I'll let them know,' his lordship said with a dismissive wave of his hand.

Diana, who was by now well into her cups, called after the departing Annabelle, 'Run away, little code girl, go and join the riff-raff.'

Annabelle passed Ruby, standing by the hot serving trays, as she left the room. She grinned at the boggle-eyed girl, who, having heard the entire conversation, gave the discreetest of nods. Of course Ruby would keep her ladyship's secret – anything had to be better than living upstairs with this bunch of spiteful toffs!

Once she was out in the corridor, Annabelle punched the air in triumph. 'Yes! Yes! Yes!' she chanted, as she ran to her room, where she wasted no time packing a suitcase. Then she slipped down the stairs, went out into the yard, where she collected her bike from the bicycle shed. She balanced her suitcase across the handlebars and, with a grin on her face, cycled out of Walsingham estate the back way.

Half an hour later, a smiling young woman with soft, blonde hair and pale blue eyes cycled up to Walsingham Hall, passing the ornamental gates on her way. She stopped to read the family motto emblazoned underneath the ancestral coat of arms.

'*Prudens qui patiens eternim durissima coquit* – the prudent one is the patient one because he digests the hardest things.' She murmured the words she knew so well under her breath, then shivered as a tingle of excitement slipped down her spine. 'I have been prudent and I have been patient and now I'm damn well going to do what I want!'

7. An Army Marches on Its Stomach

Bella wasted no time in phoning her former headmistress at Cheltenham Ladies' College, who promised an excellent reference by return of post then she made an appointment for the following day with her doctor in Fakenham, after which she reported back to the brigadier, who looked surprised by her speedy return.

'You'll have all the official information you require by next week,' she promised. 'Please may I report for duty right away, sir?'

The brigadier appraised the keen young woman standing before him, her chin thrust firmly forward as if she wasn't going to take no for an answer. The War Office was on the lookout for bright young code girls, and if this determined girl had the right qualities he'd certainly recommend her for code-breaking ops at Bletchley Park.

'Miss Cox won't like it,' he said, as he packed the bowl of his pipe with tobacco. 'Better tell her I said it would a pity for you to miss out on the start of the course while we wait for the paperwork. Have you decided on a name?'

'Wells,' she answered with a grin. 'Bella Wells.'

The brigadier couldn't help but smile, which lit up his dark brown eyes and softened his usually firm mouth.

'I'm sure your parents will love that,' he remarked.

Bella shrugged and cheerfully replied, 'They don't like anything about me, so it doesn't really matter.'

The brigadier wisely refrained from making any comment;

instead he nodded towards his open office door, and Bella quickly took her leave.

Miss Cox, a stickler for protocol, *was* quite put out.

'It's rather out of the ordinary to start without papers.'

Bella repeated the senior officer's words. 'The brigadier thought it would be a pity to miss out on the start of the course.' Seeing Miss Cox's grumpy expression, she quickly added, 'I could collect my reference and copies of my examination results at the weekend, if that would suit you better?'

'And the doctor's report?'

'I've arranged for an examination at the Fakenham surgery in the morning,' Bella answered politely.

'You seem to have thought of everything, Miss Wells,' Miss Cox answered grudgingly. 'There are a few empty beds in the south wing. Settle yourself in there and we'll see you at teatime, four thirty sharp. Oh, and take your ration book to the cook,' she added.

Bella left the room and, in the empty corridor, hugged herself with joy. 'Goodbye, Your Ladyship,' she said gleefully. 'Hello, Bella Wells!'

Later, Bella made her familiar way below stairs, where she found Ava and Ruby, flustered, loading the teatime trays with bread, butter, jam and jars of meat paste.

'Hello, I'm Bella Wells.' She winked as she caught Ruby's amused expression. 'I've brought my ration book,' she added politely.

'Pleased to meet you,' said Ava, taking it. 'Thanks for dropping this off – the more the merrier!'

Bella turned curiously towards the scrubbed wooden kitchen table where Maudie was pounding dough.

'Hello, again,' she said with an easy smile. 'What're you making?'

Maudie wiped a speck of flour off her nose and replied, 'Rye bread.'

Bella smiled. 'It smells good.' She sniffed appreciatively. 'Where did you learn to bake rye bread?'

'In my parents' bakery in the East End of London,' Maudie replied, with undisguised pride.

'S'cuse me, miss,' said Ruby, as she hurried by with a heavy tray.

Bella quickly corrected her. 'It's *Bella*, Ruby. Please forget the "Miss" bit.' She held out her hands. 'Here, let me take that, you've got more than enough to do.'

Ruby didn't argue. 'Ta, Bella,' she chuckled.

Bella also chuckled as she carried the tray upstairs. If only her mother could see her now!

Over tea, which was noisy with the chatter and laughter of twenty-five women, Bella introduced herself as a late-comer local girl. She made a point of asking her companions about their families and their lives prior to arriving at Walsingham Hall. She'd learnt from experience that people liked to talk about themselves, which suited her, as she definitely didn't want to talk about herself or her family!

Throughout tea, Bella was aware of Ruby, Maudie and Ava coming and going, carrying huge teapots and urns of hot water.

'Poor things, they've got a lot on their plates,' she thought sympathetically.

The girls below stairs worked far longer hours than the code girls above stairs. Their day could be anything from fifteen to eighteen hours long. Maudie even set an alarm clock to wake her up in the middle of the night to put a batch of risen bread into the oven so it was cooked and ready for breakfast.

On top of the cooking, serving and clearing away, the three girls slavishly worked their way through the set menus, which, out of boredom, they had started to vary.

'I'll go mad if I have to look at another bloody Lord Woolton pie,' Ava joked.

They really appreciated Peter's daily offerings, which greatly enhanced their larder, especially when he turned up with the odd treat of seasonal game: hare, rabbit, pigeon, sometimes pheasant. Although Ava and Maudie were squeamish about the plucking and skinning – they left it to Ruby and Peter – they were clever and inventive with the meat, making tasty stews thickened with root vegetables and Oxo, or casseroles with herb dumplings, and the game stock made a rich broth.

Ava's big grocery order was delivered every week: tins of corned beef, Spam, beans and peas; bags of flour, sugar, salt and dried pulses. Everything had to be unpacked and stored away in the warren of cupboards and pantries below stairs. One morning, as Ava headed to one of store rooms, she tripped over a mountain of laundry that had been carelessly dumped outside the laundry room, which housed washing dollies, washboards, tin baths, wooden tubs, wringers and a boiler that only Ruby could coax into life.

'Who's put this lot here?' Ava exclaimed.

'Me,' Timms replied, as she dropped another dirty load. 'The woman who's been doing the washing has been taken into hospital.'

'But . . .' Ava retorted, flabbergasted. 'I'm a cook not a washerwoman!'

'Cleaning goes on below stairs, your domain!' said Timms, with an ill-disguised smile.

Ava didn't waste her breath on peevish Timms. Instead, she went straight away to see the 'Brig', as everybody below stairs now called the brigadier.

'Sorry to bother you, sir, but Timms has decided the below-stairs staff are responsible for the laundry as well as everything else. We really haven't got the time to wash and iron *and* cook.'

'I never expected you to do the laundry, Ava!' the Brig exclaimed in astonishment.

Ava sighed with relief. She really was beginning to like this man, who, above all things, was fair. Thinking of her fury when she first met him, Ava smiled to herself; how wrong first impressions can be.

'Ignore Timms,' the Brig answered brusquely. 'I'll deal with her.'

'With pleasure, but what about the laundry?' Ava laughingly replied.

'I'll get some of the local estate women to do it,' he replied. 'I'm told there's plenty of them eager to make a few extra bob or two.'

Ava returned to the kitchen wearing a triumphant smile. 'The laundry's being outsourced,' she announced.

'Where's that?' Ruby asked naïvely.

'Anywhere but here!' laughed Maudie.

'Thank God!' cried Ruby.

Leaving Maudie in the kitchen making a gigantic apple strudel, Ava and Ruby cleared away the remains of lunch to the strains of 'Workers' Playtime' blasting out on the Bakelite radio. Ruby stopped wiping down the tables when she saw through an open window an RAF jeep bouncing up the drive.

'Looks like an officer's heading into the west wing,' she remarked.

Ava peered out of the window, too.

'There must be so many men at Holkham airfield,' she said wistfully. 'You'd think they'd organize a dance night every so often.'

'I've never heard of anything like that going on up there,' Ruby replied as she resumed wiping the table-tops. 'Anyway, RAF officers aren't likely to fancy lowly scullery maids.'

Ava held her right hand up in the air. 'Stop right there, Ruby Marsden!' she declared. 'I might be a cook below stairs but I'm a woman with a brain and a mind of my own, and I don't like being done down by my own sex. If this rotten war's taught us anything, it's that women can and have stepped into men's shoes to do jobs nobody five years ago would have thought possible. As Maudie would say, "We're all equal!"'

Ruby giggled as she replied, 'Sorry, Ava, I'm just learning how to be – thanks to you two.'

Ava threw a dishcloth at Ruby, as she said, 'You're beautiful enough for any RAF officer, Ruby. Never forget that.'

Ruby blushed, but she looked pleased by Ava's compliment.

Less than half an hour later, a shy young man came hesitantly into the kitchen.

''Scuse me, please,' he mumbled self-consciously. 'I am Polish driver from airfield. My officer in bed here sent me for food.'

Maudie and Ava smiled, not unkindly, at his grammatical mistakes, which Ruby seemed oblivious of. Gazing raptly at the tall, pale-haired young man with shy blue eyes, she asked, 'Did they send you down for sandwiches?'

The young man's smooth brow crinkled in concentration as he laboriously translated what she'd said.

'Sandvitches . . . yes! They ask for these things.'

He smiled nervously at Ruby, who pointed to a chair beside the big wooden table.

'You sit, and I make sandvitches.'

Hearing Ruby speaking pidgin English to the Polish driver sent Ava and Maudie rushing into the pantry, where, covering their mouths, they rocked with laughter.

'Did she really say "sandvitches"?' Maudie tittered.

'Let's stay out of the way,' Maudie whispered. 'If we start giggling, we'll only embarrass the poor boy.'

Chatting in pidgin English to the young man who was called Rafal, Ruby made a pile of sandwiches, which she handed over to him.

'Come back here, to me,' she said, pointing to herself. 'I make sandvitches for *you* to eat!'

Rafal looked blank but nodded politely, then, with a grateful smile, he made his way upstairs. Ruby waited ten minutes and, when he didn't return, she hurried to the front door, from where she saw Rafal climbing into the jeep.

'*No!*' she yelled, and ran out on to the drive, where she flagged down the jeep.

Rafal turned off the ignition and got out. Taking him firmly by the hand, Ruby led him back to the kitchen, where she put a plate of sandwiches and a pot of coffee before him.

'Enjoy!' Ruby said kindly.

'For me, driver?' he asked incredulously.

'Yes, for *you*!' she giggled.

Rafal grinned, then enthusiastically started on the sandwiches.

'Good, very good,' he said, as he admired her small, shapely figure and the swing of her long, bobbed hair. 'Thank you.'

Ruby gazed into his wide, innocent eyes. 'You're more than welcome,' she replied with a warm smile.

8. Call the Vet

Though she was rushed off her feet, Ava really missed Shamrock and the rides they'd had over the Lancashire moors. It wasn't as if she had any free time at Walsingham Hall or, even more to the point, a horse to ride – she simply missed the exercise and the unforgettable smell of the stables: saddle soap, hay, leather, grooming brushes and oats! It was exactly that combination of smells that attracted Ava to the Walsingham stables shortly after she arrived at the hall; the aroma of straw and horse muck drew her like a magnet!

When she entered the airy stables, still wearing her cook's uniform, she was greeted by a tubby little Shetland pony and a handsome chestnut, both of whom popped their heads over their stable doors and neighed softly.

'Hello, lasses,' a delighted Ava said gently, as she reached into her pinafore pocket for the apples she'd brought along with her. 'Who are you, greedy guts?' she went on, as the Shetland bit into the apple cradled in her palm. 'Sorry, I can see you're not a lass.' Ava chuckled as she peered over the stable door and saw that the handsome chestnut was indeed a gelding.

Later, she discovered from Ruby that the Shetland was called Tara and the gelding Lucas. Ruby also told her that all the Walsingham children had been taught to ride on Tara.

'Lady Annabelle and Lord Edward lost interest when they got into their teens, but Lady Diana enjoyed hunting – well, she enjoyed meeting the lords and ladies of the county in the saddle,' Ruby added with a cheeky wink. 'So his lord-ship bought Lucas for her, but she hasn't ridden him for years. Shame, he's a fine hunter. He's wasted these days, with nobody to exercise him.'

'I'd willingly exercise him in my spare time,' Ava immediately responded.

'What spare time?' mocked Maudie.

'I'm sure I could snatch a few hours a week to ride – if I was allowed to.' Ava's face fell, and she shook her head. 'Forget it, I can't see Lady Diana doing me any favours, though I feel sorry for that fine chestnut of hers.'

Nevertheless, Ava was a frequent visitor to the stables, and the paddock, too, where the horses were turned out every morning in the summertime. One afternoon, after clearing lunch and leaving Ruby and Maudie preparing tea, Ava dashed across to the yard to give the horses their daily treat. They'd only to see her approaching and they'd toss their heads and neigh excitedly. Greedy Tara thrust her muzzle in Ava's pinafore pocket, while well-mannered Lucas stayed back until Ava held out his apple on the palm of her hand for him to bite into. One day, seeing Lucas's mane knotted and tangled, Ava collected a dandy brush and a currie comb from the stable, then spent half an hour brushing and combing his golden mane until it glowed.

'Aren't you the handsome boy?' she whispered.

As she swept the dandy brush in wide, even strokes across Lucas's flanks, the horse snickered softly.

'Oh, this is nice,' Ava sighed, laying her head against his warm chest and inhaling the sweet smell of his body.

Lucas bent to gently blow into her dark hair, which billowed out as she resumed grooming him. Drawing the dandy brush back and forth across Lucas's withers, Ava got so into the rhythm of the process she hardly heard the sound of a car drawing up. Lucas did, though, and his sharp neigh quickly brought Ava to her senses. She looked up as a Land Rover came bouncing down the track leading to the paddock, then stopped by the five-bar gate. When a tall young man got out, the horses tossed their heads in excitement.

'Hello, there!' he called to them.

Ava felt silly wearing her servant's pinafore, and with her dark hair falling untidily around her shoulders, her first reaction was to run, but the tall, good-looking stranger blocked her path by standing close to the fence in order to pat the necks of the eager horses.

'All right, all right,' he said softly, and reached into the top pocket of his open-necked shirt and drew out some mints. 'One each and no more,' he said with a smile.

Ava couldn't help smiling, too; she was almost as taken as the horses by the handsome man with a mop of thick, tawny hair and warm, hazel eyes.

'They never believe a word I say,' he said, as he indulgently fed all the mints to the horses. 'I'm so sorry,' he said, turning to Ava with a wide, relaxed smile. 'I haven't introduced myself.' He held out his hand to her. 'I'm Tom Benson, the local vet. Pleased to meet you.'

Ava took his warm, tanned hand in hers. 'Ava Downham,' she replied, then, in order to explain the servant's uniform, she added with a shrug, 'Cook at the hall.'

Tom's eyes widened in surprise, 'What happened to Timms?'

'She's still there – unfortunately!'

'So how long have you been at the hall?'

'I can't recall exactly; it feels like for ever.' Ava laughed.

Tara and Lucas, cross that they were being ignored by their visitors, started to stamp their feet and whinny impatiently.

'OK, OK,' said Tom.

As he unhooked the gate and walked into the paddock, Ava noticed he walked with a distinct limp. 'I've got to check Tara's feet and give her an injection,' Tom said. 'Would you mind holding her for me?'

Even though she knew she should be setting the tables in the dining room by now, Ava nevertheless clipped a lead rope to Tara's halter and stroked the impatient mare as Tom bent to pick out her hooves.

'She likes you,' he said, without looking up.

Watching Tom kneeling on the warm grass just inches away from her, Ava had an irrepressible urge to run her fingertips through the shock of golden-auburn hair which fell over his eyes. She started self-consciously when Tom stood up and stretched his long, muscular back.

'Do you ride?' he asked.

'I did when I lived at home, in Lancashire.'

'I thought you didn't sound like a local,' he said, taking a syringe out of his bag. 'Just got to give Tara a shot in her bottom. Hold still, old lady,' he said, and patted Tara's flank, then gently inserted the needle into her hefty rump. 'All done.'

Ava handed him the halter rope. 'I'd best get back to the kitchen,' she said, feeling a blush rising from her neck upwards.

'That's a shame,' said Tom, as he took the rope from her rather shaky hand. To Ava's astonishment, he suddenly said, 'Would you like to come for a ride on Holkham beach tomorrow?'

'I'd love to, if only I had a horse,' she replied with a smile.

'There's Lucas – he'd love the exercise.'

Ava shook her head. 'I can't do that. He belongs to Lady Diana.'

'Who's asked me to exercise him,' Tom replied. 'You'd be doing both me and Lucas a favour.'

Wide-eyed, Ava looked from gorgeous Tom to gorgeous Lucas; this really was an offer she couldn't refuse.

'Well, if you put it like that.'

Tom grinned. 'Good! Two o'clock, here, tomorrow?'

Ava panicked. Two o'clock was the time she was usually prepping supper.

'Er, how about three?'

'You're on!' laughed Tom.

Ava literally erupted into the kitchen, where, in front of her startled friends, she flung her arms in the air and shimmied around the kitchen.

'Have you been on the bottle?' Ruby teased.

'I've just met the vet!' Ava replied.

'Tom Benson?' Ruby asked.

Ava nodded. 'He's very nice, good-looking, too – spoken for, no doubt.'

Ruby's brow crinkled as she answered, 'As I recall, I think he probably is.'

Ava's heart sank. 'Stupid me!' she thought. There were hardly any young men around, they were all away fighting the war; of course a good-looking man like Tom Benson would have a girlfriend, if not a string of them.

'Well, that's awkward,' she said with a shrug. 'He's just asked me to go horse riding with him tomorrow.'

'Horse riding, by definition, must classify more as a date with the horse rather than the bloke. After all, it's the horse you're sitting on!' Maudie joked.

Ava giggled as she replied. 'I am *definitely* not giving up my date with Lucas; he's my total dream boy!'

In between clearing tea and serving supper, Ava worried about leaving her friends in the lurch.

'I'll only go if I've finished all my work,' she assured them.

'You sound like Cinderella,' teased Maudie. 'You *shall* go to the ball, but only after you've made breakfast, lunch and supper – and swept the chimney!'

'You *must* go to the ball,' Ruby declared. 'It's about time we all started having a bit of fun!'

The next morning, Ava was first up and busy making pastry for the cheese-and-tomato flans.

'Guess what day it is,' she laughed, as her friends entered the kitchen.

Ruby and Maudie looked at the ingredients on the table-top.

'If it's cheese and tomato, it's Thursday!' Ruby laughed, too.

'Lucky for me Maudie's the apple-strudel maker today,' Ava said, now lining metal tins with pastry, then cracking eggs into a bowl of milk. 'Pass me the whisk, lovie,' she said to Maudie, who was standing closest to the long row of hooks from which numerous kitchen utensils dangled. 'I've already made the mock turkey salad for teatime. It's on the cold slab in the pantry.'

'You're ahead of yourself,' said Maudie.

'I have to be,' said Ava, as she busily whisked the egg-and-milk mixture. 'I want to give Lucas a good grooming before Tom arrives.'

'You might need grooming yourself if you carry on slopping stuff about,' Maudie teased, as a blob of egg yolk splashed up into Ava's face. 'Here, let me,' she said, relieving Ava of the whisk. 'Grate the cheese, and mind your fingers!'

'I'll start laying the breakfast,' said Ruby, and loaded the trays with Maudie's soft, warm rolls, marge and rhubarb-and-ginger jam. 'Put the kettle on,' she said, as she headed for the stairs. 'We'll have a brew when I get back.'

As Ava grated the strong Walsingham Cheddar cheese, she blurted out what had been worrying her all morning: 'I haven't got any trousers!' she wailed.

Maudie burst out laughing. 'It's not funny!' Ava exclaimed. 'I can't go riding in a skirt. It'll blow up with the first breeze and my knickers will be on display for the whole world to see!'

'I've got some trousers,' Maudie volunteered.

'My hips aren't as slinky slim as yours,' Ava said, dropping the grated cheese into the milk mixture, along with a generous sprinkling of salt, black pepper and some fresh parsley.

A wicked smile crept across Maudie's mouth. 'I know somebody who must have more than one pair of jodhpurs.'

Ava looked blank. 'Who?'

'Lady Diana, of course.'

Ava's jaw dropped. 'I can't go borrowing her horse, and her trousers, too!' she spluttered.

Maudie raised her beautifully arched eyebrows as she replied, 'I really don't see why not.'

When Ruby came rushing back for another tray-load, Ava dropped three heaped teaspoons of tea into the big kitchen teapot as she said, in all innocence, 'Would you know where Lady Diana keeps her old jodhpurs?'

Ruby nodded as she loaded the tray with more bread rolls.

'In a box of junk that's been sitting at the back of her wardrobe since she was moved to the suites upstairs. Why?'

'I haven't got anything to ride in,' Ava explained.

'Do you think you could liberate a pair of jodhpurs for our head cook?' Maudie asked with a wry smile.

Ruby grinned and nodded. 'I could nip up and get you a pair after we've finished clearing breakfast.'

'Will they fit?' Ava asked. 'I've got a bigger bum than Lady Diana!'

'They stretch quite a lot, so even somebody as fat as you will be able to squeeze into them!' Ruby joked. 'Now, in return for stealing from her ladyship, you can carry the rest of those damn heavy trays upstairs while I'll stay here and drink my tea!'

'Deal!' said Ava, and loaded two more trays with bread and butter. 'I might even give you a Woodbine to accompany your tea break!'

When breakfast had been cleared and the savoury flans were cooking in the slow oven, Ruby, with a mischievous look on her pretty face, skipped up the back staircase.

'I hope she won't get into trouble,' Ava murmured, watching her go.

'Stop worrying. Lady Diana's never sober long enough to miss anything,' Maudie answered knowingly.

While Ava was busy in the large pantry, stacking the latest delivery of sugar and flour on the stout wooden shelves that ran around the small room from floor to ceiling, Ruby returned with a pair of jodhpurs.

'Come out of there and try them on for size,' she called.

'Thank you, Ruby, you're a pal,' said Ava. She stripped off her uniform and stood before the hot Aga in only her bra and knickers.

'I only hope Peter doesn't come waltzing in with a delivery of cucumbers!' Ruby chuckled.

Ava wriggled into the jodhpurs, which were a snug fit.

'They show your bum off a treat!' Ruby said.

'That wasn't the look I wanted,' Ava said, stretching down to touch her toes. 'I hope they don't split when I'm in the saddle,' she added anxiously.

'As long as they don't split when you're out of the saddle, you'll be fine,' Ruby teased.

As Ava whipped off the jodhpurs and slipped back into her uniform, Maudie smiled mischievously at Ruby. 'You and that sweet-looking Polish boy seemed to get on well the other night.'

Ruby blushed. 'He's a nice lad, but we barely understand each other,' she giggled.

'I could teach you how to say, "Have a sandvitch with me" in Polish,' Maudie teased. *'Ma sandwicz z mna.'*

Ruby's dark eyes widened as Maudie slipped effortlessly into her mother tongue. 'Could you really teach me Polish, Maudie?'

'Of course,' she replied. 'We could start right now, naming things in the kitchen. Cup and saucer: *filizanka i spodek.'* She nodded to the large dresser stacked with crockery. 'Knife and fork: *noz i widelec,'* she went on, as she picked up some cutlery. *'Meko i cukier*: milk and sugar.'

Bewildered, Ruby put her head in her hands, 'Slow down!' she wailed. 'You're getting me all confused.'

As soon as lunch was cleared, Ava headed off to the bedroom she shared with Ruby, where she stripped and washed herself down with warm water. Then she pulled on Lady Diana's jodhpurs and a white-and-pink striped crêpe blouse, which she tucked into the waistband.

'I hope I don't look fat,' she fretted, peering over her shoulder, trying to get a view of her backside.

Next, she cleaned her teeth and brushed her hair. She didn't apply any make-up – what she had was old and greasy;

and, anyway, as Maudie had pointed out, this wasn't exactly a date. She took a quick glance at herself in the tiny bathroom mirror. Her dark blue eyes were glowing with excitement, her lips were full and pink and her long hair floated in a cloud around her smiling face. When Ava walked back into the kitchen, her friends nodded in approval.

'You look like you've just walked off the set of a cowboy film!' Ruby teased.

'I'm a nervous wreck – and I think my bum looks big,' Ava blurted out.

'Stop worrying. You look all curvy and sexy, like Jane Russell!' Ruby assured her.

Ava dashed into the cold store to collect two apples before leaving. 'Have fun! Don't fall off!' Maudie yelled after her, laughing.

When the back door banged shut and Ava was well out of earshot, Maudie turned to Ruby.

'So what makes you think this vet of Ava's is spoken for?' she asked.

Ruby was sitting, smoking, in the old Windsor chair by the Aga, and lowered her voice when she replied.

'I remember, when he made his first visit to the hall, he was definitely with a tall, dark, snobby woman, more a Lady Diana type than a vet's wife,' Ruby said. She stubbed out her cigarette in the ashtray. 'I've never seen her with him since, but a handsome man like him is never short of girlfriends.'

'Let's hope he's not the flirting kind,' Maudie said thoughtfully. 'Because from the smile on her lips and the sparkle in her eye, Ava has definitely taken a shine to Mr Tom Benson!'

9. Holkham Beach

Ava chattered away happily as she groomed Lucas's chestnut coat until it shone like burnished gold. 'You've got to look your best, young man,' she said, as Lucas, searching for treats, pushed his muzzle into her jodhpur pockets

She jumped when she heard the sound of an approaching car. Turning quickly, she saw Tom driving his Land Rover, with a horsebox in tow. Her heart lurched as he jumped out of the vehicle. Her reaction to the sight of his golden hair, smiling, bright eyes and strong, tanned body suggested that this meeting was more than 'just a ride on the beach', no matter what her common sense told her.

Tom grinned as a thump and a shrill neigh emanated from the horsebox.

'Drummer's in a pig of a mood,' he said. As he walked round to the back of the horsebox, Ava again noticed the distinct limp in his right leg. 'He hates being cooped up, even though I told him it would be worth it in the end.'

'Drummer . . . ?' she queried.

'Drummer Boy, my horse,' Tom explained.

Intrigued, Ava watched Tom lower the ramp to the horsebox.

'Come and meet Ava,' he said to the sixteen-hand dark bay gelding that trotted down the ramp, tossing his silky black mane and waving his long black tail.

'Oh, he's beautiful!' Ava cried, and hurried over to stroke the frisky young horse. 'How old is he?'

'Four years old,' Tom replied. 'I delivered him when he was born to a breeder in Fakenham and, for a reduced fee, I bought him and broke him in. I know both the dam and the sire, so I knew he'd be a beauty, but I never dreamed he'd be as fast as he is. Believe me, give him a free rein and he goes like the wind.'

Lucas, in the paddock, fed up with being overlooked, neighed and pawed the ground.

'Don't think we should keep these two impatient creatures waiting much longer,' said Tom, as he tied Drummer's lead rope to the fence. 'I'll just get his saddle from the horsebox.'

Ava quickly tacked up Lucas, who was nudging Drummer's nose and sniffing his nostrils. Wearing tightly fitting jodhpurs and a soft, cotton open shirt that showed off the golden hairs of his tanned chest, Tom laid the saddle over Drummer's back, then looked over to Ava, who sat mounted on Lucas, her hair flying around her face.

'Ready?' he asked.

'Ready as I ever will be,' she answered, with an excited smile.

Five minutes later, Ava and Tom were trotting side by side down the curving drive that led out on to the quiet main road. They crossed it, then continued up an even longer drive, flanked on either side as far as the eye could see by fertile water meadows, where groups of honking geese waddled between grazing cattle. Ava's eyes grew wide as she gazed around.

'This is amazing!' she exclaimed. 'Right outside the front door and I've never even seen it.'

Tom, who was having trouble reining in feisty Drummer, looked surprised.

'You mean you've never ventured down to the sea?' he asked.

Ava shook her head.

'I've hardly ventured out of the kitchen,' she admitted.

'Oh my, are you in for a treat,' he promised. The muscles on Tom's arms strained as he continued to rein in his horse. 'I can't give him his head yet – the drive is used by pedestrians and farm traffic. Whoa, there, boy,' he said, in a firm but soothing voice.

Ava bent to pat Lucas's neck. Even though he was excited, he kept calm and didn't react to Drummer's high-pitched squeals. 'My lovely boy is happy to be out,' she said fondly.

Tom nodded, and smiled at Lucas, who was sniffing the air curiously.

'He's a fine horse. Pity he's so neglected.'

'Not any more,' Ava replied happily.

When they reached the belt of pine woods, she inhaled the sweet smell of pine resin mixed with the salty tang of the sea. This was nothing like riding out on the wild, wet northern moors. This was a cool, still, dark green world, where all sounds were muted; even Drummer stopped his impatient head-tossing as they walked deeper into the woods. A woodpecker's sharp call startled the horses. The pine trees were replaced by rolling sand dunes that hedged the wide sweep of Holkham beach.

'Hahhhhhh!' she gasped, in a low, rapt voice.

Tom nodded and said, 'I knew you'd like it. It's my favourite place on earth.'

The perfect, white, sandy beach, hardly marked by a footprint, merged with the distant, churning sea, which fused with the arching, blue sky, creating an image so pure and light it almost hurt Ava's eye to gaze too long at it.

'It's like paradise,' she whispered.

Paradise or not, Drummer, by this time, was almost apoplectic.

'If I don't give him his head now, he'll throw me.' Tom laughed as he slackened the reins. Drummer took off like a flash of lightning.

Lucas tossed his head and whinnied, desperate to catch up with the dark bay whose hooves were pounding the compacted sand.

'OK, baby, your turn now,' said Ava, as she slackened her reins and gently pressed her heels into Lucas's flanks. 'Come on, let's have some fun!'

Neighing with pleasure, Lucas tossed his head then broke into a gallop. There was no way he was ever going to catch up with Drummer, who was well ahead, but that didn't stop Lucas opening out his long legs and thundering after him. Sitting tight in the saddle, Ava marvelled at Tom's riding skills. He was a natural: graceful, bold and completely at one with his mount. She wondered what he'd think of her. Was she sitting erect and riding well? Were her feet pressed neatly into the stirrups or did she look like a sack of potatoes flopping around on top of Lucas? She needn't have worried. As Drummer slowed his pace, Tom turned to see Ava galloping towards him, her glorious hair lifted by the sea breeze.

'God! What a woman,' he murmured under his breath.

As Lucas caught up with speedy Drummer, they both slowed their pace. Snorting and tossing their heads, they walked companionably side by side in the shallow waves breaking on the white sand.

'I don't know who's happier,' Ava said, 'Lucas or me.'

Tom's eyes roved admiringly over Ava's open-necked blouse. He could see the soft swell of her full bosom, and forced himself to turn away.

'So what do you think of Holkham beach?' he asked.

'Paradise!' Ava replied, with a happy, carefree smile.

Tom nodded to the sand dunes that fringed the edge of the dense pine woods. 'Shall we dismount and let the horses cool down?'

Ava smiled as she replied. 'We'd better tie them up, though. We don't want Drummer bolting off and joining the Hunstanton donkeys!'

They tethered their mounts to stout pine trees in the shade, then made their way to the sand dunes, where Tom threw himself down, as carefree and relaxed as a boy. With his hands folded behind his head, he stretched luxuriously in the warm sand and sighed with pleasure. Ava, suddenly awkward, sat rather primly, with her arms laced around her legs, looking out to sea. Sensing her discomfort, Tom sat up and took her hand.

'News travels fast in the country,' he started. 'So I'm going to come straight out with it – I was married; I'm not any more. Divorce isn't common in Norfolk, so it was quite a local scandal when my ex-wife and I split up last summer. After Edith returned to London, I stayed on here, which is when people started asking why I wasn't serving at the front. Altogether uncomfortable,' he added, patting his right leg. 'Polio,' he explained. 'Unfit for duty.'

Ava's eyes opened wide. 'Did you catch it as a child?' she asked.

Tom nodded. 'I tried to join up. If I'd been accepted, I would have had officer status in the army, but they wouldn't let me in.'

'You're doing essential work here,' Ava said staunchly.

'I'm the only vet within a radius of fifty miles,' he informed her. 'But it doesn't stop the clicking tongues and pointing fingers.' Tom gazed thoughtfully out to sea before he continued. 'The divorce is going through. The only obstacle is parental custody.'

'You have a child?'

'A son, Oliver,' Tom answered proudly.

Ava sensed that he felt vulnerable now that he'd shared his secrets with her. Squeezing his hand, she said softly, 'Thank you for telling me, Tom.'

Looking her straight in the eye, he added, 'So now you know all there is to know about me, and you can be prepared for the local gossip.'

'I'm a big girl, I can handle that,' she retorted. 'But I do want to know one more thing,' she said with a giggle.

Tom lifted her chin and stared into her honest, shining eyes. 'And what might that be?' he asked.

'That we're going to ride out here again soon,' she answered softly.

'That can easily be arranged, young lady!' he replied, and pulled her closer to him on the warm sand. 'Now I want to know all about you, Ava Downham. How come you're so far away from home?'

Ava sighed. 'It's a long story with the wrong ending.'

Stroking her hair, Tom said, 'Tell me.'

So Ava told him her story.

'That's rotten luck,' he said when she'd finished.

'It was, for sure,' she replied. 'But, if I'm honest, I love working with Maudie and Ruby. We laugh ourselves silly below stairs!'

'So you're not resentful?'

'Not any more. I think I secretly enjoy the challenge,' she admitted, for the first time.

But talking about her friends made Ava suddenly remember the time. 'Bugger!' she cried, and jumped to her feet. 'I should be back by now.'

Tom reluctantly rose and accompanied her to the waiting

horses. 'I promise you, this is the first of many gallops we'll have on this glorious beach.'

Ava gazed into his hazel eyes, which were flecked with gold lights. 'I hope so,' she answered, with a happy smile.

After a quiet ride back, the contented horses snickering and nudging each other like playful children, they arrived at the stables, where Tom said, as he lifted Ava from the saddle, and held her briefly in his strong arms, 'Off you go, I'll see to the horses.'

Ava gazed into his tanned, handsome face. 'Thank you for a wonderful afternoon,' she whispered.

'Thank *you*,' he said, and gently traced a finger down her cheek.

Ava dragged herself away, and walked quickly back to the hall, where, below stairs, she stood smiling and radiant in the doorway of the kitchen. Her happy smile rapidly faded when Ruby ran towards her, almost in tears.

'What's happened? What's wrong?' Ava cried.

'It's Maudie!'

Dreadful thoughts rushed into Ava's head. Had she had a row with Lord Walsingham and run away from the hall? Had she had an accident, cut herself with the carving knife, got run over, been electrocuted? Was she in a hospital bed in King's Lynn?

'What's the matter with her? Where is she?' Ava demanded.

'Maudie's fine,' Ruby quickly told her. 'It's her dad. He's had a stroke.'

Ava covered her mouth with her hand and gasped, 'Is he alive?'

'Yes,' Ruby told her. 'He's been taken to hospital.'

Ava immediately imagined the danger of being in a London hospital. It could be hit by one of the German bombs that rained down every night on the war-ravaged capital.

'Poor man,' she whispered.

'Maudie left an hour ago,' Ruby concluded. 'Rafal gave her a lift to the station. They went off, nattering in Polish. She was in tears, he was being really kind to her, calmed her down, I think – though I haven't a clue what he was saying.' She couldn't resist a little joke as she added. 'It certainly wasn't about cups and sauces or knives and forks! That much I do know.'

Apart from worrying about Maudie, who, the girls knew, was devoted to her father, there was also the overwhelming prospect of how were they ever going to manage without her. Everything would take so much longer: setting the trays, carrying them upstairs, cooking, prepping and serving all the meals, and the endless, endless waves of clearing away and washing up.

'We've got to put our best foot forward and get on with it, Ruby,' Ava said, lighting up a Woodbine. 'Poor Maudie's dodging bombs in London, and there are brave pilots flying out on bombing raids every night from Holkham airfield.'

Ruby nodded. 'You're right, Ava; the worst thing that could happen to us is breaking our necks running up and down those damn stairs,' she chuckled.

For all their brave words and determination, there was no denying that, without Maudie, their workload was virtually impossible to manage.

'I could get Mum to come and help with the washing-up,' Ruby suggested, as she set the supper trays with the Spam salad that Maudie had prepared before she got the bad news about her father.

'That'd help,' Ava replied.

They staggered upstairs with the loaded supper trays. At the top of the stairs, they bumped into Rafal, who firmly relieved Ruby of her tray.

'Rubee, I take, *tak*?'

Ruby nodded gratefully.

'Thanks, Raf. I'll go back and get another load.'

Rafal helped the girls lay out the supper, then he said, 'Maudie in London. Her father, sick. I know'

Ruby was right: he'd obviously got all the relevant information from Maudie on his drive to King's Lynn station.

'I gives help to you this night,' he added, then tapped his watch. 'I go, nine o'clocks.'

Ruby and Ava hugged him.

'Thank you, Raf!' they cried, as the gong for six-thirty supper rang and the hungry code girls filed into the canteen.

With Rafal's generous help, supper went almost to plan, though none of the diners could have been unaware of a breathless Rafal frantically running up and down the kitchen stairs with empty trays and dirty dishes.

'You're down on numbers,' the Brig remarked to Ava.

Without stopping to clear away, she quickly replied, 'Maudie's had to go home.'

'Can you manage?' he asked.

'No! But needs must.' Ava bustled off with more dirty dishes.

Bella, sitting at a table with a group of chattering trainees, also noticed the cook's frenzied activity and the fact that a young man in RAF uniform was clearly helping out.

'Looks like the cooks are overstretched,' she observed.

'Don't look at me!' her companion exclaimed, pushing aside her empty plate and lighting a cigarette. 'I've got to practise my Morse code for tomorrow's test.'

Below stairs, Rafal insisted on washing up with Ruby.

'Please rest,' Ruby begged, and tried to sit him in a chair by the Aga. 'You're on duty all night, you'll be worn out.'

Rafal didn't understand, but it didn't matter, as he had no intention of sitting and resting.

'I wash for you!' he announced, and stuck his hands into the sink, which was brimming with soapsuds.

Ruby smiled fondly at him. She loved Rafal's sweet mistakes and his determination to communicate, even if he did say the wrong things. Turning to Ava, who was wiping down the worn wooden tops with a damp cloth, Ruby said, 'What do you do with a fella like this?'

'Give him a big kiss,' Ava joked. 'We would never have got through supper without his help.'

Rafal was surprised when Ruby took his hands out of the water and turned him to face her.

'Thank you,' she said. She held his face and softly kissed his warm cheek.

Blushing and laughing, a delighted Rafal dabbed soap bubbles on Ruby's nose, then kissed her cheek, too. *'Tak*, thank you, my Rubee!'

10. Another Pair of Hands

Bella had worked out an effective way of avoiding her family, who would resent spotting her mixing with 'commoners'. By confining herself to the south wing and the utilitarian dining and recreational areas, she'd managed to avoid them, though she had half glimpsed Edward on the grand staircase and seen her mother being chauffeur-driven by Dodds down the wide sweep of the drive.

'We're like ships in the night,' Bella thought to herself, with a relieved smile.

She loved the communications course. It suited her analytical, mathematical mind; she always got top marks at the end of every test, which her colleagues good-naturedly teased her about.

'Brainbox!' they called her or 'teacher's pet!'

Seeing her potential, the Brig singled her out for advanced training. Thrilled to be asked, Bella immediately agreed to attend extra classes outside of the scheduled timetable. Without mentioning his work at Bletchley Park, the Brig explained to Bella that when she had completed her advanced-skills course she would be eligible for top-secret work in a communications centre which specialized in cracking German codes. Bella's cheeks blazed bright pink with excitement when she heard this; doing high-priority war work was more than she'd ever dared dream of.

Bella looked forward to her twice-weekly meetings with the Brig. During the day, he was always brisk with his trainees, sometimes to the point of brusqueness, plus, he was always accompanied by Miss Cox, who guarded him like a terrier guards a bone. In the early-autumn evenings in the south wing library, with a fire (lit by Bella!) crackling in the hearth, Bella saw another side of Brigadier Charles Rydal. He was a quiet, intellectual man with strong views on politics and religion; he was also a brilliant teacher. Bella loved the intriguing challenge of learning the codes and then the even harder job of decrypting them. Sometimes the coded messages he set her were funny and made her laugh out loud; at other times, they were so difficult she entirely failed to decrypt them, which put her in a bad mood.

'There are too many combinations,' she moaned.

'That's the whole point of code-breaking,' he said. 'You've only got to break one word, like "Hitler", then, with time, the rest will fall into place.'

'But it's not that simple!' she cried.

'I never said it was simple. It's a question of elimination. It's a slow, tedious process, like doing a crossword – you keep cancelling out until you've completed the puzzle.'

Bella threw back her head and laughed at this. 'It's a thousand times harder than any crossword, even the *Times*',' she objected, pointing at the newspaper lying in his lap.

'You're clever enough. You'll work it out,' the Brig said, admiring her eyes, which always lit up with excitement when she was working alongside him.

Bella particularly enjoyed their time after the lessons, when the Brig would build up the fire, pack his pipe with cherry tobacco and sit back in a battered old leather armchair, cradling in his hand a small tumbler of Scotch. Bella loved to watch him relax. His dark brown eyes became soft and dreamy as he stared into the flames, and all the tension of the day flowed out of him. It was on one of these occasions, when she wasn't quite sure whether to chat or keep quiet, that the Brig suddenly said, 'Your parents should be very proud of you.'

Bella literally hooted with incredulity. 'Quite the opposite!'

The Brig gazed at Bella, curled up in an armchair. With her soft, blonde hair framing her sweet face, she looked as innocent as a child.

'Then they should be thoroughly ashamed of themselves,' he said, more forcefully than he'd meant to.

'I can sort of understand it. I've always let them down,' Bella tried to explain. 'They never wanted a plain, dowdy daughter like me.'

'God spare us!' he cried. 'You are neither plain nor dowdy. You're beautiful and extremely clever.'

Bella's heart pounded so loudly she was sure the Brig would hear it through her ribcage. At school she'd been told she was clever, but nobody had ever said she was beautiful. As he gazed into her wide, staring eyes, a slow smile spread across his face.

'Would you like me to inform them that you're the brightest trainee I've ever taught?'

'Believe me, they wouldn't be impressed, though they'd love it if you could find me a husband with a title,' she said with a mischievous smile.

'Waste of a fine brain,' he said, and returned to rekindling his pipe.

They sat on in companionable silence, the Brig reading his newspaper and Bella pretending to read the decoding manual they'd been working on. In fact, she hardly read a word. All she could think of was the Brig's words: 'You're beautiful and extremely clever.' That was praise indeed.

At breakfast the next day Bella saw Ava and Ruby struggling to serve, this time without Rafal to help them. When she caught sight of Ava hauling the hot-water urn on to the serving table, she abandoned her breakfast.

'Let me help,' she said, and took hold of one of the handles.

Too tired to protest, Ava smiled gratefully.

'Are you short-staffed?' Bella asked, as they settled the urn on the large serving bench.

Ava nodded. 'You could say that,' she said, as she hastily laid bread and marge on the tables. Until Maudie returned, there'd be no soft, warm breakfast rolls.

'Our second cook had bad news from home and had to return to London.'

'So it's just you and Ruby downstairs?' said Bella.

'Just the two of us,' sighed Ava, and hurried below stairs.

Bella hung about in the dining room, waiting for Miss Cox to leave the Brig alone for a few minutes. When she did so, Bella dashed to his table.

'Would you mind if I helped the girls in the kitchen?'

The Brig lowered the newspaper he'd been reading and gazed up at Bella, who was breathless.

'They're short-staffed,' she added.

'I know,' he replied.

'I promise you my work won't suffer,' she assured him. 'I'll only spend my spare time helping out.'

Knowing how capable she was, the Brig made a suggestion. 'You could skip the classes that you're well ahead in – Morse code and signalling, for instance?'

Bella's face melted into a warm, happy smile as she realized he *wanted* her to help the girls below stairs.

'Yes! Yes!' she answered eagerly.

'I'd prefer you not to skip your advanced classes with me,' he added quickly.

Bella gazed into his soft brown eyes. 'I'd rather die than give those up!' Blushing, she immediately tried to rectify her outburst. 'They're my top priority, I'd never miss them,' she added primly.

The Brig was surprised at the relief that flooded through him; he would have been very disappointed if she'd ask to suspend her one-on-one classes with him, and not just because of the progress she was making; the hours he spent with her in the library were some of the happiest of his week.

'Are you a good cook?' he joked.

Bella gave him a big, confident smile. 'Just you wait and see!'

A little later, Bella skipped below stairs and presented herself for work.

'Give me a pinafore, and I'll fill in for Maudie,' she said, with a winning smile.

Although they were astonished, Ava and Ruby didn't argue; instead, they gave Bella a pinafore and a long list of jobs to do. Over the next few days, they quickly learnt to value Bella's presence. For one thing, she was fit and strong and could run up and down stairs with vats of stew, several pies and a loaf tucked under her arm! Bella, of course, had to keep up with her own work; she only skipped the classes the Brig suggested and never missed a single private class in the library; in fact, she enhanced them by bringing slices of cake or some nutty cheese and warm bread for him to eat.

'Are you trying to fatten me up, young lady,' the Brig teased as he ate whatever she'd brought.

'Just building up your strength for code-breaking,' she said, admiring his long, lean body, stretched out in the battered old armchair.

'Get over your pathetic schoolgirl crush,' she told herself firmly, tearing her eyes away from him. 'The man's nearly double your age!'

As the days turned to weeks, Bella revealed her real culinary talent, which was cooking game. Unlike squeamish Ava, who was revolted by blood and innards, Bella could skin rabbits and hares, pluck pheasant and wild duck, make pâté from mackerel and crab, and her game pie was to die for. Nobody would argue that Maudie and Ava were good cooks, but Bella's flair and creativity took below-stairs cooking to another level. When her fellow trainees were upstairs making bedtime cocoa, Bella was to be found below stairs, happy in the kitchen, making pies, bottling or jamming leftover fruit, boiling chutney made from anything she could find; apples, pears, carrots, cabbage, beetroot, onions, vinegar, ginger and dried fruit.

'You're the queen of making do in wartime, lass,' Ava said, as they sat around the kitchen table one afternoon, smoking Woodbines and drinking scalding-hot tea. 'You could make summat from nowt, as mi mam would say.'

'I really enjoy the challenge,' Bella admitted.

'By the way,' said Ruby, as she topped up her tea from the big brown kitchen teapot. 'His lordship said to congratulate the cook on yesterday evening's venison casserole.'

Bella rolled her eyes. 'He'd choke if he knew his youngest daughter had cooked it!'

'Thank God it's autumn,' Ruby said gratefully. 'There'll be more game after his lordship's seasonal shoots. It should keep us going until well into the New Year.'

'Nineteen forty-two!' said Ava with a heavy sigh.

'And still fighting,' Bella added. 'The Germans are bombing the living daylights out of our cities.'

'Pity the poor sods living there, bombed out of house and home,' said Ava, as she lit up another cigarette.

'I'm grateful Raf's a mechanic and not a pilot,' Ruby said earnestly. 'At least he's safe on the base.'

'When I lived upstairs I used to see the planes flying out over the North Sea. It made me shudder to think how many would never come back,' Bella said sadly.

Ruby raised her brimming teacup. 'Here's to our brave lads in the RAF!'

'*Cheers!*' her friends replied in earnest.

On a dank and misty November morning, grim news was announced on the radio; the British aircraft carrier *Ark Royal* had been torpedoed and sunk by a U-boat just off Gibraltar.

'My God!' Ava cried as they listened to the BBC news announcer. 'The crew survived. They played a big role in the sinking of the *Bismarck* in May.'

'But the ship's gone down, that'll hurt our national pride,' Bella observed.

'Sounds like it sank quickly,' Ruby said. 'I'm glad the crew got safely away.'

The kitchen phone shrilled out.

'I'll get it,' said Ava. 'It's probably the Fakenham grocer wanting more ration coupons.'

When she recognized the warm voice on the other end of the line, Ava smiled in delight.

'Hello, Tom!' she said softly.

'Have you been avoiding me?' he teased.

'Of course not,' she replied.

'I've decided I'm going to put in an official complaint to His Majesty's government,' Tom joked. 'It's outrageous to keep a beautiful woman chained to a hot Aga!'

Ava laughed and explained: 'Maudie had to go home and we've been rushed off our feet.'

'Well, I'm certainly not waiting till Maudie comes back to see you again,' Tom said firmly. 'I'll be at the Walsingham stables this afternoon. Can you pop over at four, just to say hello?'

'I'm sure I can be spared for half an hour,' she replied.

'See you later,' he finished cheerily.

Ruby and Ava were concerned about losing Bella, who they'd come to like very much in the brief time Maudie was away. Apart from being grateful for her help and enthusiasm, Ava was, frankly, amazed by Bella herself.

'She's a fantastic cook and a lovely, kind, generous woman. I can't believe she's a Walsingham. She couldn't be more different from the rest of her rotten family.'

'She's had a tough time, poor kid,' Ruby told her. 'When I came to the hall at fourteen, I envied the gentry but, as I got to know the family, I felt sorry for Lady Annabelle, as she was then. Her bloody family never stopped criticizing her. She couldn't get anything right for trying, and that bitch of a sister picked on her for everything; she took a real pleasure in mocking her hair, her clothes, her weight. She made poor Lady Annabelle cry nearly every day. Wealth doesn't always bring happiness,' Ruby concluded, with a heavy sigh.

'The Walsinghams are a mystery to me,' Ava said. 'Why is Lord Edward not in the armed forces? And how come his sister's dodged female conscription? She might be drunk from dawn till dusk, but she's young and strong enough for factory work.'

Ruby burst into a fit of giggles. 'Oh, I can just see her driving a farm tractor or making bombs in a munitions factory! She'd get her hands dirty or, worse still, break a precious fingernail!'

Maudie's compassionate leave only extended to a week. Even though she begged for more, hard-hearted Miss Cox refused, saying her duty was to her war work, not her family. She also insisted that Bella's place was above stairs, though the Brig didn't seem too fussed.

'Just as long as you keep up with your course work, you can do what you want in your spare time,' he said to Bella, in the privacy of the library. 'Don't make it too obvious or you'll have Cox on your back and, for God's sake, don't stop making your game pies. I'd go to prison for one of those!' he joked.

Bella smiled happily. After a compliment like that, she'd make the Brig a game pie every week until the day she died!

When Bella heard about Maudie's imminent return, she didn't, as her new friends expected, sigh with relief and make plans to rejoin her fellow trainees. Instead, she said, 'I intend to continue working below stairs with you, if you'll have me?'

'How can you do that?' Ruby exclaimed.

'Don't you have to finish your course?' Ava asked.

'Please don't think I'm being big-headed,' Bella begged, 'but, in Maudie's absence, I proved that I could study *and* cook. The Brig doesn't have a problem with me helping out, as long as I keep on top of my work and –' she blurted it out – 'I absolutely love being down here. We have great fun, and we make great food, which I love eating!'

'We've loved it, too, our lass,' Ava answered fondly. 'Don't know what we would have done without you, especially when it came to gutting those blasted hares!'

Looking suddenly self-conscious, Bella asked an awkward question. 'Do you think Maudie will mind me being in the kitchen?'

'No, not at all!' Ava cried. 'She'll be thrilled to bits to have an extra pair of hands.'

'She won't think I'm posh and bossy?' Bella asked shyly.

'Probably, but she'll get used to it,' Ava teased.

Ruby's face lit up as she realized that, with Maudie back and Bella helping out, they might finally reduce their long hours.

'Maybe we'll have a bit of spare time for canoodling!' she joked, then asked, in all seriousness, 'Have you got a boyfriend, Bella?'

Bella shook her head and shrugged dismissively. 'Too busy,' she replied. 'And anyway, let's face it, no man I chose would ever be up to scratch for my family. Only a crown prince or a head of state would bring a smile to their miserable faces!'

'You're pretty and clever – you should have a boyfriend,' romantic Ruby insisted.

Bella kept her thoughts to herself; the only man who'd ever made her heart skip a beat was Brigadier Charles Rydal, and he was nearly old enough to be her father.

'I'd rather roast a goose or bake a pie – and eat it, of course!' Bella retorted.

'Well, if you're that keen to stick with us, can I beg a favour?' Ava asked, nervously watching the kitchen clock ticking its way up to four. 'Can you help Ruby with tea while I run over to the stables to meet Tom for half an hour?'

'Sure,' Bella replied. 'Is he checking the horses?'

Cheeky Ruby giggled, 'More like checking out Ava!' she joked.

Ava was already on her feet, heading for the back door. 'Got to rush. It'll be dark soon,' she called over her shoulder.

'Don't do anything I wouldn't do!' Ruby called after her, but the bang of the closing door announced that Ava was gone, winging her way across the icy yard to Mr Tom Benson.

11. Made with Love

It was wonderful to have Maudie back.

'How's your dad?' Ava and Ruby asked as soon as she walked through the kitchen door.

'Much, much better,' Maudie replied, with a relieved smile. Draping her coat over a chair, she sat at the table, where she sipped the hot tea that Ruby had poured for her. 'He'll never regain full strength in his right arm, but he's strong enough to argue about politics, his favourite subject,' she said with a fond smile. 'He's worried sick about his relatives in Kiev. He's not heard a word since the Germans took the city in September.'

'It's beyond human belief that the Germans just marched in and slaughtered thirty-three thousand Jews just because of their religion,' Ava cried.

'They can't possibly kill all the Jews in Europe,' Ruby murmured incredulously.

'I think Adolph Hitler is evil enough to have a good try,' Maudie replied angrily.

As a heavy silence descended, Ava lightened the mood by squeezing Maudie's hand. 'We missed you soooo much,' she said.

Maudie, who looked tired after the anxious days she'd spent looking after her father, warmly returned her squeeze.

'And I missed you, too. Can you believe, I missed my life of drudgery? I must have gone soft in the head.' She pointed her forefinger at her smiling friends. 'I blame you two for making below stairs a happy place.'

'It's even happier these days, now we've got extra help,' Ruby told Maudie.

'Has Timms had a mid-life crisis and agreed to peel potatoes for us?' Maudie joked.

'No, much better than that,' Ruby cried. 'We've got Lady Annabelle on board.'

'Or Bella Wells,' Ava corrected her

'Didn't she drop her posh title so she could join the trainees?' Maudie recalled.

'That's right,' Ruby said. 'She noticed we were in a flat spin after you'd left; she walked into the kitchen, put on a pinnie and got stuck in. She's a brilliant cook and she loves her grub, too.' She chuckled. 'If she fancies anything, like soup at the end of the day, she just pops into the larder, collects some vegetables and, before you know it, there's a bowl of tasty, hot soup on the table with a bit of cheese on toast. Nothing seems to be an effort. Cooking's as natural as breathing to her.'

'She told us her parents never allowed her near the kitchen, they thought an interest in cooking was below her,' Ava told Maudie.

'What a bunch of snobs!' Maudie scoffed.

'Actually, Bella secretly spent a lot of time down here when she was little,' Ruby informed her friends. 'It was her escape from her nagging parents. When Cook was off, she'd mess about in the kitchen, trying out recipes. 'Course, Timms always shooed her back upstairs, but she always managed to sneak back down again.'

'She sounds good news,' Maudie replied, then added with a mischievous smile: 'As long as she doesn't take over my baker's role, she's more than welcome!'

Maudie turned her sparkling green eyes on her friends,

who were busy lighting up their Woodbines. 'So . . . what have you two been up to while I've been away?'

'I had a lovely time with Tom,' Ava answered dreamily.

'Well, now I'm back and Bella's joined the team, you should be able to grab a couple of hours a week to go riding,' she said with a smile.

'I'd *love* that!' Ava exclaimed.

'And what about you, Ruby' Maudie asked.

'I wish you'd teach me some more Polish, then I could get to know Rafal a bit better! We communicate mostly in stupid sign language.'

'You don't need words for kissing,' Maudie giggled.

'Rafal's so shy,' Ruby told her friends. 'I think he's frightened of kissing me.'

'So kiss him instead!' Ava cried.

'I don't want to shock the poor lad by throwing myself at him,' Ruby answered primly.

Ava nodded sympathetically. 'It's difficult, especially now there's a war on; the news we hear, day in and day out, of death and destruction, loss and hardship, makes you think, why shouldn't we grab life by the throat and enjoy every moment, because who knows what tomorrow might bring?'

'My body's a temple, according to Rafal,' Ruby sighed.

'And I'm taking it carefully with my handsome divorcee,' Ava admitted.

'What about you, Maudie?' Ruby asked. 'Have you ever had a boyfriend?'

'Never!' Maudie laughed. 'There were boys at home that I kissed and cuddled, but I've never met anybody who took my breath away.'

'It would have to be a very special man to catch you, Maudie,' Ruby said fondly.

'He'd have to be clever, strong and sensitive to handle you,' Ava said, with a knowing smile.

'And handsome and left wing and working class,' Maudie chipped in.

'We're talking about a likely lover, not a politician!' Ava joked.

'That's the trouble – I want all of those things,' Maudie answered truthfully. 'I'm sure I'll never find the right man, because I'm looking for Mr Perfect, and men like that just don't exist.'

Changing the subject, Ava asked, 'How was the East End? Is the bombing as bad as we're told?'

Cradling her mug of tea, Maudie shook her head sadly. 'It's like one big building site. Rubble everywhere, buckled metal, gaping holes, shattered churches, whole neighbourhoods razed to the ground, most of the kids have been evacuated now, thank God,' she added fervently.

'You must be worried sick about your parents?' Ruby asked.

Maudie nodded. 'I am, but they'll never leave the East End. The community there is strong, and they watch out for each other, and they need to at the moment,' she added grimly. 'Oswald Mosley might be in prison, but he's still got a lot of supporters.'

'Prison's the best place for the likes of Mosley – behind bars and out of trouble,' Ava said angrily.

'It's impossible to believe they openly support the Fascists,' Maudie seethed. 'Honestly, I could throw a brick at them!'

'Don't,' Ruby warned. 'You could finish up behind bars, too.'

'While I was at home I saw a fight break out between some Mosley supporters and soldiers in uniform; the soldiers were so incensed, they just went for them. The police quickly broke it up, but it was ugly.'

Ruby glanced nervously over her shoulder. 'Sometimes I think Lord Edward is a bit that way inclined,' she whispered.

Stunned, Maudie stared at her. 'Do you think he's a fascist?'

Ruby dropped her voice. 'I don't know what he is, but he's an odd bugger. Mum overheard him speaking German to one of his Cambridge pals. It's the language of the enemy!' she added in a shocked whisper.

'Don't be daft! I speak German, too,' laughed Maudie. 'And Polish and Yiddish. Does that make me the enemy?'

Still whispering, Ruby continued, 'One night at the start of the war, before you came here, he was raving about the Nazis over dinner. He'd had a few but, nevertheless, the things he said shocked me.'

'Like what?' asked Maudie, wide-eyed.

'How high-minded the Germans were, how focused and determined, not like us Brits, shilly-shallying about starting the war. He even said the government should take a leaf out of Hitler's book.'

'I don't think so!' Maudie retorted indignantly. 'I'll never understand how he's managed to skip conscription.'

Ava reluctantly rose to her feet. 'Come on, lasses, them apple fritters aren't going to fry themselves, and Bella's vegetable stew smells like it's beginning to catch.'

Maudie took a spoon and dipped it into the bubbling pan on top of the Aga. Her eyes widened as she savoured the rich flavour of Bella's stock.

'You're right. Bella's very good,' she said appreciatively.

Ruby chuckled as she dropped the battered apple rings

into a pan of sizzling oil. 'You can tell Maudie's back – politics is *big* on the menu when she's around!'

As Ruby and Ava had predicted, Bella and Maudie got on like a house on fire. They'd met briefly before and had liked each other in a passing, casual way, but now they were working together their friendship blossomed. They were both young women with strong views. Sometimes, it was hard to get a word in edgeways when the two of them got going on politics, religion, the war, Hitler, Churchill, female conscription . . . the list was endless. They shared a bedroom and swapped notes on the books they were reading as they snuggled down at night.

'Go to sleep!' Ava often called out, as she tapped on the adjoining wall. 'You'll never get up in the morning!'

When Bella and Maudie cooked together, Ava and Ruby had to hide their smiles as both girls sparred to try to create more appealing meals from the rations and the food from the estate.

'You're giving me a headache,' Ava complained. 'A pie's a pie at the end of the day. The people upstairs will wolf down anything we give them.'

Maudie threw up her hands. 'That doesn't mean we've got to be dull.'

'Not when Peter's picked up a couple crabs, which are right now sidling around the pantry,' laughed Bella, who'd earlier seen Ava running screaming down the corridor, away from the scuttling crabs.

Ava threw an oven glove at Bella, who was doubled up with laughter. 'Nobody told me there were crabs on the loose!'

'It was one of the funniest sights I've ever seen.' Bella hiccupped as she wiped tears of laughter from her face.

'I can tell you one thing, the Brig's loving Bella's fine fare,' Ruby said cheekily. 'I think your wild-duck pâté is made with a dash of *love*.'

This time, it was a blushing Bella's turn to whizz the oven glove across the room. 'Shut up!' she cried.

With four of them working in the kitchen, the girls did now get some time off. Ava wasted no time in arranging a few hours riding on Holkham beach one bright clear winter morning.

'God, I've missed this,' she said, as she and Tom trotted past fields where grey lagged geese honked and marsh harriers circled high overhead, hunting for voles in the ditches.

An icy cold wind blowing in from the east didn't stop Drummer and Lucas breaking into a gallop and pounding across the wide sweep of the empty beach. Later, with the frisky horses safely tethered, Ava laid out the picnic lunch she'd prepared for Tom: boiled-crab sandwiches, hot coffee spiced with brandy, and mince pies. Delighted and surprised by the spread, Tom leant over impetuously and kissed Ava on the cheek.

'Thank you,' he said softly. 'It's a long time since somebody made a fuss of me.'

Ava blushed. She felt hot, even though the wind whistled around them as they snuggled down in the sand dunes facing the turbulent North Sea.

'Hard to think, with all the peace and beauty around us, that soldiers are fighting on the other side of that sea,' Tom said, as they rose from the shelter of the dunes and returned to their horses.

'God help them,' Ava said fervently.

As they trotted slowly back through the pine woods, pheasants flapped and fluttered in the undergrowth. They disturbed a sleepy owl, who hooted in the swaying treetops, and a deer with her baby shot out from behind a belt of trees, startling the horses, who snorted as they pawed the ground. When they reached the hall, Tom helped Ava dismount. This time, he held her in his arms.

'Ava,' he said, staring into her sparkling blue eyes. 'I'm growing very fond of you.'

Even though she was supported in his strong arms, Ava felt her body going limp.

'I know it's complicated because of my divorce, and there will inevitably be scandal, but would you consider being my girl?'

Ava hadn't a single doubt in her head. 'Yes!' she said, with ringing sincerity. 'I can live with scandal for a good man like you.'

Seeing him standing speechless before her, with tears stinging his hazel eyes, Ava reached up and kissed him briefly on the lips. It was so good, she kissed him again. Sighing with pleasure, she clung to Tom for support.

'I think I might faint!' she giggled.

Tom gently lifted her chin. 'You're so beautiful,' he murmured.

Before he could kiss her again, Lucas and Drummer, impatient for their supper and a warm stable, whinnied shrilly, their hot breath flaring in the frosty air.

'I'll see to the horses,' Tom told Ava, as he reluctantly released her.

Dizzy and dazed by his kisses, Ava nodded.

'See you soon, darling,' he called, as he led the horses, clip-clopping, across the icy yard.

Ava hugged herself as she ran laughing to the kitchen door. 'I'm Tom Benson's darling!'

When Ruby had a night off, she took Rafal to see *Gone with the Wind* at the old picture house in Wells. Rafal hardly understood a word of the film, but it was clear he adored Brett Butler. He had Ruby helpless with laughter as he mimicked him, and said, 'Frankly, my dear, I don't give a damn!'

'You don't even know what it means!' Ruby teased.

'I know he fed up with stupid Scarlett woman!' Rafal replied, looking into Ruby's dark eyes. 'I never like this Brett with my Rubee,' he said, and pulled her to him, he kissed her on the lips for the first time.

Astonished and delighted, Ruby closed her eyes and abandoned herself to this first glorious blast of passion with Rafal.

'Bloody hell!' she thought to herself. 'Maybe we should watch *Gone with the Wind* a bit more often!'

12. De-mob Happy

With the code girls' course coming to an end, Ruby wondered where they'd all go.

'I looked into where I might be sent after my training,' Ava said with a wry smile. 'I tell you, these girls are needed *everywhere*! Tracking, signals, administration, interception, radar imagery, postal communications . . . I fancied myself in mapping,' Ava said, and struck a pose, one hand on her hip, the other holding up her mass of thick, dark hair. 'Imagine me in a utility suit, waving a stick around and shouting instructions.' She dropped the pose and grimaced as she looked down at her cook's uniform. 'And what did I get? A cook's pinnie and my dreams in pieces!'

'Stop moaning,' Ruby teased. 'You might not have met Tom Benson if you were a code girl upstairs.'

'I suppose that's one good thing about being a skivvy!' Ava laughed.

'Won't you be moving on soon, Bella?' Maudie asked.

'Actually, I'm staying here,' she replied.

Maudie gave her a long, sideways look. 'Why?'

'To do further advanced code-breaking with the Brig,' Bella answered, rather shyly.

'*Oooooh!* Is that what you call it?' mocked Ruby.

'Training you up for spy work, eh?' Ava joked.

'Let the poor girl speak,' Maudie cried, as Ava and Ruby started giggling.

'He obviously can't bear to lose you,' Ava teased.

'Put a sock in it, Ava,' Bella cried. 'The Brig's almost old enough to be my father!'

'You don't look at him the way a daughter looks at a father,' Ava remarked.

'He's keeping you here because he doesn't want to lose a great cook!' Ruby laughed.

'We're *all* brilliant cooks – the best in the world!' Maudie added, with a dramatic flourish of her hands.

'Seriously, Bella,' Ava said, 'I thought you wanted to get away from this place and your family?'

'I did – I do – but if further training is going to help me get a better placement, then I don't mind staying on a bit longer, especially now that I work below stairs with you interfering old bats!' she added with a giggle.

'We're glad you're staying, Bella,' said Ruby, and gave her friend a big hug. 'We love you to bits!'

Not used to open shows of affection, Bella, clearly touched by Ruby's emotional outburst, quickly wiped a tear away. 'Thank you, Ruby, I love you all, too.'

Ava surprised them all by suddenly saying, 'Shall we cook a farewell dinner for our first official code girls?'

Bella, Maudie and Ruby nodded.

'Why not?' said generous Ruby. 'They've worked hard enough these last six months.'

'We'll have to come up with an extra-special menu for the night,' Maudie said. 'Nobody will want macaroni cheese for the hundredth time!'

'Let's see what Peter can rustle up,' said Bella. 'I'm already fantasizing about roast goose and apple sauce.'

'A goose in Norfolk in December – dream on!' Ava mocked.

As they started to prepare the teatime trays, Ruby said

excitedly, 'Just think. Once the trainees have left, we can start to look forward to our own Christmas. I'm going to spend every free minute with Rafal.'

'Don't get too carried away, Ruby. There's still the Walsinghams to feed.' Realizing what she'd said, Ava quickly apologized. 'Sorry, Bella.'

'You're right,' Bella responded. 'They will need feeding – if they're here. With a bit of luck, they might go to their club in London, but, even then, we've still might have the RAF officers.'

'Christmas doesn't stop the war for them, that's for sure,' Maudie said compassionately. 'Poor chaps, they'll still be flying out on bombing raids.'

Ava nodded. 'Let's not get too de-mob happy, we've a few more weeks to go till Christmas.'

Bella and the Brig decided on 7 December for the code girls' final dinner. Over the next few days, everybody got into the Christmas spirit. The excited trainees decorated the drawing room and library with paper chains they'd made from strips of brightly painted newspaper. Peter brought holly and mistletoe from the estate, and hung it around the doorframes, and tantalizing seasonal smells of steaming puddings and baking cakes drifted up from the kitchen.

Predictably, as Ava had foretold, there wasn't a goose to be had in Norfolk, but Peter somehow got hold of a hare, a rabbit and a pheasant. Even with Peter's contributions, though, the girls would have a job spinning out the meat between the number of diners.

'Don't worry. I got some tripe from the butcher in Wells,' Bella told her astonished friends.

'*Tripe!*' shrieked Ruby. 'How's that going to work with game?'

'It'll be fine once it's all cooked down with a good slug of sherry,' Bella answered confidently. 'Thank God I can still use Pa's vintage booze.'

Bella was right. The mixture was gently stewed with thyme, a splosh of Lea and Perrins sauce and an even bigger splosh of very expensive sherry, then Bella left it to cool and later she and Ava pulled the cold meat into a shape that roughly resembled a goose's breast.

'Depending on the angle you look at it,' Ava giggled, 'it could be a mock turkey, duck, cat or goose!'

Smeared with sausage meat flavoured with fresh sage and rosemary, it smelt wonderful.

'But there are no legs,' Ruby cried. 'How can we offer them a legless mock-goose?'

Ava smiled and held up two large parsnips. 'I read in a magazine about cooking on rations that parsnips tucked into a piece of meat looked a bit like drumsticks.' As she spoke, she stuffed the parsnips either side of the fake goose's breast. 'They might look better once they're roasted,' she giggled.

When evening came, menus embellished with pictures of Father Christmas were left on the tables of the festively decorated dining room. Maudie had written on each in her best swirling script: *First course: mackerel pâté and rye bread. Main course: mock-goose, roast potatoes, carrots, turnips and sprouts, rich gravy and stuffing. Dessert: apple pie and custard.*

'A feast!' Maudie declared, as they laid the hot dishes on trays ready to be taken into the dining room, where they had also set up a gramophone (borrowed by Bella from upstairs) so the diners could be entertained by Bing Crosby and Frank Sinatra as they ate their supper.

'I wish we'd thought of paper hats,' said Ruby, as she and

her friends entered the room. The mood was not quite what they'd expected.

'I thought we might get a cheer, or a burst of party poppers,' Ruby whispered. 'Everybody looks like a bomb's dropped.'

The code girls raised a smile when they saw the piping-hot food, but they certainly didn't stand up and applaud the hard-working cooks.

'What's going on?' Ava muttered to Maudie as they set the dishes down, ready for serving.

The Brig enlightened them. Rising to his feet, he said solemnly, 'Thank you for all your efforts, we really do appreciate it, but before we eat, can we stand in silence and pray for the many souls lost today in the bombing of Pearl Harbor.'

The jolly, festive meal the girls below stairs had worked so hard to produce, and which the trainees had been looking forward to, was eaten in subdued silence. Bella didn't dare to play the gramophone on such a tragic day. The trainees thanked the cooks as they left the dining room, but there was no getting away from the fact that the meal they'd planned with such excitement had fallen on a bad day.

'How were we to know the Japs were planning on bombing Pearl Harbor the very day we'd set for the leavers' dinner?' Ruby said sadly.

'Better we hadn't bothered at all,' sighed Maudie, as they staggered back downstairs with the dirty dishes. 'It's not exactly a night to celebrate, is it?'

When the Brig saw Bella's weary expression, he couldn't stop himself from relieving her of the tray she was holding, loaded up with greasy plates.

'I'll take that.'

Bella was too sad to argue. With tears in her eyes, she gratefully handed him the tray. 'How many died?' she asked.

'Not clear yet, but it must be thousands,' he replied. 'And no warning – though it looks like the scheming Japs have been planning it for months.'

Below stairs, Rafal and Tom were waiting for the girls in the kitchen.

'We needed company,' Tom said, pointing to himself and then at Rafal, who looked even paler than usual.

Like an unhappy child, Ava plonked herself down on Tom's knee and buried her face against his shoulder. 'We've been down here cooking all day and completely missed the news,' she said guiltily.

'I've been in the surgery all day, I've only just heard the news myself,' Tom said.

Rafal was holding Ruby in his arms. 'So many dead,' he said sadly. 'I pray God to help.'

Ruby stroked his silky fair hair. 'Come on, sweetheart. Sit yourself down and I'll make some tea.'

As she put the kettle on the Aga, the Brig appeared with the loaded tray. 'Mind if I join you?' he asked politely. 'I think we all need company tonight.'

Introducing himself as Charles Rydal, he shook hands with Rafal and Tom.

'You Mr Brig?' Rafal asked.

Looking a little uncomfortable, the Brig replied, 'Upstairs, I am the Brig but down here –'

He didn't get to the end of the sentence.

'You Brig – up and down, too!' Rafal insisted.

Clearly amused, Charles Rydal smiled across at Bella, who was covering her mouth, trying not to laugh.

'"The Brig" it is, then,' he chuckled.

As Ruby poured strong tea for everybody, Tom asked,

rather apologetically, 'You wouldn't have anything stronger than tea on offer, would you?'

Ruby turned to Bella, who nodded; she knew exactly what they all needed.

'I could beat my sister Diana to a fine bottle of brandy,' she said, and she set off purposefully towards the wine cellar.

Maudie, Bella and the Brig, Ruby and Rafal, and Ava and Tom sat around the kitchen table drinking tea and sipping the very best Walsingham brandy for well over an hour.

'One thing's for sure, America is up to its neck in the war now,' said Tom, draining his glass then, holding it out for a top-up. 'Here's to the Yanks!'

'*To the Yanks,*' came back the collective response.

Tom was right. A few days later, Adolf Hitler declared war on the United States of America.

13. Walsingham Christmas

As the departing code girls packed their cases and booked their train tickets home, the girls below stairs felt like a heavy weight was slowly lifting from their shoulders.

'I can hardly believe it's almost six months since I arrived here,' Ava said, brewing up for her friends.

Peter arrived with a couple of fresh mackerel.

'*Yum!*' said Bella, happily.

'You can thank the local fisherman for these,' Peter explained. 'He's always had a fancy for you, miss,' he told Bella with a cheeky wink.

Not a vain woman, Bella pulled a funny, flirty face. 'My God! Me and my Norfolk sex appeal!' she giggled.

Bella washed her hands and gutted the mackerel. 'We'll serve hot toast with mackerel pâté tonight. Once I've bulked it out with egg and oatmeal, it'll go a lot further,' she said, gleefully scooping out the innards and ripping off the greasy skin.

'I'm sure you were an executioner for the Spanish Inquisition,' Maudie teased, wrinkling up her nose at the sharp, tangy smell of the gutted fish.

'Be sure to keep some of that back for Rafal and Tom,' Ruby begged. 'They need feeding up.'

Bella laughed out loud. 'If ever two men were well fed, it's Rafal and Tom!' she exclaimed.

Whenever Raf wasn't on duty at Holkham airfield, he drove over to Walsingham Hall to spend every spare minute with his beloved 'Rubee!' He was there so often, he seemed like part of the furniture, though, being the gentleman he was, he never took advantage of his situation. He was always helpful and considerate, carrying heavy sacks of food and vegetables to and from the pantry. He sometimes gave Peter a hand in the vegetable garden, and he always 'brew tea', as he called it, for the tired girls after they'd finished serving.

Bella envied Raf and Ruby their ease and familiarity together. She wished the Brig would pop down to the kitchen, like he had the night they'd heard about the bombing of Pearl Harbor. It had been a sad but companionable evening. It was clear that everybody had liked the Brig, and Bella had felt inordinately proud of him. He was so clever and wise, but he was funny, too, and seemed to enjoy the company below stairs as much as they enjoyed his. Maybe he was too busy, or wary of intruding? Bella thought. Or maybe Miss Cox had tied a ball and chain around his ankle!

She wondered what the Brig would do over Christmas. Did he have a bachelor flat in London? Did he have an old mother to visit, or a sister with a large family who took care of him over the holidays? She realized that, though they'd spent many evenings together in the library, she really knew very little about him, while he seemed to know almost everything about her. Not that he'd asked – she'd chatted openly and easily about her home, her education and, though her family were not her favourite subject, the Brig knew everything he needed to know about them.

Fortunately, her family weren't about very much these days. His lordship was off on shooting parties up and down the county, and her mother was in London with Diana, who was busy pretending to look for war work. Astonishingly, Edward had – finally – got a job working for the War Office.

'Doing what?' Bella asked her mother, who'd telephoned to tell her what had been happening.

'Intercepting and translating German memos,' her mother had replied. 'At least I no longer have to hang my head in shame whenever friends enquire about my son.'

When Bella told the Brig of her brother's new post, he grinned. 'I wonder when that wayward sister of yours will snap into action?'

Bella shrugged. 'Probably the day peace is announced.'

The suppertime gong curtailed their conversation. Bella hurried to the kitchen, where she loaded the mackerel pâté and hot toast on to trays, then dashed upstairs, followed by Ruby, who was carrying Maudie's spicy cinnamon rolls.

Behind her, Ava chuckled to herself breathlessly.

'I'm looking forward to not running up and down these flaming stairs every five minutes during the Christmas break,' she declared.

The following morning, Dobbs drove Lord and Lady Walsingham home from their London flat, then, to the girls' surprise, he appeared, rather breathless, in the kitchen.

'Her ladyship has asked me to inform you that she will be hosting the traditional Walsingham Christmas dinner this year.'

'They're staying?' gasped a stunned Ava.

Dodds nodded. 'Yes, those are her ladyship's plans.'

'We thought they might be going to London,' Ruby said, hopefully.

Bella quickly took control of the situation.

'Thank you, Dodds,' she said, firmly but politely.

When Dodds had slipped away, the four girls stared at each other.

'I didn't think her ladyship would throw a traditional Walsingham Christmas dinner, not when there's a war on,' Ruby said incredulously. 'We could end up cooking for the county!'

'I'd imagined we'd have a few days off – not necessarily Christmas Day, but some time to ourselves,' Ava admitted. 'I thought I might go home, or at least spend a bit of time with Tom.'

'I was thinking the same about me and Raf.' Ruby sighed glumly. 'Looks like there's going to be no rest for the wicked.'

'They can't force us to cook for a bunch of aristocrat toffs! It's slave labour – insufferable,' fumed Maudie.

Without saying a word to her friends, Bella ran up the back stairs to the first-floor library. She knew that at this time of the day her mother would be there, writing letters. Throwing open the door, she burst into the room, exclaiming, 'Mummy! Are you seriously expecting the girls below stairs to cook for you and your guests over Christmas?'

Her mother laid down her pen and turned to her daughter, who looked flushed and untidy. 'Of course,' she replied coldly. 'I am allowed to re-inhabit my home now that the ghastly brigadier and his dreary trainees are leaving, at least for a while.'

Gritting her teeth, Bella slowly repeated herself. 'But they've spent the last six months working flat out!'

'That was not my decision!' he mother snapped. 'As far as I'm concerned, it's the least they can do. I think I deserve my home back sometimes, however briefly,' she added haughtily.

'But they were hoping to have some time off!' Bella cried.

'They'll do as they're told – they're my servants!'

'They are *not* your servants!' Bella protested. 'They're

hard-working young women who have been conscripted by the Brig – the brigadier,' she quickly corrected herself. 'Their remit does not extend to cooking for you and your guests on Christmas Day.'

'I have checked with Brigadier Rydal,' her ladyship retorted.

'You've talked to the him?' Bella gasped.

Her mother nodded curtly. 'He agreed he couldn't leave us without cooks at Christmas,' she finished, with a triumphant smile.

Bella felt like she'd been punched in the stomach. Seeing there was nothing she could do, she spun on her heel and walked out of the library, slamming the door hard behind her.

Seething, she ran back down the stairs, her heart hammering in her ribcage.

She found the Brig in the library, puffing on his pipe as he read *The Times*. He looked up as Bella barged, red-faced, into the room.

'You gave my mother permission to exploit my friends below stairs, even though you know full well how hard they've worked and how much they need a holiday!' she raged.

Dropping his paper and removing his pipe from his mouth, the Brig strode over to Bella in three quick steps. 'I had no choice.'

'*Rubbish!*'

Grabbing her by the shoulders, he stared hard into Bella's pale blue eyes, which were blazing with anger.

'You should know your mother better than anybody!' he said, in a hard, quiet voice. 'She has rights in her own home, and she is determined to exploit them. She said that she'd put up with six months' incarceration upstairs and she wanted to celebrate Christmas in the traditional Walsingham style. The only compromise I could get out of her was that the staff would be granted some leave – but only after Christmas. If your mother had had her way, she'd have had them working up until New Year's Eve,' he concluded, as he dropped his hands from Bella's shoulders.

Bella knew, of course, how difficult and demanding her mother could be. She knew that Lady Walsingham would give the Brig no leeway but, perversely, she was angrier with the Brig than her mother.

'I thought you were a bigger man than that,' she said, and walked out of the room.

Below stairs, Bella burst into tears. Rafal, who'd arrived a brief half-hour early to pick up some RAF officers, immediately put the kettle on.

'Looks like news is bad,' he said quietly.

'Is it true?' Ava asked.

Now slumped at the kitchen table, Bella nodded her head. 'Sorry,' she answered flatly.

Faced with the reality of the situation, Ava, typically, got down to brass tacks. 'How much work is it, really?' she asked.

Ruby, who knew from years of experience exactly what a Walsingham Christmas involved, replied, 'Formal candle-lit Christmas dinner for at least twenty, a Christmas tree as big as a house, cocktails, tiaras, house guests – a *lot* of bloody hard work!'

'I've a damned good mind to walk out right now!' Maudie said, pacing the kitchen floor in a blind fury.

'I wouldn't do that,' said a stern voice from the stairs.

Surprised, they turned as one to see the Brig standing there.

'I know how hard you've worked, and with a good and generous spirit, too. You deserve a rest but, unlike the trainees, who are free to go when their course is finished, you remain part of the Walsingham household.'

'I never signed up to be a servant!' Maudie protested. 'It's unjust! We are, by rights, allowed some time off – it's not such an unreasonable thing to expect.'

The Brig repeated what he'd told Bella. 'Lady Walsingham has rights which she is allowed to exercise in her own home.'

'Without even thinking to consult us?' Maudie demanded.

'Yes,' the Brig bluntly replied.

Bella's heart sank. It was an agony to see the Brig being yelled at, even though she'd been doing exactly the same thing herself only ten minutes ago! Now she was no longer in a raging temper, she could see it wasn't his fault; it was her family's determination to have their damn grand, traditional Walsingham Christmas, to show off to the county, to reclaim their aristocratic status and act as if they were important again. It was all such a mess. Pushing back the chair, she walked over to the Brig.

'If you're going to blame anybody, blame *me*. It's my family who demanded this; it's they who put pressure on the Brig, and then he's had to put pressure on us.' Without thinking, she took hold of the Brig's hand and stood firmly by his side. 'Please yell at me, not him,' she said, tears spilling from her eyes.

Not daring to look at Bella's sad, sweet face the Brig added, 'I'll work down here with you. I'll do everything I can to help,' he promised.

'I, too,' said Rafal.

Ruby swiped him playfully with a tea-towel. 'You daft sod, you might be on duty,' she giggled.

'My Rubee, I no sod!' he declared.

As the tense atmosphere lifted, Maudie sighed. 'I apologize, too. Jesus knows why I'm fussing about Christmas Day – I'm a Jew!'

With that remark, everybody started to laugh, and as they laughed they knew that, together, they'd get through the Walsingham Christmas route march!

It turned out the Brig was planning on staying in one of the estate cottages for most of the Christmas break.

'I wanted a bit of time on my own before I put in a visit to the family,' the Brig told Bella. 'And,' he added as he took her soft, white hand in his and kissed it, 'to be honest, I hated the thought of being far away from you,' he said gently.

Woozy with joy, Bella swayed and gripped the Brig's firm, warm hand.

'I enjoy your company, Bella Wells,' he added softly.

Bella felt tears filling her eyes. 'Nobody has ever said that to me in my whole life,' she replied, in an awed whisper. 'Nobody has ever wanted to hold on to me.'

'Oh, but I do! I do, so very much,' he said, pulling her into the warmth of his arms and pressing her shapely young body against his own.

Bella had to stand on her tiptoes to reach up to stroke his happy, smiling face.

'Dearest, dearest girl,' the Brig murmured, as he bent to kiss her tenderly on the lips.

Bella had never been kissed before. For the first time in her life, passion blazed through her like a flame. It seemed to melt her bones as it coursed through her body, then it settled somewhere low in her stomach, where she literally ached for the Brig. When they drew apart, she was trembling so much she had to lean against him.

'Wow, young lady,' he whispered into her soft, blonde hair. 'It's definitely the right decision to stay close to you. With kisses like that, you could set the world on fire!'

After several more kisses Bella asked him to show her where he was staying. It was an estate cottage just behind the Victoria Arms pub, freezing cold and basic. It was the kind of cottage she'd visited dozens of times with her mother when she was acting out her role of Lady Bountiful, bearing a basket of fruit from the greenhouse or freshly baked short-bread for the poor, grateful servants. Bella had hated what she thought were condescending, embarrassing visits, par-ticularly when her mother dragged her along to visit Ruby's family, who were her friends. Now she found the Brig's rented cottage charming, like a setting from 'The Three Bears' or 'Little Red Riding Hood'. The Brig, standing before the empty hearth and gazing at her with a mixture of joy and delight, held his arms out wide.

'Come here, sweet thing.'

Bella rushed towards him, rubbing her face against his rough, tweedy jacket, which smelt of cherry tobacco and lemon soap. She gave a blissful sigh.

'Promise you'll visit me in my hovel?' he teased.

Bella nuzzled her face against his. 'Yes, yes, yes!'

The Brig faithfully joined the team below stairs, who worked like slaves in the run-up to Christmas, and Ruby's predic-tions were spot on; it was candle-lit dinners for twenty, lunch for at least a dozen house guests, and teatime was re-established as well as the cocktail hour. House guests expected spotless linen sheets, fresh flowers and a fire in their room and breakfast (on request) to be served on a tray. Their former routine of feeding thirty people four meals a day seemed a breeze compared to the constant demands of the pampered Walsingham guests. There was always one bell or another dinging for attention behind the servant's baize door.

Maudie, who was ready to shoot the lot of them, threw up her hands and cried, 'God! Do they *ever* stop making demands?'

Dodds and Timms willingly took charge of the linen, the silver, the flowers, wine and glassware.

'I'll suggest wines to accompany the Christmas Day meal,' Bella firmly said to Dodds, who looked distinctly put out.

When he'd gone, she told her friends, 'I'm sick and tired of being told what Dodds recommends. He must have served the same wine since the Crimean War! Time for a change.'

Everybody pitched in. Ruby's mum and her auntie, and Rafal, when he was off duty, helped wash up.

'Well,' giggled Ruby. 'I suppose that's one way of getting to know my young man, though it's not quite what I'd planned!' she said, rolling her eyes at Raf, her mother and auntie, all chatting non-stop in pidgin English in the back scullery.

'How are you coping with the language?' Ruby's mum said loudly and slowly, as if Raf was deaf.

''Scuse me, Rubee's mama, what is "copping"?' Raf asked in baffled ignorance.

Ruby's mum frowned as she tried to find an alternative.

'Managing,' she tried. 'Is speaking our English a bugger for you, lovie? Hard work, like?'

'Ah, Engleeesh is hard; I stand on the ceiling, I sit on the floor.' Rafal laughed. 'But is the language of my Rubee, so I learn,' he ended, with a bright smile.

Tom helped, too, when he wasn't on call; he delivered calves all over the county. The Brig, too, wearing a pinafore and occasionally a Christmas paper hat, was kept busy, clearing away, making a toast, stirring soup, pouring drinks, rolling pastry or making a 'brew'. The male volunteers didn't put in a public appearance in the dining room; they left that to Ava, Maudie, Ruby and Dodds. Bella stayed below stairs, too, as most of the guests knew her – and the sight of her dressed as a servant might possibly kill her father stone dead! There were, however, several occasions which Bella simply couldn't get out of, Christmas dinner being one of them.

'Come with me – be my shield,' she begged the Brig. 'If you're beside me, they won't pick on me.'

'It's about time they stopped picking on you altogether,' he growled angrily.

It was bizarre to sit in the candle-lit dining room, where the fire of seasoned logs that Raf had laid earlier crackled in the huge grate. The food that Bella and her friends had produced tasted like sawdust in her mouth; all she could think of was the hours they'd spent working on a feast that everybody seemed to take totally for granted.

For this occasion, Peter had managed to find a goose. He had been under strict instructions from his lordship to scour the county for one. The bird, which had been well hung in the pantry, had been marinaded with dried prunes and port, and was accompanied by Norfolk duckling – Ruby's neighbours' ducklings, to be exact – stuffed with sage, lemon and onion. The foul were then roasted in the slow oven for most of the day, lovingly basted by Ava. The brandy-soaked Christmas puddings, which contained more breadcrumbs and grated apple than usual this year, to make up for the lack of dried fruit, were simmering on top of the Aga in bowls tightly secured with stout linen cloths. Local Walsingham cheeses were accompanied by port and Madeira from the Walsingham cellars.

'Not a bad spread for wartime, eh?' said Ava, as they surveyed their splendid efforts.

'I'd call it a bit more than "making do",' Ruby remarked. 'I wonder if the toffs upstairs will appreciate just how lucky they are!'

Dodds and Timms had done a great job of setting the long dining-room table. It obviously gave them huge pleasure to return, however briefly, to the impeccably high standards of pre-war days. The spotless, white damask cloth ran the length of the table, which easily seated twenty; it fell in snowy-white folds to the floor and was laid with the Walsinghams' finest silver and cut glass. In the centre of the table was a three-tiered, solid-silver Victorian dish holding grapes from the hothouse which dripped in delicate clusters over the fluted edges. At its base were this year's walnuts, picked on the estate and kept in the cellar especially for Christmas. Sweet-smelling lilies from the greenhouse were arranged in vases on the tables and around the room were festive bouquets of holly and mistletoe. Bella smiled as she admired the impressive preparations: her parents would be the talk of the county and, for a short time, before they were kicked back upstairs, they would feel grand again. Not for a minute did she want to return to her Lady Annabelle days; she had spent too many miserable Christmases around this very table, sad and lonely, alienated from her family. But not any more; not now that she had her friends downstairs and her beloved Brig at her side.

As the courses were brought in by Maudie, Ava and Ruby,

Bella smiled gratefully at her friends, who looked red in the face after running up and down stairs with trays of boiling-hot food. When they set down the roast goose, Bella couldn't believe that the guests didn't thank the cooks or even seem to notice their efforts.

'I feel like standing up and saying, "Hey, there's a war on, you know!"' she seethed. '"Savour the fine food and thank the hard-working cooks below stairs."'

The Brig gripped her hand under the table. 'Forget it, darling. This lot take it all in their stride. By the way,' he said, leaning in closer, 'you look amazing tonight.'

Bella blushed with pleasure. For six months, she'd worn a cook's pinafore in the kitchen or tweed skirts and woolly jumpers for classes. Now, for the first time in her life, she wanted to wear something that made her feel like a woman. She'd gone into the small market town of Holt to buy a new egg whisk but instead she'd bought a full-length, pale pink crêpe evening gown. When she saw her reflection in the shop mirror, she couldn't believe the lusciously feminine woman she was looking at really was her.

'You've gone to quite an effort,' Diana had said, as she tottered past her sister in a silver, sequinned, backless gown that revealed her slender, elegant body. She'd stopped in her tracks when she saw the brigadier sitting beside Bella.

'Oh, you're here!' she'd said rudely. 'I thought you'd left with those dreary girls you teach.'

'I invited him,' Bella had said, as she took a sip of champagne.

'Talking shop, are we? Morse code, tip-tap-tap,' Diana mocked as she swanned off back to her place at the far end of the table.

*

Later, over port and cheese, Lord Edward searched out the Brig. As he topped up his glass, he said, rather pompously, 'I'm sure you've been briefed about my recent appointment at the War Office?'

'I'm aware you're working for MI5,' the Brig replied.

'None of my family, including Annabelle, is aware of my new role. They think I'm translating German memos,' said Edward, a little too self-importantly. 'For obvious reasons,' he added, his gaze landing on Diana, who was laughing over-loudly at something said by the handsomest young man in the room.

The Brig held his gaze but didn't respond.

'Maybe we could discuss some issues connected with my operations?' Edward suggested.

'I think those issues are best dealt with by your contacts at the War Office, sir,' the Brig replied. 'Now, if you'll excuse me . . .'

Leaving Edward looking a little put out, the Brig rejoined Bella.

'What did he want?' she asked.

'He wants us to be friends,' the Brig told her.

Bella's eyes widened in surprise. '*Friends!* You and my brother?'

'Don't worry, darling, it's never going to happen,' the Brig replied.

The Brig and Bella slipped below stairs just as soon as they could. Bella ate some Christmas cake, then covered her pink dress with a big black pinafore and helped with the washing-up.

'It's so much happier down here than up there,' she said, smiling at the Brig, now also wearing a pinafore and drying the dishes she'd washed.

'I was hoping a couple of those obnoxious upper-class

twits might choke to death on the goose's wishbone,' Maudie giggled as she poured out glasses of sloe gin, which she'd made in the autumn.

'It was a wonderful feast,' Bella said.

'You cooked most of it,' laughed Ava.

Then Ruby made them all jump by clapping her hands. 'Listen,' she called. 'We've got something to tell you.' She turned to Rafal, who was blushing and smiling self-consciously.

'I ask Rubee to become wife!' he said.

A roar of approval from everybody in the kitchen went up.

'*Yeaahhhh!* Well done!'

'*Wonderful!*'

'*Congratulations!*'

As more sloe gin was poured, Ava, who was standing with her arm around Tom, asked, 'When did all this happen?'

'This morning, at Mass,' Rafal answered.

Smiling, radiant Ruby burst out laughing. 'It's true! Rafal took me to Mass at the Walsingham shrine. It's sooooo beautiful! We sang carols and said prayers, in Latin – no idea what they were on about,' she joked. 'We stayed on to light candles and, as they burnt, Rafal asked me to marry him and I said *yes* – definitely *tak!*'

Maudie raised her glass high. '*Do długiego i szczęśliwego życia. Powodzenia, Bóg błogosławi!*' she cried, then added in English: 'To a long and happy life. Good luck and God bless!'

'*God bless!*' came the resounding reply.

It was a happy time, despite the hard work, with all of the girls working together, laughing at their mistakes, getting up in the middle of the night to check the bread was rising on the hot plate, going out in the icy-cold mornings to pick up the milk, stealing kisses in the kitchen, hiding Christmas presents, drinking Maudie's sweet sloe gin, making cocoa around the Aga, and discussing politics till late in the night. Above all, the girls enjoyed the laughter and camaraderie brought about by their situation.

Ruby summed it up: 'It's a Christmas I'll never forget!'

When it was finally over and the last guests had driven away, Dodds and Timms retreated into their bolt-holes, the Walsinghams went to London for New Year, the Brig, reluctantly, left Bella to visit his family in Lincoln, Maudie took Bella to her home in the East End, Ruby stayed, happily planning her wedding with Rafal and her family, while Ava and Tom rode out daily on a snowy Holkham beach.

The new year opened with the signing of the Declaration of the United Nations by twenty-six Allied nations on 1 January 1942, shortly after which the first American forces arrived in Britain. The people prayed that the involvement of the US would radically alter the course of the war that had raged in the Germans' favour for well over two years.

PART TWO

1942

14. Squadron Leader Kit Halliday

Squadron Leader Kit Halliday had fallen asleep on the job – again! His long, lean, muscular frame was stretched out the length of the rickety old office chair that creaked and threatened to fall apart as he was roused from an uncomfortable sleep by Air Mechanic 1st Class Rafal Boskow arriving early with a brimming, pint-pot mug of strong tea.

'Here, sir,' said the eager young lad, setting the tea down without slopping it over the paper-strewn desk.

'Cheers, Raf,' Kit replied, smothering a yawn.

'Why you keep to sleep here, sir?' Rafal enquired. 'I take you with other officers to Walzing Hall?'

Kit nodded. It would be a lot more sensible to head off to the officers' billets at Walzing Hall, as Raf always called the requisitioned stately home, but he'd been so busy over the last few months he'd had no choice but to work through the night, every night, even when he was supposedly on leave.

'Want bacon buttee, sir?' Rafal asked.

Kit nodded again.

'Two please, Raf!' Kit said hungrily and held two fingers in the air to make his point.

As Rafal hurried off, Kit smiled to himself and rubbed some life back into his cold, numb arms; the young Pole's English had come on in leaps and bounds since he'd been courting the maid at Walsingham Hall – and Rafal had proudly told Kit she was now his fiancée. The pale-haired, blue-eyed and earnest young man clearly didn't hang about when it came to women:

rumour had it that he'd snapped up one of the best-looking local girls almost as soon as he had arrived at the airfield.

Kit had a lot of time for the Polish servicemen stationed at Holkham. Reliable, hard-working and loyal, Raf, along with some of his fellow countrymen, had joined the RAF to fight alongside the British after they entered the war following Hitler's invasion of Poland in 1939. Rafal was one of the talented mechanics who worked with the ground crew, diligent guys who knew the workings of a Spitfire, a Hurricane and a Wellington like the back of their hands. They scrupulously prepared the planes for take-off and could literally reassemble them when they came limping back after a brutal night raid over Berlin, Cologne or Leipzig. They could weld the bodywork of any shattered plane, seal holes made by a battery of bullets in the fuselage, replace broken glass in the rear gunner's tower and reload ammunition at lightning speed, ready for the next take-off. For every pilot in any plane, there were ten men and women working on the ground to keep that plane flying; when there was a fatality and the pilot went down, the ground crew took the loss deeply and personally.

Kit stood up and straightened his back. What wouldn't he give for a long soak in a hot bath! Rafal was right, he should take advantage of the officers' billets, of the clean sheets and home-cooked meals served by Raf's pretty fiancée. It would be a damn sight better than camping out in his office and surviving on bacon butties and tea! His brief was to establish Bomber Command at Holkham. Volunteer pilots from New Zealand, Poland, Canada, the United States and Australia, plus regular RAF pilots, were undergoing gruelling physical training which would prepare them to fly the mighty Lancaster bombers due to arrive at RAF Holkham in the spring. As officer in charge, Kit was responsible for timetables, training and billeting, but sitting behind a desk doing paper-work for eighteen hours a day was not his forte.

In the early days of the war, he'd been commended for bravery after intercepting a German fighter plane intent on blowing up the B-17 bomber he was accompanying across the English Channel. As the B-17 headed safely on its way to Hamburg, Kit realized there was a hole in his tank and the plane was losing fuel fast. He crash-landed just off the coast of Dover, where he was found unconscious and bleeding heavily from head wounds. For his brave action, he was awarded the Distinguished Service Order, which he'd hidden in his sock drawer at home. The last thing Kit was interested in was rib-bons and gongs. As far as he was concerned, he had simply been doing his duty as an officer for his king and country.

Once the Lancasters arrived, the RAF would have a better chance against the Luftwaffe, who, up until now, had been winning the war for the Germans. No matter how devoted Kit was to Whitleys and Wellingtons, he knew they didn't stand a chance against the might of the German Messer-schmitts. The RAF needed heavier fighter planes with bigger engines and a bigger fuselage to house a bigger bomb load. It wasn't until the Germans razed Coventry to the ground in November 1940 that the Prime Minister decided that if the Hun could wreak havoc, so could he. In his typical, bullish way, Churchill commissioned the building of seven thousand Lancaster bombers, a great number of which were allocated to airfields along the east coast, with instant access to the North Sea. Kit was counting down the days till he could get his hands on his first Lancaster and take to the skies over Germany.

As Kit was shaving the thick golden-blond stubble from his chin, Rafal returned with another pot of tea and two bacon butties, which a ravenous Kit fell on immediately.

'So what's it like at Walsingham Hall?' he asked between enormous mouthfuls. 'You seem to be there most of the time.'

'Upstairs is bloody trainees,' Rafal replied, using one of Ruby's favourite expressions. 'Plenty code girls.' He blushed then quickly added, 'I have my Rubee, so no interest, maybe you like?'

Kit shook his head.

'Definitely no interest.'

'Below stairs is three very beautiful cooks.'

Kit smiled indulgently. Beautiful cooks below stairs didn't normally come in threes, but he didn't say anything that would disillusion Rafal. Instead he said, 'Can you bring the jeep round? I need to take a quick look at the new operational building.'

'Right away, sir,' Raf replied with a smart salute.

The drive in the open-topped jeep quickly blew away the cobwebs brought on by lack of sleep. Kit pulled up the fur-lined collar of his leather flying jacket as a sharp east wind whistled around his ears.

'Polish wind!' Raf joked, as they bounced along the mile-long runway that ended by a turnip field. 'Straight from the Balkans.'

'Bloody freezing, wherever it's coming from,' Kit chuckled, looking out proudly over Holkham airfield, which, when he'd arrived, had been little more than a few derelict Nissen huts surrounded by turnip fields.

The Met Office, signals room, rest rooms, control centre and operational centre surrounded the newly built control tower and runway where Spitfires, Whitleys and Halifaxes stood ready for take-off. The guard house, hospital, NAAFI, chapel and post room were housed in newly built, spacious, red-brick houses, beyond which stood the renovated Nissen huts that provided accommodation for the hundreds of men on site. The next stage of building work was the erection of domestic blocks for the WAAFs who would shortly be arriving at Holkham; women who would be working around the clock plotting the course of outgoing and returning planes on huge mapping tables and operational wall charts.

Raf pulled up outside the new block, which was presently being fitted out with teleprinters, radio transmitters, radar detection screens, decoding machines and a row of telephones. Pleased with the progress going on all around him, Kit nodded. 'We're just about ready for action,' he said.

'Thank God for that!' laughed Raf. 'All we need is planes to boom-boom Fritz!'

'The Lancasters will be here soon enough,' Kit promised.

On their way back to Kit's office, they drove past the big hangar which housed the training unit. Outside, hundreds of airmen were doing their gruelling daily exercises, essential for the maintenance of their fitness levels: only the physically fit could tackle the arduous task of flying long hours through enemy territory on dark nights in sub-zero temperatures. When the airmen weren't on route marches or cross-country runs, they were being prepared for combat: night-vision tests were carried out and regular swimming classes were held in a freezing-cold swimming pool, where servicemen in full RAF kit practised the drill of ditching into the sea. Kit gave a cheery wave as they passed by the square-bashing airmen.

'Keep it up, fellas,' he hollered. 'It'll be worth it in the end!'

'Yeah, try telling that to Hitler!' one of the pilots yelled back.

By late afternoon, with the winter sun going down over the flat fields like a ball of orange fire, Kit, struggling to keep his eyes open, shoved away the pile of order sheets he'd been ploughing through all afternoon.

'Time for a hot bath,' he told Johnny, his second-in-command, who was working at his desk at the other end of the room.

'Don't do anything I wouldn't do,' Johnny joshed, as Kit reached for his flying jacket and headed for the door.

'Chance would be a fine bloody thing!' Kit laughed.

Kit went outside and squeezed into the bucket seat of his ancient MG. He murmured encouraging words as he tickled his precious car into life by teasing the throttle.

'Come on, girl, you can do it. Come on,' he urged, his breath turning to steam and misting up the windows. Suddenly, the MG juddered, then, with a roar, she burst into life and rattled down the drive. As she gathered speed, Kit put his foot down, then, with his headlights off, he drove blind along the dark, narrow lanes which wound their circuitous way to Walsingham Hall.

The officers had all been given keys to their billet in the west wing of the hall, which had its own entrance. Kit parked his MG, grabbed his kit bag from the back seat and headed indoors, where he bumped into one of his fellow officers.

'If you want a good supper, make it quick to the dining room,' the officer suggested.

His flying jacket thrown over his shoulder, Kit wasted no time in sniffing out the dining room, which was now empty. A small, slim, dark-haired girl wiping down the table-tops called out, 'You've missed supper.'

Frustrated and starving, Kit swore under his breath, 'Damn! That was a bloody waste of time!'

Seeing his tired, disappointed face, Ruby said, 'Wait, I'm sure the cooks can find something.'

With a reassuring nod, she hurried below stairs, leaving Kit alone in the empty canteen. He appraised the family portraits which hung across the length of the once beautiful dining room. He was so engrossed in studying a grumpy Elizabethan Walsingham that he barely heard Maudie approaching with a loaded tray. After cooking and serving her tasty tomato, paprika and fish pie, which the trainees had hungrily polished off, Maudie was distinctly irritated by the thoughtless officer who'd turned up late and given her even more work to do.

'We usually finish serving at seven o'clock,' she said sharply, as she set down a slice of Bella's famous game pie, a baked potato and a mountain of sprouts and, to follow, a slice of her delicious apple strudel. 'You're lucky Ruby took pity on you.'

Kit stared incredulously at the food; the sight of it was making his stomach rumble.

'Oh, my God! This is wonderful. Thank you.' He laughed in delight and turned to the girl who'd served him.

When his sky-blue eyes locked with Maudie's mesmerizing green ones, Kit stopped laughing and Maudie stopped complaining. For a few seconds, they simply took each other in. Maudie thought he was without doubt one of the most handsome men she had ever seen, while Kit simply gazed, rapt, into her beautiful pale face, framed with tumbling, golden-red curls.

'Thank you, thank you so much,' he said, repeating himself.

Maudie nodded curtly. He might be gorgeous, but she couldn't spend all night gawping at him! Remembering her dignity, she reluctantly turned and walked away, aware as she retreated of his eyes following her across the room. Once he was alone, Kit devoured the delicious food, which he could easily have eaten fifty times over. It was so good to have hot, freshly cooked food. Raf was quite right, he really should use the facilities more often; after all, the hall was less than a ten-minute drive away from the airbase.

'You were lucky,' Ruby said, when she reappeared to clean the table-tops.

'I certainly was,' Kit said. As he lit up a Craven A, he took in the girl's glossy, dark hair and beautiful eyes and smiled to himself. She was the same girl Raf had proudly showed him a black-and-white photograph of just that week. 'Am I right in thinking you're Raf's fiancée?' he asked.

'Indeed I am,' Ruby proudly retorted. 'We're getting married soon,' she added, with a sweet, excited smile.

'He's a good man.'

'He's lovely!' Ruby giggled.

Sated and happy, Kit ran himself a hot bath, which he wallowed in until it turned tepid. Wrapped in a bath towel, he headed to his room, where the bed seemed to rise up and greet him. Still in the damp towel, Kit fell face down on to the mattress and slept soundly for fifteen hours.

When he awoke he couldn't make out what time it was. He was so used to waking in a dark, cold dawn, stretched out on his office chair, Kit now took a few minutes to luxuriate in the clean sheets and the warm eiderdown. Snuggled deep down under his bedding, he peeped out to see bright morning light filling his room. Reaching for his watch, he gasped when he saw it was nearly midday.

'Gotta get back to base,' he mumbled to himself, and jumped out of bed. Then, looking at his watch again, he thought with a smile that he might just have a spot of lunch before he left. The idea of another meal served by the willowy, green-eyed beauty was enough to keep Kit in the hall for at least an hour longer.

After a quick wash and a shave, Kit donned his light blue uniform, then set off for a quick tour of the hall. In the library, which was chillingly cold and smelt of stale cigarettes, Kit went along the shelves, admiring the leather-bound first editions of Shelley, Wordsworth, Dickens and Thomas Hardy. He flicked through a copy of *Far from the Madding Crowd* and jumped at the sound of a silky, soft, caressing voice,

'I hope you weren't thinking of removing that?'

Stung by the thought that somebody might think him a thief, Kit turned angrily, and said, 'I certainly was not!'

The voice belonged to a slender, beautiful woman with shoulder-length silver-blonde hair, wide blue eyes and high cheekbones. She was impeccably dressed in a lavender-blue tweed suit, with the wartime regimental short swing skirt, brogues and nylon stockings, a luxury for most women, but not this one, who oozed wealth and style. Her smile was slow and slightly mocking as she studied Kit's indignant face.

'I'm not in the habit of stealing other people's belongings,' he added, less hotly.

'Forgive me,' the languid, smiling woman murmured. 'So much goes missing in a requisitioned house full of women with no breeding.'

Kit's thick blond eyebrows flew up. 'And also men with no breeding?' he asked.

Her eyes fixed on his lapels, where his squadron leader's badge denoted his officer status.

'I'm sure a man such as you does not belong in that category,' she replied, and extended her hand to Kit. 'Lady Diana Walsingham. Pleased to meet you.'

'Kit Halliday. Pleased to meet you, too,' he replied. He shook her firmly by the hand and smiled, a smile that crinkled the corners of his eyes and revealed his strong white teeth and full, generous mouth. 'I'm billeted in your impressive west wing, for which I am extremely grateful.'

Gazing at the well-spoken, polite and stunning-looking young officer standing before her, Diana could barely believe her luck. Compared to the men she socialized with in Norfolk, Kit Halliday was a young god – *and* he lived right under her roof. He was perfect material to accompany her on long walks by the sea, for cocktails, shoots, dinners – and for bedding, too!

Taking a cigarette from a packet in her crocodile-skin handbag, Diana inserted it into a silver holder, which she held out, clearly expecting Kit to light her cigarette.

'I can't tell you how uplifting it is to meet somebody of interest. This dreary war has stolen our *joie de vivre*,' she drawled.

Kit lit the cigarette, which she inhaled deeply, then blew the smoke out through her aquiline nose.

'Sorry to disappoint,' Kit answered, 'but I'm really not at all interesting. I'm just an officer at Holkham airfield, where I sit all day, checking order forms and building regs for the new base. I call that very boring!' he said, with a self-deprecating shrug.

Rather embarrassed by the fact that Lady Diana's big blues eyes were raking up and down the length of his body, Kit mumbled on, 'I am, however, most grateful for your hospitality.'

'I'd like to say the pleasure's all mine, but that would be a big bloody lie!' Diana continued. 'You've no idea how ghastly it is to be told what to do in your own ancestral home,' she added, with a little moue of her voluptuous mouth.

Kit checked the clock on the mantelpiece. He really

needed to get a move on if he was going to have lunch before reporting back to the base.

'We're starved of company upstairs,' Diana said, with a bewitching smile. 'Do promise you'll join us whenever you can?'

Kit made a slight bow. 'I'm rarely here, but thank you for your kind invitation. Excuse me, but I'm afraid I really do have to go now.'

As he hurried away, Diana flung her half-smoked cigarette into the empty fireplace.

'You're just the kind of man who could make this place tolerable,' she murmured underneath her breath, as she moved towards the door, a scheming smile on her perfect face.

Meanwhile, below stairs, the cooks were setting the trays for lunch.

'That handsome RAF officer's here for lunch,' Ruby informed her friends. 'You should clear away his plate, Maudie, and sneak another look at him!'

Maudie blushed. Nobody could deny that the man was attractive, but she wasn't the kind of woman to be seduced by good looks alone.

'Hearts and minds are more important than charming smiles,' she replied. 'Anyway, I don't see why I should clear away for him,' Maudie added, as she left to go upstairs with bowls of steamed jam roly-poly and custard. 'He's got arms and legs. He can clear away himself.'

In the dining room, wearing her cook's dowdy black dress and frilly lace cap, which barely contained her wild, red-gold curls, Maudie felt cringingly self-conscious as she served dessert. Without even looking up, she knew Kit's eyes were watching her all the time. When he approached to collect his pudding, he held on to the bowl she offered longer than was necessary.

'I must say, the food here is stunning,' he said gratefully. 'Don't know how you manage it, with rationing getting harder by the day.'

'We're inventive below stairs!' she replied briefly.

'Geniuses, I'd say! I'm Kit Halliday, by the way. I'd love to shake your hand, but I daren't let go of my jam roly-poly!'

Maudie burst out laughing.

'It's my favourite,' he added, sounding like a hungry little boy. 'I could eat it till the cows come home.'

Maudie smiled at his enthusiasm for her food.

As they gazed at each other, Kit noticed the charming spattering of golden freckles across Maudie's small nose. But a high, brittle voice behind Kit instantly wiped the smile off Maudie's face.

'Dahling! I hoped I'd catch you before you scuttled off back to that ghastly old airfield,' Diana gushed, and reached up to peck Kit on the cheek.

Embarrassed, Kit turned from a red-faced Maudie, who could barely conceal her irritation, to Diana, who, though he barely knew her, was treating him like her new best friend.

'Mummy and Daddy are simply agog to get to meet you,' she simpered, as she slipped her arm through Kit's, causing him to slop custard on to the serving counter. 'We wondered if you'd like to join us for dinner tonight. It won't be anything special, just the usual grim slop the dreadful cooks produce.' She stared in disgust at the dish of jam roly-poly he was holding.

Feeling awkward and embarrassed, Kit looked apologetically over his shoulder to Maudie, but she was dashing towards the stairs.

'Damn! Damn! Damn!' she seethed furiously under her breath. 'I should have known better. Stupid, stupid me!'

Once in the kitchen, she slammed the door so hard Ava and Ruby jumped with fright.

'What's the matter with you?' cried Ava, when she saw Maudie's face, which was as dark as a thundercloud.

'Nothing!' Maudie snapped, and started to pace around the kitchen table.

'Looks like more than nothing to me,' Ruby said knowingly.

'Spit it out, lass, or you'll curdle the cream,' Ava added briskly.

Maudie threw her hands up in the air and replied, 'I was having a chat with that "handsome RAF officer", as you call him, Ruby, just joking about the bloody pudding, of all things, when up swans damn Lady Diana, who, right in front of me, told him our food was basically pigswill!'

She stopped short as Bella came out of the cold store with two dead hares. 'Sorry, Bella, I'm talking about your cow of a sister!'

'Talk away, sweetheart. Nothing you say about Diana could ever upset me,' Bella reassured her. 'What's she up to now?'

'Just being rude and offensive,' Maudie answered.

'Oh, she's good at rude and offensive,' Bella chuckled.

'So who is this RAF officer that you and Ruby are going on about?' Ava asked.

'His name's Kit Halliday, and he's clearly a pal of Lady Diana,' Maudie snapped irritably.

'All right, all right. Keep your lacey hat on!' Ava giggled.

Still livid, Maudie bristled as she ranted on, 'The way that blasted woman treats people! She seems to have nothing but contempt for anybody not of her social status. I'm not used to being addressed like a second-class citizen, and I don't see why I should take it now, just because I've been forced to work below stairs. There's a war on, we're all making sacrifices – unlike "Fancy Pants Posh Face", who swans about like Marie Antoinette before they chopped off her head!'

Bella threw back her head and laughed in delight. '"Fancy Pants Posh Face" says it all! I wouldn't waste your breath, Maudie. Believe me, my sister will never change. She's wilful, vain, dim and ruthless – and that's the truth.'

'I don't know how you got to be a Walsingham,' Maudie marvelled.

'I think somebody made a mistake and swapped me in the hospital,' Bella answered good-naturedly, reaching over Ava's shoulder to take a sharp knife from the rack that ran along the length of the kitchen wall.

Maudie gaped at the knife and then at the hares. 'Oh, God! Don't start skinning and gutting those things in here!' she begged.

'Wimp!' giggled Bella, as she walked out, swinging the hares. 'I'll hide in the back kitchen so you won't have to smell their nasty little innards!'

'We'd better clear away,' said Ruby.

Maudie hesitated. 'They might still be up there.'

'They'll have gone by now,' Ruby assured her, and they went upstairs together.

Diana and Kit had left the dining room, but Maudie and Ruby caught sight of them strolling in the garden.

'He doesn't look very happy,' Ruby remarked.

'That's his problem,' Maudie answered, as she turned up 'Worker's Playtime' on the radio and started to wash down

154

the table-tops vigorously, to the cheerful rhythm of Glenn Miller's 'Little Brown Jug'.

Outside, Kit wasn't at all happy. He felt like he'd upset the sweet, green-eyed cook, who had just been beginning to loosen up and chat when Lady Diana barged in and rudely insulted the work of the staff below stairs. Now the wretched woman was intent on making all kinds of complicated arrangements, none of which he felt like falling in with.

'You must have a few hours to spare,' Diana said, in a voice that had lost its sweetness as she realized she was getting nowhere fast with this ravishing officer. 'Do the RAF tie you to your desk with a ball and chain?'

'I do have a heavy timetable and hardly any free time,' Kit answered firmly. 'Now, if you don't mind, I really have to be making my way back, otherwise I shall be late for duty.'

Not getting her own way, Diana looked suddenly sulky. 'Promise you'll at least pop upstairs for a glass of champagne next time you're in the west wing. It would be rude not to,' she said, with a limp smile.

Not wanting to give her the slightest opportunity to think he might be available, Kit gave a curt nod and said farewell. 'Good afternoon, Lady Diana. It's been a pleasure.'

She coquettishly offered him her hand to kiss, but he shook it firmly instead, then walked away. Frustrated and bored, Diana kicked the turf.

'God damn this bloody place,' she seethed, then headed indoors in search of the sherry bottle.

15. Back to Business

Kit found Johnny Hibbert looking a bit the worse for wear.

'Been on a bender?' Kit enquired, as he hung his flying jacket on the back of the office door and dumped his kit bag on the floor.

Johnny just grunted and gazed blankly out of the window.

'Well, speak!' Kit laughed, as he started to go through the pile of mail on his desk.

When Johnny still didn't reply, Kit joined his friend by the window, which gave extensive views of the runway and the new control tower.

'What's up, man?'

'Jenny,' Johnny replied, and turned to Kit with tears in his eyes.

Kit felt the muscles in his stomach clench in fear. 'Is she OK?'

Johnny shrugged hopelessly. 'We don't know.'

Jenny, an experienced WAAF pilot, worked as a ferry girl. She was one of many accomplished female pilots who delivered newly built planes to airbases up and down the country. It was a service the WAAF fulfilled while the majority of male pilots were on active service.

'Last thing I heard, she was delivering a Halifax to an airbase in Grimsby. All of their Halifax bombers were shot down over Belgium, and Jen and a couple of other ferry girls, were replenishing their depleted stock.' Johnny took a deep, shuddering breath and put his head in his hands. 'For some reason, Jenny's radio cut out. The other ferry girls arrived safely at their destination, but not Jenny.' He looked up at Kit with haunted eyes. 'They can't trace her.'

Kit put a reassuring hand on Johnny's chunky shoulder. 'Come on, it could be nothing, especially with those damn new Halifaxes. Maybe she discovered a faulty switch or had a leak in her fuel tank – she could be bailing out in a parachute over a potato field in Hull right now,' he added, with an attempt at a smile.

'But we'd know by now. Jen's a real pro. She knows the routine, she'd have radioed in before bailing.'

Kit nodded. Johnny was right. Jenny had ferried more planes around Britain than any other female pilot he knew. Dropping the cheerful façade, he squeezed his friend's shoulder hard. 'We'll just have to hope and pray,' he said fervently.

As Kit sat back down at his desk, Johnny took himself off to the communications centre, where he hoped he might pick up some information from central control. Raf quickly appeared with a pint mug of strong tea for his commanding officer.

'So you like my Rubee?'

'I most certainly do,' Kit replied, and Raf glowed with pride. 'And I like her red-headed friend, too.'

Raf nodded knowingly. 'Ah, Maudie,' he answered. 'Clever girl, speak Polish too, good cook.'

'Very good cook . . . with beautiful green eyes,' Kit added.

'*Czarownica!*' Raf pointed to his own pale blue eyes. 'She has eyes like witch. Magic, yes?'

Kit dreamily recalled Maudie's cloud of golden-red hair and delicate pale face, spattered by a few golden freckles.

'She's magic all right,' he thought, but he wasn't about to launch into further discussion with Air Mechanic Rafal Boskow. 'Thanks for the tea,' he said briefly, and turned his attention once more to the pile of unopened letters. When Johnny returned, his face even paler than when he'd left, Kit stood up, grabbed his flying jacket and headed for the door.

'Come on, old chum, you need a drink!'

In the officers' mess, holding a whisky and soda each, the two senior officers stood side by side at the bar. Determined to take his friend's anguished thoughts, however briefly, off his girlfriend, Kit discussed the imminent arrival of Canadian airmen.

'They're an experienced bunch, I'm told. Years of active service, with a good number of gunners, too – guys we're desperately short of.'

Johnny's eyebrows flew up. 'I'm a rear gunner down,' he admitted. 'Lost all of my Tail-end Charlies on bombing missions. They're always the first to get shot at – poor buggers. The last one we literally hosed out of his turret.'

Kit grimaced as he took a good slug of his whisky. 'Tail-end Charlie' was the RAF's nickname for rear gunners, which was without doubt the loneliest and most dangerous job. The Lancaster's seven-man crew consisted of pilot, navigator, bomb aimer, wireless operator, flight engineer, rear gunner and side gunner. Tail-end Charlies squashed themselves into the narrow gun turret at the back of the plane, hardly able to move, and working at times in sub-zero temperatures, with only a sheet of glass to protect them from an oncoming Messerschmitt blasting bullets from a machine gun aimed directly at the rear of the plane. They were unquestionably the bravest men in the crew; because of the nature of their job, their life expectancy was often short. They were incredibly heroic.

'Here's to them,' said Kit, as he and Johnny chinked glasses, then drained them in a gulp.

Setting his glass down, Johnny clapped Kit on the back. 'Thanks, old man, I needed that. Think I'll take a walk over to the control room, just in case,' he said, then turned and left the bar.

As Kit watched him go, he murmured, 'Fingers crossed, mate.'

When Johnny returned to their office with a plate of Spam-and-mustard sandwiches and a mug of tea, Kit's heart lifted. Johnny usually had the appetite of a horse: the sandwiches had to be a good sign.

'She's safe,' Johnny said, as he clinked mugs with Kit. 'Bailed like you said – bloody engine failure. She was picked up in a ploughed field in Lincolnshire, freezing, but safe, thank Christ.'

'Glad to hear it, chum,' Kit replied, lighting a cigarette.

Johnny bit into his sandwich, devoured it a blink, then started on the second.

'Jen will have something to say to the ground crew who assembled that duff Halifax she was ferrying. Poor bastards, she'll have the skin off their backs for a cock-up that could've cost her her life!'

'Those ferry girls are amazing,' Kit replied, as he took a drag of his cigarette. 'Flying all over the country, delivering new stock to airbases – don't know what the RAF would do without them.'

Johnny grinned as he polished off his second sandwich. 'I

bet bailing into a ploughed field pissed Jen off. She hates anything dirty.' He chuckled.

'She's alive and well. That's all that matters,' Kit answered.

As Johnny sat down at his desk, he winked cheekily. 'Maybe you'll land yourself a pretty ferry girl when they start delivering planes here?' he teased.

Kit shrugged his shoulders as he stubbed out his cigarette. 'Maybe.'

He'd never been really interested in having a relationship. Not that he wasn't interested in women – there was nobody more appreciative of a lovely woman with a fine pair of legs than Kit Halliday – it was the ability to commit that he lacked. His life had always been planes. His father, a pilot in the First World War, called his son a grease monkey because, even as a little boy, he was never happier than when he was taking an engine to bits. Kit had his first flying lesson when he was sixteen, which was when his love affair with planes began in earnest. He was already at Cranwell College training to be a pilot when war broke out. There, in the service hangars with the ground crew, he'd spend every spare moment fine-tuning the beautiful engines of the Rolls-Royce Merlin Spitfires. Apart from flying itself, there was nothing in the world Kit liked more than getting down and dirty, helping the ground crew to dismantle and reassemble damaged Spits, which he knew every working part of.

There was precious little time left for 'canoodling', as the chaps called it, though Kit had met a rather gorgeous brunette WAAF at one of the Cranwell dance nights. He'd enjoyed the kissing and cuddling, but she'd quickly cooled off when Kit repeatedly chose to spend his free time in the service hangar rather than walking out with her. As he cleared the report sheets and order forms off his desk, Kit let out a heavy sigh. Women! They were a mystery to him.

At Walsingham Hall, the below-stairs staff had swung effort-lessly back into their work routine. Bella kept to her word and cooked alongside Ava and Maudie, but she begged that they changed the weekly menus.

'Why? What does it matter,' Ruby said impatiently. 'Any-way, I really want to talk about something else.'

'I know set menus help but, honest to God, if I have to live through another shepherd's pie Monday, or a cheese-and-tomato flan Saturday, I think I'll have hysterics!' Bella groaned.

Maudie nodded. 'We could vary things, just to ring the changes.'

'We're still basically stuck with meals we can make from the rations,' Ava cut in.

'But variations on a theme might stop us from going nuts with boredom!' Maudie chuckled.

'Don't forget the lovely seasonal produce Peter brings,' Bella reminded them.

Ruby smiled to herself; she knew she wouldn't get a word in edgeways while Bella was on a roll, talking about menus!

'But we never know what and when, so we can't rely on it on a daily basis,' Ava pointed out. 'How can we plan some-thing when we can't be sure of having the ingredients?'

'I've been thinking that we could create menus based on rationed food but then change them if something else turned up,' Bella quickly replied.

'Like what?' Ruby questioned.

'Well, we could carry on cooking normal stuff – pies,

pasties, flans, rissoles using mock-mince, cheese, root veg – but if we had a windfall from Peter,' Bella said with a wink, 'we could use minced rabbit and hare, pheasant and partridge – depending on the season, of course. It's excellent meat and it's free!'

Ava smiled fondly at Bella. 'There's a war on, rationing is getting stricter by the day, and there you are, dreaming up treats for the new code girls, who would eat anything you put in front of them.'

'Come on, dinner ladies!' urged Maudie, as she reached for her notebook.

'Oh, God, here we go again!' chuckled Ruby.

With her pencil poised, Maudie began to call out the days of the week. 'Monday?'

All eyes turned to Bella.

'You started this, lady, so you'd better get the ball rolling,' Ava joked.

Bella didn't hesitate for a second. 'Curried-corned-beef meatballs – or curried-game meatballs.'

Maudie continued. 'Tuesday?'

'Savoury pancakes filled with mock-mince –' Bella paused and smiled at her friends. 'Or hare, spiced with fresh thyme and sage and a dash of Lea and Perrins, wrapped in a big fluffy pancake – gorgeous!'

Relentlessly, Maudie pressed on. 'Wednesday?'

'Stuffed cabbage, or marrow later on in the season,' Bella answered.

'Stuffed with what?' Ruby enquired.

'Sausage meat, when we can get it, mixed with a bit of bacon, parsley, Worcester sauce, breadcrumbs and chopped onion. Some weeks we might have to be creative, but we'll make sure it's always tasty.'

'Thursday?' Maudie rattled on.

'Meat-and-potato pie,' Bella replied.

Ava held up a hand. 'It's OK, we can all guess what the meat will be if you send Peter out with a shotgun!'

'It could be a road-kill pigeon!' Bella giggled. 'Anything free has got to be good.'

'Friday?' Maudie interrupted.

'Fish pie – if we land a local catch – or cheese and onion, if we don't,' Bella answered.

'Let's keep the weekend meals as they are,' Ava suggested. 'Cheese-and-tomato flan, and everybody loves Sunday's mock-roast followed by fruit pie and custard. So we're done!'

'Puddings!' Maudie cried.

'You're the master confectioner.' Ava laughed. 'Get on with it!'

Maudie frowned as she considered the possibilities.

'Starting from Monday,' she said, as she scribbled in her notepad, 'custard tart with cinnamon and vanilla flavouring. Tuesday, spiced fruity swirls. Wednesday, sticky gingerbread slices. Thursday, jam roly-poly – we introduced that last term and the trainees loved it.' She stopped to look down at her notepad. 'Where am I? Friday . . . ah, apple strudel.'

'Depends on how many apples are left in the apple store in the cellar,' Ava cut in.

'Loads!' Maudie retorted. 'I've checked.'

'Thank God,' cried Ruby. 'There'd be a riot if we dropped strudel from the menu, led by Raf and me. We love it!'

'Saturday,' Maudie ploughed on, 'mock-chocolate mousse – and jelly and custard on Sunday. Done,' she announced, dropping her pencil on to the table.

'Teas?' Ava asked.

'They can stay as they are. I'm exhausted.' Bella yawned.

Ruby pulled herself up to her full height. 'Have you quite finished?' she asked, barely able to suppress her excitement.

Ava half rose in her chair. 'I was just thinking of making a brew.'

'No, not yet!' Ruby cried.

All eyes turned to her, and she looked suddenly flushed and nervous.

'We've booked the Catholic shrine for our wedding, and I want all of you to be my bridesmaids,' she blurted out.

The girls, as one, rushed to hug little Ruby, who disappeared from sight as they gathered her into their arms.

'Let me come up for air,' Ruby laughed, as she surfaced from their embrace.

'What date did you fix?' Ava asked.

'The first day of spring – 21 March,' Ruby replied.

Looking panicked, Ava exclaimed, 'Bugger! We need to get organized, there's the wedding breakfast, the venue –'

She was interrupted by a loud yelp from Maudie. 'The cake!'

'The dresses!' Bella added, and turned to Ruby. 'Do you know what you're going to wear?'

'I thought I might wear a suit.'

'No! You can't!' Bella exclaimed.

'Where am I going to get a wedding dress at such short notice?' Ruby asked.

'If we pooled all our clothes coupons, would that be enough for a wedding dress?' Maudie asked, then giggled as she joked, 'You're so small, Ruby, you wouldn't need much material!'

'That's sweet of you to offer,' Ruby said, 'but then, what would you all wear?'

'We could never get together enough clothing coupons for all of us to have new frocks,' Ava pointed out.

'Maybe we should all wear suits?' Maudie said glumly.

'There's nothing wrong with Fashion on the Ration!' Ruby announced staunchly. 'Thousands do it without any complaints. Why not me and Raf?'

'How about borrowing somebody else's wedding dress?' Ava suggested.

'I've put the word out among friends and family,' Ruby replied. 'We might get lucky,' she added doubtfully.

Bella suddenly said, 'There's a wardrobe in the attic that's stuffed with old ballgowns!'

Ruby, who knew the contents of the attic as well as she knew the contents of the scullery, stared at her incredulously. 'You wouldn't dare?' she gasped.

With her blue eyes glittering brightly, Bella nodded. 'Nobody's been near that stuff for years, apart from me! I used to sneak up there and dress up on rainy days,' she confessed.

Maudie sprung to her feet. 'Let's go and take a peek,' she cried. 'There might be stuff that we could use.'

'Not now, it's nearly supper,' Ava said firmly. 'Time to warm up the macaroni cheese.'

'Slave driver!' teased Bella. 'When can we take a half-hour off to investigate?'

Now crouched on the floor, sliding huge trays of macaroni cheese into the Aga, Ava looked up and grinned at Bella. 'Straight after lunch tomorrow,' she replied, without a moment's hesitation.

The following day, the girls flew through serving lunch, causing the Brig to remark, 'What's going on? I'm in terror of blinking in case you take away my delicious apple strudel.'

'We're on a secret mission,' Bella whispered conspiratorially.

Ruby led the way up the back stairs to the large attic at the top of the house, which had high windows giving on to views of the parkland and the vast Walsingham estate.

'Look!' Ava cried, standing on her tiptoes and peering out. 'I can see the path that Tom and I take when we ride down to the sea.'

'You won't see the sea today,' Ruby joked. 'It's about two miles out at this time of the year.'

'Come on,' urged Bella, as she threw open the wardrobe doors. 'We're not here for the view!'

'*Pooh!* What a pong!' gasped Ruby, as the acrid smell of mothballs filled the room.

'Hopefully, it's kept the moths away,' said Bella, as she pulled out one gown after another. 'They're all quite dated, but that doesn't matter if the fabric's good,' she went on, flinging the dresses on to an old chaise longue. 'Green, blue, silver, peach, gold.' She paused and smiled. 'I knew it – white!' Holding a heavy white satin cocktail dress aloft, she examined the length of the train, which was edged with white velvet interlaced with tiny, glittering stones. 'This could be made into the perfect bridal gown,' she said, thrusting the dress into Ruby's arms.

'Oh, God, it's gorgeous,' Ruby sighed, with tears in her eyes.

'Take your clothes off,' Bella instructed. 'Try it on.'

Ruby whipped off her work clothes and slipped into the slithery, satin cocktail dress, which drowned her small, slim frame.

'It's too big!' she wailed.

'Of course it is.' Bella laughed. 'Mother's nearly twice as tall as you.'

'Don't worry, it can be altered,' Maudie assured her.

'I could have a go at altering it on the old Singer machine in the sewing room,' Ava volunteered, then her face fell. 'Though, if I'm honest, I'd be terrified of making a mess of it,' she confessed.

'And there's all the bridesmaids' dresses to make, too,' Ruby said, as she longingly fondled the wonderful dresses draped over the chaise longue. 'There just isn't enough time,' she concluded, with a heavy, resigned sigh.

Maudie shook her head, and a slow smile spread across her pale face. 'I know exactly who could run up five dresses in record time,' she said quietly.

'*Who?*' they all cried.

'Mama.'

'Your mum?' exclaimed Ava.

Maudie nodded and continued, 'She used to be a seamstress in Krakow, before she met Papa. After they married, she became a baker and worked alongside him. She made all my clothes when I was a little girl,' she added proudly.

'We couldn't ask that of your family, though?' Ruby said in an anxious voice.

'She could come here,' Maudie suggested.

'Is your father well enough for your mother to leave him?' Ava asked.

Maudie nodded thoughtfully. 'It would take some planning, but I think I know how it could be done,' she said, with a confident ring to her voice.

'So, if we managed to get the dress-making sorted,' Bella said, 'how do we decide which of these dresses to use?' She pointed at the array of frocks. 'There are at least three pink dresses, but none of them is the same shade of pink.'

'Why should that be a problem?' Maudie asked.

'Because bridesmaids usually wear matching colours,' Bella replied.

'I know I'm in danger of repeating myself, but this is Fashion on the Ration,' Ruby chided.

'Point taken,' Ava conceded. 'So tell us, what would *you* like, Ruby?'

Ruby wriggled uncomfortably. 'I wasn't expecting this much, so I don't want to sound picky . . .'

'You're only a bride once,' Bella reminded her.

'If you're lucky!' Maudie quipped.

'Well, if I'm honest, I'd love it if you were all in the same colour,' Ruby confessed.

'Oh, so you don't fancy your three bridesmaids wearing clashing green, silver and black dresses?' Maudie teased.

Bella looked thoughtfully at Ruby. 'What happened to those silk curtains that hung in Mummy's dressing room years ago? They didn't get thrown out, did they?'

'They were too good to be thrown out,' Ruby replied. 'They're probably stored away somewhere.'

The two girls looked at each other, then spoke at the same time. '*Timms!*'

Later that day, Bella was delegated to sweet-talk Timms.

'At least she won't spit in your face,' giggled Ava.

'Thanks for that,' Bella retorted. 'Wish me luck as I enter the dragon's den.'

Timms was simperingly surprised when Bella knocked gently on her parlour door, bearing a Victoria sponge cake, which she knew from years past that Timms adored.

'We had extra eggs from Peter's estate hens,' Bella explained, as she cut a large slice for the former housekeeper. She didn't add that she'd given up her week's sugar ration to make the cake. 'There you go,' she said, presented it to Timms, along with a large glass of her father's vintage sherry.

After eating half of the Victoria sponge cake and drinking a second large glass of sherry, Bella had all the information she needed.

'The curtains are in the chest in the small back-attic room,' she told Ruby, when she came rushing back into the kitchen.

The two girls dashed up the back stairs and returned laden down with bundles of heavy silk curtains.

'*Pink!*' a delighted Ruby cried, as she twisted the fabric around her body.

Ava sneezed as dust flew up. 'Ugh, they'll need a bit of a wash!'

'I can sort that out,' said Ruby confidently.

'And Mama can do the rest!' Maudie said happily.

16. Mumia

Rafal drove Maudie to Wells railway station to pick up Mrs Fazakerley, who, unlike her slender-hipped, willowy daughter, was small and squat, with a face like a soft baked roll and topped by a mass of short, grey curls. Alternating between English and German, she staggered off the train, talking nineteen to the dozen.

'*Schätzel!*' she cried, as Maudie ran into her arms. 'Darling girl, how are you?'

'All the better for seeing you, Mumia,' Maudie replied happily.

'Let me help you with those,' Rafal said in Polish, pointing at the two huge suitcases Mrs Fazakerly had lugged all the way from London.

'You speak Polish!' she exclaimed, and clapped her hands in delight. 'I lived in Krakow before I met Maudie's father and moved to Hamburg,' she gabbled. 'Fazakerley is not our real name?' she continued, scrambling into the jeep. 'Our family name is Fazhlo, but nobody could pronounce it, so we anglicized it to make life simple.'

Rafal grinned as he replied in his mother tongue, 'Madam Fazhlo, welcome to beautiful Norfolk!'

The journey back to the hall was astonishing for Mrs Fazarkery, whose knowledge of England was strictly limited to the East End of London, though, when Maudie was a little girl, she had travelled to Luton for her friend's wedding.

'Where is the sea?' she exclaimed, as they bounced along in the jeep, passing the marshland that edged the coastline.

'Miles and miles away,' Maudie replied with a laugh.

Before they reached Walsingham Hall, Maudie asked who was looking after her father.

'All arranged,' Mrs Fazakerly announced. 'Miriam across the street – you know, the one that used to be a nurse?'

Maudie nodded.

'She'll be keeping an eye on Papa. Don't worry, she'll keep him in his place,' her mother added, with a knowing wink.

'And the shop?'

'We hired a baker to come in for a few days.'

Maudie gasped in dismay when she heard this. 'You can't afford to pay somebody to help you!'

Her mother waved one hand dismissively in the air. 'Hey, it's Joseph, Papa's old friend, and he's lonely after the death of his wife. He said he'd enjoy the change, but we insisted on paying him something. Anyway, dearest, I needed a holiday, and where better to be than with my daughter?' Seeing Maudie's anxious expression, Mrs Fazakerly planted a kiss on her cheek. 'Stop worrying, child, it's only for three days. Papa will be fine.'

When they reached the ornamental gates that led on to the drive and parkland of the hall, Mrs Fazakerley's jaw dropped.

'Oh, *mein Gott*!' she gasped. 'Is this where the king lives?'

As they passed the perfect Palladian front entrance, Mrs Fazakerly shook her head in wonder. 'You never told me you were living in a palace, *liebling*!'

'We go in the back way, Mumia,' Maudie explained. 'We live below stairs.'

'Upstairs, downstairs! Who cares? It's all sooooo beautiful!' raved Mrs Fazakerly.

Rafal dropped his passengers off by the back door, then, after unloading the luggage, he drove off, but not before kissing Mrs Fazakerly on both cheeks.

'A pleasure to meet you, ma'am,' he said in Polish.

Maudie's mum pinched his pale cheeks and replied in the same language, 'Whoever the bride is, she's lucky to have such a handsome *Polski* boy.'

Bella, Ava and Ruby warmly welcomed Mrs Fazakerly, who hugged and kissed them all.

'Thank you for coming all this way to help us, Mrs Fazakerly,' Ruby said gratefully.

'It's a pleasure. Anything I can do for Maudie's friends, I will do – and please call me Mumia.'

Her gazed travelled from the smiling girls to the vast scullery, which was dominated by several tall Welsh dressers piled high with crockery, then to the old Aga range, already loaded with bubbling supper pans and, finally, to the long kitchen table surrounded by upright wooden chairs.

'Even the kitchen's like a palace,' she murmured.

'There are a dozen more rooms below stairs,' Ruby told her. 'Maudie got lost all the time when she first arrived.' She giggled.

'So now, little bride, show me what we have.'

Ava and Ruby dashed out of the kitchen and returned with the roll of washed pink silk and the white satin cocktail dress. Holding the dress up against her body, Ruby said excitedly, 'This is for me! And that,' she added, pointing to the silk that Ava laid on the table, 'is for my bridesmaids.'

Mrs Fazakerly popped a pair of steel-rimmed spectacles on to her nose and ran an expert hand over the silk and the satin.

'What do you think, Mumia, will it work?' Maudie asked.

'Don't hurry me, child,' her mother replied, as she unwound the roll of pink silk that spilled over the sides of the kitchen table in soft, delicate folds. Nodding her head, she smiled. 'It will do, but for how many?'

Ruby pointed to her friends. 'Bella, Ava and Maudie – my three bridesmaids.'

'Time to do some measuring,' said Mrs Fazakerly. 'Clothes off!'

Standing close to the Aga in order to keep warm, the girls stripped down to their underwear so that Mumia could measure them from top to bottom. While they were putting their uniforms back on, Mrs Fazakerly asked, 'So where would you like me to work? I'll need a big, clean space.'

'There's a sewing room just along the corridor,' Ruby replied.

'Show me the way,' Mrs Fazakerly replied with an excited smile.

The sewing room contained a high, wide table with a brass tape measuring a yard built neatly into a side panel.

'Perfect for cutting out paper patterns!' Mumia exclaimed.

There was a Singer machine with a heavy treadle, which Mumia's feet just reached. There were several tall chests of drawers containing bolts of material for making tea-towels and sheets, an ironing table, two full-length mirrors and a modern electric iron, the sight of which filled Maudie's mum with relief.

'Thank God I don't have to use an old flat iron,' she said. 'I've scorched too many things in my life with those heavy metal things.'

The wooden pulley hanging from the ceiling delighted Mrs Fazakerly. 'Excellent!' she cried. 'I'll be able to hang all the dresses up there, and they won't get creased or dirty.' She turned to her daughter. 'Bring me a pot of strong black coffee, *schätzel*, and I'll get started right away.'

The days that followed were wonderful. It was exciting for all of them, especially Ruby, to see their gowns being made, but it was the company of Mumia that made the girls so happy and strangely carefree. Their days, as ever, were dictated by the routine of cooking, cleaning, preparing food and clearing away but, with Mrs Fazakerly below stairs, they were like light-hearted, giggly schoolgirls. Every time they passed the sewing room, where the door was always left wide open, they'd pop their heads in and smile at the little lady working on the sewing machine, singing Polish folk songs to the rhythm of the clattering treadle.

'Come see, *liebling*,' Mumia would cry when she caught sight of a curious girl. 'Please, no dirty hands, though,' she warned.

The fitting sessions were a riot of laughter. The girls stood in bra and knickers, shivering in the sewing room, which wasn't warmed by a wood-burning Aga, and turned this way and that as Mumia pinned the slippery, cool, pink silk to their bodies.

'My Maudie is so tall and skinny compared to you two soft, curvy girls,' she told Ava and Bella, as she smoothed the silk bodices over their full breasts.

'Are you saying I'm flat-chested?' Maudie joked.

'Not flat, just not much,' her mother chuckled. 'Don't worry, the heart-shaped neckline I've cut out will make up for that.'

Bella, who'd had many expensive dresses made for her by bossy seamstresses, was especially impressed by Mrs Fazakerly's easy creativity.

'I love the off-the-shoulder puffed sleeves,' she said, as she twirled in front of one of the full-length mirrors.

'And the full-length skirt – I feel like a princess!' raved Ava, who looked gorgeous in the figure-hugging silk.

But it was Ruby who stole the show. Once Mumia had cut down and refitted the white silk, the bride-to-be looked stunning. The slashed neckline, the tight sleeves (fastened by tiny, silk-covered buttons) and the fitted waist emphasized Ruby's small, slender frame, while the skirt cascading in thick, silky folds gave her some height. A tear rolled down Ruby's cheek as she stared in wonder at her reflection in the mirror.

'Oh, God,' she sobbed. 'It's all my dreams come true.'

'No tears, sweetheart!' Mumia cried. 'They'll wet the dress and make a mess!'

As she turned Ruby around in order to make tiny alterations to the gown, Mumia said, through a bunch of pins she was gripping between her teeth, 'A bride must have a veil.'

'No, really, Mumia, I'm happy with what I've got,' Ruby insisted.

Mrs Fazakerly shook her head vehemently.

'You *must* have a head-dress and a veil; a traditional *Polski* groom will expect to see his virgin bride blushing behind her veil.'

Ruby's face flushed with colour. Lucky she was still a virgin, she thought to herself. Rafal might have high religious principles, but she was longing to experience the full joy of their love-making. Another month of waiting might have pushed her over the edge. As far as she was concerned, the sooner she was wed, the better!

'Where am I going to find a head-dress and veil?' she exclaimed.

Ava and Maudie turned to Bella, who burst out laughing. 'I'll work on it,' she promised.

Later that evening, after they'd cleared away the trainees' supper, Bella showed her friends what she'd found in the chest of drawers in her upstairs bedroom.

'A tiara I was forced to wear for a debutante's ball years ago. It's a bit tainted round the edges, but if we wash it in hot, soapy water and rub it with silver polish, it should come up as good as new,' she said, as she handed the tiara to a smiling Ruby, who placed it on her swinging black hair, then danced around the kitchen wearing it.

'It's gorgeous!' she cried.

'While I was upstairs, I searched for anything vaguely resembling a veil, but I only found a silk scarf decorated with a fox-hunt print,' Bella said with a giggle. 'Not quite wedding material.'

In return for Mumia's hard work, Ruby suggested they have a special supper party just for her.

'Do you think she'll like a proper Lancashire hotpot?' Ava asked Maudie, who nodded eagerly.

'She'll love it,' she replied.

'If only I could get a crab from the fish shop in Wells, I could make crab cakes with mashed potatoes and onion,' Bella said wistfully.

'I'll make her a nice egg custard with some of mum's bantam eggs,' Ruby announced.

'And I'll make an extra-big apple strudel that we can serve Mumia, and, use the next day for the trainees' lunch,' Maudie told her friends.

'I'll get a good bottle of Daddy's red wine from the cellar,' Bella promised, with a mischievous wink.

*

Mrs Fazakerly finished the bridesmaids' dresses just before they had their supper. Ruby, who had set a large jug filled with bright yellow Norfolk daffodils on the table, beckoned to her to come and eat.

'This is very kind of you all,' Mumia said, as she took her place at the head of the table.

'We want to thank you for everything you've done for us,' Ruby said, blushing. 'Done for *me*, in particular!'

'It's been a pleasure, *liebling*,' Mumia said, raising her glass and sipping the fine Bordeaux Bella had supplied.

The supper went down a treat. Bella hadn't managed to get a crab from the fishermen in Wells, but it didn't matter. Mumia had two helpings of Ava's delicious Lancashire hot-pot, followed by two helping of Ruby's rich custard tart and Maudie's apple strudel, based on Mumia's very own family recipe.

'I couldn't have done better myself!' she cried apprecia-tively. 'Thank you, *lieblings*,' she said, her eyes sweeping fondly over Ruby, Bella, Ava and Maudie. 'Please thank your mother for the fine eggs, Ruby,' she added.

'Mum also gave me something else,' Ruby said with a twinkle in her eye. 'Wait there. I'll show you.'

Five minutes later, as Ava was pouring hot tea for everybody, Ruby swanned in, wearing Bella's tiara and a long, floating veil. As she posed with a virgin smile before them, Ruby said, 'Mum bought this for sixpence at a church jumble sale in Fakenham!'

Mrs Fazakerly clapped her hands in delight. 'It will look perfect after it's been washed and starched,' she announced. 'I'll see to that before I leave tomorrow.'

Mumia completed all her tasks the next day. She sewed fifty tiny, silk covered-buttons down the back of Ruby's wedding gown and left the washed and starched veil hanging from the wooden pulley in the sewing room.

'I shall miss you all,' she said, as she hugged Maudie, Ava, Bella and Ruby tightly. 'Send me photographs of your wedding day,' she added, as she pecked Ruby on both cheeks.

'Thank you,' said an emotional Ruby, with tears in her eyes. 'I'll never forget what you've done for me.'

'You will make a beautiful bride,' Mumia promised. 'Rafal will be very proud of you.'

Smiling, she turned to her daughter. 'Perhaps one day my Maudie will marry a fine young man and I will make her a bridal gown.'

Maudie laid her arms around her mother's shoulders and, looking down into her kind eyes, she answered softly, 'You know I'm not ready for anything like that, Mumia.'

Mrs Fazakerly gave her characteristic philosophical shrug. 'Ah, my *liebling*, I wonder if you ever will be?'

17. Our Lady of Walsingham

It felt quiet after Maudie's mum left. They all missed the cheery rattle of the treadle sewing machine and Mumia calling them into her room for a fitting. As the days lengthened out and buds appeared on the oaks lining the driveway, Ava announced one morning, 'We've got to turn our attention from wedding clothes to the wedding breakfast. W*hat* are we going to eat and *where* are we going to eat it?'

Ruby laid the tray of dirty breakfast plates she'd brought down from the dining room on the kitchen table. 'I've been talking to Mum. She said folks won't expect much when there's a war on; it's more a question of making do,' she said, quoting an expression the government had promoted.

Ava, Bella and Maudie's startled expressions reflected their thoughts on Ruby's words. Ava spoke first, and quite forcefully. 'But that doesn't have to stop us from trying to do something a bit special for you, does it?'

Ruby gave Ava a big, warm hug. 'You are such a good friend!'

'I always like a challenge!' Ava retorted.

A loud male voice rang down the long kitchen corridor. 'Anybody home?'

'That's Peter with the estate delivery,' said Bella, and eagerly dashed out of the kitchen.

'Let's discuss the wedding later,' Maudie added, as they disbanded to do their morning tasks.

'After lunch, over a brew!' Ava laughed.

*

'So, I've been thinking,' Bella said.

'You do surprise me,' teased Maudie.

'Hold on, you two!' Ava cried, as she brewed tea in the old brown teapot. 'I've hardly had time to light up a fag!'

Looking flushed with excitement, Ruby set out mugs, milk and sugar, then sat down at the head of the table.

'I'm in charge!' she joked.

As Ava poured tea, Bella excitedly launched into what she wanted to say.

'Spring's a great time of the year!' she exclaimed. 'Peter will have some good seasonal veg by then, and he's bound to have some fruit growing in the hot house.'

'Let's get to the meat and potatoes before we worry about the frills and fancies,' Ava replied, lighting her cigarette and sitting back in her chair with a contented sigh. 'I was thinking along the lines of mock-turkey, potato salad, fresh salad – depending on Peter, of course – pickles and chutneys. A cold spread. What do you think?'

'Fantastic!' cried Ruby. 'We wouldn't have to worry about heating anything up.'

Ava glanced at Bella, who looked seriously underwhelmed.

'I'd love to get my hands on a lamb!' Bella announced.

'Here we go!' Ava teased. 'We're only in the middle of a war, why not a herd of ostriches?'

Ignoring Ava, Bella continued to fantasize. 'Imagine roast lamb, mint sauce, potatoes, seasonal local veg and rich, thick gravy,' Bella murmured, her mouth watering.

'That's Plan B,' Maudie retorted. 'Until you find a lamb that you can buy with wartime rationing coupons, I suggest we stick with Ava's Plan A – a tasty mock-turkey buffet.'

Bella nodded. 'Over-ambitious, I know,' she admitted. 'But I've never cooked for a wedding party before!'

'A wedding in *wartime*,' Ava pointed out.

'My family said they'll donate their ration coupons towards the wedding breakfast,' Ruby told her friends.

'And we'll donate ours,' Maudie added.

Still on a roll, Bella said, 'It would be nice to have hot soup for starters.'

Maudie nodded enthusiastically. 'Peppery pea soup!' she exclaimed. 'With fresh poppy-seed rolls.'

'Sherry trifle for pud,' Ava said, topping up her mug with tea. 'Jelly's not a problem, there's enough sherry in the cellar to float a boat, and we could scrounge cream from the estate dairy for the topping.'

'What about the wedding cake?' Maudie asked.

'We'll never be able to buy enough sugar for the icing, not if we're to comply with the Sugar Restriction of Use guideline,' Ava stated flatly.

'It's not a problem. I'd settle for a fake cardboard cake, like most couples do,' Ruby answered realistically.

'You really are the Make-do Queen!' Bella teased.

'We could compromise and make an iced cardboard cake,' Maudie replied, tapping the table-top thoughtfully. 'But we'll decorate it with something original.' She clicked her fingers as she had a thought. 'I could make a gingerbread bride and groom, Polish style, to go on top, and little gingerbread boys and girls dancing in a ring around the cake's base.'

Ruby clapped her hands in delight. 'Raf would love that!'

Ava checked the kitchen clock. 'Before we start on tea, let's talk about the reception. What are your thoughts, Ruby?'

'Mum made enquiries about the village hall. The roof leaks a bit, but so long as there's not a thunderstorm, it'll do.'

Before anybody could speak, Bella said quite firmly, 'I think it should be here.'

Ruby's dark eyes shot wide open. 'Her ladyship won't be best pleased, hosting a servant's wedding party in her stately home!'

Bella looked thoughtful as she replied, 'I'm not quite sure, but I think that decision might lie with the Brig.'

Her friends, gathered around her, burst into laughter.

'In that case, lassie, over to you!' chuckled Ava.

Bella and the Brig met most evenings in the library. He always began by checking her homework, then went through any material she was having difficulty with.

'Poem codes!' Bella laughed incredulously.

'You'll get the hang of it,' the Brig said, smiling at her sweetly frowning expression.

'Say it all again,' she begged.

'All right, from the top,' he agreed. 'This is how you create a cypher which the sender and the receiver agree on in advance – the poem you both choose is your cypher.'

'A poem's much simpler to remember,' Bella said. 'Saves the trouble of carrying around a cypher book.'

'Pick a poem from the poetry book I gave you,' he instructed.

As Bella flicked through the book the Brig advised her, 'Don't pick something predictable like '"God Save the King"' –, anybody could easily break that code because the words are so well known. It's quite a challenge to crack the code of a really obscure poem.'

Looking up, Bella said with a grin, 'How about Browning's "Home Thoughts from Abroad"? The poem that begins, "Oh to be in England now that April's there"?'

The Brig nodded. 'OK. Write out the first line on a sheet of paper.'

Bella quickly did as she was told.

'"Oh to be in England now that April's there."'

'Now, underneath each letter, and space, too, write out the alphabet. Write neatly so you can keep track of your changes, making sure each letter represents only one other letter,' he advised.

Muttering out loud, Bella did as she was told.

When Bella had completed her writing, the Brig said, 'So now you have your cypher,' he pointed at the letters on the page. 'You, the sender, and the receiver on the other end now know that O is A, H is B, space is C, T is D, then another O, so that's A again, and another space, which is C again . . . so the next letter, B, has to be E, and so on. Keep going, darling. Once you know the cypher by heart, it's as easy as riding a bike.' The Brig chuckled as he lit his pipe, leaving a muttering Bella struggling on the task he'd set her.

It was only after she had successfully completed her assignment that the Brig poured them both a whisky. Bella always brought some to their evening 'meetings'.

'Well done, darling,' he said, toasting her coding success. 'From here on in, it just gets harder!'

'Cheers!' said Bella, with a cryptic smile.

Sitting side by side on the sofa, they laughed and chatted, kissed and cuddled as the crackling fire warmed the room.

'You know, sweetheart, you could call me Charles occasionally,' he said, as he stroked her soft, blonde curls.

Bella shook her head. 'I love Brig,' she giggled, kissing his earlobe. 'Anyway, the title keeps me in my place!'

'Which is right here beside me,' he replied, in a mock-stern voice.

'Do you think the new code girls have guessed we're "walking out"?' she asked.

'They'd know right away if they walked in here and saw us canoodling on the sofa,' he chuckled. 'How would they guess during work hours, when you're slaving away below stairs and I'm trying to dodge Miss Cox!'

'She's *definitely* guessed,' Bella declared.

'You've ruined her love life,' he teased, pulling her close to his broad chest.

Bella suddenly pulled apart from the Brig as she remembered the task she'd be given by her friends. 'Whose permission do we need for Ruby to have her wedding reception here in the hall?' she asked.

The Brig took a sip from his Scotch.

'Let's see,' he said thoughtfully. 'The date falls during the official period of training, so I suppose, in theory, it's down to me.'

Bella leapt to her feet and punched the air. '*YESSSS!*'

'If it was in the gap after their training, before the next trainees arrive, it would be up to his lordship to decide. Same thing that happened at Christmas, when your parents took over the hall for their own personal use.'

Bella grimaced. 'Ugh! Don't remind me,' she grumbled.

Laughing, the Brig pulled her back on to the sofa, where he playfully tickled her.

'You look lovely when you're cross!' he teased, as she wriggled and jiggled underneath his fingers, helpless with laughter.

Gasping for breath, Bella came up for air. 'I must tell Ruby right away.'

Pulling her to her feet, the Brig put his arm around her waist as he replied, 'Come on, let's both go and tell the bride-to-be.'

*

With the venue finalized, Ruby and Raf sent out the invitations.

'It's a shame Raf's parents can't come,' said Ruby, as she and Maudie washed the supper dishes late one evening while Bella set the breakfast trays.

'So, will he have no guests at all?' Maudie asked.

'He's invited his pals from the base,' Ruby replied. 'English and Polish, and Captain Kit, too, as Raf calls him.'

Maudie's heart gave an involuntary jump. 'Oh, him,' she answered dismissively.

Oblivious of Maudie's reaction, Ruby rambled on, 'He might not come, especially if the Lancasters arrive, but Raf would love it if his superior officer was there . . . bet you would, too!' she added with a cheeky wink.

Maudie forced herself not to retort with a sharp comment like, 'Make sure he doesn't breeze in with Lady Diana in tow!'

She knew that would upset dear Ruby, who was as happy as a songbird these days. Fortunately, they were interrupted by Ava, who walked in with another load of dirty dishes.

'If I carry on washing pots at this rate,' Ruby joked, 'my hands will be so chapped and swollen I'll never get my wedding ring on!'

The four girls had their own individual tasks to focus on for the forthcoming wedding. Maudie made gingerbread whenever she could scrounge a bit of sugar from the week's rations. She took great delight in decorating the little gingerbread boys and girls in traditional Polish costumes, icing these details on to the figures using a mixture of glycerine and flour. She made sure she kept the gingerbread figures in a tightly sealed tin in order to keep them fresh and crispy for Ruby's wedding day.

Bella's priority was *meat*! She asked the Walsingham estate shepherd again and again if there was any way she could secure a lamb. Ava, sticking with her Plan A, discussed at length with Peter what seasonal vegetables or salad he might have in late March. As for the Brig, he was planning how to decorate the dining room for the wedding breakfast.

Ruby, who'd planned to carry a simple bouquet of Walsingham daffodils, was stunned when Kit sent a message via Raf one night asking if he might be allowed to order a bridal bouquet for her from Covent Garden in London.

'I can't accept!' she told her friends, after she'd rushed downstairs to share her surprising news.

'Why not?' Bella asked. 'It's a genuinely kind offer. He can't exactly offer Raf a bouquet, can he!' she joked. 'It's a sweet tribute to both of you.'

Maudie, who was working hard on really disliking the smooth-talking Flight Captain Kit Halliday, felt her heart skip a beat. *What* was happening to her? *Why* did she get goosebumps every time his damn name was mentioned?

When Ruby asked Raf if he thought a bridal bouquet from his boss was appropriate, he nodded with pride.

'Sure, Rubee, Captain Kit is generous man, he ask what flowers are favourites for you.'

Unused to so much fuss and attention, Ruby flung her arms around her fiancé's neck. 'You choose!'

He traced a finger gently over Ruby's soft, red, pouting lips before bending to quickly kiss them. 'Red roses, red lips!'

So Ruby gratefully accepted Kit's offer. After this, she and Kit regularly chatted when he was staying in the west wing – about the wedding plans, the Lancaster bombers and the progress of the war. Maudie coolly circumnavigated the pair of them whenever she saw them together.

'I don't know what's wrong with you,' Ruby said one

morning as she and Maudie set the breakfast trays with the usual rhubarb-and-ginger jam and marge. 'He's a nice man, but you treat him like he's dirt.'

Maudie flushed as she replied, 'Why should I want to talk to him?'

Seeing her friend's cheeks grow pink, Ruby retorted in a teasing voice, 'Who are you kidding?'

Furious at herself, Maudie answered sharply, 'Don't you realize he's going out with Lady Diana?'

'He is *not*!' Bella exclaimed.

'I saw them together. She was all over him like a rash, and he certainly wasn't fighting her off!'

Ruby shook her head. 'You must have got it wrong – he never even mentions her name.'

'And what does that prove?' Maudie demanded.

'That he's got his eyes on somebody else!' Ruby answered with a sly smile. 'I think you're missing a great opportunity.'

Stung by her words, Maudie reacted crossly. 'A great opportunity to – what? – mix with people better than us? Is that what you mean?'

'Keep your political hat on, missus!' Ruby replied light-heartedly. 'I've not got an ulterior motive. I think he's a genuinely nice man, and so does Raf.'

Maudie pressed her lips firmly together; she had to stop talking like this; railing all the time about a man everybody but her thought was wonderful. 'I'll go and see if the dough's risen for the rye bread,' she said, and strode out of the kitchen.

As the short, dark winter days gave way to longer, lighter days, Tom and Ava were able to ride out almost weekly. Their time together was always limited because of Ava's work load, and Tom's, too; he never had a day off and often worked through the night, delivering lambs and calves up and down the Norfolk coast.

'Promise you'll make the wedding?' Ava pleaded, as they sat in their favourite sand dune, with the horses, Lucas and Drummer tethered to a nearby pine tree, rubbing each other's muzzle.

'I'll try, darling,' he assured her.

'I'll hit you on the head with mi rolling pin if you don't!' she joked.

Tom buried his face in her long. dark hair. 'Feisty Lancashire lass!'

'I think I'm losing my northern accent.' Ava laughed. 'The other day, I heard myself saying "graaaas" instead of "grass"! I don't stand a chance, do I? Surrounded by all you posh southerners!'

'I don't care if you say "arse" or "ass",' he chuckled. 'You're perfect.'

There wasn't time for a leisurely picnic but they shared a flask of hot coffee and a spiced apple pasty, which Ava had made that morning. As they sat contentedly side by side, gazing out at the churning, metal-grey North Sea, which, on a dull spring morning, reflected the darkness of the sky and the scudding clouds.

'Did you hear the planes flying out from the airbase last night?' Ava asked.

Tom nodded as he topped up their coffees. 'I was driving home late from a farm visit and I saw them taking off. One after another – *whoosh! whoosh! whoosh!* as they left the runway. It's always an exciting sight but, after the first thrill, I wonder how many of those poor sods will come back alive?'

'Thank God you're not a fighter pilot,' Ava murmured, and snuggled up even closer. 'At least the Huns can't touch you!'

Tom threw back his head and laughed out loud. 'I'm hardly going to get shot down for neutering a cat!'

As they trotted slowly back, they were the only people on the beach. The sharp call of dunlins and oystercatchers and the screech of swooping seagulls merged with the softly breaking waves that swept sideways over the vast expanse of clean, white sand.

'I never thought I'd love a place so much,' Ava said, as she bent to lay her head on Lucas's warm, golden mane. 'I loved the moors and the valleys which were so much part of my childhood, but this is different.' She raised her head to take in the majestic sweep of pine trees on one side of her and the sea meeting the sky on the other.

'It steals your heart away,' Tom replied. 'I can't wait to bring Oliver back here. Maybe in the summer, if all goes well.'

Ava smiled hopefully. 'I'm sure his mum will want him to stay with you,' she said. 'It'll give her a holiday, too.'

Tom gazed out to the far horizon. 'I want Oliver to grow up with a knowledge of the countryside.' He turned towards Ava and added, 'I want my boy to meet you.'

'And I can't wait to meet him,' Ava replied. 'We can play football and rounders, and fish for crabs on the quay at Wells.' Her blues eyes sparkled with anticipation. 'We can teach him to ride, right here on Holkham beach!'

Tom grinned at her glowing, excited face. 'You're just a kid at heart yourself,' he said fondly.

'I like children, they're good fun.'

For a second, they stared at each other, both thinking the same thing but not daring to say it. Would they one day have children who would grow up in a country that was at peace?

*

Bella's friends should have known that Bella would, eventually, get what she wanted. It was Tom who found what she'd been searching for.

'It's an old girl who died of natural causes. Probably worn out by pushing out lambs every year. But she's more mutton than lamb, I'm afraid,' he warned.

'I can do mutton!' a happy Bella answered.

'I'll drop the carcass off with the butcher in Wells; he'll prepare it for the table,' Tom replied.

'Thank you, Tom. I'll make sure I give the farmer a good price,' she promised.

Back at the hall, Bella flounced into the kitchen, flushed with success.

'Drop Plan A! It's roast mutton stuffed with garlic and rosemary.'

Ruby flung her arms around Bella. 'A feast and a treat for everybody! Just wait till I tell Raf.'

'So how are we going to handle a hot roast dinner if we're needed at church?' Maudie asked with a sardonic smile.

Utterly undaunted, Bella replied, 'We'll serve it up when we get back.'

'In our bridesmaids' dresses?' gasped Ava.

Bella nodded. 'It's not a problem – we can cover them with our enormous kitchen pinafores.'

Ava burst out laughing. 'Bloody hell, lass, I'm going to use a bedspread to cover my precious bridesmaid's frock!'

The first day of spring, 21st March, Ruby's wedding day, dawned bright and beautiful, with songbirds singing their hearts out in every treetop surrounding the hall.

'I'm so nervous and excited I'm shaking all over,' Ruby confessed.

'Thank God the Brig's given the trainees cash to go into town and buy their own meals today,' Ava said, taking the rollers out of her long hair, which fell in charming ringlets around her shoulders.

'The bride gets the first bath,' said Maudie, steering Ruby towards the bathroom. 'I left the immersion heater on over-night, so it'll be piping hot, and there's some bubble bath by the sink. Off you go – enjoy!' she giggled, as she closed the door on Ruby. 'Let's spin a coin for who gets the second bath.'

Bella got the raw deal – the fourth to bathe, and in tepid water, too – so she nipped upstairs to her old bedroom, where she soaked in luxury for a good half-hour. The girls sat in their bras and knickers around the kitchen table, on which was placed a large looking-glass that was circulated as they took it in turns to do their make-up. Ruby, who was a dab hand with rouge, eye liner, lipstick and foundation, helped her friends with their make-up, and with their hair. Mumia had made the sweetest little head-dresses from the left-over bits of the pink silk curtains, and the bridesmaids clipped them into their hair, along with several pink rosebuds.

'What would we do without Peter's greenhouse blooms?' Bella said, as she stared at her glowing, excited reflection.

As if he'd heard his name, Peter popped his head round the kitchen door. His eyes just about popped out when he saw four half-naked ladies sitting at the table.

'*Oooh!*' they screamed in unison.

'Wish I had my camera,' he chuckled, then quickly said to the bride-to-be, 'I took the flowers for the altar over to the shrine earlier.'

'Thank you, Peter. See you in church,' Ruby answered, and gestured to him to shut the door and leave them to get dressed.

Ruby helped her friends slip into their lovely dresses, then they helped her into the glistening white bridal gown. After securing the seemingly endless silk buttons on the sleeves and down the back, Maudie carefully lowered the veil over Ruby's glossy, dark hair, which she'd looped into an elegant chignon, to which the glittering tiara was tightly secured. Standing back, the smiling bridesmaids admired the beautiful bride, who was blinking back tears behind her drifting white veil.

'God! You look gorrrrgeous!' Ava cried, as she brushed tears from her own eyes.

'Take a look in the mirror,' Bella said, and led Ruby into the sewing room, where the two full-length mirrors stood. 'I can show you a back view,' she added, turning one of the mirrors so Ruby could see the back of her gown and the white train edged with velvet and tiny, glittering stones.

'Don't even ask,' Bella joked. 'Your bottom *definitely* doesn't look big in that dress!'

Ruby started to shake with laughter.

'Oh, heck!' she gurgled. 'It's going to take Raf all night to undo all those tiny buttons and get the damn thing off!'

Just before they left, Maudie handed Bella the beautiful bridal bouquet Kit had bought for her. Gazing at the shower of fragrant red roses intertwined with fern and myrtle, Ruby gasped with pleasure. 'It's soooo beautiful!'

Afraid she'd become over-emotional, her three friends fluttered lace handkerchiefs in the air.

'Don't cry!' they said.

Ruby nodded as she wiped away a tear with the nearest lace hankie. 'Don't worry, I won't – it'll ruin my make-up!'

*

Bella had persuaded Dodds to drive the bridal party to the church in her father's Bentley. With her parents safely out of the way in London, Bella assured Dodds that it would only be a question of driving them into Walsingham then home again after the service. What she didn't know was the nuptial Mass would be an hour long and Dodds would be stuck outside in the Bentley for the duration.

Quite a crowd had gathered in the tiny Roman Catholic slipper chapel, which flickered with the light from a hundred candles and smelt of fragrant narcissi and hyacinths. The beautiful bridesmaids preceded Ruby down the aisle to the strains of 'Here Comes the Bride'. Trembling on her father's arm, small, slender Ruby looked exquisite, and when she reached the groom's side, Raf, his handsome face suffused with love, took his bride's hand and gently kissed it.

'My Rubee, my beauty.'

The Latin Mass was long indeed. Full of blessings and clouds of perfumed incense, it had an ancient rhythm that thrilled Maudie, in particular. A staunch agnostic, she had never thought she would be so intrigued by a service that she didn't understand a single word of! The dark chapel, glowing with candlelight, and the stained-glass windows, rich with jewel-dark colours, reminded her of the Polish icons her mother treasured at home.

When the final hymn was sung and Mr and Mrs Boskow walked down the aisle arm in arm, the entire congregation applauded, then followed them into the chapel garden, where they showered the newly-weds in drifts of confetti. Maudie flushed when she noticed Kit Halliday, handsome and arresting in his RAF uniform, walking out of the church with a group of Raf's pals from the airbase. One of Raf's friends who owned a Brownie box camera took some group photographs, then Ava, Bella and Maudie jumped into the Bentley, which Dodds drove home at break-neck speed. Back in the kitchen, they donned their striped pinafores and started to unload the piping-hot food from the Aga oven.

'Wait till all the guests are sitting down, then we'll get the dishes on to the hotplate and serve immediately,' Ava said, steam from the vegetables clouding her beautifully made-up face.

When the wedding party returned to the hall, the girls were called outside for more photographs. In a flutter, they joined the guests, and the first photograph taken was one of all the bridesmaids wearing blue-striped kitchen pinafores!

'I'll frame that one!' Ruby giggled, as her friends hastily ditched their pinnies to pose in their pink silk bridesmaids' dresses.

'All together now!' Raf's pal called out. 'Let's get you into a tight group.'

As everybody jovially shoved and shuffled closer, Maudie found herself pressed against Kit, who, in order to make room for others, had to put an arm around her waist. Maudie suppressed a gasp at his touch. It was if an electric current had travelled from his body to hers, leaving her limp and breathless.

'You look lovely,' he murmured.

Blushing to the roots of her loose, red-golden curls, Maudie was utterly tongue-tied. Taller by four inches than Maudie, Kit bent to speak to her and, in doing so, he inhaled the sweet perfume of her hair. 'I was hoping to catch up with you,' he added.

'I've been busy,' Maudie answered weakly.

'Maybe we can chat later?' he asked tentatively.

'I've got work to do,' she replied, and the group photograph was taken with her frowning crossly.

'Why do you keep avoiding me?' he asked sadly.

'I think that's a question you already know the answer to,' she retorted. She picked up her discarded pinafore and hurried back indoors.

The Brig had done a great job on the dining room. He'd covered the Formica-topped tables with white crêpe paper and put jars of daffodils on each one. Bella, Maudie and Ava served the lunch, helped by the Brig and Tom, who'd also donned aprons, like the bridesmaids. The peppery, thick pea soup warmed everybody up and the roast mutton, served with a rich gravy, mint sauce, roast potatoes, estate-grown carrots and cabbage, just about fed the sixty hungry guests. The trifle, heavily doused with Walsingham sherry, went down a treat, and everybody loved Maudie's wedding cake, topped with a gingerbread Polish bride and groom.

Rafal had managed to get a bottle of black-market vodka, which he instructed his guests to knock back in one gulp in a toast to the happy couple.

'*Dobre zdrowie i szczęście na wieki!*' Raf cried as he downed his vodka shot.' Good health and happiness for ever!'

'Whoooh!' giggled Ruby, as she downed hers, too, and swayed giddily. 'I could get used to this. Makes a nice change from Dad's home-brewed stout.'

By five in the afternoon, the newly married couple had left for their three-day honeymoon in Hunstanton, and Maudie had managed to ignore Kit throughout the entire meal. Seeing him driving out of the estate gates in his old MG, she slumped with relief; she needed to avoid Flight Captain Halliday if just his touch set her tingling with desire. Best to let him devote his energies to Lady Diana; they made the perfect match.

18. Bomb Raid

Edward came home briefly one weekend before Easter.

'God!' Bella cried, as she returned to the warmth of the kitchen after a brief visit above stairs to have tea with her family.

'The fuss they're making up there – you'd think the son and heir had won the Military Cross!'

'I suppose they're glad he's doing his bit for the war effort at last,' Ruby said.

Bella gazed fondly at her newly married friend. It was a couple of weeks since she'd come back from her honeymoon, and she still had the glow of love.

'You always have something nice to say about everybody,' she said. 'Honest to God, I truly believe that if Goebbels walked in with a machine gun, you'd put the kettle on!'

'Don't be daft!' Ruby giggled, as she drained water from the vast pan of potatoes she was about to mash for the shepherd's pie, which contained more root vegetables and Oxo than minced meat.

'I bet you can't wait to leave us and go and live with your husband, Mrs Beskow?' Ava joked.

'Will you please shut up?' Ruby cried, throwing her hands up in the air. 'I'll miss you all – when and *if* we get an estate cottage of our own.'

'Until then, you'll have to put up with us spinsters!' Maudie laughed.

'With Raf working all the hours God sends now that the

Lancasters have arrived at the airbase, I'd be lonely if I was miles away in an estate cottage' Ruby confessed.

'You could always make friends with a badger!' Ava teased.

Before she could stop herself, Maudie asked. 'Have you seen the Lancasters?'

Ruby nodded her head and rolled her eyes. 'They're *huge*! You should see the size of the fuselage; Raf said they can get twenty times more bombs in a Lancaster than you could in a Spitfire or a Halifax. 'Course, Raf adores them. Him and his ground crew have been allocated Captain Kit's Lancaster, which they wash and polish every day.'

Maudie couldn't stop herself from asking yet another question. 'When is the captain taking one up?'

'He's been up four times already on practice runs,' Ruby laughed. 'He's like a kid with a new toy!'

'Have they been on any bombing raids?' Maudie persisted.

Ruby gave her a smiling, quizzical look. 'You're asking a lot of questions about somebody you claim not to like,' she teased.

Maudie answered with an airy wave of her hand, 'Oh, you know, those blasted bombing raids keep the entire county awake all night.' Grabbing a basket of parsnips, she hurried out of the room, saying, 'I'd better get these into the cold store.'

Ruby shook her head as she turned to Ava and Bella, who were putting trays of shepherd's pie in the Aga in readiness for lunchtime.

'She can lie all she wants, but our Maudie's got a real thing for Captain Kit.'

'She insists he's going out with my sister.' Bella laughed in disbelief. 'Diana should be so lucky! Captain Kit would be a real improvement on her usual goofy, chinless wonders.'

With her back pressed against the warm stove, Ava lit up a Woodbine.

'So are you saying that Kit's not going out with Diana?' she asked.

'Of course he's not!' Bella exclaimed. 'Believe me, Diana would be announcing it from the rooftops, if they were.'

'Then why is Maudie so convinced he is?' Ava asked.

'I think she's trying to protect herself,' Bella replied thoughtfully.

Rummaging around in the cutlery drawer, Ruby said, over the metallic, clattering noise, 'Protect herself from *what*? A kiss and a cuddle?'

'You know how proud and independent Maudie is,' Bella retorted. 'She's not going to drop her guard lightly, even if the man in question is as handsome as a movie star.'

'You'd better not let the Brig hear that,' Ruby giggled. 'He might get jealous.'

'Change the conversation,' Ava whispered, as she heard footsteps in the kitchen corridor. 'Maudie's on her way back.'

That night, Maudie's words about bombing raids keeping the county awake all night came tragically true. Unfortunately, it wasn't the Lancasters flying out on a night mission to bomb Berlin, it was German Messerschmitts flying in to bomb the Holkham airbase.

The deafening thunder of planes flying over the hall woke the entire household. In their bedrooms, the girls felt the ground and the walls shake as bombs were dropped less than five miles away.

'Jesus Christ Almighty!' screamed Ava, leaping from her bed.

'Get out! Get out!' yelled Bella.

Wearing only their cotton nighties, with their hair flying wildly about their faces, the four of them ran out of the back door, where, in the pitch dark, the sight that met their eyes made their blood run cold.

'They planes are flying *inland*!' Maudie gasped in horror.

'The Germans are bombing the base!' Bella cried.

Almost fainting in terror, Ruby fell against the wall, clinging to it for support.

'Raf's on the base! My Raf's there!' she shrieked.

Several figures dashed out of the west wing. As they ran towards their vehicles, Maudie, even in the dark, made out the tall, athletic shape of Kit Halliday. So did Ruby, who, barefoot and hysterical, ran across the yard towards him.

'Take me with you! Please take me with you!' she implored, flinging herself on Kit.

Maudie, right behind Ruby, grabbed hold of her friend, who was sobbing uncontrollably.

'I'll look after her,' she told Kit, who was in the driver's seat and trying to reverse out with his headlights and rear lights switched off.

He nodded tersely and roared away, leaving Maudie clutching Ruby. It was only after the sound of Kit's MG had faded into the darkness that Maudie realized the top of her nightdress was wide open, revealing the soft curve of her small pert breasts.

'I must look like the mad woman in the attic!' she thought to herself, as she buttoned up her nightie. 'Thank God he didn't turn his lights on!'

It wasn't just Ava, Bella, Ruby and Maudie who were outside in the dark, all the trainees were in the garden, along with the Brig and Miss Cox. If the trainees hadn't guessed the Brig's relationship with Bella, there was no doubting it that night. He tore across the lawn towards her and held her tightly against his warm chest as she shivered in her thin nightdress.

'Those poor men on the base,' she murmured.

As flickering orange flames licked the dark sky, the Brig answered grimly, 'God help them all.'

As the bombs continued to rain down on their targets, Ava said grimly, 'That'll be the end of the Lancasters.'

'And the base, too, by the looks of things,' Maudie added grimly.

After what seemed like hours, the Messerschmitts suddenly stopped pounding the base.

'What's happening?' Ruby cried, as they stood in the thick pall of smoke that had drifted over from the burning airbase.

With their ears still ringing from the thunder of continual bombing, they waited in a tense silence. The sound of roaring engines made them all look up into the sky, where they could see the low-flying Messerschmitts heading out over the North Sea.

'It's over,' sighed Bella in relief.

'They're going!' cried Ruby.

'For now,' added the Brig darkly.

As day dawned, soft and pearly pink, the birds seemed too stunned to sing. Slowly, one by one, as the sun rose, they picked up their dawn-chorus serenade. It was only then that Bella saw her brother and sister returning to the hall in the half-light.

'They must have been watching the bombing raid, too,' she thought to herself, as she led a sobbing Ruby indoors. None of them could even think of going back to bed.

'If only you'd let me go to the airbase,' Ruby begged. 'I'd be fine if I could only see Raf.'

The Brig was adamant. 'Nobody can leave this house

until we get the all-clear,' he said firmly. 'The airbase isn't safe right now – for all we know, the Germans could be reloading for another hit.'

'God help us all,' whispered Ava, crossing herself.

'If a flying ember should go anywhere near the bomb store, it could blow half the county to kingdom come,' the Brig said ominously.

Bella put a warning finger to her lips and pointed towards Ruby. Getting the message, the Brig nodded his head as he said, 'I'd better get back to the trainees.'

'We'll bring up tea and toast for everybody right away,' Bella called after him.

Having something to do centred the girls' thoughts. As they toasted bread and boiled the huge kettle on the Aga, they heard the familiar *pop-pop* of Raf's old jeep. Ruby dropped her empty tray and went flying out of the front door as if she had wings on her feet. With the engine still running, Raf leapt out of the driver's seat and hurled himself into Ruby's open arms. Weeping and kissing, they clung to each other, then they both began to gabble at the same time.

'I thought you were dead!'

'My Rubee, my love!'

'The Lancasters?'

'All gone – *boooom!*'

Ruby stared into Raf's pale blue eyes, which were ringed with soot and dirt. 'You look exhausted,' she whispered.

Laying his head against her soft shoulder, he sighed. 'My God, Rubee, it was very bad.'

Ruby took him by the hand. 'Come on, sweetheart, let's get you a nice cup of tea.'

Below stairs, the girls fussed around Raf, feeding him fried eggs on toast, which he devoured, along with hot, sweet tea. Now that Raf was safe and sound, Ava confessed she was worried about her Tom.

'I can't get through on the phone – the lines must be down. I just hope he was safely home in Wells and not driving near the base when the bombing started,' she said fervently.

Maudie put an arm around her drooping shoulders. 'Do you want to jump on the bike and cycle over there?'

With tears in her eyes, Ava nodded gratefully.

'I'll help start the lunch, then I'll go,' she replied.

After Raf had finished his food, he sat back in his chair and shook his head as he recalled the attack.

'They came – no warning,' he said. 'How come bloody Jerry know exact location of base?'

'Bang on bloody target,' Ruby muttered angrily, topping up her husband's mug with more hot tea.

Having seen the jeep on the drive, the Brig came rushing downstairs to talk to Raf as soon as he was free.

'How bad is it?' he asked urgently.

'All bloody bad, Brig, sir,' Raf replied. 'Captain Hibbert, blown up, dead. Many others dead, too. Buildings burning all over place. Captain Kit, he ask how Jerry know to find Lancasters?'

'My thoughts exactly! That was precision bombing, without a shadow of a doubt,' the Brig said angrily. 'It's got to be an insider's work, for sure.'

'You mean, somebody's feeding the enemy information?' Bella gasped.

'That – or bloody amazing radar technology,' the Brig replied.

Raf dragged himself up on to his feet. 'I go back to base now,' he said.

'But you've been up all night!' Ruby cried.

'Thank God, I still here, not dead. Need to help injured,' Raf answered wearily.

Suddenly galvanized, Bella declared, 'We could help, too! We could nurse the sick in the west wing.'

'You're right,' Maudie cried. 'This huge house could accommodate so many injured men!'

Bella put a hand over her mouth to suppress an inappropriate giggle. 'Stay right away from my parents' suites!'

'With pleasure!' Maudie laughed.

'We can't contact the base – the telephone lines are down,' the Brig pointed out.

'I tell Captain Kit right away,' Raf said.

On the verge of tears, Ruby held on to Raf's arm.

'Sweetheart, you're in no fit state to drive!' she cried.

'I'll go!'

At the sound of a man's voice ringing out, they all turned to see Tom Benson descending the kitchen stairs.

'*Tom!*' cried Ava.

Crossing the room in two quick strides, Tom took Ava in his arms. 'Darling, I've been trying to get through to you all morning,' he said, burying his face in her long, dark hair.

'Thank God you're safe,' she whispered, as she clung to him.

Giving Ruby a passionate farewell kiss, Raf tore himself away from her grip. 'Get ready for injured,' he said, as he headed for the stairs.

Reluctantly releasing Ava, Tom dashed after him. 'Wait, Raf! I'm coming with you.'

By the time the two men returned to the hall with two army trucks full of injured airmen, Ava, Bella, Maudie and Ruby had laid out mattresses, filched from all over the house, in the west wing.

'The dead and the badly wounded have been taken to Wells and King's Lynn hospitals,' Tom told the Brig as they helped the injured out of the trucks. 'These men need their wounds cleaned and bandaged. They'll require painkillers, too.'

'We can rip up sheets for bandages,' Bella replied. 'There are plenty in the sewing room.'

'I can pick up painkillers from my surgery,' Tom added, then his face dropped. 'Bugger, my car's at the base.'

'Saddle up Lucas and ride him into town,' Ava suggested. 'Be as quick as you can, sweetheart.'

Grinning, Tom gave her a quick peck on the cheek. 'Don't worry, I won't go for a gallop on Holkham beach on the way!'

As Maudie, Bella and the Brig helped the wounded men to their makeshift hospital beds, Ava and Ruby held the fort below stairs. Chopping a huge pile of peeled potatoes and root vegetables, which she dropped into a pan of water on top of the Aga, Ava said to Ruby, 'With all the extra mouths to feed, we'd better keep a stew going night and day.'

'What're we going to put in it?' Ruby asked, standing by the larder door, surveying the half-empty shelves.

'Anything we can lay on hands on: barley, beans, lentils, more spuds, whatever Peter can dig up in his garden, Oxo cubes, Marmite, mince, marrow bones,' she said breathlessly. 'We've got to keep the injured warm and fed after what they went through last night.' Unexpected tears stung the back of Ava's eyes as she murmured, 'Poor buggers.'

'Do you think the Jerries will bomb every airbase where there are Lancasters?' Ruby asked, wide-eyed, as she added Marmite and Lea and Perrins sauce to the stew pot.

Ava pressed a finger to her lips and said in a low voice, 'Loose lips sink ships – or, in our case, bombers.' She dropped her voice even lower and added, 'I'd say, the less we know the better.'

Kit arrived with the next truckload of wounded. Jumping out of the cab, he hurried round to the back to help his men out.

'Take care now. Watch out, mate,' he said tenderly, as he guided them into the west wing, where he found Maudie, with blood splattered on her face, bandaging an airmen's gashed arm.

She caught her breath at the sight of him in his filthy, ripped uniform. His face was smeared with grease and dirt and he had a deep cut across his forehead. Her heart ached at the sorry sight of him and, after bandaging the arm of the injured man she was attending to, Maudie rose to her feet.

'You need treatment,' she said softly.

Kit shook his head.

'It's just a cut from a piece of flying metal,' he said dismissively. 'I must get back to the base to prepare in case there's another attack.'

Maudie gazed at him incredulously. 'But there can't be anything left to bomb?' she cried.

'The enemy seem determined to blow Holkham right off the map, but it'll be bloody well over my dead body!' he said grimly.

Leaving Maudie, he dashed outside to bring in more wounded. When he returned, he was less terse. 'Thank you for helping my men. It's not as if you haven't got anything else to do,' he said with an understanding smile.

'Everyone's doing their bit. Even some of the trainees are washing up.' She chuckled. 'Please let me at least clean your wound?' she begged, before he dashed off again. 'If you leave it too long it could get infected,' she warned.

'OK, thanks,' Kit said, slumping into a chair and closing his eyes.

When Maudie came back with hot water, antiseptic cream and cotton wool, she found Kit fast asleep in the chair. Smeared with dirt as he was, his face in repose looked beautiful; high, sculpted cheekbones, dark hair falling softly over his forehead, long, dark lashes that hid his penetrating blue eyes and a full, soft mouth, now slightly parted as he breathed heavily in his sleep.

'Poor chap,' Maudie muttered under her breath.

Knowing there was no time to spare, she squared her shoulders as she dipped cotton wool into the hot water and gently started to clean the gash on his forehead. Kit woke with a start and grabbed her wrist so tightly that Maudie squealed in pain.

'*No!*' he yelled, then, looking around, he blinked in confusion as he took in his surroundings. 'I'm so sorry,' he mumbled, wiping his head and in doing so smearing fresh new blood into his hair. 'I . . . I . . .' He broke off as his face convulsed in grief.

'I was dreaming of Jimmy, my second-in-command, my friend.' Tears streamed down Kit's face and he sobbed helplessly. 'He . . . he . . . he ran out – he burnt to death.'

With her compassionate heart aching, Maudie did the most instinctive thing any woman would do when standing before somebody in pain. Laying aside the bowl of water and the cotton wool, she put her arms around the heartbroken man and held him close. Wrapped in Maudie's slender arms, with her wonderful hair pressed against his face, Kit slowly began to breathe more easily.

'Your friend was doing his duty,' she said, in a soft, soothing voice, as she rocked Kit gently back and forth. 'God help him. May he rest in peace.'

Neither she nor Kit knew how many minutes passed before they pulled apart, but when they did there were tears in both their eyes. Still holding hands, they stared with undisguised emotion at each other. Taking a deep, shuddering breath, Kit said, 'Why have you been so angry with me?'

Maudie blushed. She was embarrassed, but she was determined to spit it out. 'I didn't like you flirting with me when you were courting Lady Diana!' she blurted out.

Kit's blue eyes opened wide in disbelief.

'*Lady Diana?*'

Maudie nodded. As a big grin spread across Kit's face, she asked nervously, 'Aren't you?'

In answer, he drew her face close to his and kissed her gently on the mouth. For Maudie, the universe she had previously known fell away; she floated on air, every nerve in her body tingled, her pulse raced, her heart pounded: she felt like she'd left her world and found a new one. As Kit pulled away, she made strange, whimpering noises, 'Aaaah . . . no . . .'

Maudie wanted to grab him and kiss him till she fainted away. At this point, she really didn't care about Lady Diana, or any other woman, for that matter.

'*Never!*' He laughed. 'You silly, adorable, beautiful, green-eyed witch!'

'Kit . . .' When she spoke his name for the first time it felt almost like an act of love.

'Maudie . . .'

Ridiculously, she giggled. She was in a room full of wounded man who needed her attention. She pulled herself together. 'I have to dress your wound, or attend to another patient.'

Not wanting her to go to another man, not right at this moment, Kit picked up some cotton wool, which he dunked in the now-cool water, then laid it against his gashed brow.

'Jesus, that hurt!' he cried, grinning. 'Come on, sweet nurse, attend to me!'

By the time Kit drove back to the airbase, Maudie was reeling. She hadn't slept for twenty-four hours and had hardly eaten, but the truth was she was on an emotional tidal wave. When would she see Kit again, touch him, kiss him? she wondered, as she tended one injured airman after another. A terrifying thought almost immobilized her: could the Holkham base be hit again tonight? Kit had survived one bombing raid. Could he survive another, or would he burn in the flames, like his poor friend Jimmy? Seeing Maudie looking white and pale, Tom, who was assisting the duty doctor, suggested she took a break.

Once out of the west wing, Maudie stood on the driveway, staring blankly at the park, over which a pall of smoke still hung. She jumped when she heard somebody calling her name.

'Maudie! Come inside and get something to eat,' Ruby cried from one of the open dining-room windows.

Below stairs, Maudie couldn't face the stew she was offered, but she was grateful for the strong tea and Marmite on toast Ruby made for her. Ava and Ruby raised their eyebrows at their unusually quiet friend.

'Do you need to rest, lovie?' Ava asked.

Maudie gazed up at her. Her green eyes were wide and sparkling with happiness. 'I've just kissed Kit Halliday!'

Ava and Ruby burst out laughing.

'That's been a long time coming!' Ruby giggled.

Ava smiled at the love-struck Maudie. 'What made you finally drop your guard?'

'He was asleep . . . he looked so lovely,' Maudie confessed. 'I couldn't be angry with him any more.'

'I don't know why you were angry with him in the first place,' Ruby teased.

Laughing with happiness, Maudie cried, 'He's not going out with Diana!'

'Told you so!' laughed Ruby.

Ava lit up a Woodbine and leant against the warm range.

'Well, that's one mystery cleared up at last!' she chuckled.

The Germans didn't come back for a second raid. They didn't have to, they'd successfully destroyed every Lancaster on the airbase, and most of the official buildings, too.

As Raf stood beside his senior officer, tears filled his eyes. 'God Almighty,' he murmured, as he stared at the once-mighty planes that now lay smouldering on the runway like shattered metallic dinosaurs.

Kit took a deep breath. 'We did it once, we'll do it again.'

Raf nodded. 'Start all over, eh?'

Kit nodded back. 'It's our bloody duty, Raf. We have to beat the enemy.'

'How we do this, sir?' a bemused Raf cried.

Kit replied through gritted teeth, 'We rebuild the base . . . and bring back the Lancasters.'

19. Lord Edward

Early summer found all four women below stairs in love, or in the process of falling in love. The mood in the kitchen was light-hearted, giggly and romantic.

'Do you think we're going the same way as the swallows, coupling up and nest-building?' Ruby joked.

'Well, I wouldn't go that far,' giggled Maudie, who, at that particular moment, had more stars in her eyes than anybody.

'Considering we've got a lot to worry about, what with the bombed-out base and more mouths to feed, you'd think we'd be as miserable as sin,' Ava said, as she whisked the mixture for the savoury pancakes they'd be serving up for lunch.

'I suppose we've got far better things on our minds,' Ruby said, with a knowing wink. 'I know I have!'

Ava grinned at Ruby, who was glowing with love.

'Can we turn our minds to the here and now instead of the joys of a double bed?' Ava teased. 'I was thinking of filling the pancakes with corned beef and baked beans.' Seeing Bella's disapproving look, she added, 'Got any better ideas, lady?'

'Peter shot some pigeon in the barley field – they were eating all the ripening grain. Don't panic, they're plucked!' She laughed when she saw the look on Ava's face. 'I could casserole them with some beans and tomatoes, that might work.'

'Pigeons, yuk!' Ava grimaced.

'Honestly, you squeamish town girls, you don't know what's good for you,' Bella teased.

'I'd prefer to eat meat that's not wearing feathers or a fur bonnet!' Ava retorted.

The girls continued chatting as they went about their different jobs.

'I was so scared when I thought I'd lost Raf,' Ruby said, putting the bowl of pancake mixture she'd prepared in the cold larder. 'It made me think we've got to live every moment as if it's our last.'

Ava smiled as she lit up two Woodbines, one for herself and one for Ruby.

'You're dead right, lovie,' she said, exhaling cigarette smoke. 'God only knows what tomorrow will bring.'

On a regular basis, to keep the Walsinghams and Timms sweet, there were certain duties the girls below stairs had to carry out, even though they were forever pushed for time. Maudie and Ruby usually took on these duties. Bella was exempted, as her parents would be mortified to find their daughter making their bed. Ava was also exempted, as she was 'Top Cook', a title Ruby had bestowed on her after Maudie arrived.

'Top cook, second cook, skivvy,' Ruby often chanted, as she pointed first to Ava, then Maudie, and then herself. 'And Bella the Game-pie Queen!'

On this particular lovely summer morning, Ruby was clearing ashes out of the various fireplaces in the Walsingham suites and relaying fresh wood and newspaper to be lit for later use. Maudie was assigned to tidy Lord Edward's suite. To her surprise, she found him in his study, packing his bags.

'Sorry,' she said. 'I was told by Timms that you'd left for London.'

Edward's irritated expression changed when he saw that

the intruder was the attractive new maid with the stunning long legs and bewitching green eyes.

'I'll be out of here soon,' he said, with a charming smile, 'if you'd like to make a start on the bedroom.'

Maudie hesitated. She instinctively felt uncomfortable at the thought of going into a man's bedroom when he was there; then she remembered the curried-game meatballs she'd promised to help Bella with in a short while and realized she had no choice. Without saying another word, she opened the door to his bedroom, which smelt of cigarette smoke and Brylcreem. Admiring her shapely hips and perfect calves, Edward sauntered into the room, where Maudie was now busy stripping his bed.

'Forgotten something,' he said casually, as he approached his bedside table.

Maudie carried on stripping the bed, but as she did so, Edward suddenly lurched at her. 'You're not like the usual girls we employ,' he said, grabbing her by the waist and pushing her down on to his bed.

Frightened and furious, Maudie pummelled her fists against his chest. 'Get off me!' she cried.

'Don't be like that,' Edward replied, as he tried to kiss her.

Repulsed by his full, wet lips and flushed, red face, Maudie put up a fight. Struggling and writhing underneath his overweight body, she tried to bite his hands, which were pressing her down on to the bed.

'Ouch!' he exclaimed, as he held her more firmly. 'I like a woman who can fight. I should have guessed when I saw that flaming-red hair that you'd have a temper, eh?'

By this time, Maudie was really panicking. She was finding it hard to breathe, with him almost smothering her, and he was groping his way up her body, feeling for her breasts.

'No harm in a little farewell kiss,' Edward murmured, as he sucked on her soft white neck.

Maudie wanted to scream, but she was so flattened by him she couldn't, so she did the only thing left to her: she kneed him hard in the balls.

'*Aghhhh!* You bitch!' Edward cried in agony, and leapt away from her.

Seeing his bright red face and little piggy eyes flaming with anger, Maudie sprang up and ran to the door.

'Help, Ruby! *Help!*' she screamed.

'Not so quickly, lady,' Edward roared, catching up with her and grabbing her by the hair.

'*No!*' Maudie gasped in pain as he yanked her backwards into his arms.

At that moment, Ruby, who had heard her friend's call from the end of the corridor, flung open the door. She gasped at the sight of a dishevelled Maudie being groped by Lord Edward, who was puffing and blowing with excitement and exertion. At the sight of wide-eyed Ruby, Edward let go of Maudie, who dashed to her friend.

'You brute!' Maudie cried, once she'd put a distance between herself and her attacker. 'How dare you touch me!' she raged.

Lord Edward shrugged, took a cigarette from a solid-gold case and lit it with a matching gold lighter.

'I'll do whatever I please in my own house,' he snarled at Maudie, and blew smoke in her face. 'If you don't like it, bugger off.'

Back in the safety of the kitchen, Maudie was a wreck, intermittently raging and weeping.

'I feel dirty,' she said, as she rubbed her lips clean with

cold water. 'He touched me all over, like I was a whore he'd paid for – the pig!'

Ruby sat Maudie, now sobbing, down at the table as Ava poured some strong tea for her.

'Don't tell Bella – she'll kill him,' Ruby whispered.

'I'll kill him first!' Maudie seethed.

'Don't tell Kit – he'll go mad,' Ava said.

Maudie's face fell, and tears slipped down her cheeks.

'It wasn't like that with Kit – it was so beautiful, I couldn't get enough – but *him*!' She shuddered. 'Fat and sweaty – he stinks of booze, too – pushing up my skirt, trying to get into my knickers. Ugh, it was nauseating!'

Ava and Ruby comforted their friend as best they could.

'Don't keep thinking about it,' Ava advised. 'He's gone. You're safe now.'

Still in shock, Maudie murmured, 'If Ruby hadn't come to my rescue, I think he would have raped me.'

'I wouldn't put it past scum like him,' said Ava. 'I thought he was a bit of a nancy boy, him not going to war, but clearly I was wrong,' she added.

They all stopped talking when Bella, blissfully unaware of what had just taken place, walked in and set a big pan of stew on the table. Seeing their flushed faces, she immediately asked, 'What's wrong?'

Ruby, Ava and Maudie looked at each other.

'Tell me!' Bella demanded.

'Nothing,' Maudie prevaricated.

'It doesn't look like nothing from where I'm standing,' Bella retorted, as she eyeballed her friends, who shuffled uneasily. 'For God's sake, tell me!' she begged.

Ava and Ruby turned to Maudie.

'You'd better tell her,' Ava advised.

'Your brother's just tried to rape me.'

Bella went as white as a sheet. Gripping a chair for support, she stared at Maudie with tears in her gentle blue eyes.

'I . . . I'm so sorry.'

Maudie laid a hand on Bella's arm. 'It's nothing to do with you. Please don't take responsibility for him.'

'How can I not when he behaves like a beast?' Bella cried. 'He's loathsome.'

'Don't feel bad about it, Bella,' Ava said softly. 'You're the pick of the bunch – better than the whole bloody lot of them put together!'

As usual the sheer amount of work to be done drove the girls back into the daily grind. They simply didn't have a minute to themselves, or to think about the distressing events of the past few days. On the day Edward left for London, Bella followed him on to the drive, and watched him throw his suitcase into the back of his sports car.

'I want a word with you, Edward,' she called.

'What if I don't want a word with you, kitchen maid?' he sneered.

Ignoring his look of contempt, Bella said coldly, 'If you attempt to molest any of the girls below stairs again, I'll report you to the police.'

Edward rolled his eyes in mock-fear. 'Well, well, been sharing stories, have we?' Lighting a cigarette, he lazily blew a smoke ring into the air, before adding, 'She was asking for it, little tart!'

'That's what most rapists say,' she snapped, and turned on her heel and left him smoking in the drive.

'Bloody good riddance, scumbag!' she mumbled under her breath. 'London and the War Office are welcome to you!'

20. Beach Ball

When the injured airmen finally returned to their base, the work load for the girls in the kitchen, mercifully, decreased.

'Maybe we could snatch a few hours off,' Ruby said, as she polished the Walsinghams' silver cutlery service. 'I'm glad we were able to help those poor injured men but, my God, it did make a lot more work for us,' she added.

'Worth it, though,' said Ava, stirring a meagre-looking stew in a pot on the hot plate. 'Nice to see the men get back to health and walk out of here smiling.'

Maudie and Ruby hardly saw Kit and Raf, as everybody on the airbase was working around the clock in order to bring the Lancasters back to Norfolk. Bella saw the Brig every day, mostly below stairs, when he rolled up his shirt-sleeves and helped her wash up or mop the kitchen floor at the end of a long shift. So it was Ava who got the first afternoon off and, this time, she and Tom didn't go for a romantic ride on the beach, even though the sky was blue and it was gloriously hot; instead, Ava met Tom in his flat over his veterinary practice in Wells. After parking her rickety old bike, she skipped up the stairs to Tom's flat where she found her boyfriend glowing with excitement. Rushing towards her, Tom picked Ava up in his arms and twirled her round in dizzying circles.

'Stop it!' she laughed.

'Wonderful, wonderful news!' he exclaimed, as he set an unsteady Ava down. 'Oliver's coming at the weekend. Edith's agreed he can come here for the first two weeks of his summer holiday.'

Ava was almost as excited as Tom. She was dying to meet the little boy, who Tom obviously adored.

'That really is wonderful news,' she said with a happy smile. Looking around the rather grubby bachelor flat, she asked. 'Where's the little lad going to sleep?

Tom's face fell. 'I know what you're thinking – it's not great for kids here, is it?'

Because most of their previous dates had been in the Walsingham kitchen or on Holkham beach, Ava wasn't at all familiar with the flat.

'Give me a tour?' she said.

Tom winked as he answered, 'Believe me, it won't take long.'

He was right. There was a small kitchen, a sitting room with a view of Wells harbour and the busy quay, a bathroom built under the eaves and a spare bedroom packed to the ceiling with junk and empty boxes.

'I thought Ollie might sleep in my bed,' Tom explained. 'I can kip on an army camp-bed in the sitting room for a couple of weeks.

Ava shook her head. 'No, Tom. Ollie needs to feel he belongs here. He must have his own space, and it must be a nice one, too, a place he'll always want to come back to.'

Tom slowly nodded his head. 'You're right, sweetheart, I'm just a bloke – I can only do one thing at a time!'

Ava put her arms around his neck and buried her face against his warm shoulder.

'I'm a woman and a cook – I can do lots of things at the same time!'

Tom kissed her down the line of her slender neck, then nuzzled her glorious hair, which always smelt of flowers and cake. It was tempting to spend the afternoon wrapped in each other's arms – how often did they get the chance for sweet-talking and romance? Ava, however, was on a mission. With an effort, she pulled away from Tom, who groaned as he reluctantly released her.

'He can sleep in here,' Ava said, pointing to the packed box-room.

'But it's full of junk!' Tom exclaimed.

'Then let's get rid of it!'

Ava wasted no time. She and Tom stuffed his Land Rover with rubbish from the spare room and, while Tom drove to the local tip, Ava bought some blue and white paint from a small ironmonger's shop on the high street. After wiping down the dusty walls, she painted them, and the ceiling, while Tom washed and polished the worn lino floor. Leaving the paint to dry, they drove into Fakenham, where they scoured the second-hand shops for a single bed, a chest of drawers and a rug. They found an old brass bed with knobs on the bed rails and a charming chest of drawers which was painted white and decorated with little blue stencilled sailing ships. Finally, they purchased a bright, multicoloured rag rug.

'It's perfect!' Tom enthused, as they arranged the furniture in Ollie's new room.

'There's plenty of material in the sewing room at the hall,' Ava said, as she wiped down the metal bed with warm disinfected water. 'I'll knock up a pair of black-out curtains tonight, and that'll finish the room off nicely,' she said excitedly.

Tom removed the cloth from her busy hands and turned her to face him. 'You've done so much for me, darling.'

Ava nodded. 'And for your little lad, too,' she replied.

Tom drew her down on to the narrow bed, which creaked under their joint weight.

'You are a wonder,' he murmured, as he stretched his long, muscular body against Ava's voluptuous curves. 'God, you're gorgeous.' He ran his hands down her strong back.

A sharp knock at the door made them both jump.

'Damn!' Tom cursed. He got up reluctantly and went to open the door.

Ava groaned and lay back on the bed, with her arms stretched out.

'Who is it?'

'I'll soon find out,' Tom answered.

When he returned a few minutes later, he was scowling. 'A mare's having difficulty delivering her foal. The farmer's outside, waiting for me in his car. I've got to go, sweetheart,' he grumbled.

Ava dragged herself up off the bed, smoothing down her clothes, which were creased and rumpled after their passionate embraces, and sighed. 'Never mind, at least it stopped us doing something we shouldn't have been doing,' she giggled.

They quickly kissed goodbye, then Ava cycled home in the evening sunshine. As she pedalled slowly along the winding coast road, she thought about their love-making. Everybody knew the dangers of abandoning themselves to a moment of passion; the young women up and down the land giving birth to illegitimate babies were clear proof of that. Unlike many who condemned these women as immoral and flighty, Ava had real compassion for them. She was lucky enough to see Tom almost every other day, even if it was only for a swift cup of tea and a hasty cuddle, but millions of young women saw their boyfriends and fiancés only when they were home on leave for a brief twenty-four hours, twice a year, if they were lucky. When they said their goodbyes, they never knew whether they would meet again. How did they control the urge to possess their beloved in every sense of the word? War denied them the luxury to develop a relationship and at the same time propelled them into situations that were fuelled with passion and desire. It was so unfair, so impossible and so frustrating!

'Bloody, bloody, rotten war!' Ava raged, pressing down hard on her bicycle pedals and racing past the pine forest, where owls hooted deep in the woods and the first stars peeped out in a navy-blue sky.

Early the next morning, straight after breakfast, Ava bicycled back to Tom's flat to hang the black-out curtains she'd made the night before.

'There's clean bedding, too,' she said, showing Tom the sheets, pillows, pillowcases, towels and thick, warm blankets she'd borrowed from the well-stocked Walsingham airing cupboards. 'We've got to keep the little lad warm, otherwise his mum won't let him visit you again.'

'Darling,' Tom murmured, kissing her.

'I can't stop, as much as I want to,' she said breathlessly.

'Have you time to make the bed with me?' Tom asked.

Ava nodded and smiled. 'Of course.'

When the single bed was made, Tom slipped his arms around Ava's slender waist. 'Sure you don't want to slip between those crisp, laundered sheets?'

Ava flushed with desire as she stared into his golden-hazel eyes.

'Tom . . .' she groaned, as she leant against his chest. 'We've got to be sensible.'

'I know, I know,' he answered softly, as he held her at

arm's length so he could gaze into her beautiful face. 'But it's hard with a woman as lovely as you.'

'I've got to get back to bake the mock-roast!' Ava giggled as she slipped from his grip and ran downstairs.

'When will I see you?' he cried after her.

'I'll wangle an afternoon off this week so I can meet Ollie,' Ava called back to him. 'Phone me, lovie. Let me know how it goes.'

As the ancient church bells rang out from Little Snoring to Great Snoring, from Burnham Norton to Burnham Deepdale, Ava lifted her radiant, happy face to the heavenly blue sky and prayed out loud. 'Thank you, God, for my life! Thank you, God, for my Tom!'

On Tuesday, Tom phoned Ava in a flat spin.

'Sweetheart, I've got a problem tomorrow morning,' he started. 'I've had an urgent call from a farmer near Docking – his prize bull's fallen ill.' He paused to take a breath. 'I can't take Ollie. It's dangerous hanging around a bull with a bellyache!'

'Bring Ollie here!' Ava exclaimed. 'He can stay in the kitchen with me, or help Peter in the garden. I'll keep an eye on him – it'll be a pleasure,' she assured Tom.

The next morning, Tom appeared in the kitchen just after breakfast. Holding his son's hand, he introduced Ollie to Ava, who was instantly captivated by the boy, who had Tom's wonderful hazel eyes and wide, infectious smile.

'I'm Ava,' she said, kneeling down so she was on the same level as Ollie, who hid behind his father. 'We could make some jam tarts for when your dad gets back from work?' she added persuasively.

Ollie peeped out from behind Tom and smiled a charming, gap-toothed smile.

'Please can I have a jam tart, too, please?'

That morning, using the strawberries that grew in profusion on Ruby's dad's allotment, Ava and Oliver managed to make a few jam tarts before Ava had to help with serving lunch to the code girls upstairs. After lunch, Bella suggested that Ava took the little boy on to Holkham beach for a play. 'He's been cooped up all morning – he'll enjoy a romp on the beach in the sunshine.'

As Ava dithered, Bella spun her around to face the back door. 'Off you go, we can manage the tea,' Bella insisted.

'Don't forget to take a picnic!' Maudie called.

'And a beach ball,' Ruby added. 'There's an old one in the bicycle shed.'

So, in the heat of the day, with the giggling little boy perched on the back of her bike and clutching a small picnic basket, Ava cycled down the long, tree-lined path that led to Holkham beach.

'*Wheee!*' squeaked Ollie as they bounced over the dry, rutted track.

At the end of the drive, the path divided: one way directly to the beach, the other way through the dark pine forest.

'Let's cut through the forest, it'll be cooler,' Ava suggested, as she propped the bike up against a tree and helped Ollie climb down.

When she held out her hand for his, Ava wondered if he'd take it. When he did, quite spontaneously, she smiled with pleasure. Clutching his little hand in hers, they skipped along the criss-crossing paths that led up and down and round and round the dense forest. The tall pines soughed in the warm breeze blowing inland from the sea. Feeling like a six-year-old herself, Ava said, 'Let's play hide and seek!'

'*Yes!*' he squeaked.

'You run and hide,' she said. 'I'll stay here and count to twenty, then I'll come and find you.'

Ollie grinned, showing the sweet gap in his front teeth. 'Start counting, Avie!' he yelled, and ran into a belt of trees and disappeared from view.

With her eyes closed Ava counted, ' . . . fifteen, sixteen, seventeen, eighteen, nineteen, *twenty*!' she bellowed. 'Coming, ready or not!'

Ava cocked her head as she listened out for tell-tale sounds. Thinking she'd heard a little cough, she bounded over a sandy hill, then ran down it and stopped short. Before her stood a ring of trees: was Ollie there, or was he hiding further on, in the sand dunes?

'I'm coming to get you!' she cried out in a spooky voice.

Hearing a high-pitched squeal, Ava raced towards the trees, where she found the little boy hiding in some bushes growing around the base of the pines.

'*Got ya!*' she giggled. 'Now it's your turn to find me. Close your eyes and count to twenty,' she instructed, as she skipped away.

Terrified that she might lose sight of the little boy in the dense forest, Ava made sure she stayed within eye contact of Ollie when he came searching for her.

'*Got ya!*' he cried, copying her words to him. 'I'm a good finder,' he added proudly.

'And I'm not a very good hider,' she joked.

After a few more games of hide and seek, they came out of the forest and on to the sand dunes, where they ran along narrow, silvery rabbit paths which, after a while, led them to the sea. Ollie's eyes widened in wonder when he saw the sweeping, vast arc of Holkham's glorious golden beach, which ran down to the edges of the softly lapping sea.

'Can we play football?' Ollie asked politely, longingly eyeing the ball they'd brought along with them.

'Of course, but have a drink first, lovie,' Ava suggested. 'You need plenty of liquid, or you'll get a headache in this heat.'

Ollie impatiently gulped back mouthfuls of barley water before grabbing the beach ball from the picnic basket and booting it to Ava, who booted it back.

'Run after it!' she cried, as Ollie tore along the dazzling golden beach in pursuit of the rolling ball.

Ava watched him go with a lump in her throat. Ollie was wearing a pair of white plimsolls and ran as fast as his little legs would take him. Squeaking and squealing with joy as seagulls wheeled over his head, he looked so small and vulnerable against the backdrop of the majestic, sweeping shore.

'Yeahhh!' he laughed, as he raced away.

Filled with the same childlike *joie de vivre*, Ava dumped the picnic basket in a nearby sand dune and, laughing too, she gave chase.

'Wait for me!'

She caught up with Ollie near the water's edge. Breathless from running, she called out, 'Take your shoes and socks off, then we can paddle in the shallows.'

As the ball floated on the gentle waves, they both made lunges to pick it up. Suddenly, Ollie's attention was caught by something round and grey floating close by.

'Look, Avie, another ball!' he cried.

Ava squinted at the round thing he was pointing to. As it drifted inland, she frowned. It didn't look much like a beach ball, and there was an odd, pointy thing poking out of the top of it. As over-excited Ollie raced to pick it up, Ava realized that the ball was a landmine.

224

'Oh, Jesus, *no!!!!*' she screamed. '*Ollie! No!*'

Either he couldn't hear her warning over the crashing waves or he was too excited to listen. Ollie waded on.

'God help me!' Ava gasped, as she splashed after the boy. As the water got deeper, she threw herself fully dressed into the waves and swam, all the time calling out, 'Get back, Ollie! Get back!' As soon as she had caught up with him, Ava flung an arm out and pulled him backwards. '*Run!*' she screamed, as she leapt to her feet and ran with him. '*GO!!*'

Making sure she was between the incoming landmine and the terrified boy, she cried out to him.

'Don't stop, Ollie! Run back to the hall!' she screamed, frantically waving her arms as she urged the breathless child to run for his life.

When the landmine rolled on to the shore, it exploded, sending showers of shrapnel everywhere. With her back to it, Ava caught the full blast and fell to the ground. Seconds before losing consciousness, she saw Ollie in the distance, running for the sand dunes.

Back at the hall, Bella was beginning to worry about Ava and Ollie. 'They only went for a picnic, but they've been gone for hours now.'

'Maybe Ava's bike's got a puncture,' Maudie suggested. 'She might be pushing it back. I don't envy her, in this heat.'

As Maudie, Ruby and Bella were busy making the trainees' tea, little Ollie came staggering into the kitchen. Having run all the way across the wide beach, then down the long drive, the boy was virtually on the point of collapsing. Maudie grabbed hold of him as he swayed in the kitchen doorway.

'Lovie! What's happened?'

Maudie settled him in one of the Windsor chairs then brought a mug of cold water, which he downed in one.

'Take it easy,' she said, wiping his damp forehead. Gradually, Ollie's breathing steadied.

'Can you tell us where Ava is, sweetheart?' she asked softly.

Looking petrified, the poor child burst into floods of tears. 'Avie blown up on beach!'

The terrified girls forced themselves to stay calm.

'Did you see her getting hurt?' Maudie pressed on.

Ollie nodded. 'She told me to run away, then the beach ball blew up.'

'Oh, dear Jesus!' Bella cried, heading for the door. 'I'll get Peter – and the jeep.'

'I'll stay here with the child,' Ruby said, putting an arm around the sobbing boy.

'Get hold of Tom!' Maudie said, as she and Bella headed for the door. 'And phone 999!'

Peter drove them at break-neck speed across the wide beach, where they spotted a small group of anxious holiday-makers. As they got closer, they could see they were trying to cover the body lying prone on the beach with blankets and coats.

'Stand back!' yelled Peter as he pulled up, and Maudie and Bella jumped out of the cab.

'Oh, God!' Bella gasped, as she raced towards her friend. 'Please be OK, Ava. Please don't be dead.'

Crouched beside Ava's body, Bella gently felt her pulse. 'She's alive!' she sobbed.

Maudie tenderly touched Ava's marble-cold face. 'She's soaking wet – she'll freeze to death!'

'We wrapped blankets around her to try to keep her

warm,' an anxious woman said, 'but her clothes are wet through.'

'We can't move her,' Bella said tensely. 'We have to wait for the ambulance.'

The sound of a distant siren, when it came, was music to their ears. After making its way across Holkham beach, an ambulance stopped close to Ava. Two sturdy females, a nurse and a driver, swiftly stepped out of the cab and, with impressive expertise, lifted Ava on to a stretcher, which they then loaded into the back of the ambulance. Slamming the doors, the nurse joined the driver in the cab.

'Where are you taking her?' Bella cried. 'Where are you going?'

As the siren shrieked out and the ambulance pulled away, the nurse yelled out of the open window, 'Wells Cottage Hospital.'

When Ava came round just over an hour later, Bella was on one side of her and Maudie on the other. Through cracked lips, she whispered hoarsely, 'Ollie . . . ?'

'He's safe with Ruby,' Maudie answered gently.

'Tom . . . ?'

'On his way.'

Seeing Ava stirring, the sister bustled the two girls out of the ward and quickly drew the curtains around the patient's bed. Maudie and Bella sat in the waiting room holding hands, hardly able to talk. Tom arrived about half an hour later, looking wild with fear.

'I got here as soon as I could – how is she?"

'We don't know,' Maudie answered.

Seeing Tom's terrified expression, Bella quickly said, 'She's conscious.'

Trembling, Tom sat down beside them. 'The police told me it was a landmine.'

'It looks like Ava took the force of the blast, but not before telling Ollie to run away, to run back to the hall,' Bella told Tom.

Tom put his head in his hands and wept. 'My beautiful, brave girl . . .'

Maudie and Bella put comforting arms around his shaking shoulders.

'Typical of Ava to think of herself last,' Maudie said, as tears stung the back of her eyes.

As they waited for what seemed like hours, they all began to worry about Ruby and Ollie back at the hall.

'It's not fair to leave Ruby holding the fort,' Maudie fretted.

'And she's got Ollie, too,' Tom said. 'I hope she'll be all right?'

Bella, who was resolute about not leaving, replied firmly, 'The Brig's there, too. They'll sort something out between them.'

Just before seven o'clock, the doctor and the ward sister joined them in the waiting room.

'She's going to pull through,' the doctor announced.

Maudie, Bella and Tom grabbed hold of each other. 'Thank God!' they cried in unison.

'She took a huge hit,' the doctor continued. 'Flying shrapnel hit the back of her skull, and she has some very deep lacerations.' Seeing that Ava's tense friends hardly dared to breathe, the doctor quickly added, 'She's young and strong. She'll make it.' He gave a brief, reassuring smile. 'I should warn you before you see her: we had to shave off her hair to stitch the wounds at the back of her skull.'

The stern ward sister allowed the three visitors five minutes with Ava, who'd been heavily sedated. They hid their shock at the sight of her shaved head, criss-crossed with dressings.

'Darling . . .' Tom said, and fell to his knees at the side of her bed so he could kiss Ava's limp fingers.

Tears trickled softly down her pale cheeks as she whispered, 'Sorry . . .'

'No, no,' Tom whispered, softly and urgently. 'You saved Oliver's life. You saved my son, Ava.'

Ava smiled weakly as sleep engulfed her.

21. Summertime

Ava was hospitalized for three weeks. She was allowed a limited number of visitors, but strictly no children were allowed on the ward. As much as Tom begged and pleaded, the ward sister was intractable.

'But my son wants to thank the woman who saved his life,' Tom implored.

As the granite-faced sister turned away from Tom, she caught sight of the small boy at his side. He had a wide, gap-toothed smile and arresting hazel eyes, and in his hands he clutched a small bunch of crumpled roses.

'Please will you give these to Avie,' he mumbled.

There was no guile in the child, just simple gratitude, which touched the sister, who for five minutes every day slipped Ollie on to the ward so he could have a cuddle with Ava. He didn't mind her shaved head and bandages, he just wanted to hold her hand and talk about playing hide and seek in the pine woods, which he solemnly told Ava was much more fun than playing with the beach-ball bomb!

'You're right there, lovie,' Ava said, smiling at Tom over the top of Ollie's head. 'That beach-ball bomb was no fun at all!'

Tom kissed her outstretched hand. God, he was falling head over heels in love with her before the accident, but now he unequivocally adored the brave, beautiful woman lying on the hospital bed before him. The ward sister called father and son 'the fan club', because they both spent their brief visiting time staring in delight at their adored Ava. Ollie's last visit before going back to his mother was hard – he, Tom and Ava all fought back tears when the little boy said his final farewell.

'I'll ask Mummy if I can come back soon,' he promised.

'My hair might have grown back by then,' Ava joked.

'Next time, we'll all go riding on Holkham beach,' Tom announced.

'Really?' Ollie cried.

Ava's lovely deep blue eyes lit up with excitement as she said, 'We'll borrow Tara, the Shetland pony, from the Walsingham stables. She's a bit tubby at the moment, but I'll have her trimmed down for your next visit,' she said, then, pulling the child to her, she added, 'Now, come on, give us a big kiss before you go.'

With tears in her eyes, Ava blew kisses as Ollie left the ward.

'Safe journey home, sweetheart, God bless.'

Ava was allowed to phone her family while she was in Wells Cottage Hospital. Her mother was desperate to visit, but Ava sensed she was frightened of the long journey into the unknown, and her father, warden of several local bomb shelters, certainly couldn't take time off. She assured her parents she was making a good recovery and promised she'd let them know as soon as she was discharged.

When Ava was allowed home, the doctor made it crystal clear to Tom, Bella, Maudie and Ruby that she had to rest.

'She absolutely cannot go running around,' he stated.

'Try stopping her,' Ruby chuckled under her breath.

'I'm deadly serious,' the doctor added. 'She's had eighteen

stitches across the back of her skull, and more subcutaneously. I can only allow her home if you promise to keep an eye on her – the more rest she gets, the sooner her wounds will heal.'

'We'll make sure of it,' Bella promised. 'Even if it means strapping her to the bedpost!'

It was a gloriously hot day when Ava arrived back at Walsingham Hall. As Tom drove up the winding drive, Ava, who'd been hospitalized for weeks, blinked in the bright sunlight and gasped at the sight of the fragrant summer flowers growing in tumbling abundance in the gardens: roses, larkspur, delphiniums, peonies, phlox, lilies and carnations.

'The world's so beautiful,' she sighed, leaning against Tom's strong shoulder.

'The world's more beautiful for having you in it, my sweet,' he murmured, stroking her hand.

When Tom pulled up at the front door of the hall, Bella and the Brig, Maudie and Kit, and Ruby and Raf cheered in delight.

'Welcome home, Ava!'

The young woman who Tom helped out of the Land Rover looked quite unlike the laughing, long-haired girl who'd cycled down the drive to take Oliver for a picnic less than a month ago. As well as her shaven head, Ava had lost weight during her stay in hospital. Her high cheekbones were more pronounced and her clothes hung off her slim frame.

'Home . . .' Ava smiled as she stared up at the golden stone Palladian columns of the beautifully proportioned hall. 'Who would ever have thought I would call this stately pile my home?' she joked.

After a cup of tea and a slice of seed cake in the kitchen, Ava was shown to her bed, where she was instructed to lie down and rest.

'I'll go mad, staring at the bloody ceiling,' she complained.

'I'll go mad if you so much as lift a spoon!' Maudie threatened.

Ruby pointed at Ava's bedside table, where they'd placed a vase of pink-and-white roses, alongside a jug of lemon-and-barley water, and a copy of *Gone with the Wind*. On the floor beside the bed the girls had put the big Bakelite kitchen radio.

'I can't have that!' Ava protested. 'You need it to listen to "Music while You Work!"'

'You need it more,' Bella answered firmly. 'Now, *rest*!'

Left alone, Ava did sleep. When she was awake, however, there was always somebody keen to pop in and chat to her, and her friends went out of their way to make her treats to tempt her rather weak appetite. Using their own sugar rations, they made little fruit jellies and soft blancmanges, while Peter brought a few fresh raspberries or a little bunch of redcurrants from his greenhouse. Bella picked some salty samphire from the marshes, which she served on toast, with some home-potted shrimps.

'Got to build up your strength,' she told Ava, placing a tray on her lap, then perching on the bed beside her.

'Where did the yummy shrimps come from?' Ava asked, as she wiped the bowl clean with warm toast.

'Blakeney – I twisted a friendly fisherman's arm,' Bella giggled. 'In exchange for one of Maudie's warm poppy-seed loaves, I got a dozen shrimps, just for you, dear girl!' she said, with an emotional catch in her throat. 'God, Ava, we missed you so much,' Bella added, removing the tray and gripping her friend's hand. 'The kitchen just wasn't the same without you bossing us about and making us laugh.'

'I'll be back in there soon, so enjoy the peace while you can,' Ava said, as she reached for a Woodbine and lit up. 'God, when I think of that day on the beach!' She shuddered at the memory. 'One minute we were laughing and splashing in the shallows, the next I was throwing myself between Ollie and a German landmine.'

'You were so brave,' Bella said softly.

Ava shook her bandaged head. 'You know what? I never even thought about it – it was pure instinct. I prayed it would be a duff bomb that would just roll away, but the minute it touched shore there was no doubting it was a live one. It would definitely have killed Ollie if he'd picked it up.'

Seeing tears filling Ava's eyes, Bella said briskly, 'It's all over now, and the good thing is, as a consequence of your accident, the coastguards have been up and down the coast line from Cley Next The Sea to Hunstanton, checking for any more landmines that the Germans might have sent our way.'

Ava stubbed out her Woodbine. 'Did they find any?'

Bella nodded. 'A dud one just off Brancaster beach. Now, come on, lady, get some sleep, or I'll get a ticking-off from the Brig for keeping you talking too long.'

As Bella rose to go, Ava pulled her back on to the edge of the bed.

'How are you and the Brig?' she asked.

Bella's eyes grew large and dreamy as she replied, 'Wonderful!'

'We're all so lucky to have our loved ones close to us,' Ava said. 'It must be unbearable for those girls who only see their boyfriends once or twice a year.'

'Poor souls. I'd go mad,' Bella admitted. 'Mind you,' she said, as she dropped her voice to a confidential whisper, 'There are times when we're kissing that I'm tempted to go further – even all the way,' she confessed with a blush.

Ava nodded. 'I know what you mean. I daren't, though. Imagine if I fell pregnant – Tom's still married. I'd be shunned by good society,' she added, with a melodramatic smile.

Bella looked thoughtful. 'You know, I really do wonder about my sister. She's never made a secret – at least not to me, because she likes humiliating me – of how many lovers she's had. She's got to have sorted out the contraceptive problem – I just wonder what she does?'

'Probably had something like a coil fitted,' Ava replied knowingly. 'She could afford to have it done at some fancy private clinic in London. I couldn't afford it – and, anyway, if you love and respect somebody and want to live with them for ever, isn't it worth waiting till the wedding night?'

Bella burst out laughing. 'Just so long as the wedding night isn't ten years away!'

As Ava lay on her bed one sunny August morning, she heard on the radio that General Montgomery had taken command of the Eighth Army in North Africa. When Tom arrived with flowers and some black-market chocolate for the patient, he was alight with excitement.

'The tide's turning, at last!' he said, kissing his girlfriend while gently stroking the thick tufts of dark hair that were quickly growing back on Ava's head. 'Der Führer's getting it from both sides now,' he added gleefully. 'What with Montgomery pushing north into Tunis, and Stalin and Churchill meeting up in Moscow to discuss the German's drive on

Stalingrad, the Third Reich are going to feel a draft – about time, too!' he finished passionately.

Good food and rest certainly helped Ava regain her strength, but the best tonic was the wonderful summer weather and the tranquillity of the Walsingham gardens. As Ava's strength returned, she was allowed to walk outside and sit in a deckchair under the shade of an ancient oak. She was regularly visited by one friend after another, Peter always dropped by with a bunch of sweet peas or a ripe peach from the greenhouse and, one day, Tom brought Lucas to see Ava.

'Surprise! Surprise!' Tom laughed, as Ava's jaw dropped in amazement. 'Don't jump up,' he warned, as Ava struggled to stand. 'We'll come to you.'

Lucas was ecstatic to see Ava, who he'd missed over the weeks since her accident. He blew softly against her cheek and greedily chomped on the apples Tom had slipped Ava to feed to him.

'Lovely boy,' she murmured, as she caressed his velvety-smooth neck, then tickled his pink muzzle. 'We'll go riding soon, I promise.'

Ava suggested to Bella that, while she was sitting sunbathing in the garden, she could help in a small way.

'Just bring me a pan of water and a knife, and I'll sit here and prep the veg.'

'Are you sure?' Bella asked.

Ava burst out laughing. 'I'm not exactly going to bust a gut peeling spuds!' she joked.

So her friends appeared in the garden with baskets of fruit and veg, which Ava peeled, or topped and tailed, and she spent hours shelling peas. The sun caught her skin, turning it brown and golden, and her hair grew quickly in the sunshine.

'You look like a pixie sitting there, shelling peas, with your dark hair and tanned skin!' Ruby teased.

'I feel so well!' Ava assured her.

'Don't run away with yourself,' Ruby warned. 'You're definitely not ready for standing on your feet all day.'

'But I worry about you in the kitchen,' Ava fretted. 'Don't give me the party line, Ruby, I know you're doing everything you can not to worry me, but I also know what it's like below stairs even when there are four of us working flat out. How you manage with only three, I simply can't imagine.'

'We manage – that's all that matters,' Ruby answered firmly.

Ava was right: Bella, Maudie and Ruby were stretched to breaking point below stairs. The Brig helped out every night with the washing-up and setting the breakfast trays, but it was, nevertheless, a strain on the three girls, who had scarcely any free time at all. Ruby and Maudie had hardly seen Raf and Kit; Raf managed to sneak a quick visit to his wife when he was on chauffeur duty, but Kit, who couldn't be spared for a moment, was back to sleeping in his office. The only chance Maudie got to see her handsome pilot was when she cycled over to the Holkham airbase, which she'd managed a few times between serving lunch and preparing tea. Kit's tired face lit up when his girl arrived.

'Maudie!' he cried, swinging her in his strong arms.

Pressed against Kit's warm chest, with his blue RAF shirt unbuttoned at the top, Maudie wriggled in delight. 'You smell nice,' she said.

'I stink!' he exclaimed. 'I wash in the sink in the lavatory, and I've been nowhere near a bath in weeks. Come on, love,' he added excitedly. 'Let me show you how much progress we've made.'

Holding his hand, Maudie ran with Kit across the base to the runway. 'Look, it's as good as new!' Kit declared proudly. 'We've been working round the clock on twelve-hour shifts, but it's been worth all the hard slog – we'll soon be operational again.'

'Then you'll get your Lancasters,' she said.

'Yes, yes, yes!' Kit cried, and thumped the air. 'My beautiful Lancasters.' His voice dropped and he muttered, 'It's top secret, sweetheart, no loose lips, eh?' He kissed her lovely, pouting, full lips. 'The bloody Huns are not going to get a chance to bomb my babies again. Oh no! This time it'll be the other way round – we'll be bombing those bastards!' Remembering his manners, he checked himself. 'Whoops, 'scuse my French.'

Maudie shook her golden-red hair, which today was held back with a blue silk headscarf that bought out the colour in her brilliant green eyes.

'Don't worry. You can call the Germans any name you like – it won't upset me,' she assured Kit.

They sat on a wall close to the barrage balloons that floated overhead to hide the runway from enemy planes. Maudie reached into her basket and drew out a warm cheese-and-spinach pasty she'd made that morning.

'Not only are you beautiful and clever, you're also an amazing cook,' Kit said, as he ravenously devoured the pasty.

'I should have made more.' Maudie laughed.

They made the most of her free hour, kissing, laughing and chatting in the sunshine. Kit talked excitedly about the first all-American air attack in Europe.

'Thank God for the Yanks,' he declared. 'At long last, we're giving Jerry a run for his money. When my Lancasters arrive, I'll make the most of their bomb load. It'll be pay-back time, when I take to the skies!'

Maudie's eyes went dark with foreboding. 'Kit, please don't talk like that – you frighten me,' she murmured, and reached for his hand.

'Sorry, love,' he replied. 'We took a hell of a hit, and it hurts a man's pride.'

'Just the thought of you flying over Germany makes me feel sick to my stomach,' she confessed.

'It's what I was born to do, Maudie, you must understand that . . . ?' He looked at her closely, waiting for an answer.

'I understand, Kit, but it doesn't stop me from being frightened.'

When Maudie arrived back at the hall, she was surprised to find Ava sitting at the kitchen table.

'What are you doing here?' Maudie exclaimed.

'I've had enough of lolling about,' Ava announced. 'The doctor said I could do some light work, so I can sit here and roll pastry or peel vegetables while keeping an eye on you lot! I might not be able to run up and down stairs, but I can certainly offer you an extra pair of hands.'

'And we're grateful,' Bella said, with a warm smile. 'But we're going to watch you like a hawk. Any sign of stress and fatigue, and you're straight back to bed, OK?

Ava gave a smart military salute as she replied, '*Ja, ja, mein Herr!*'

As August came to an end, the fine sunshine still held out, so when Ollie returned for a second visit to Norfolk the weather was perfect for their first ride on Holkham beach.

'I'm definitely not riding Drummer,' Tom assured her. 'His high spirits will wind everybody up.'

Much as Ava loved the beautiful Arab, she entirely agreed with Tom. 'Let's keep it calm,' she replied. 'You lead Ollie on Tara, on the loose rein, and I'll ride beside them.'

'Sure you're up for it, darling?'

'I wouldn't miss it for the world! Anyway!'

Oliver couldn't believe his eyes when he saw pretty Tara tacked up and waiting for him. After running to hug Ava and give her a big kiss, he stood transfixed before the cheeky little Shetland, who impatiently nudged the boy's tummy.

'What does she want, Daddy?' he asked.

'An apple, a carrot, a mint – or all three!' Tom laughed. 'Tara will eat anything!'

After feeding Tara a carrot, they set off down the drive to the sea. Ollie looked adorable in his riding hat, and the sight of his little legs poking out over Tara's wide girth gave Ava and Ollie the giggles.

'She's too fat for you to put your legs down her sides!' Ava laughed.

'She's bouncy, too, like a ball!' Ollie chuckled, as he bounced up and down on Tara's wide back.

Sitting up straight and holding his reins, as his daddy had taught him, Ollie smiled proudly. 'I'm a proper horse-rider!' he told Ava.

Tom led Ollie along the track, with Ava, mounted on bomb-proof Lucas, riding right beside him. Lucas's calm presence kept the flighty Shetland steady as a rock, even when she waded through the shallow waves that lapped on to the beach. Seeing Ollie's anxious eyes straining into the distance, Ava said gently, 'There aren't any more beach bombs, Ollie, lovie. They've all gone. We're completely safe.'

Ollie's eyes turned to her, full of trust. 'Really, Avie?'

'Scout's honour – really,' she assured him.

They tethered up Lucas and Tara to the pine trees close to the sand dunes, and quenched their thirst with lemon-and-barley water, then shared some left-over sticky gingerbread slices from the trainees' lunch.

'I missed you, Avie,' Ollie said, in between bites of cake.

'Missed you, too, sweetheart,' she replied, as she leant over to hug him.

Tom gazed from the woman he loved to the son he adored. Even though there was a war raging just across the North Sea and the Germans were doing untold damage to the Russians in Stalingrad, Tom felt a rush of happiness that simply took his breath away. Mesmerized by the vast expense of shimmering blue sea that merged with the blue of the sky, Tom realized that he wanted to marry Ava and live with her for ever. He wasn't yet a free man but, as soon as his divorce came through, he would go down on his bended knees and ask beautiful Ava Downham to be his wife.

22. Lancasters

The Lancasters arrived in late autumn. Maudie heard them before she saw them. The distant hum of the engines turned into a mighty roar as the first half-dozen bombers flew low over Walsingham Hall on their way to Holkham airbase.

'Jesus!' Ava exclaimed, as they all rushed outside to squint up at the Lancasters. 'How's anybody ever going to keep those noisy buggers a secret?'

Shading their eyes against the low autumn light, they watched the planes lose height, then disappear behind the Norfolk turnip fields.

'God! They're *huge*,' Ava said in an awed voice.

'They certainly look the business,' Bella commented.

The Brig and the code girls had also come outside to observe the Lancasters fly past.

'Churchill wasn't messing about when he commissioned those,' the Brig said with a grim smile.

'Let's hope the blasted Germans don't get wind of the new arrivals. It would be a double tragedy if they destroyed those, too,' said Ava.

As Maudie stared into the now-empty sky she said thoughtfully, 'I bet Kit wastes no time in getting them airborne.'

'Raf said the ground crews have to do routine checks before they can take to the air,' Ruby said knowledgeably.

Ava chuckled as she lit up a Woodbine. 'Do you two talk planes even when you're in bed?' she teased.

Ruby replied with a cheeky wink, 'A kiss and a cuddle takes my husband's mind off twin engines in a blink!'

Later that evening, just after supper, Kit came roaring up to the hall in his noisy old MG.

'Darling!' he said, swinging Maudie around until she was dizzy. 'They're here!'

'I know, I heard them – along with the rest of the county!' she joked.

'Come and see them for yourself,' Kit urged, and dragged her towards his convertible.

Maudie pulled him away from the car as she said firmly, 'Not until you've had something to eat.'

Impatiently, Kit shook his head. 'I'm not hungry.'

'Yes, you are. You don't eat enough. Come on – five minutes, max,' she promised.

Below stairs, in between mouthfuls of the remains of supper – Lord Woolton pie and fruit crumble – Kit eulogised about the Lancasters to the girls, and to the Brig, who'd dashed down to see him.

'They're beautiful!' he cried. 'The bomb bay can carry up to twenty-two thousand pounds of bombs and still travel at two hundred and seventy miles an hour when fully loaded!'

Maudie chuckled. 'You're losing me, darling!'

'Four propellers and eight machine guns – we'll be rulers of the skies!' Breathless with excitement, Kit swallowed his mug of tea then stood up and took Maudie by the hand. 'I've finished my supper – now, please can we go?' he asked, like an impatient, over-excited child.

'When's your first sortie?' the Brig asked, as they headed for the stairs.

Kit drew a hand across his mouth as if he were securing a zip. 'Top secret,' he replied with a grin. 'Not even Maudie knows!'

When they got to the airbase, Maudie stood wide-eyed before the line of mighty Lancasters ranged along the runway.

'They're *spectacular*!' she gasped.

'See! Didn't I tell you?' laughed Kit proudly. 'Come on, I'll give you a tour.'

For all their enormous size on the outside, Maudie was surprised at how cramped the Lancasters were inside.

'The bomb bay and the two gun turrets take up a heck of a lot of room – there's only just enough space for the seven-man crew,' Kit explained. 'Just look at the dashboard, darling.'

Maudie stared in bewilderment at the range of dials, levers and switches on the elaborate control panel. 'I'd be terrified to fly this,' she confessed.

Totally elated, Kit's sky blue eyes burnt with passion. 'My God – I can't wait to get this baby off the ground!'

Seeing tears trembling in Maudie's eyes, Kit gently gathered her into his arms and kissed her glowing golden-red hair. Gulping back tears that were threatening to overwhelm her, Maudie blurted out, 'I'm sorry to be pathetic when you're so happy but . . . I'm frightened!'

Holding her at arm's length so he could look her levelly in the eye, Kit said, 'Listen to me, Maudie. I've never had anybody to rush home to before, but in the short time I've known you, I've come to realize how precious life is when you care for someone as much as I care about you. I'm not in a rush to throw away my life. I'll do my duty along with all my brave men, but I want to come home to you,' he concluded, as he kissed her sweet, pouting lips.

'But you sound so gung-ho and reckless,' she whispered.

'That's excitement, that's *now* – but, believe me, the mood changes on a raid,' he explained. 'Generally, we're silent. Apart from the navigator giving his readings, we're focused and intense, a team on a mission.'

There was a long silence as they clung to each other in the cockpit.

'It's taken me so long to find somebody like you, Kit,' she sighed, as pressed her face against his warm neck, feeling his pulse quicken. 'I really don't want to lose you.'

Taking her face into his hands, Kit held her gaze as he said, 'Do you know the RAF motto, *Per ardua ad astra*?"

Maudie shook her head.

'I've never heard of it.'

'It means "through adversity to the stars",' Kit continued, as he took hold of her right hand and slowly kissed her fingers one by one. 'Whatever troubles may befall me, whatever difficulties may arise, I will *always* come back to you.'

Maudie raised his hand to her lips. 'I have my own motto for when you fly, darling,' she whispered, as tears trembled in her green eyes. 'To the stars . . . and back.'

Kit nodded as he repeated her words,

'To the stars . . . and back, my love.'

Maudie woke to the sound of the Lancasters taking off. Reaching for her dressing gown, she slipped outside, where she stood in the dark, west-facing garden and watched the squadron fly low over the pine woods. Then, gathering height and speed, they flew out over the North Sea. With her pulse racing and her heart thudding, Maudie felt so frightened she could barely breathe.

'Oh, my God,' she whispered to herself. 'Why didn't he

tell me it would be so soon?' She wrapped her arms around her trembling body. 'Why didn't he warn me?' She chided herself as she thought, 'Don't be stupid! As if he ever would blab! Loose lips sink ships,' She murmured out loud, recalling his words of warning.

She stayed out in the garden until the sound of the Lancasters' engines faded away. As silence returned, she could hear owls hooting in the pinewoods and, somewhere in the garden, two foxes exchanged shrill barks as they vied for a mate. Maudie shivered, as if somebody had walked over her grave. Looking up, she blew a kiss into the starry sky.

'*Per ardua ad astra* . . . God speed, my love.'

Back in bed, Maudie didn't sleep a wink. Three months ago, planes taking off from the airbase wouldn't have kept her awake all night, but things were different now. She felt like her heart was in her mouth; she'd never know peace until she knew Kit was safely home again. Just before dawn, as the sky was turning light, Maudie heard the distant throb of the returning Lancasters; she knew immediately there weren't as many planes coming back as there had been going out. Not stopping to think, she threw off her nightdress, pulled on her clothes and, slipping out of the hall by the back door, dashed across the yard to the bike shed. Jumping on to her bike, Maudie set off down the narrow country lanes, which were filling up with sunlight and birdsong.

When she reached the airbase, Maudie stood by the locked metal gates. She grasped them hard and peered through them, hardly daring to breathe. She gasped in shock as she saw only three Lancasters standing on the runway. As the sun came up over the turnip fields in a blazing orange ball, Maudie could clearly see the ground crews doing their routine checks on the planes that had returned safely. She had no idea which, if any, of the three Lancasters was Kit's plane. Her instinct was to rattle the fence until somebody let her into the base, but she suddenly thought that if every woman in Britain reacted to battle in the same way, the country would be in utter chaos. She had to stay brave and focused, even though she wanted scream.

'Is he alive or dead?' she murmured, over and over again.

Fortunately, Raf caught sight of Maudie by the gates and, seeing her tense, white face, he hurried over to her.

He knew exactly what she was going to ask him, so he said as he approached, 'He came back. He's OK.'

Weak with relief, Maudie sagged against the metal fence. 'Thank God . . . '

'You want to see Captain Kit?' Raf asked, gently patting her hand through the gates.

'No!' she exclaimed. 'He'll have enough to do. I just wanted to know he was safe.'

She turned to pick up her bike, which, in her haste, she'd thrown to the ground. She leant against and stared at the planes on the runway. 'They were lucky.'

Raf nodded, but he couldn't help but smile proudly. 'It was big success, Maudie. We surprise bloody Jerry, eh?'

Maudie nodded. She didn't feel any thrill, just a huge sadness. There would be mothers, brothers, sisters, wives and lovers weeping in German towns and villages for loved ones who would never come back to them. Somebody would be knocking on a door in Essen or Munich, Cologne or Berlin, passing on a message that would break another's heart. As Maudie cycled back through the beautiful morning, golden and shimmering in the low autumn sun, she wept. She knew she had to keep strong, it was her patriotic duty, but in her gut she detested this war and the millions of lives it was savaging all over the world.

Maudie's mood wasn't much improved when, bone-tired and over-emotional, she got back to the hall and found Bella with a face like thunder.

'Edward's back!' she seethed, as she made toast on the Aga hot plate. 'He arrived last night, apparently, with a crony of his from Cambridge.' She turned to drop hot toast on to a warm plate, and saw Maudie's face, haggard from lack of sleep. 'Heavens above!' she exclaimed. 'What've you been up to?'

'Tell you later,' Maudie replied, as she tied an apron over her dress, then, on automatic pilot, grabbed a loaded tray and headed upstairs.

'Why's the lecherous creep back again so soon?' she called over her shoulder.

Bella grimaced as she replied, 'Who knows?'

Maudie had carefully avoided mentioning her nasty encounter with Edward to Kit, and she intended to keep it that way. There was no point in stirring things up; Kit had enough on his plate.

'The less Kit knows about Edward, the better,' Maudie told her friends, as they cleared away breakfast.

Bella, Ava and Ruby exchanged an awkward glance. None of them liked the idea of protecting Edward. Seeing their mutinous expressions, Maudie begged them to keep her secret. '*Pleeease.*'

Ruby broke the silence. 'Don't go anywhere near his rooms,' she said sharply. 'Leave that to me.'

Bella grabbed a long brush and started to furiously sweep the kitchen floor. 'My brother's an animal!'

Ava, standing in her favourite spot, with her back to the

Aga, blew out cigarette smoke as she said, 'Calm down, missus. Dodds told me he'll only be here a few days.'

'The sooner he's gone the better!' Bella snarled.

'We could always slip a drop of strychnine into his pea soup,' Ruby said, with a wicked giggle.

The girls might have made a pact to keep Maudie's secret to themselves, but nobody had mentioned this to Raf, who thought it was his duty to inform his senior officer that the young lord was back.

'This Edward lord no good for Maudie.'

Riding along beside Rafal in the RAF jeep, Kit did a double-take. 'What's that supposed to mean?'

'You know, remember what he tried on last visit to hall?'

Kit shook his head. 'Spit it out, man,' he snapped.

'You don't know?'

'Know *what*?'

Realizing he'd put his foot in it, Raf sighed and prevaricated. 'Better for you to ask Maudie.'

Grabbing the wheel, Kit shouted, 'Tell me!'

Raf slowed down and put the handbrake on. 'He try to have Maudie, he try raping her.'

Kit went deadly white, then bright red. 'Drive me over there, right now!' he commanded.

When they reached the hall, Kit was out of his seat before Raf had even pulled up. 'Wait for me,' he called over his shoulder.

Raf slumped back in his driver's seat. 'Oh, my God! Rubee, she will kill me!'

Kit went in the back way, scaring the living daylights out of the four girls when he threw open the kitchen door.

'*Maudie!*'

Hearing his tone and thinking there'd be an accident at the base, Maudie dropped the pan of potatoes she was moving from the sink to the Aga.

'I need to speak to you – *please*.' He added the word as an afterthought.

Taking her by the hand, he led her outside, where they passed a white-faced Raf, who was on his way inside. Ignoring his crew man, Kit asked, 'Where's private?'

Maudie pointed towards the stable block and said, 'Kit, what is it? What's happened?'

When they were in the stable yard, Kit turned to Maudie. 'Why didn't you tell me about Edward Walsingham?'

Maudie went white with shock. 'Who told you?' she gasped.

'Raf. He thought I knew.' Tilting her face so he could peer into her eyes, he said, '*Why* didn't I know, Maudie?'

She shrugged and tried to make light of it. 'I didn't want to worry you.'

Kit grabbed her wrists and said angrily, 'Anything that concerns you concerns me, Maudie – especially an attempted rape!'

Maudie burst into tears as she replied, 'For God's sake, stop yelling at me!'

Seeing her crumple into tears, Kit caught her into his arms and smothered her tear-stained face with kisses. 'Darling, darling, I'm sorry. Please don't cry.'

Maudie swiped away her tears and tried to explain. 'He jumped on me while I was tidying his room. He threw me on the bed and was pulling at my underwear. Thank God Ruby heard me struggling. She rushed to my rescue and he backed off.'

'*Bastard!*' Kit raged. 'Total bloody bastard!'

'He seemed to think it was his God-given right to maul any maid under his roof,' Maudie added. 'I did give him an almighty thump in the balls!' she said, managing to break into a laugh at the memory of his anguished face. 'He looked like a fat, pink pig with his eyeballs popping out!'

'I'm glad you can laugh at it,' Kit said, with the trace of a smile. 'I'd seriously like to shoot him.' He lit a cigarette, and drew on it deeply. 'And now he's back, right here under the same bloody roof – he might try again.'

Maudie shook her head vehemently. 'I'm banned from even going upstairs to the Walsingham suites,' she answered quickly. 'Ruby's covering for me while he's home.'

Kit ground his cigarette out with the heel of his boot. 'They're all the same!' Kit cried furiously. 'Bloody snobs and aristocrats demanding their *droit de seigneur* – it makes me sick!'

'Hey, be fair – Bella's not like that. She's given up her position and title in order to break away from her ghastly family.'

Kit nodded in agreement with her. 'Yes, you're right.'

'Apart from that, your words are music to my ears,' Maudie chuckled. 'Bring on the revolution, brother.'

Kit grinned. 'Not sure I want heads to roll – just *his*!'

Taking Maudie in his arms, he kissed her long and tenderly. 'You're so precious to me, the thought of any man's hands on you, apart from mine, totally incenses me. Promise you'll take care of yourself?'

Maudie nodded. 'Of course,' she assured him.

'Especially at night, lock your door and keep a hammer under the bed.'

'I'll certainly lock my door, but I might not go as far as the hammer.' She giggled. 'Anyway, he won't be here long, thank

God! He'll be going back to his safe desk job at the War Office,' she added contemptuously.

Kit stared thoughtfully at the last of the climbing roses that grew in profusion up the red-brick wall, warmed by the late autumn sun.

'Why isn't he out there, fighting in the army? It's what his sort do. Why's he shuffling piles of paper around a desk while the Germans and Italians are invading Vichy France? How does he get away with it?'

'He's probably a coward as well as a bully,' Maudie replied. 'Come on, let's stop talking about him. It spoils the loveliness of the day.'

Taking his hand, she kissed it softly, then they walked back to the jeep, which was standing empty in the drive at the back of the house. When Raf saw his boss approaching, he ran out to join him.

'Thank God you're back. Rubee go up the wall for me spilling beans!'

Dodds was right; Edward's stay was short. After he'd driven away in his noisy, expensive sports car, life quickly returned to normal. Ruby had apologized to Maudie on Raf's behalf.

'He shouldn't have blabbed to Captain Kit,' she said, then added fondly, 'The boy can't lie – he's got "true" and "honest" running through him like a stick of Great Yarmouth rock.'

'Don't worry, Ruby, it's good Kit knows.' She burst out laughing and added, 'Though thank God Walsingham's gone – Kit was itching to shoot him!'

23. Farewell Code Girls

As November turned into a frosty December and the code girls approached the end of their training, they each received information about their official placements. There was a buzz in the dining room as excited young women swapped notes on their next move.

'I feel envious when I hear them talking about their postings,' Ava admitted after they'd cleared supper and were having a tea break before they launched into the mountain of washing-up piled up in the scullery sink.

'Me, too,' said Maudie. 'I overheard one girl saying she was being sent to the filter room of Fighter Command.'

'Wow!' giggled Ruby. 'She'll be one of those smart-suited woman like you see in the war films, waving a stick at a massive wall map while other smart girls push toy tanks and guns across a big table.'

Bella laughed out loud. 'It's not quite like that, Ruby,' she cried. 'Fighter Command is more about getting a range on incoming bombing raids.'

'God! I'd love to have worked in RDF,' Ava said wistfully.

'What's that when it's at home?' Ruby asked.

'Radio Detection and Ranging,' Maudie explained. 'Radar signals can pick up information on enemy activity even when they're flying over France on their way here; they give advance warning of what's coming our way.'

Ruby smiled as she took in the information. 'That's clever,' she remarked. 'Give us time to organize a bloody big welcoming party for the Luftwaffe as they come sweeping in across the Channel!'

'It's code-breaking I love,' Bella enthused. 'It's so devious and complicated but, once you get the crib, it's fantastic. Everything just clicks into place – like that,' she said, as she snapped her fingers with a loud click.

'You're wasted here, sweetheart,' Ava said, lighting a Woodbine.

'We're all wasted here!' Bella exclaimed.

'Not me. This is my home and I love it – especially now that you're here to keep me company,' Ruby replied staunchly.

'And that's the heart of it, isn't it?' Ava said, exhaling cigarette smoke. 'We're all happy here. I never imagined I'd ever hear myself say that,' she said, with an amused sigh.

Gathered around the table, the girls exchanged secret smiles.

'We've met wonderful men – even Fussy Drawers Maudie has finally dropped her guard and has fallen for her handsome bomber boy,' Ava teased.

'And you've got your Tom and his sweet little boy,' Maudie pointed out.

'Bella's got the Brig, and I'm a married woman,' Ruby added, with a bright smile.

'But it's not just about men, is it?' Maudie continued thoughtfully. 'I love the camaraderie we have below stairs, we look after each other and share the load. I know it's our war work but I wonder, in the future, if we'll ever find such intense friendship again?'

Ruby quickly wiped a tell-tale tear from her brimming eyes. 'I've never known friendship like this – and I've never laughed as much, either!'

'We're the girls that feed the code girls!' Ava declared.

'Without food in their bellies, they wouldn't be much good to anybody – we should be proud of what we do.'

'Who knows, if this wretched war goes on, maybe we'll be offered the opportunity to become code girls, too,' Maudie said.

'Bella's really the only one of us who could move on,' Ava remarked.

'You could be doing finer things for your country than plucking pheasants and disembowelling hares, missis!' Ruby teased.

Bella shook her head, as she answered with real passion, 'I want to get *much* better. I really want to be able to send and break complicated codes – maybe even work undercover,' she added, flushed with excitement.

'You won't be able to take the Brig with you when you go,' Maudie said with a smile.

Bella groaned. 'I've spent my whole life longing to get away from this place, and now I dread leaving.' She winked and went on, 'Imagine leaving the Brig with twenty-five young women – and Miss Cox!'

'I'm glad you're not in a rush, lovie,' Ava joked. 'God knows, there'd be hardly any meat on offer if you left. No bloody way am I skinning ferrets and funny fluffy things!'

Maudie, Bella and Ruby howled with laughter as squeamish Ava shuddered at the thought.

'They're not ferrets, you silly bugger!' Ruby chuckled.

As their laughter faded away, Bella added solemnly, 'If a placement comes up with my name on it, I'd have to go immediately.'

'We could always lock you in the wine cellar and throw away the key,' Ruby joked.

Bella grimaced and shook her head. 'No, thanks, Ruby.

I'd bump into my rotten sister, who spends more time down there than anybody I know!'

The below stairs staff held their breath as Christmas approached: were they going to get put upon again? Would they have to work round the clock, providing a Christmas feast for the Walsingham table, when rationing was getting harsher by the day? Bella broke the tension by rushing down the back stairs one evening, her cheeks flushed bright pink as she announced to her friends, 'The parents are going to Northumberland for Christmas!'

Whooping with joy, she skipped around the kitchen table, where her friends joined her in a happy, triumphant dance.

'*Yeah!!*' they cheered.

When they stopped, out of breath and smiling, Maudie cried, 'Christmas to ourselves! I can go home.'

'Me, too,' Ava added.

'Imagine having the freedom of the hall, with no grumpy parents in it,' Bella sighed.

'The problem is,' said ever-candid Ava, 'I should go home . . . but do I really want to leave Tom and miss out on seeing Ollie in the Christmas holidays?'

Maudie nodded. 'I feel guilty about it but, actually, I agree with you, Ava, it would be wonderful to spend time here with Kit.'

'If he's here,' Ruby interjected. 'He might have a family to visit or . . .' Her voice trailed away in embarrassment.

'He might be on a bombing raid,' Maudie starkly finished the sentence for her. 'Which is all the more reason why I want to stay.'

'We could do both,' Ava continued. 'I could spend Christmas and Boxing Day at home, then dash back here and spend the rest of my holiday with Tom and Ollie – though I would be two whole days on a train,' she added with a grimace.

'That's if they're running,' Ruby remarked.

'The trains always run, they're needed to move troops up and down the country,' Bella pointed out.

Later, when all four girls were cleaning the trainees' dining room, which, now empty, echoed to the sound of their cheery voices, Ava laid aside her mop to ask Bella and Ruby a question,

'What will you two do over the break?'

'I'll be here all the time,' Ruby replied. 'Below stairs is like a second home for me and Raf.'

'And without us breathing down your neck, you'll be able to get up to all sorts of hanky-panky!' Maudie teased.

'For all I know, Raf might be on duty over Christmas, though I'm sure he'll insist on us going to midnight Mass at Our Lady's shrine on Christmas Eve,' Ruby said fondly.

Bella's eyes glowed as she imagined the time she'd spend with her beloved Brig. 'We'll go for lots of walks on Holkham beach and build up the fire in the library every evening. Bliss!' she sighed.

The day before she left for the East End, Maudie cycled over to the airbase with Kit's Christmas present.

'It's nothing much,' she said, handing him the gift-wrapped present.

Kit smiled with pleasure as he unwrapped a copy of John Buchan's *The Thirty-nine Steps*.

'Thank you, darling,' he exclaimed, kissing her. 'I'll take it to bed every night and think about you.' Taking Maudie by the hand, he added with a twinkle in his eye, 'Your present's outside.'

Looking mystified, Maudie followed Kit on to the runway, where he positioned her in front of a bright yellow Tiger Moth.

'Surely you're not giving me a plane for Christmas!' she giggled.

'No, she belongs to me,' Kit replied, leading her towards the aircraft. 'And I'm taking you for a spin.'

Maudie gaped at him in disbelief. 'But . . . I've never flown in a plane before!'

'Then it's about time you did!' He laughed and bundled a warm jacket around her shoulders.

Maudie was horrified when Kit popped her in the front seat of the open-cockpit bi-plane. 'It looks like it's made of wood and wires!' she exclaimed.

'She goes like a bird,' Kit said, sitting in the seat behind her. 'Put these on,' he instructed, giving her some earphones. 'I've got a pair too,' he added as he adjusted his own. 'We're connected, so now we can chat during the flight.'

Staring at the wide expanse of the engine bonnet looming up in front of her, Maudie began to panic. 'Why am I in the front seat?' she cried.

Kit burst out laughing at the sight of her petrified face. 'Don't worry, sweetheart. Believe it or not, I'm in the pilot's seat! Ready?'

Shaking with nerves, Maudie adjusted her flying goggles. 'Ready as I ever will be!' she squeaked.

Kit gave Raf, who was standing on the runway, the thumbs-up, and Raf swung the propeller.

'Chocks away!' called Kit, as he released the throttle and the Tiger Moth started to taxi down the runway.

Maudie gasped as the plane bounced along, then gathered speed as they approached the turnip field that began where the runway ended. Thinking they'd go crashing headlong into the muddy field, she closed her eyes and prayed but, suddenly, she felt the Tiger Moth lift and, with graceful ease, she took to the wide, open skies. Opening her eyes Maudie laughed out loud with joy and wild exhilaration.

'Hahhhhh! It's so beautiful!' she cried. Her fears fell away and she gazed in wonder at the world below.

Behind her, Kit smiled. 'There's nothing in the world like it!'

They flew out over the pine woods that fringed Holkham beach, then soared over the sweeping arc of dazzling white sand before gathering height and flying out to sea.

'We can't go too far out,' Kit explained. 'We don't want to fly into enemy territory!'

Maudie was mesmerized by the dazzling light above her and the flat expanse of dark sea below her. 'I feel like I'm in heaven!' she giggled.

With the wind whipping around her, she peered over the side of the small plane as it lifted gently on the changing air currents. Excited as a child, she pointed down to the wild coastline they were passing over. 'Burnham Overy Staithe and Brancaster,' she called out to Kit.

They swooped over miles of marshland, then circled around Hunstanton before heading out over King's Lynn. Maudie was disappointed when she realized that Kit was swinging inland and they were heading for home.

'Shall we loop the loop?' he asked, as they climbed into the sky.

'*No!*' she screamed.

Her stomach churned as, on a breathtaking nose-dive, they dropped height, before Kit took the Tiger Moth curling up and up again.

'*Wheeee!*' laughed Maudie, as they dipped and soared.

'Feeling sick?' he asked.

'No! I love it,' she replied.

Their journey back, in contrast to their coastal journey out, was idyllically green and pastoral. They flew over farms and churches, villages and grazing cattle, and followed criss-crossing lines of railway tracks and roads, where the few vehicles way below looked like toys in a child's picture book. When they swooped over the Walsingham estate, Maudie could see the stable block and the formal gardens, the sweep of the long, winding drive and the high rooftops of the hall. She waved wildly as they passed overhead.

'Hi, Ava, Ruby and Bella! Look at me – I'm flying!'

As the airbase loomed up and they skimmed over the turnip fields, Kit made his descent downwind. Closing down the throttle, he reduced speed and, with professional expertise, skilfully landed the plane back on the runway. They disconnected their earphones and he hopped out of his seat before helping Maudie out of hers. When she was once more safely on terra firma, Maudie, elated, rapturously flung her arms about Kit's neck and kissed him long and hard on the mouth.

'That was *wonderful*!' she exclaimed.

Holding her close, Kit gazed into her green eyes, which sparkled more than ever with sheer exhilaration.

'I've never know anything like it,' Maudie babbled on. 'The sky and the light, the sea and the shore, the wind . . . oh, it was so amazing,' she finished, running out of breath.

'I knew you'd love it,' Kit said happily.

'I was scared stiff to begin with,' she admitted. 'Especially when you plonked me in the front seat – I thought you were expecting me to fly!'

'You should have seen your face.' Kit chuckled as he recalled her terror.

'But once we were up there, swooping and diving, I felt like I was an eagle soaring higher and higher into endless space.' She sighed and slumped against him. 'How am I ever going to go back to work when I've just nearly touched heaven?' she murmured.

'I'll take you up whenever you want – within reason, of course,' he quickly added. 'Wouldn't want you on a bombing raid,' he said, with a half-laugh. 'You'd be too much of a distraction!'

Kit drove Maudie, who was chattering like an over-excited child, back to the hall, where she said a reluctant goodbye to him.

'Thank you for an unforgettable afternoon,' she whispered, as they kissed goodbye.

'It's the first of many flights,' he replied.

'Promise?'

Kit kissed the line of freckles speckling the bridge of her nose. 'Cross my heart and hope to die,' he replied.

24. New Year's Eve

Walsingham Hall was a proper little love nest the Christmas of 1942. Raf's spent his only day off in bed with his wife. In the room she usually shared with Ava, Ruby pushed the two single beds together so she and her husband could roll around in blissful abandon.

'I might lose you in the night if these beds drift apart,' Ruby joked, as she made up the iron-framed beds with crisp white sheets and newly starched pillowcases.

As she covered their improvised double bed with warm blankets and a blue satin eiderdown, Raf smiled adoringly at his young wife.

'I hold you tight all night, my Rubee love,' he promised.

Ruby smiled back at her husband, who she loved more with every passing day. She loved his pale, gentle eyes, his young, smiling face, the way he looked at her after they'd made love and his unconditional devotion to her. There wasn't a single thing about Air Mechanic Rafal Boskow that she would change; he was simply the light of her life.

Bella and the Brig had more suitable sleeping arrangement for a couple who weren't even engaged. Bella returned to the luxury of her own room upstairs, while the Brig slept in his room in the communications centre. Since Timms had taken herself off to some relations in Norwich, the two couples had the hall virtually to themselves.

'God help the poor buggers in Norwich having Timms,

the Wicked Witch of the West, for Christmas!' an irrepressible Ruby joked.

Dodds wasn't around either. He'd driven the Walsinghams up to Northumberland and remained there until it was time to drive them back.

As Christmas approached an icy wind blew in from the North Sea.

'Straight from Stalingrad,' Raf said sadly. 'Poor Russkis they must freeze to death.'

The fire was permanently stoked high in the library, where the two couples gathered for chats and cups of tea.

'I can't believe we're doing this,' Bella laughed, lying flat out on one sofa, while Ruby lay prostrate on the one opposite.

'I'm too relaxed to stand up and toast a crumpet!' Ruby giggled, and nodded lethargically at the plateful they'd brought into the snug library, along with a pot of tea and some Walsingham estate honey. 'We'd normally be dashing about like blue-arsed flies at this time – supper done, washing-up to do and breakfast to prepare – but here we are, in the lap of luxury, snug as bugs in a rug!'

'I'm loving my holiday, but I do miss Ava and Maudie,' Bella admitted. 'I hope they're enjoying being with their families. Mumia will be ecstatic to have her *liebling* home.'

'I was thinking,' said Ruby, as she eventually stretched out to pour some tea. 'Shall we ask Kit and Tom and a few lonely lads from the airbase to Christmas dinner?'

Bella nodded, as she speared two crumpets with a toasting fork and set them close to the fire. 'That's a nice thought, though we haven't got much food,' she warned.

Ruby struggled to sit up so she could smear honey on the crumpet Bella dropped on to her plate.

'I could ask around the estate to see if there are any pheasants going spare.'

'Or we could do another mock-turkey with parsnip legs!' Bella giggled.

'It'll be a treat for the lads and get them out of the airbase for a few hours,' Ruby said happily. 'And, let's be honest, cooking for less than ten has got to be a piece of cake after what we're used to!'

The snow was deep on Christmas morning, but Raf dug the jeep out of a drift and drove with Ruby to Our Lady of Walsingham's shrine for Christmas Mass. Ruby had prepared the bread sauce and roast potatoes before she left, and Bella had strict instructions to baste the birds, a pheasant and a scrawny partridge, and keep an eye on the pudding, bubbling away on the back of the Aga. Low on dried fruit, they had been considering just a simple apple tart for afters but, luckily, Bella found a Christmas pudding wrapped in a white cloth at the back of the larder.

'It's one of the puddings I made last year,' she told Ruby in delight. 'I put one by, because they're always better after a bit of ageing, but I completely forgot about it.'

'Won't it be crawling with maggots?' Ruby asked, wrinkling her small nose.

'No, they keep beautifully. The booze preserves them,' Bella assured her.

They served a late lunch below stairs to Raf, Tom, the Brig, Kit and a couple of RAF officers, colleagues of Kit's who were on duty over the Christmas break. Everybody brought a small gift: a bottle of red wine, some black-market bananas, a piece of Stilton, and Raf had procured Polish vodka for the seasonal toasts. Though their portions of poultry were meagre, their plates were piled high with crisp roasted potatoes, bread sauce, sprouts, parsnips and stuffing made from rabbit meat and sage and onion.

'I couldn't eat another thing!' Kit announced when they had finished their meal, and passed around the cigarettes. 'Thank you, Ruby and Bella, that was delicious.'

They took their coffee and the brandy that Bella had looted from the cellar into the library, where a log fire crackled in the large hearth.

'This would be next to perfect if Ava was here,' Tom said, as he settled back on one of the sofas.

'And Maudie, too,' Kit said with a sigh.

'I'm sure they're having a great time, being fussed over by their families,' Ruby chuckled.

'They're due back the day after Boxing Day, so not long to wait,' Bella added, as she poured brandy into crystal balloon glasses.

'Then Ollie arrives, too,' Tom said happily. 'Both my favourite people home at the same time.'

The Brig passed around the glasses then raised his own. 'Here's to the finest cooks in Norfolk. Cheers!'

'*Cheers!*' voices chorused around the room.

Late that night, after the guests had departed in the falling snow and Raf and Ruby had wandered rather blearily off to bed, the phone shrilled out in the marble hallway.

'Who on earth is phoning at this time of the night?' Bella cried, as she dashed to answer it.

Ten minutes later she returned to the library with a face like thunder.

'Who was it, sweetheart?' the Brig enquired.

'My mother,' Bella replied with a grimace. 'They're coming back for New Year.'

'So soon?'

Bella nodded and added, 'They've decided on the spur of the moment to host a New Year's Ball in Norfolk – the invitations have already gone out.' Furious and disappointed, she bit back tears. 'They've gone and done it again!' she cried. 'Disregarded everybody's plans in favour of their own.'

The Brig pulled her down beside him, stroking her soft, blonde curls, and said, 'There's not much we can do about it, darling.'

Soothed by his calm words and gentle hands, Bella nodded. 'You realize there'll be no more time off?' she asked.

He nodded. 'You'll be swept up in elaborate preparations.'

'More than that, darling, Maudie and Ava will be looking forward to spending the rest of their Christmas break with Kit and Tom and little Ollie.'

'There's no chance of that now,' he retorted.

'Oh, God!' Bella wailed. 'They're going to be sooooo disappointed.'

Ruby hit the roof when she was informed of the Walsinghams' change of plans.

'They can't!' she exploded.

'They can – and they have!'

'But there's no food!' Ruby cried.

'That's exactly what I told my mother,' Bella said. 'She seems to think she can buy whatever she wants on the black market.'

Ruby shook her head in disbelief. 'It'll cost them hundreds of pounds,' she exclaimed.

'And a few years in prison, if they're discovered buying black-market goods,' the Brig added grimly.

Ruby gave a heavy sigh, then, characteristically, came up with a positive thought. 'At least it's only a ball,' she laughed.

'*Only a ball!*' Bella repeated incredulously.

'Well, it's not as bad as twenty guests for Christmas dinner, like last year,' Ruby reminded her.

'But it will still be a lot of work, and . . . Ava and Maudie are in for a big shock.'

Ruby put a hand to her mouth. 'We should let them know right away!' she cried.

Bella shrugged and replied, 'What's the point? They're due back tomorrow, anyway.'

Raf drove to Wells railway station to pick up Maudie at midday, then returned later to pick up Ava. Ruby and Bella had decided to tell the returning girls the bad news together.

'I'd never have gone home in the first place if I'd known,' Ava cried in disappointment.

'Me neither,' Maudie added. 'I thought I'd have at least a few days with Kit. Now I'll be lucky if I get a few hours.'

Typically, the girls buckled down to the job in hand. Numerous dust sheets had to be removed from the marble statuary positioned in cornices around the ballroom. As Ruby skipped up a ladder to remove one draped over a priceless biblical oil painting, she called out to Ava, who was standing below, gripping the ladder, 'Hold on tight!'

'Don't worry, lovie, I won't let you tumble to your doom like the poor buggers in the picture, drowning in the Red Sea!' Ava chuckled.

The ballroom floor was swept, mopped and polished, evergreen garlands were looped around the room, sofas and chairs were pushed back against the wall and a dais was erected at the far end of the ballroom for Sydney Lipton and his Grosvenor House Band, who were travelling down from London to entertain the Walsinghams' many guests. Dodds drove the family back in the Bentley two days before the event. Lady Diana followed in her smart Daimler, and Edward showed up with a couple of pals from Cambridge.

'Can't you tell they're back!' groaned Ruby, as she lit fires in various bedrooms on the first floor.

'Yes!' giggled Ava. 'You can hear Lady Diana five miles before you see her – she's got a voice like a high-pitched foghorn.'

The girls were shocked by the sight of the first black-market delivery, of foie gras and champagne.

'Typical Mummy, throwing money away. Bloody useless!' Bella scoffed.

'They must have taken a loan from the Bank of England to pay for this lot,' Ava spluttered.

'And paid a fat fee under the counter to the thieving spiv who found it!' Ruby added.

'You know your parents could go down for ten years for dealing with black-market crooks,' Maudie said, in all seriousness.

Bella rolled her baby-blue eyes. 'I should be so lucky!'

'But seriously, kids,' said Ava, as she surveyed the expensive but totally inadequate goods sprawled across the kitchen table. 'This isn't going to feed a mob.' She pointed at the champagne. 'They'll be legless, but starving!'

Bella pulled out a chair and slumped down at the table. Seeing their dear friend sitting with her head bent, ashamed and embarrassed, made Ava, Ruby and Maudie feel very sorry for her.

'I've had an idea,' said Ava, winking at Ruby and Maudie. 'Let's give the toffs what we give the code girls!'

Catching her drift, Ruby and Maudie nodded and smiled.

'Lord Woolton pie, sausage rolls with no sausage, fritters and pasties,' giggled Ruby.

Maudie grabbed hold of a large tin of foie gras. 'Let's trade this rubbish in for real stuff – Spam, corn beef, lard, beans, peas, sugar and flour.'

Bella looked at her amazing, supportive, wonderful friends and, though tears filled her eyes, she smiled. 'Thank you, thank you,' she sobbed, and stood up and embraced them. 'What would my life be without you?'

Ava laughed as she hugged Bella long and hard. 'What's good enough for the code girls is good enough for them!'

In between cooking and cleaning and looking after the Walsinghams upstairs, Ava stole a few precious hours so she could see Ollie before he returned to his mother in London. The biting wind was almost unbearable on Holkham beach, where they were the only people in sight, but the little boy, with his cheeks blasted bright cherry-red by the north-easterly, laughed and giggled as the tubby little Shetland pony trotted along the water's edge, tossing her thick mane and neighing with excitement.

'Giddee-up!' he chuckled, as Tara gathered speed and broke into a lumbering canter.

When it got too cold to be on the beach, they tethered the horses to a pine tree and the three of them snuggled down in Tom and Ava's favourite sand dunes, where Ava produced a Thermos of home-made vegetable soup and a mock-chocolate cake, which Ollie fell on ravenously. Tom lovingly ran his hair through her newly grown, thick, brown hair.

'I adored your long hair, but I love your new look,' he murmured as he kissed her pouting lips. 'I'd love you even in sackcloth.'

Ollie wiped smudges of cocoa off his mouth, then turned to Ava with a bewitching smile. 'Come home with us, Avie,' he begged.

'I can't, lovie. I've got to work,' she replied sadly.

'But it's the Christmas holidays,' Ollie cried indignantly.

Ava bent to cuddle him. 'Try telling that to the Walsinghams, sweetheart.'

New Year's Eve was cold and chilly, but the snow had cleared and the main roads in and out of Norfolk were open.

'Thank God for small mercies,' Ruby said, as they ran up and down stairs with crockery and cutlery. 'Imagine if the guests were snowed in and holed up here for a week!'

'If that happened, I'd move into the stable bock with the horses,' Ava said, removing a tray of fairly meatless pasties from the bottom oven of the Aga. 'The only thing that's getting me through this blasted event is knowing that, by this time tomorrow, it will all be over and done with.'

'And the day after that the new code girls arrive and it's back to the grindstone for another six months,' groaned Ruby.

Maudie frowned as she deep-fried parsnip fritters.

'At least we're dry and warm, unlike the poor Russkis holding back the Huns in Stalingrad . . . God help them,' she said, with a heavy sigh.

Looking anxious, Bella came hurrying into the kitchen after paying her parents a brief visit above stairs.

'Well, I've told them,' she announced.

'And how did they take to the idea of a rationing party?'

Ava chuckled, as she leant against the warm Aga and lit up a Woodbine.

'They didn't,' Bella retorted. 'Diana and Edward said they wouldn't touch fritters and pies with a barge pole.'

'Who bloody cares?' Maudie snapped. 'They can choose to choke on foie gras or Spam!'

The band arrived and were given supper below stairs, then they set up their instruments in the ballroom, where Dodds had put silver candelabras on tables and in cornices. As the girls finished laying out the last of their wartime food on a long table decorated with Union Jack flags, the band started to tune up and, in the empty ballroom, lit by dozens of glowing candles, Bella, Ava, Maudie and Ruby joined hands and danced to the strains of 'In the Mood', 'Little Brown Jug' and 'Hang Out Your Washing on the Siegfried Line'. Laughing and gasping for breath, they jived and waltzed till the first guests arrived. When they were forced to stop dancing, the orchestra applauded them.

'Hey, I've never seen kitchen girls dance as well as you do,' the leader of the orchestra cried. 'Pity you have to go – you look so cute be-bopping in your lace hats and pinafores!'

'Come back later and put on a show,' the drummer called out. 'Show the old stuffed shirts how to really let their hair down.'

Ava winked as she said, 'We'll be busy till midnight, but we might sneak back for the last dance.'

Bella stayed below stairs with Ava, serving up food, while Ruby and Maudie replenished dishes in the ballroom, where the buffet was laid out under the high leaded windows that looked out on to the dark garden. Timms hadn't yet returned from her Christmas break, for which the girls were eternally grateful, but Dodds was on hand to serve champagne. Both Maudie and Ruby were flabbergasted by the guests' response to their buffet supper.

'Rationed goods!' a portly man with flushed cheeks and monocle boomed. 'Gets one into the wartime spirit, what ho?'

Ruby stifled a snort of laughter, which exploded out of her once the man had blustered off. 'It's clear he's never had Lord Woolton pie before!'

'He's wolfed all the parsnip fritters,' Maudie whispered, as she stared askance at the empty silver dish.

'And now he's eyeing up the curried-rabbit meatballs!' Ruby chuckled.

It wasn't just the man with the huge appetite who appreciated their efforts. Maudie and Ruby overheard many of the guests congratulating Lord and Lady Walsingham on their wise decision to serve rationed food. The girls hid their smiles as Lord Walsingham said, 'It seemed the right thing to do in the circumstances, don't ya think?'

The woman he was talking to nodded her tiara-topped head and earnestly replied, 'It makes one quite sick to see people eating to excess while the poor Russians are starving to death.'

Lord Walsingham, who was clutching a rather soggy corned-beef fritter, took a deep slug of his champagne before answering gruffly, 'Disgraceful! It's sacrifices across the board, the Dunkirk spirit, hey what?'

Ruby couldn't resist running downstairs to tell Ava and Bella. 'They're loving the grub up there,' she cried. 'They think the Walsinghams are setting a fine example by serving rationed food.' Holding her sides, she broke into peals of helpless laughter. 'Oh, you should have seen his lordship's face when some posh woman praised him for his heroic war effort.'

'*His war effort!*' Bella shrieked. 'I've got to take a sneak peek,' she said, and nipped upstairs into the ballroom, where, standing in the shadows, she listened in on various conversations.

'I say anybody who uses the black market should be flogged and sent to prison,' a man talking to her ladyship bellowed.

'P–p–prison!' Lady Caroline stammered, as she nervously eyed the champagne she'd had Dodds purchase at a high price from under the counter.

'Quite! Banged up along with the spivs who are lining their own miserable pockets on the back of the war.'

By this time her ladyship was looking white and quite unwell. 'If you'll excuse me,' she murmured, and moved on.

Bella was spotted by one of the guests, who was deep in conversation with Diana.

'I have to hand it to you Walsinghams, you're putting us to shame with the sacrifices you're making – even your younger sister is hard at work,' he said, pointing at Bella, who was desperately trying to make a quick exit.

Diana, who was three sheets to the wind on champagne, glared at her sister, who was dressed in her servant's uniform.

'It'll be you next,' the guest guffawed. 'You'd look a picture in a pinnie!'

Tom, the Brig, Raf and Kit arrived at different times during the evening.

'We give hands with washing-up,' said Raf, grabbing a dishcloth and sticking his arms up to his elbows in warm suds.

Once supper was served and cleared, the girls could finally let their hair down. As the clock in the echoing marble hall chimed out midnight, Ava, Ruby, Maudie and Bella joined their partners and, in a circle, they sang 'Auld Lang Syne'. As the strains of 'Yours till the Star Lose Their Glory' drifted down the stairwell, the Brig took Bella by the hand. 'Care to dance, darling?'

Smiling, the four couples joined the guests on the dance floor, where, by candlelight, they danced until they were the only people left in the ballroom. As the orchestra played them out to Vera Lynn's 'We'll Meet Again', Bella laid her face against the Brig's shoulder and sighed with sheer happiness.

'We're in the middle of a war, and I don't think I've ever been as content in my entire life,' she whispered.

The Brig bent to kiss her blonde curls. He didn't want to spoil Bella's perfect moment, but his heart was heavy. Could the year 1943 be the turning point of the war, as everybody hoped and prayed? Or would Hitler finally cross the Channel and occupy the country he loved with every bone in his body?

PART THREE

1943

25. Walsingham Shoot

After dancing in the New Year, Ava, Maudie, Ruby and Bella and their devoted partners cleared away the remains of the ration-themed buffet and said reluctant farewells to each other. The exhausted girls fell into their beds at three in the morning.

'The alarm's on for seven,' Bella yawned.

'I don't want to know about tomorrow,' Maudie groaned, pulling the eiderdown over her head and falling into a deep, dreamless sleep.

Diligent Ruby was up first. Having brewed up, she woke the other girls with steaming mugs of hot tea and a brusque, 'Get up! We've got three hours till the shoot party arrives.'

Bleary-eyed, the girls washed quickly, then struggled into their uniforms.

'How can these people eat and drink so much and still get up early?' Maudie grumbled, as she struggled to push her blazing, unruly hair under her lace cap.

'Years of practice!' Bella joked. 'Breakfast, elevensies, lunch, tea, dinner, supper – toffs can pack it away for England.'

'The sausage rolls – whoops, correction!' Ava chuckled, as she lit up her first Woodbine of the day and inhaled deeply, '– the wild-bunny-rabbit rolls shot by Peter only last week – are in the oven. We'll serve them with the punch.'

Ruby, who'd done many a Walsingham Shoot, explained the procedure.

'Leave Dodds to mix and serve the spiced rum punch,' she said. 'I'll whip round with the rolls while you three press on with the shoot lunch. It's served in the lake house, usually around midday.'

'How do the shoot party get to the lake house?' Ava asked.

'Peter said he and my brother will drive them there in the blood wagons,' Bella replied.

'*Ugh!* Disgusting,' Maudie cried.

'Don't panic,' giggled Ruby, who loved teasing squeamish Maudie. 'They're just a couple of old Land Rovers, dripping with the blood of dead pheasants!' she added naughtily.

'Please, spare me the gory details,' Maudie begged.

'But we'll have to cycle over there with the food. Peter can't manage that, too.'

'That should be a challenge,' cried Maudie. 'Balancing sprouts, mashed potatoes and a casserole in our bicycle baskets.'

'Not to mention the coconut tarts and custard!' Ava added. 'How're we going to warm it all up?' she added as an afterthought.

'There are a couple of old Primus camping stoves kept in the lake house for just that purpose,' Bella replied. Seeing Maudie's anxious face, she said, 'They do work, promise.'

'It's not the food I'm worried about,' Maudie admitted. 'It's being anywhere near your brother that's troubling me.'

Bella looked her friend levelly in the eye. 'I'll stand between you and my foul brother,' she promised.

Maudie put an arm around Bella, whose blue eyes were already burning with anger. 'Thank you, darling, I'll be safe with a lioness like you at my side!'

Late morning, with everything prepared, just before they set off, Ava gave Ruby strict instructions about the teatime menu. 'Meat-paste sandwiches and scones with rhubarb jam – and go easy on the sugar, we don't want the toffs taking our code girls' precious sugar rations,' she said firmly.

Laughing themselves silly, Ava, Bella and Maudie jumped on their bicycles and cycled through the pine woods, balancing pans of food in their wicker baskets.

'I don't dare to try overtaking either of you in case I lose one of the courses en route!' Bella joked.

It was a clear, bright, freezing-cold January day, which brought roses to their cheeks and a sparkle to their eyes.

'It's the kind of weather that whips up an appetite,' Bella announced, as they parked their bikes by the lake house, which Peter had left unlocked after sweeping it out and setting up the long wooden trestle tables and benches. Propped up on one of the tables was a scribbled note left by Peter, which Ava picked up.

'Looks like Peter's got a problem,' she said, as she read the letter. 'Lord Edward's not showed up all morning, so Peter will have to deliver the shooting party to the lake house in two trips.'

'Trust bloody Edward to ruin the arrangements,' Bella fumed.

'It's a real nuisance,' Ava grumbled. 'It'll take us twice as long to serve two separate groups, and the food will have to be reheated – not great for dumplings, they'll be so hard we'll be able to bounce them off the wall!'

Maudie, who could drive, quickly said, 'I can go and collect the second Land Rover and help Peter with the driving.'

Ava and Bella glanced at each other and nodded. 'Good idea,' said Ava.

'The Land Rovers are kept at the estate office,' Bella told her.

'You start heating up the lunch,' Maudie said, as she dashed out of the open door. 'Won't be long.'

Mounting her bike, Maudie cycled back to the office, where there was a Land Rover parked on the drive. Relieved to find that Peter had left the keys in the ignition, she started up the rickety old vehicle, then headed off across the estate towards the sound of loud, blasting guns. As she bounced along the rutted track that ran alongside the pine woods, Maudie spotted two men in blue RAF uniforms hurrying through the bushes. Thinking they might be on their way to Holkham airbase, she drew up and called out to them. 'Want a lift?'

The men turned to scowl at her, then, muttering to each other, they disappeared behind the thick bushes. Instantly suspicious, Maudie stepped out of the Land Rover and approached the bushes that fringed the track. Though the men had moved on, she could still hear them talking.

'We've gone too far,' one of them insisted.

'No, Walsingham told us to take a right turn and cut through the woods to get to the airbase.'

'I wonder if Kit knows about them,' Maudie thought. as she got back into the Land Rover and drove away.

Less than a hundred yards down the track, Lord Edward himself stepped out in front of her, with a gun slung over his shoulder.

'Oh, Jesus!' Maudie cried, as she dropped gear in an attempt to swerve around him. The engine stalled and the Land Rover shuddered to a halt.

The sight of his bloated red face only a few feet away brought Maudie out in a hot sweat. She tried desperately to restart the car.

'Shit!' she cried.

Suddenly, a hand with a grip of iron grabbed her by the shoulder and yanked her out of the driver's seat. 'What the hell are you doing in my vehicle?' Edward Walsingham demanded harshly.

Though she was terrified of Edward touching her, Maudie wasn't going to cringe and quake in front of such a disgusting, blustering bully. 'I'm going to pick up the shooting party you seem to have forgotten about,' she snapped.

'Bugger off!' Edward snarled.

Shoving her roughly away from the car, he climbed in and turned the keys in the ignition. 'You can walk back to where you came from!' he sneered, roaring away at break-neck speed.

'*Brute!*' Maudie screamed after him.

Struggling to her feet, she dusted herself down, then breathed a sigh of relief. She certainly had a long walk ahead of her, but at least Edward hadn't tried to molest her. Maudie broke into a run but stopped short when, yet again, she spotted the two RAF men slinking through the forest undergrowth. Suspicious of their furtive behaviour, she muttered out loud, 'What *are* they up to?'

Holding her breath, Maudie slipped behind a belt of pine trees, then crept as close as she dared to the men, who had stopped to have a cigarette. Hidden, Maudie listened in on their conversation.

'I wish Walsingham hadn't left us to it.'

The second man shrugged. 'He had to go to the shoot, otherwise it would arouse suspicion.' He carelessly flicked his cigarette butt away as he added, 'We have our orders, we know what to do – get the information and report back without being seen. We can do that with or without Walsingham.'

Maudie froze as the implications of what the men were discussing, and Edward's obvious involvement at some level, sank in.

'Mother of God!' she thought.

Trembling, she waited until the men stubbed out their cigarettes and went on their way. As soon as it was safe, she shot out of her hiding place. 'I've got to tell Kit what I've just heard!' she gasped under her breath.

When she heard the sound of an approaching vehicle, she whirled around to see who the driver was and gasped in relief when she saw it was Peter.

'Jump in!' he called.

Breathless, she asked, 'Can I borrow the Land Rover? It's urgent, I need to get to the airbase.'

Peter looked surprised. 'I've got to get this lot to the lake house for lunch.' He nodded to the passengers in the back. 'But you can have it after I've dropped them off.'

Flushed and panting, Maudie jumped into the passenger seat. 'Thanks,' she muttered.

Sitting tensely beside Peter, she willed him to drive faster. All she wanted was to get to Kit, but she couldn't kick everybody out of the vehicle without causing alarm.

When they reached the lake house Maudie's heart sank: Edward was there, drinking heavily with his loud-mouthed chums. As she moved into the driver's seat, which Peter had vacated, Edward bellowed, 'Where do you think you're going, girl?'

Before Maudie could answer he yanked her out of the cab and steered her into the lake house.

'Serve our lunch, girl! That's your job, isn't it?'

Maudie threw his hand off her. 'If you touch me one more time, you'll be sorry,' she threatened.

Edward's piggy little eyes brightened with desire. 'Mmmm, I recall you like a fight, a bit of rough,' he whispered lasciviously into her ear.

Disgusted, Maudie turned away, just as Bella stormed up.

'Leave her alone, Edward!' she commanded.

'Quite the little proletariat these days aren't we, Lady Annabelle?' he retorted, in a loud, mocking voice. 'You've spent too much time below stairs, mixing with guttersnipes. In fact,' he said, as he gave a loud sniff, 'you're beginning to smell like them.'

'You unutterable bastard!' Bella seethed.

Before a fight broke out, Ava loudly announced, 'Lunch is served!'

Though Maudie's instincts were to run out of the lake house and drive straight to the airbase, she knew such action would make Edward suspicious. The best thing she could do was serve lunch quickly, then the shooting party would be on their way. Luckily, they were all starving, so they demolished what was on their plate, along with a crate of fine red wine. Maudie gave drunken Edward a very wide berth but as she cleared away the casserole pot, he reached out and stroked her bottom. Incandescent with anger, she gasped and whirled around to face him.

'Nice arse!' he leered.

'How dare you?' she cried, and 'accidentally' dropped the half-empty pot on to his lap.

As the remains of the cold casserole dripped down Edward's tweed trousers, he jumped to his feet.

Raising a hand as if to strike Maudie, he yelled, 'Bloody stupid bitch!'

Completely unafraid, Bella stood between her brother and her friend. Edward's hand hovered in the air, then dropped. Grabbing his shotgun, he threw it over his shoulder and stormed out of the lake house.

'I'll see your servant friend fired!' he yelled over his shoulder to his sister, who angrily yelled back: 'Try it!'

As soon as Edward and his chums had driven off, Peter winked at Maudie. 'Take the Land Rover,' he said. 'The rest of us can make our way on foot.'

Ava and Bella were astonished when Maudie drove off without any explanation.

'Where's she going?' Ava asked Peter, who shook his head.

'I've no idea,' he replied. 'But she said it was urgent.'

Maudie drove like a bat out of hell. Screeching into the airfield, she pulled up sharply, switched off the ignition then sprinted to Kit's office, where she found him leaning back in his chair, smoking a Craven A with his feet up on the cluttered desk. Seeing her face, Kit instantly jumped up.

'Darling!' he said, taking hold of her shaking hands. 'What's the matter?'

'There's something strange going on, Kit!' she blurted out.

After Maudie had recounted what she'd seen and heard in the woods, Kit's blue eyes widened in alarm. 'Are you sure?'

She nodded grimly. 'I saw them twice,' she confirmed. 'I'm absolutely sure – but *wh*y would Walsingham be involved with two such shifty-looking characters?'

'Because he's a bloody shifty character himself!' Kit said as he slammed his fist angrily on his desk. 'He'd better stay well away from here, or I'll have him behind bars!'

Agitated beyond words, Maudie cried out and pointed to the window 'Kit! Those men could be snooping around the base already!'

'Calm down, darling. Interfering nosey parkers are quickly picked out.'

Maudie shook her head. 'Believe me, they won't be easy to spot – they're both wearing RAF uniforms.'

Kit took hold of her hand, saying, 'Come with me, we'll need a description.'

As they hurried over to the officers' mess, Kit asked tensely, 'Did you have any trouble with Walsingham at the shoot lunch?'

When she admitted what had happened, Kit's face tightened in fury. She squeezed his hand and she gave a wicked smile. 'But I got my own back, I poured the remains of the casserole into his lap!'

Kit gazed at her with a mixture of shock and pride. 'Really?'

'I only regret it wasn't boiling hot. I'd like to have set fire to his posh Crown Jewels!'

Kit ground his teeth in fury, 'One day, I'll beat the living daylights out of Walsingham, I swear to God I will!'

In the officers' mess, Maudie described the rogue airmen to the officers, who listened intently as they smoked their cigarettes or puffed on their pipes.

'Average height, average build, short hair, both wearing RAF uniforms. Sorry, I know it's not much to go on,' she finished apologetically.

'It's the unit leader's primary responsibility to know every man in his squad. If there're any oddballs, we'll track them down,' Kit assured her, then, turning, he gave rapid instructions to his men. 'Organize search parties to scour the grounds, hangars, bomb stores, Nissen huts, communications centre, control tower – everywhere. Right, men – scramble!'

Kit would not entertain the idea of Maudie driving back to the hall alone and in the dark. 'Raf will drive you home in the Land Rover,' he said firmly.

'You need all your men here,' she reminded him.

Kit took her in his arms and kissed her briefly but passionately. 'And you need protecting, my darling spy girl,' he said hoarsely. 'Take a torch and check out the woods on your way back – the men just might be holing up there till morning.'

'What about Edward?' she asked. 'Shouldn't somebody be tailing him?'

Kit nodded. 'I'll get Raf to shadow him. Now, off you go, Maudie. I'll feel happier once I know you're back with your friends.'

Secretly grateful that she was being escorted home, Maudie shone Kit's torch into the woods and bushes as they drove by, but saw nothing other than a startled fox and a barn owl that floated out of the forest as silent as a ghost.

'Good news about Soviets,' Raf said, as he drove, with no headlights, in the pitch dark.

'I've not had time to hear much news today,' Maudie said with a wry smile.

'Soviets on offensive against bloody Hun in Stalingrad,' Raf explained. 'Bloody freeze there but they fight, they tough, the Red Army.'

When they reached the hall, Raf opened the car door for Maudie, then got back into the passenger seat.

'I keep eyes peeled for bloody bastard Edward!' he told Maudie, settling as he pulled his leather flying jacket closely around him.

'I'm sure your wife will be out with a brew for you soon,' Maudie said, with a smile.

A few minutes later, as the girls gathered around the warm Aga, Maudie told her story.

'I'm so sorry, Bella,' she said, when she had to reveal the embarrassing truth to friend. 'It looks like your brother's up to no good.'

'Nothing that Edward does can shock me,' Bella replied with a heavy sigh. 'He's always been ruthlessly out for himself.' Turning to the Brig, whose brow was furrowed with concern, she added, 'We should search his room as soon as we can – we must find out exactly what Edward's up to.'

26. Cracking the Code

It was decided that Ruby would be the one to search Lord Edward's rooms. 'We can't have Maudie going in there, he might jump on her again,' she said.

'You'll have to tell me what I'm searching for, though,' Ruby said practically.

'Anything suspicious,' the Brig replied. 'But what we're really looking for is a radio transmitter which, if he does have one, he'll certainly have hidden.'

'And what does one of these radio thingummies look like?' Ruby enquired.

'Basically, it's a small radio built into an ordinary-looking suitcase,' Bella elaborated.

Ruby's dark eyes grew round with awe. '*Ooooh!* Like one of them radio sets that you see in scary spy films!' she exclaimed.

'You've got it, Ruby!' the Brig chuckled. 'A spy radio set.'

'You must only search his room when it's safe, Ruby,' Bella warned.

'We mustn't arouse suspicion,' the Brig added. 'The last thing we want is Edward to know we're on to him.'

With the new code girls already installed, domestic life below stairs was getting back to normal, apart from one startling piece of news.

'Timms isn't coming back!' Bella informed her friends one morning.

Ava, Ruby and Maudie gaped open-mouthed at her.

'You're kidding!' cried Ava.

Bella shook her head. 'Mummy's just received a letter from her. Listen to this!' she said, smothering a giggle. 'Timms is getting married! She met a retired vicar when she was staying with her relatives in Norwich over Christmas.'

'Well, good luck to the poor vicar,' Ruby chuckled. 'He's got the housekeeper from hell!'

As Ruby waited for a good time to search Edward's rooms, Raf remained on guard outdoors.

'Edward will rumble you if he catches you in your RAF uniform,' Bella told Raf, who crinkled his brow as he asked, 'What is "rumbles"?'

Bella laughed as she apologized.

'Sorry, Raf. You need to be in disguise – you need to get rid of the uniform.'

When Ruby saw her husband dressed in an old and grubby boiler suit that Bella had borrowed from Peter, she screamed with laughter. 'Oh, my God! You look like Worzel Gummidge!'

To complete his rustic image, Raf donned a battered tweed cap.

'Nobody rumbles Rafal Boskow now,' he joked.

'I'm your wife, and I wouldn't recognize you,' Ruby giggled, as she stood on her tiptoes to kiss Raf's cheek. Growing serious, she sat Raf down at the kitchen table. 'Now, listen, lovie, we've wasted too much precious time hanging around waiting for Walsingham. We've got to seize the moment,' she said, bunching her small fist. 'The sooner I can get into his bedroom, the better. Understand?'

'I understands you, Rubee,' Raf answered, uncurling her

fist and kissing her soft, pink palm. 'I give you nods when all is clear, OK?'

Ruby had her opportunity the very next day.

'He leave now, in car!' Raf cried, rushing into the kitchen. 'Go, quick!'

Ruby grabbed a mop and duster from the cleaning cupboard and crept up the back stairs. She opened Edward's door, stepped inside and immediately shot the bolt. Hurrying to the chest of drawers, she searched each drawer in turn but found nothing odd or unusual. Then she tried to search the desk, which was locked.

'*Damn!*' she muttered, as her eyes scanned the room. They landed on the large mahogany wardrobe which almost ran the length of one wall. She riffled through the rails of coats and suits, then spotted Edward's expensive leather-bound suitcases stacked beside the hanging rails.

'Oh, God,' she whispered, as she nervously removed the smallest case, which was on top of the pile, and flicked open the brass clips. 'Nothing,' she murmured, then laid it aside and opened the next.

It was when she came to the fourth case that she found exactly what Bella had described: a radio set neatly built into an ordinary-looking suitcase. As Ruby gazed in amazement at the transmitter, with its panel of bewildering controls and switches, she heard a tinkling sound at the window. With her heart pounding, she jumped to her feet and ran to the window, where she saw an agitated Raf waving to her from below.

'Edward back!' he called up to her.

'Jesus Christ!' she gasped.

Breaking into a hot sweat, Ruby neatly returned all the cases, including the crucial one, to their original positions.

After closing the wardrobe, she dashed across the room to slide the bolt on the door and, just in time, she snatched up her duster, which she was busily wiping across the dressing table as Edward burst in.

'What the hell do you think you're doing in here?' he snapped.

Ruby turned her honest brown eyes on him and answered with a simple smile, 'Dusting, Your Lordship; it's Tuesday, we always dust on a Tuesday.'

Edward scowled. 'Well, get out!' he barked. 'I've work to do.'

Ruby gave a little bob as she replied, 'Yes, your lordship.'

Grabbing her mop, she exited the room, then hurried down the length of the corridor. She walked slap-bang into Raf, who was skulking in a dark corner. Covering her mouth to stifle a scream, Ruby fell against her husband. 'What are you doing, hiding there?" she whispered.

Raf tapped the top pocket of his borrowed boiler suit. 'I have gun here. If bastard lordship lay hand on my Rubee, I blow bloody brains out,' he answered grimly.

Ruby stared at her young husband, whose sweet face was creased with anxiety.

'You're my knight in shining armour,' she whispered fondly.

'What is "shining night"?'

'My hero!' she said, as grabbed his hand and headed for the back staircase. 'Come on, I've got news for the Brig.'

When everybody was gathered in the kitchen and the doors were firmly shut, Ruby informed the tense group seated around the table.

'I found a radio set in a suitcase in his wardrobe. It looks exactly like you said, Bella. There are wires leading out of it, and a headset, too. There's even an instruction manual.'

'Excellent work, Ruby,' the Brig said, as he and Bella exchanged a meaningful look.

'He's transmitting from here!' Bella cried incredulously. 'From his own home! The bare-faced cheek of him!' she raged.

The Brig nodded slowly, as he tamped down the tobacco in his pipe.

'A bold move, even for Edward,' he said quietly.

'So, what now?' Maudie asked, baffled.

'Inform Kit, of course,' the Brig answered.

'But what about the police?' Ruby cried. 'Shouldn't they be told there's a spy in Walsingham Hall?' she asked melodramatically.

'We don't know exactly what he's up to yet, Ruby,' the Brig replied with a smile. 'We need to be patient.'

'Well, he's not got a bloody radio set hidden in his room to listen to "Workers' Playtime", that's for sure,' Ruby answered robustly.

Everybody burst out laughing.

'Oh, Ruby, you're a card!' Ava chuckled.

'First we've got to find out if Edward is actually transmitting,' the Brig continued. 'If he is, then we've got to find out who's he's communicating with. If we find anything incriminating, then we'll alert the appropriate authorities.'

'How will you be able to make those checks?' clever Maudie asked.

'We have our own transmitter which we use for training purposes. I keep it under lock and key in my office,' the Brig explained. 'If Walsingham does transmit, Bella and I will listen in and work on cracking his code. We'll work in shifts, day and night – one of us will even sleep next to the damn transmitter,' he said with a low chuckle.

'What happens when Walsingham leaves here?' Ava asked. 'How do you keep tabs on him then?'

'If he's operational, we can pick up his messages anywhere,' Bella replied. 'As long as we've set our receiver to the frequency he's using, we can pick him up wherever he is.'

Ruby's eyes were wide with amazement. 'How long will it take?'

'It all depends on how good we are at breaking his cypher,' the Brig replied.

Ruby, who'd been agog with curiosity since she found the 'spy suitcase', as she always referred to it, asked, 'What's a cypher?'

'It's the rule you use for decrypting and encrypting,' the Brig answered.

Ruby looked baffled. '*Huh!*' she grunted.

Recalling the problems she'd had a few months before when the Brig was teaching her how to decrypt a poem code, Bella smiled as she sat down at the table and gestured to her friends to sit down, too.

'Come on,' she said excitedly. 'I'll show you how to create a cypher based on a poem. First of all me, the sender, and you, the receiver.' She pointed at Ruby. 'We two have to agree on a poem.'

'Oh, dear,' Ruby giggled. 'I'm rubbish at poetry!'

'Don't worry,' Bella assured her. 'I've recently been working on a poem by Robert Browning,' she said, as she wrote out the first line on a piece of paper.

'Oh to be in England now that April's there.'

'Now underneath each letter, and space, too, write out the alphabet,' she said to a nervous Ruby. 'Write neatly so you can keep track of your changes, making sure each letter represents only one other letter,' she advised.

Muttering out loud, Ruby did as she was told. '"Oh to be in England now that April's there."'

'So now you have your cypher,' Bella said, as she pointed at the letters on the page. 'You, the sender, and your receiver on the other end now know that O is A, H is B, space is C, T is D, then another O, so that's A again, and another space, which is C again . . . so the next letter in the poem, B, has to be E, and so on.'

Ruby put her hands to her head and groaned. '*Stop!* You're giving me a headache,' she cried.

'That's amazing!' Maudie enthused. 'So clever, yet so simple, too!'

Ava burst out laughing. 'We're turning into code girls, after all!'

'Poem codes are a very basic way of working,' the Brig said. 'Once our trainees are qualified, they'll be working in code-breaking centres with sophisticated machines that have in-built cyphers which are much, much faster.'

'Why don't you have one of those machines?' Maudie asked.

'We're only a training centre, we're not operational,' the Brig explained. 'I don't think the War Office would run to providing us with such an expensive machine while we're working at this level.'

Looking anxious, Bella fretfully drummed her fingers on the table. 'Shouldn't you report this to Military Intelligence?'

The Brig shrugged then answered her question. 'The same applies to them as the police – we need more information. Right now, all we've got to go on is an insubstantial link with two strangers who might have infiltrated the airbase. If we do establish that Edward is transmitting, we'll be able to pass on documented evidence to Military Intelligence.'

'God!' Ruby exclaimed, lighting another Woodbine. 'Now I understand what important work our code girls do, and why you two were so disappointed not to be training with them,' she added, with a glance at Ava and Maudie.

'I don't know what the country would do without them,' the Brig said. 'There are thousands of women working in secret locations all over Britain, breaking codes and tapping into enemy information. Nice feeling to think we've trained some of them,' he said, with a proud smile.

Later, as Bella was collecting her notebook and pencil from the bedroom she shared with Maudie, her friend slipped in for a quiet word. 'This must be awful for you, Bella,' she said earnestly.

Bella cocked her head as she considered the question. 'It's sweet of you to say so but, to, be brutally honest, it's not so awful.' She sighed heavily and continued. 'I've been dislocated from my family for so long, I feel like a stranger when I'm with them. I'm the outsider and I always have been.'

'But he's still your brother!' Maudie insisted. 'He might get arrested, imprisoned – even hanged!'

'Brother or not – if he is a spy, the sooner he's locked away the better!' Bella replied bitterly.

Bella was worried about using the Brig's transmitter in the south wing.

'It'll arouse suspicion if I'm constantly wandering in and out of your room,' she pointed out. 'Wouldn't it be better to move it below stairs? We could hide it in the sewing room, which is next to the kitchen, then we could all keep an eye on it.'

So the Brig's transmitter was hidden in the sewing room, beneath a pile of sheets in a big blanket box, and Bella and the Brig manned it around the clock. It wasn't long until they picked up Edward's signals on their transceiver – evidence that he was transmitting.

'Right!' Bella announced, with a blaze of determination in her blue eyes. 'Now it's our job to decrypt the code and find out *what* he's transmitting to *who* and *where*.'

But after two days they were none the wiser. On the third morning, as Bella continued her work, the Brig walked in. 'Any luck?' he asked.

'A message came through about seven. I've given myself a headache trying to work out the cypher – I haven't even got a crib to get started,' she moaned. 'I've been working on frequency analysis, trying to find the most common German words to fit the pattern, but this is a much more sophisticated code.'

The Brig sat beside her and looked at her calculations. 'It was never going to be easy, darling,' he told her.

'The whole process takes so much time!' she cried in frustration. 'As we sit here banging our heads against a brick wall, my vile brother's as free as a bird. Honestly, Brig, I'm terrified of what he'll do next.'

'I know,' he said, and kissed her pale, tired face. 'Now, off you go, sweetheart, you're worn out. Have a kip – I'll take over.'

For the next week they wracked their brains, working on

alternative encryption methods, but drew nothing but blanks.

'He's sending out a daily message,' Bella said, studying her notes. 'I've got copies of everything he's sent – the only trouble is we can't bloody well decode them!' But, though tired and irritable, Bella refused to give up.

'You're like a dog with a bone!' the Brig teased, as he brought her a cup of cocoa late one night.

'I'll crack this if it kills me,' she said through gritted teeth.

The Brig looked thoughtful. 'I might have a word with Lionel, one of my chums in Military Intelligence. He'll be up to date on codes which have been recently cracked. He might have a few tips for us.'

'Darling! That would be wonderful,' Bella exclaimed. 'Do it right away, please.'

The Brig gave a weary smile. 'Sweetheart, it's gone midnight. It'll have to wait till morning.'

He kept his word, and phoned his chum who worked for Military Intelligence first thing the next morning.

'We're getting nowhere fast,' he went straight to the point.

After a long pause Lionel said, 'We cracked a bloody nightmare of a code a few months ago by using major street names in Berlin. You could give that a try. Worth a go, eh?'

Grateful for Lionel's advice, Bella spent many long, frustrating hours working on permutations of street names in Berlin and, finally, her determination paid off.

'I've cracked it!' she announced, hugging the Brig. 'The cypher's Friedrichstrasse, a street in Berlin. *Look!*' she exclaimed, triumphantly waving a scrap of paper under his nose. 'Just read who it's from.'

'Abwehr!' gasped the astonished Brig.

'Nothing less than German Military Intelligence in Berlin,' Bella cried, and read her decryption out loud: 'It's essential that we have the precise status of the Lancasters at Holkham airbase.'

The Brig snatched the paper from her outstretched hand. 'God Almighty, this is serious! He's providing the enemy with top-secret information about Holkham.'

Alarmed, they held each other's gaze for several seconds.

'He's *spying*, Brig,' Bella whispered. Flushing with shame, she felt tears sting the backs of her eyes.

The Brig pulled her to him. 'Darling, you don't have to go through with this,' he said softly.

Bella squared her shoulders. 'Oh, but I *do*!' she said forcefully.

'Brave little fighter,' he said proudly, then, giving her a quick kiss, he hurried towards the door. 'Kit needs to know right away.'

'Don't use the house phone,' Bella cried in alarm. 'It might be tapped.'

'I know,' he called over his shoulder, as he dashed away. 'I'll use the phone in my office.'

Hearing the commotion in the sewing room, bleary-eyed Maudie, wearing her nightdress, joined Bella, who was ablaze with both excitement and outrage.

'I cracked Edward's code!' she cried, squeezing Maudie's hands.

Maudie looked impressed. 'You clever girl!' she exclaimed.

'It's not good news, Maudie – Edward's a spy for German Military Intelligence,' Bella added in a low whisper.

Maudie held a hand to her mouth. 'God! I never thought he would sink that low.'

'Hopefully, we'll put a stop to his treacherous ways now we've cracked his code,' Bella said grimly.

But when Edward's next message came through the following morning, Bella couldn't decrypt it.

'Damn! Damn! Bloody damn!' she shouted in frustration, and threw the useless crib sheet into the fire. 'I used the same cypher as yesterday,' she told the Brig, 'but this morning the cypher's changed and nothing matches up. I'm back to square one,' she groaned.

'Say that again,' the Brig said sharply.

Bella repeated her words: 'I used the same cypher as yesterday, but this morning the cypher's changed and nothing matches up.'

'Was it first thing this morning?' he queried.

Beginning to doubt herself, Bella replied hesitantly, 'Or maybe I got it wrong in the first place?'

The Brig shook his head impatiently. 'It's nothing to do with you, sweetheart. Don't you see? Edward's changing the bloody cypher every day.'

Bella clicked her fingers with a loud snap. 'Of course! That's why it's been so damned impossible to crack – we can't keep up with him.'

Silence fell as they both considered the problem.

'If he's changing it every day, he's *got* to be using a cypher book,' the Brig said knowingly.

'Then we've *got* to find it,' Bella said, with steely determination.

After news had come through of the brutal crushing of the rebellion by the Jews in the Warsaw Ghetto, discussions below stairs grew more and more heated.

'We'll have to search Edward's room again,' the Brig informed the tense group gathered around the kitchen table.

Ruby squared her slender shoulders. 'I'll go. A dopey servant won't arouse his suspicions.'

'But you don't know what you're looking for, lovie,' Ava said anxiously.

Ruby nodded towards Bella and the Brig. 'They'll have to brief me.'

'Thank you, Ruby,' the Brig said. 'Sorry to up the pressure but, really, the sooner the better.'

'So come on, tell me – describe this cypher thing,' Ruby urged.

'It'll be a booklet, probably quite small, containing cypher text,' the Brig answered.

'And I know what a cypher is after my poetry-code lesson from Bella!' Ruby said, with a bit of a swagger.

'But this will be a bit different. It'll be a combination of groups of letters – rows and rows of them – in a notebook,' Bella explained.

Ruby stuck out her chin. 'I'll do my best to find it!' she promised.

Before he went to bed, the Brig phoned Kit to inform him of their decision to search Edward's room. 'The sooner we find the cypher book, the sooner we can nail the bastard,' he said in a low voice.

'I've got the base on high alert,' Kit told him. 'Nobody goes in or out without being questioned. No sign of the infiltrators so far, though.'

'Keep me informed, old chap.'

'Will do,' Kit replied. 'Good luck.'

'You, too,' the Brig replied with a heavy yawn. 'Goodnight.'

*

300

The following morning, straight after Raf had informed her that Edward had left the hall, Ruby dashed up the back stairs, clutching her mop and bucket.

'I keep eyes out, Rubee,' Raf anxiously called after her.

Ruby shot the bolt on the bedroom door, then scanned the room. The polished mahogany roll-top desk in front of the huge bay window drew her like a magnet. The roll-top was securely locked, but the drawers running down either side of the desk were open. After a thorough search, though, she was disappointed to find nothing. Thinking the booklet might be hidden somewhere in the bed, Ruby stripped off the bedding, checked inside the pillowcases, then crawled under the bed to see if there was anything stuffed under the metal bed springs. Next she searched all of Edward's coats and jackets that hung in the mahogany wardrobe. Her heart-beat quickened when she felt rustling paper in his green corduroy jacket, but when she reached inside Ruby found only an old train timetable.

'Bugger!' she murmured.

As she was working her way through Edward's sock drawer, she heard footsteps coming down the corridor that led to the bedroom. Ruby looked wildly about – why hadn't Raf warned her, as he had before? With her heart hammering in her ribcage, she crossed the room, slid the bolt on the door and threw herself down in front of the fireplace, where she busied herself raking out dead cinders. When Edward walked in, Ruby said in her cheery servant's voice 'Morning, Your Lordship.'

Completely ignoring her, Edward stepped over her feet in order to get to the desk. As he did so, Ruby's eye was drawn to a scrap of paper lying in the coal bucket. From where she crouched before the fireplace, it looked exactly like what

Bella had described: rows and rows of letter combinations. Glancing up, she saw Edward take a key from his pocket, which he used to unlock the roll-top desk, and as he did so Ruby quickly sprinkled a handful of cinders over the precious scrap of paper. After relocking the desk, Edward turned to find Ruby laying newspaper and kindling in the black cast-iron grate. Ignoring her still, he walked out, slamming the door behind him. Weak with relief, Ruby slumped forwards.

'Jesus!' she sighed.

She reached into the coal bucket and removed the scrap of paper, which she stuffed into the pocket of her lace pinafore. Before she got to her feet, she peered closely into the grate where she found the charred remains of sheets of cypher text; Edward had obviously thrown them into the fire to destroy them but, fortunately, a small piece had landed in the coal bucket. Checking the room was as it should be, Ruby picked up her mop and bucket and hurried down the back stairs, where she bumped into a frantic Raf.

'*Rubee!*' he yelled, as he flung his arms around her.

'You didn't warn me!' she cried.

'He leave, I see him go, he must come in round back,' Raf spluttered.

Ruby gave him a quick kiss. 'Don't worry, I'm fine,' she said with a wink. 'Let's go and get the Brig. It's urgent!'

When everyone had gathered, Ruby triumphantly laid the scrap of paper on the kitchen table.

'Is this what you're after?'

Bella's eyes grew big and bright with excitement. '*Yessss!*' she exclaimed. 'Where did you find it?'

'In the fire bucket. Himself must have thought he'd burnt it – lucky I spotted it before he did, eh?'

Bella was furiously scanning the cypher. 'It's yesterday's code!' she announced, and gave Ruby a grateful hug. 'Thank you, darling girl!'

Though pleased with her discovery, Ruby was worried. 'A scrap of paper's not much good without the code book,' she said bluntly.

Bella's happy smile faded. 'I know – I'm jumping the gun,' she admitted glumly.

'As far as I can tell, the only thing that's locked in his room is the roll-top desk. Speaks for itself, wouldn't you say?' Ruby asked her friends.

'And Edward's got the key?' Bella asked flatly.

'Don't send me back into the monster's den again!' Ruby pleaded. 'It'll give me a heart attack!'

Raf's blue eyes opened wide in shock. 'No, Rubee, enough you do, no more, I beg.'

The Brig nodded in agreement with him. 'Quite right, Raf. Ruby's stuck her neck out enough times. It's down to us now,' he said, and turned to Bella, who smiled slyly.

'Nobody can tell me off for wandering about my own house,' she said.

Seeing the glint in her eyes, the Brig said, 'What're you planning, young lady?'

'I'll get the key,' Bella announced, without the bat of an eyelid.

Ruby hooted with laughter. 'The key's in Edward's coat pocket, I saw him take it out from there.'

'I'll steal it, then put it back without him even knowing,' Bella replied, cool as a cucumber.

Ava shook her head and lit up a Woodbine. 'What'll you do, drug him or hit him on the head with a hammer?' she joked.

'Obviously, I'll have to put some thought into it,' Bella answered slowly. 'I'll need help, too, because if Edward finds me snooping in his desk, he'll kill me.'

'Just let the bastard try!' the Brig responded angrily.

Bella gnawed thoughtfully on her lower lip. 'I need to know Edward's exact movements.' Galvanized, she walked quickly to the door. 'Time to have a cuppa with Mummy!'

The Brig shook his head as his girlfriend blew him a kiss then skipped out of the kitchen.

'She's one in a million,' Ava said fondly.

The Brig's lovely brown eyes softened as he answered, with a proud ring in his voice, 'She's wonderful!'

27. The Key

'Darling!' her ladyship exclaimed, grimacing at the coconut-and-carrot buns Bella had brought along with her. 'Do you call this *cake*?'

'Don't be silly, Mummy, it's ration cake. It's the best we can do, given there's a war on and there's hardly any sugar to be had,' Bella snapped, then chided herself. The last thing she wanted to do was get her mother's back up; she'd come to winkle out information, not have a row.

'Oh, you're always so damned worthy, Annabelle,' her mother moaned, handling the lumpy bun as if it were a hand grenade about to go off.

Bella dug her nails into her palms to force herself not to get into an argument. 'How's Edward?'

Her mother shrugged and answered, 'He's been in Cambridge with that girl . . . what's her name?'

'Geraldine,' Bella replied, remembering Edward's sometime girlfriend. Keen to move the conversation forward, she pressed on with her questions.

'I wonder why he isn't back at work at the War Office?' she said, as she poured them both tea.

'He's going back soon,' her mother told her. 'Apparently, he has urgent business to see to here.'

'And I know exactly what that business is!' Bella thought to herself.

'What about you, dear?' her mother asked, taking the

305

delicate bone china teacup and saucer Bella handed her. 'Have you finished that ghastly communications course?'

Before Bella could answer her mother sighed and pushed aside her untouched cake. 'I wish you'd joined the WAAFs – *so* glamorous.'

'Working in communications is vital war work, Mummy.'

'I can just see you in a WAAF uniform,' her ladyship fantasized. 'In a roomful of – handsome, eligible men.'

'I already have an eligible man,' Bella answered sharply. 'Brigadier Charles Ryder – remember him?'

'Yes, twice your age and as dull as ditchwater!'

Before she totally lost her temper, Bella went on, 'I know how ashamed Edward is when he sees me wearing a servant's uniform,' she said, in all innocence. 'If I know his comings and goings when he's here, I can make sure I avoid him and save him the embarrassment.'

Her mother looked surprised. 'That's unusually thoughtful of you, dear,' she replied cryptically.

'Well, do you know what his plans are this week?' Bella asked bluntly.

'He's got business in Holt this morning, then he's home for lunch, and tonight he's out to dinner at the Hoste Arms in Burnham Market with Rodney Binge. He leaves for Cambridge tomorrow, then he's back to work in London,' she concluded.

Bella's mind was whirring. It would have to be tonight if Edward was leaving for Cambridge the next day. Pushing aside her chair, she took up the tea tray and made her farewells; she had a lot to do in the next few hours.

Below stairs, Bella worked out her plan with Ruby, Raf, Ava, Maudie and the Brig as they sat around the table drinking cups of hot strong tea. Ava and Ruby lit cigarettes and the Brig tensely puffed on his pipe.

'He's definitely having supper at the Hoste Arms in Burnham Market. I've just phoned, he's booked a table,' Bella informed them. 'I'll have to get the key off him before he leaves.'

'You can't go rooting through his coat while he's wearing it!' Ruby giggled. 'He'll think you're molesting him!'

'Let's assume you get the key,' the Brig pondered. 'You go to his room, open his desk, find the cypher book.'

'Crossing fingers!' Raf interrupted, and held his crossed fingers in the air.

'You can't walk out with it, and you won't have time to copy *all* the combinations before Edward gets back,' the Brig pointed out.

Undeterred, Bella smiled at Maudie, Ruby and Ava. 'Between the four of us we could copy the entire cypher book!' she announced.

Her loyal friends nodded.

'No problem!' Ava answered for them all.

'When we've finished copying it, I'll put the cypher text back and lock the desk and wait for Edward to return,' Bella concluded.

'Hopefully, he'll be rolling after five pints of the Hoste's strong beer,' Ruby said.

'And I slip the key back into his pocket before he collapses in bed,' Bella added, with a wide smile.

Raf rolled his eyes. 'God goes with you,' he said fervently.

That afternoon, everybody was on tenterhooks. Would Edward change his plans? If he did, they'd have to abandon Plan A, but nobody could think of a Plan B. After lunch, Bella heard a signal on her receiver and realized that Edward was transmitting a message – which, of course, she couldn't decipher.

'It makes me boil with rage,' she seethed to Maudie, who was sitting beside her, watching in total fascination as Bella operated the radio transmitter. 'To think he's up there!' she jabbed a finger towards the ceiling. 'Making contact with German Military Intelligence, and we can't break his damn code!'

Maudie turned to her friend, her eyes shining with barely suppressed excitement. 'Bella, I have a favour to ask,' she started. 'I want you to train me as a code girl.'

Bella did a double-take. 'Really?'

'Oh, yes, really!' Maudie laughed. 'I find the whole thing amazing, intriguing, mind-boggling, and hey, it's what I came here to do in the first place.'

'God! I'd love an assistant – but we've still got to cook for the trainees. We can't let Ruby and Ava down.'

'I'll make time,' Maudie vowed. 'I want this very much,' she added earnestly.

Smiling, Bella extended her hand. 'Deal!' she said, as they shook hands. 'Welcome to the world of espionage.'

They were all relieved when Edward's goofy, overweight chum finally arrived, just after seven in the evening.

'Your coat, sir,' Ruby said as she took the visitor's coat, then pointed him towards the stairs that led to the Walsinghams' suites.

'His friend's arrived!' she cried, dashing downstairs to announce the news to her anxious friends.

Bella smiled grimly. 'Now all we've got to do is wait till they go out.'

In between all the action, the girls, apart from Bella, were still on duty. As they prepared supper, Bella hovered close to the front door, while Raf watched the back door. When

Bella heard doors banging upstairs, she shrank back into the shadows and, holding her breath, she listened for footsteps on the grand staircase. When she didn't hear them, she knew Edward and his friend had taken the back way. Leaping to her feet, she bolted below stairs, where she found Ruby holding the back door wide open.

'*Go Go!*' she cried, ushering Bella outdoors.

Bella hurried into the yard, where she saw Edward with his friend.

'Edward!' she called.

Her brother frowned as his sister ran towards him in her black servant's uniform and white lace pinafore. 'How many times do I have to tell you that I don't want to see you when you're dressed as a grubby little maid?' he whispered angrily as she approached.

Bella feigned a smile and waved an envelope in the air. 'Sorry. I just wondered if you could post this for me,' she said, slipping the envelope into his coat pocket and at the same time wriggling around with her fingers to find the key.

'Why don't you post it your bloody self?' Edward barked.

'I can't, I'm working,' she replied. 'It's important,' she added, following him round to the driver's seat.

Before he could get in, Bella made a grab for the envelope now poking out of his pocket. 'It might be safer in here,' she said, and shoved the envelope deep inside his other pocket. Her searching fingers felt cold metal.

'Stop rummaging around in my bloody pockets, Anna-belle,' Edward cried, and pushed her aside.

Bella watched her odious brother drive away, then, smiling, she opened her hand and gazed at the precious key lying flat on her palm.

'To work!' she laughed, and ran back indoors.

Tom, Kit and Raf took up their lookout positions at strategic spots outside the hall. The Brig gave them precise instructions on what to do if Edward suddenly returned.

'Flash your torches three times in the direction of his bedroom. I'll be standing guard at the window.'

When Bella unlocked the roll-top desk she gasped at the sight before her. 'My God!' she cried.

For the benefit of the Brig, who stood on guard with his back towards her, Bella listed her findings: 'Two revolvers, a notebook written entirely in German, a German passport and German ID: Herr Heinrich Brun. Oh, my God . . .' Bella's voice trailed away in disbelief. For all her words about her brother's ruthlessness, nothing had prepared her for this: unassailable proof that Lord Edward Walsingham, her own flesh and blood, was, irrefutably, a German spy. Sick to her stomach, she studied the German passport with Edward's picture stamped on it. 'Herr Heinrich Brun,' she murmured. 'Deutsche Reich, Reisespass.'

'This will kill my parents,' she thought to herself.

The Brig's tense voice broke into her melancholy line of thought. 'The code book?'

Remembering the urgency of their mission, Bella answered quickly. 'Got it!' she said, as she lay the book down on the floor.

'We'll work in two teams,' she quickly told her friends. 'Me and Maudie, will take the right-hand pages, and Ruby and Ava, you take the left,' she instructed, as she flicked through the book. 'There are twenty-six pages – write as quickly and accurately as you can.'

They worked in total silence, copying the cypher text. The only sound to be heard was the sound of pencils scribbling on paper and Bella turning the pages. In less than an hour, the job was done.

'Let's get the code book back where it belongs,' said Bella, returned the book to the desk, and locked it. 'Done,' she told the Brig, still standing guard at the window.

'Go downstairs. I'll wait here till you're safely back in the kitchen,' he replied. 'Then I'll switch off the light so the chaps outside will know we've got what we want.'

Once safely below stairs, the girls were euphoric.

'We did it!' cried Maudie, who was flushed with nervous excitement.

'My heart was in my mouth,' Ruby confessed.

'I've got to have a fag!' Ava laughed, and lit up a cigarette. 'My hands were shaking all the time I was writing down the letter combinations.'

Bella laid the sheets in the right order on the kitchen table, then she clipped them together. When the Brig, Tom, Kit and Raf came dashing into the kitchen, Bella triumphantly flourished the copied booklet high in the air. The Brig, visibly relieved, smiled for the first time that evening.

'Now we can keep track of him,' he said.

'But, darling,' Bella pointed out, 'We have far more incriminating evidence than the cypher notebook. Edward has a false passport and a fake German identity. We must report him now,' she insisted.

The Brig nodded. 'Of course, I'll get in touch with Military Intelligence immediately, but they're not going to come marching down here and arrest him.'

'Why not?' Tom exclaimed.

'He's guilty as hell!' Kit cried.

'Nobody's arguing with that, old chap,' the Brig replied earnestly. 'I, for one, would love to see him banged up behind bars but, don't you see, it would blow his operational cover?'

Tom and the others gathered around the kitchen table still weren't convinced.

'It's too dangerous,' Tom insisted.

'I am a brigadier in the British army, and I know what Military Intelligence would say: see the mission through, find the nest, secure the spy ring,' said the Brig firmly. 'Kit and I have discussed this at length, and we both agree that the longer we can spy on Walsingham, the more information we'll get out of him. That's our mission.'

Looking uncomfortable, Tom shrugged. 'I take your point but it doesn't stop me from worrying about what we're planning to do.'

Further discussion was swept away by the girls' sudden rush of enthusiasm.

'I *definitely* want to help you,' Maudie announced.

'Me, too – if you'll teach me, as well' Ava added.

'Oh, God!' wailed poor Ruby. 'I'll be the only cook left in the kitchen!'

'Don't worry. We won't abandon you, lovie,' Avie assured her alarmed friend.

Bella smiled excitedly. 'With all of you helping, we could organize a twenty-four-hour rota.'

'Good idea!' said the Brig. 'Around-the-clock surveillance.'

'Are you in?' Bella asked her friends.

Ava and Maudie answered together: '*Yes!*'

Ruby shook her head. 'It's not that I'm unpatriotic,' she said apologetically. 'It's just that I'm really too daft to be a code girl. I wouldn't be able to get my head round all those rows of letters, day in and day out. I'd go bonkers!' she giggled. 'I'll be the code girls' comforter!' she said. 'I'll supply the brews and sandwiches, and fags, too!'

The Brig picked up the copied notebook.

'OK, let's start cracking Edward's last message!'

'I'll wait upstairs for Edward,' said Bella, as she headed towards the door.

The Brig followed her into the kitchen corridor. 'What exactly are you planning to do, darling,' he asked anxiously.

Bella smiled mischievously. 'I'll give my brother a bedtime kiss,' she giggled. 'Hopefully, he'll be so shocked by my rare show of affection, he won't even notice me dropping the key back into his pocket.'

In the days that followed, sitting in front of the transmitter in the sewing room, Bella and the Brig took it in turns to teach Ava and Maudie how to be code girls. They showed them how to pick up the date and the algorithm for the day, then how to match up the letters to the enemy's code.

'It's time-consuming – not for the impatient,' Bella joked.

Ava and Maudie were both enthralled and challenged by the complicated mechanics of decrypting.

'I love it!' Maudie enthused. 'It's like a really tough crossword – you have to find a letter or two, then everything else falls into place.'

'If you're lucky,' groaned Ava, who was struggling with her first cypher.

Even with a copy of the notebook, it took a lot of hours and patience to match the coded letters with Edward's encrypted messages. It certainly speeded things up having Maudie and Ava working alongside them, and Ruby kept her word, appearing at intervals during the day and in the middle of the night, too, with hot tea, cocoa or Bovril on buttered toast.

'Got to keep the troops happy!' she joked, as she shared around the refreshments.

It was Bella, one early dawn morning, who cracked the first message. She woke the Brig, who was having a nap in the library.

'Brig! Brig!' she whispered urgently, as she shook him awake. 'Look!'

The Brig struggled to sit up, then, rubbing his eyes, he stared at Bella's decryption.

'Jesus God!' he gasped.

'It's from Berlin again!' she exclaimed. 'Based on the information Heinrich has passed on to them – Heinrich Brun is the name on Edward's German passport – action will follow. He must have told them about the Lancasters at Holkham airbase, as they requested.'

'I'll drive over and tell Kit right away,' the Brig said, standing up and stretching himself awake. 'Are you all right to carry on, darling?' he asked, as he drew a tired Bella into his comforting arms. Laying her face against the Brig's chest, Bella inhaled the rich smell of his tweedy jacket, which always comforted her. 'I could sleep right here,' she sighed.

Tilting her face up to his, the Brig kissed her pink lips. 'Maudie will relieve you soon,' he said softly.

Bella nodded as she withdrew from the warmth of his embrace. 'And Ruby generally turns up with a brew just after dawn! Off you go,' she said briskly, as she set off for the sewing room. 'Come back soon!'

Everybody was on high alert, both at the hall and at the airbase, where Kit had extra guards and lookouts posted around the clock. What Kit most longed to do was strangle

Edward, who he hated with a vengeance; not only had he twice molested his beloved Maudie, but he had also had the audacity to threaten his precious Lancasters. Kit kept his emotions under wraps, though; he was professional enough to accept the Brig's decision, which was to continue to monitor Walsingham in order to get to the nest and break the spy ring. There would be time enough after that to have it out with him.

Over the next few days, the messages coming in for Heinrich Brun became more frequent.

'It's all a bit boring,' Bella said, reading her decryptions to the Brig. 'It's mostly stuff like this,' she said, and quoted. 'Good clear spring weather. Little activity. Await orders.'

'It's anything but boring,' the Brig retorted sharply. 'The subtext is the weather's fine for a bombing raid but no decision has been made so far – they're biding their time until they get further information.'

'Oh, dear!' Bella said guiltily. 'I never even thought of it that way.'

Looking stressed, the Brig said urgently, 'We must send Maudie to the airbase immediately – she needs to deliver a letter to Kit.'

Happy to be relieved of supper duty, Maudie hopped on to her bike. It was the most perfect spring evening, with a new silver moon, the size of a baby's fingernail, hanging in the clear, bright sky while, all around, in the hedgerows and treetops, birds sang their final songs of the day. A rush of guilt filled Maudie as she sped along the estate track, the Brig's letter firmly tucked into her cleavage. It seemed wrong to be happy when so many weren't; she thought about the thousands of Red Army soldiers slaughtered by the German army in the Ukraine, of the young British soldiers fighting in the deserts of Africa and the Allies steadfastly marching on Italy. Happiness seemed inappropriate, too, when her mission was to deliver a message that could have a huge impact on the man she loved and on his brave squadron.

When she got to the airbase, Kit hugged her tightly. 'Darling! To what do I owe this pleasure?'

Looking serious, Maudie extricated the letter from her bosom. 'An urgent update from the Brig.'

Kit's face grew grim as he scanned the message. 'Looks like Jerry's planning another hit.' Anger blazed in his eyes. 'God! I won't let them destroy my Lancasters again.'

Seeing his thunderous expression, Maudie said soothingly, 'At least you're one step ahead of the Germans; this time. You have an idea what they're planning.'

'What Jerry doesn't know is that we're planning a bombing raid, too. We've been working on a strategy to outfox the bastards. We can't just sit around here waiting for Jerry's plans to unfold.' Pulling her close, he murmured, 'We've got to act, darling – we can't be sitting ducks all over again.'

Ava realized she was starting to shake. Would she ever get used to the terror that gripped her every time Kit talked of going on a raid? Seeing her turn pale, Kit kissed her tenderly. Comforted, Maudie smiled and traced the thick blond stubble on his chin.

'You need a shave,' she said. 'Come back to the hall with me, have a bath and a good meal.'

'Don't tempt me, you green-eyed witch,' Kit murmured.

Maudie slumped in disappointment. 'These snatched moments just aren't enough!' she cried.

'Then stay, my love. We can turn off the light and lie on the floor and make love . . . ?' he added in a soft, seductive whisper.

'Kit!' she yelped in shock.

He buried his face in her rich golden-red hair. 'I want you so much . . .' he whispered, his lips moving down her neck and lingering between her breasts.'

Groaning with desire, Maudie felt herself go limp. 'Yes . . .' she murmured, and reached to unbutton his jacket.

Kissing, they started to undress each other then, just as they were down to their underwear, the door swung open and Raf walked in. Seeing them entwined, he blushed to the roots of his pale hair.

'Whoops, buggers!' he blustered, and slammed the door shut.

'Christ! That was close,' Kit laughed.

Looking shocked, Maudie stood before him, tall and slender in her silk cami-knickers and bra.

'What was I thinking of?' she cried, grabbing her dress and pulling it over her head.

'Sweetheart, it's not wrong,' Kit said, helping her to fasten the buttons at the back of her dress. 'Making love is natural – it's beautiful. Please don't be embarrassed.'

'I'm not embarrassed, Kit,' she declared. 'I'm just shocked that I could forget everything but you and how much I want you.'

Kit rocked her gently in his arms. 'It won't always be like this.'

Pressed against his cotton vest, Maudie began to giggle. 'For God's sake, put your trousers on before Raf comes waltzing in again!'

28. Bomber Moon

Holkam airbase was on high alert, with guards and lookouts posted everywhere. Security was heightened, and anybody going in and out of the base was searched and their passes scrutinized. As Kit worked on his imminent top-secret operation, the Walsingham code girls, Bella, Ava and Maudie, continued their secret surveillance in the sewing room. One particular decryption nearly gave Bella a heart attack.

'Oh, my God!' she gasped, when she'd matched up the letters to Edward's cypher. 'Get the Brig!

The message contained explicit information about Kit's squadron's next bombing raid.

'How the hell do they know this?' the Brig growled, as he read Bella's decrypted message.

'*How?*' Bella almost shouted. 'My bloody treacherous brother, of course!'

'But this is top secret!' the Brig pointed out. 'Only Kit and Intelligence are privy to this information.' He shook his head in disbelief. 'Walsingham must have a mole working for him, or he's tapped all the blasted phone lines at the airbase.'

Having been informed of Edward's latest activities, Kit arrived at the hall ten minutes later. Waiting tensely for him in the kitchen were the Brig, Bella, Ruby, Maudie and Ava.

'So Jerry knows our plans?' Kit said, as he lit up a Capstan.

'Everything, thanks to Walsingham,' the Brig replied.

Kit lowered his voice to the merest whisper. 'But

Walsingham doesn't know what *I* know,' Kit said, wagging a finger in the air. '*Two* vital pieces of information. He doesn't know the time and date of the raid, because I've just changed them to outwit the filthy traitor! Nobody will know anything until we take to the air – not even the ground crew, damn it! We'll take the bastards by surprise this time!'

The Brig didn't look convinced. 'But the minute you take off, Walsingham will know,' he pointed out. 'It'll take him five minutes to alert his source, and you'll be picked off over the North Sea!'

'True. Then we have to think of a way of preventing that happening,' Kit cried in total frustration. 'Think of a way of stopping the swine from leaking information.'

All eyes turned to the Brig. 'There is a way – jamming,' he said slowly. 'I'd have to check with Military Intelligence, of course, but if we could jam his radio frequency his transmission wouldn't get through.'

'How do you do that?' Bella asked.

'Broadcast a signal that interferes with his original signal,' the Brig explained.

'But wouldn't he suspect something was going on?' Bella asked.

The Brig shook his head. 'The jamming happens at the other end. Berlin would get a lot of interference and assume it's just a bad signal. Walsingham wouldn't have interference his end, so he wouldn't be any the wiser.'

'Could you jam his transmitter long enough for us to fly out?' Kit enquired excitedly.

'Yes,' the Brig replied. 'There are risks attached, of course – Berlin or Edward might change their signal in order to get round the problem of interference – but it takes time to do that.'

Kit lit another Capstan. 'It's a risk we've got to take. We can't go on like this, stymied at every turn.'

'I'll have to seek approval from my superiors, as I say,' the Brig responded. 'If they give us the green light, we can get on to it right away.'

Before Kit left, he and Maudie had a private five minutes in the courtyard, where Kit had left his MG. Putting his arms around her shoulders, Kit lay his tanned face against the gentle swell of Maudie's breasts.

'Remember *our* motto, darling?' he asked.

Tears rolled down Maudie's cheeks, as she whispered, 'To the stars . . . and back – please God,' she prayed.

After Kit had driven away, Maudie, red-eyed, joined Bella and the Brig in the sewing room, where the Brig was in communication with headquarters.

'There's no way Kit's squadron can take off until we've cleared this,' Bella assured her friend, who was choked with emotion. 'We have to do everything we can to protect them,' she added earnestly.

Maudie nodded. 'I know,' she said, with a gulp.

'Go and get some tea,' Bella said, patting her hand. 'And bring us some, too,' she added with a tired smile.

In the kitchen, Maudie made tea, which she delivered to Bella and the Brig, then she fastened a pinafore around her waist.

'What do you think you're doing?' Ava asked in astonishment. 'It's half past eleven at night!'

'I know I won't sleep, so I'm going to cook,' Maudie announced. 'What's tomorrow?'

Ruby and Ava looked blankly at each other.

'Wednesday,' Ava answered after a moment.

Maudie rolled up her sleeves. 'Stuffed cabbage and stewed

apple and cinnamon– that should keep me busy for a couple of hours!'

The Brig was given clearance to jam Edward's transmitter, but only he, Kit and Military Intelligence at the War Office knew the exact time and date the jamming would take place. It was only when they heard the Lancasters flying out at eleven o'clock the following night that everybody else knew that, at that precise moment, the Brig was jamming Edward's transmitter. In a blink, Maudie was outside, running in the dark so she could stand on the lawn and watch the Lancasters pass over. The others ran out after her. The noise of their twin engines was like a low growl as they climbed higher and higher into the sky, which was illuminated by a shimmering full moon.

'Look!' cried Ruby. 'A bombers' moon to light them on their way.'

Ruby counted the Lancasters, which looked like shiny black silhouettes flying across the silver face of the moon.

'One, two, three, four, five, six, seven, eight, nine, ten, eleven, twelve!' she yelled. 'God speed, bomber boys!'

'God speed, my love,' Maudie whispered.

Ruby and Ava, on either side of Maudie, squeezed her hands tightly. Nobody spoke: there were no words left to say – from this point on, they were all in God's hands. A heavy silence hung in the air as the sound of the bombers' engines faded away.

They slowly walked back to the hall, where, in the kitchen, they put the kettle on and tried, half-heartedly, to concentrate on the getting the trainees' breakfast prepared. When Bella took the Brig a cup of tea, she found him white-faced. His headset on, he was frantically trying to get a signal.

'Edward's rumbled something,' he muttered frantically. 'When he got no response from German Military Intelligence, he changed the frequency. I've been trying to jam him, but he keeps moving on to another one. God!' he said in anguish. 'I don't know how much longer I can stall him.'

Standing holding the cooling cup of tea, Bella felt faint with terror. 'We've got to stop him getting a message through, or Kit and his men will be flying into a trap.'

The Brig checked his watch. 'If he manages to alert Berlin, the Luftwaffe will try to intercept Kit's Lancasters and there will be a shoot-out over Germany.'

'Oh, God!' Bella gasped. 'What can we do?'

The Brig put his head in his hands. 'What have I done?' he cried in despair. 'I sent those poor chaps off thinking they were safe for at least a few hours.' He sprang to his feet. 'We can't play cat and mouse a moment longer,' he declared, and headed for the door. 'I'm going to stop the bastard right now!'

Bella chased after the Brig, who ran up the back stairs two at a time. When he reached Edward's bedroom, he pressed his shoulder against the door, expecting to have to break it down, but the door swung open.

'Christ! He's gone,' the Brig cried, as they surveyed the empty room.

Bella's heart sank. 'He's fled the nest!' she gasped. 'He must have realized someon was on to him.'

Filled with dread and foreboding, Maudie lay wide-eyed all night. When the birds began their dawn chorus, she slipped out of bed, pulled a coat over her nightdress and went into the garden, where she listened intently for the sound of returning aircraft. The second she heard them, her stomach lurched; the roar of their combined engines was not as loud as when they had flown out, which could only mean one thing: there were fewer planes returning to base than had left. When they burst into her line of vision, flying low over the pine woods, then swooping past the hall, Maudie counted the planes home.

'One . . . two . . . three . . . four . . . five – only five.'

That meant seven had not come back. Slumping against one of the ancient Walsingham oak trees for support, Maudie closed her eyes and prayed that Kit's Lancaster was not one of them.

'Please God, let Kit be alive. Please, save him.'

Racked with guilt that she wanted somebody else to die in preference to her beloved, a huge sob ripped through her body.

'Oh, when will this killing stop?'

When Bella woke to find her friend's bed empty, she pulled her dressing gown around her and hurried out into the garden, where she found Maudie lying on the ground, damp with morning dew.

'Darling!' she cried, holding her tightly in her arms.

Shivering with cold and fear, Maudie struggled to her feet. 'Only five came back,' she murmured.

Seeing her friend traumatized with shock, Bella gently led her towards the hall.

'Come on, you need to get warm,' she said, but before they even reached the front door they saw an RAF jeep come swinging into the drive. Almost hysterical, Maudie ran towards it and frantically flagged it down. Raf, in the driver's seat, drew to a sharp stop. Before he even said a word, Maudie knew from the harrowing sadness in his blue eyes that the news was bad. Gripping Bella's hand, she waited. Choking back tears, Raf blurted out, 'Captain Kit and crew, shot down over Germany!' Unable to hold back his grief, Raf wept uncontrollably.

Maudie swayed, then, with a high-pitched wail of agony, she fell to the ground in a dead faint.

As Bella and Ava comforted Maudie in her bedroom, Ruby, below stairs, took her heartbroken husband's trembling hands in hers. 'Captain Kit might be safe,' she whispered. 'He could have bailed out.'

Raf wearily shook his head. 'I think no, Rubee,' he answered. 'Other crews sees Captain Kit's plane shot bad by bastard Jerries, on fire it hit ground. *Boom!* Big explosion. Nobody bail out.'

'Sweet Jesus,' Ruby murmured, and lit a Woodbine, which she inhaled deeply. 'Seven Lancasters, forty-nine airmen . . . all gone.'

Ruby put her arms around her husband's heaving shoulders. 'Sweetheart, sweetheart.'

'I miss Captain Kit already,' he wept, pressing his face against her soft, warm breasts.

As Ruby stroked her husband's soft, blond hair, her thoughts flew to Maudie. How would the poor girl ever recover? How could a woman so in love survive such a tragic loss?

Upstairs, Bella sat beside the Brig, who was inconsolable.

'How did we get it so wrong?' he cried, his head in his hands. 'I sent those brave boys out there with hope in their hearts. For Christ's sake, I was supposed to be protecting them!'

Fighting back tears, Bella laid an arm around his shoulders. 'Darling, you did everything you could possibly do.' She gave a long, shuddering sigh and added, 'But Edward outsmarted us.'

*

There could be no funerals, as there were no bodies, but forty-nine airmen fighting for their country were missing, presumed dead, fallen from the skies over Germany, and their number included Kit. A commemoration service was held at the church of Our Lady of Walsingham, and on a warm spring day, with bluebells and primroses brimming in the hedgerows and birds singing rapturously in the treetops, a sad procession of mourners dressed in black – friends, colleagues and families of the lost airmen – made their way into the candlelit church, which was fragrant with narcissi and hyacinths. At the end of the service, which was loud with the sound of weeping relatives, a young airman in RAF uniform stepped into the pulpit and read a piece from Shakespeare's *The Tempest*.

> 'These our actors,
> As I foretold you, were all spirits and
> Are melted into air, into thin air:
> And, like the baseless fabric of this vision,
> The cloud-capp'd towers, the gorgeous palaces,
> The solemn temples, the great globe itself,
> Yea all which it inherit, shall dissolve
> And, like this insubstantial pageant faded,
> Leave not a rack behind. We are such stuff
> As dreams are made on, and our little life
> Is rounded with a sleep.'

Heartbroken, Maudie was strangely comforted by the words; she felt that, from now on, her life would be rounded with a sleep, because, without Kit, there was nothing for her to wake up for.

*

Nearly four hundred miles away, in an old barn in Bremen, Kit lay unconscious on a hay bale that was dirty with his own blood. Charlie, his navigator, a gaping gash across his forehead, sat staring at his superior officer as he puffed on a cigarette. The farmer, who had rescued them from a ditch, was being harangued by his furious wife, 'Get the swine out of here!' she cried, in guttural German. 'The Gestapo will have our guts for garters. We will be shot, tortured!'

'But this one,' the kind-hearted farmer protested, 'he is not conscious.'

His wife threw a bucket of dirty water in Kit's face. 'He is now!'

Kit came round and groaned in pain. 'Oh, God,' he moaned, clutching his head. 'Where am I?'

Charlie rose and stood before him. 'In the north of bleeding Germany, sir.'

'What happened to the others?' Kit demanded frantically. 'We were all going down together!'

'Jerry pumped us with bullets, blew out a chunk of the fuselage,' Charlie reminded him. 'We bailed out through the bloody hole.'

Kit shook his head in confusion.

'It didn't help that you hit a tree when we landed,' Charlie added.

The farmer's wife stopped their conversation by throwing open the barn door. 'Out!' she yelled. 'Go on, go!'

Charlie helped Kit to his feet. 'Come on, mate, lean on me,' he said, as he hauled Kit towards the door.

Concussed and hardly able to see straight, Kit moaned in pain, as he was half dragged outside.

'*Gute Nacht und viel Glück!*' the farmer said, and closed the door firmly behind them.

'Good night, and good luck to you!' Charlie snarled, giving the closed door the V sign.

Hearing the buzzing noise of an approaching motorbike, Charlie threw Kit into a nearby bush, then promptly hid behind it himself. A light blazed across the path as a German soldier flashed by, then all was darkness again. Kit groaned as he struggled to get out of the bush.

'What're we going to do?' he gasped.

'Stay under cover of darkness, and hope we can make our way to a safe house,' Charlie replied, with a confidence he certainly didn't feel. How in God's name was he going to get a wounded, semi-conscious man in RAF uniform to a safe house? As if sensing Charlie's fear, Kit staggered to his feet.

'Let's get moving,' he said feebly, and moved forward into the night.

Charlie shook his head; nobody could ever deny that Squadron Leader Kit Halliday had balls!

29. Interception

Although, with the Allied bombing of Rome, hopes of victory were high across the nation, Maudie's spirits could not be lifted. Her charm, wit, laughter, humour and passion for life dried up like water in the heat; her pale, delicate face was grey and drained and her wonderful eyes were blank and depressed. Her appetite flagged so much she looked like a bag of bones, but the one thing that remained unshakeable was her sheer determination to work. Nowadays, she worked longer hours than anybody. Because she couldn't sleep she often got up in the middle of the night to start her working day.

'Lovie, you'll drop dead in your tracks if you carry on like this,' Ava fretted.

'As if I care!' Maudie answered bitterly.

Though Edward had vanished into thin air, the girls still kept a vigilant rota by the radio transmitter.

'He might not be upstairs, but we can still pick up his messages,' the Brig said to Bella, as they sat side by side in the sewing room one night. 'My hunch is he's gone to ground as he waits for collaborators to organize his escape from England.'

'Why would he stay here when he could be partying with his pals, the evil Nazis in Berlin!' Bella seethed. 'How can he live with himself? To think he willfully conspired in a plan that would end the lives of so many of his fellow countrymen. What is wrong with him, Brig? How did he become such a monster?'

The Brig shrugged. 'Who knows what tosh was poured into him when he was groomed as a spy in Cambridge.'

'Is that where you think he crossed over?' she whispered.

'For sure,' the Brig replied forcefully.

'If he escapes to Germany, we'll lose everything,' Bella continued in a rage. 'All his contacts and their plans – everything we've worked for will go with Edward.'

'Which is why we have to stay vigilant, keep tabs on him as long as he remains in the country. And keep listening into his messages in case he gives anything away about his location. Have your parents said anything about him?' he asked.

'They think he's gone back to his desk job at the War Office. God! If they knew only half the truth about their son and heir they'd die of shock.'

'The less they know, the better. We don't want them getting in our way,' the Brig advised.

The daily rhythm of cooking, serving, cleaning, followed by more cooking, serving and cleaning, kept Maudie going through the long, long weeks when her broken heart yearned for the man who had promised he would come back.

'I'm worried she'll kill herself,' Ruby confessed. 'I don't mean top herself, but drop dead from sheer exhaustion.'

'It's upsetting watching her working herself into a state of oblivion,' Bella said anxiously. 'But in some weird way, it keeps her going.'

Their only contact these days with Holkham was Raf. The RAF base, badly depleted by frequent losses, was awaiting replacement Lancasters.

'Until they arrive we're in a very vulnerable position,' the Brig told Bella in private.

Raf arrived one morning with good news. 'Twenty planes due any day now,' he announced triumphantly. 'We don't give up, we keep hitting Jerry for Captain Kit,' he said, as tears filled his eyes.

'Poor bloody pilots, flying to their doom,' a bitter Maudie muttered, and walked angrily out of the room.

At around midsummer, just after the RAF had led a successful bombing raid on Hamburg, there was a sudden flurry of radio messages from Edward Walsingham.

'He's back!' Bella told the Brig, and gave him the thumbs-up sign. 'Please God, let my foul brother still be using the same code book, otherwise we're buggered all over again!'

'He probably will be. It takes time to set up a new cypher,' the Brig replied.

With a fiery gleam in her pale blue eyes, Bella stared at the Brig. 'He may be my brother, but I'll do *whatever* it takes to stop him killing any more innocent men.'

The Brig took her troubled face in his hands. 'I know you will, my love,' he said proudly.

Luckily, it seemed Edward had stuck with same code book the girls had secretly copied in his room, so Bella was immediately back in business.

One uneventful night, as Bella and the Brig were manning the radio transmitter in the sewing room, Maudie walked in with two mugs of cocoa.

'I want to work with you again,' she announced.

'No, Maudie,' the Brig said firmly. 'You need to rest and get your strength back.'

Maudie's green eyes flashed angrily. 'I want to bring Edward Walsingham down. He killed my Kit and forty-eight other men, and he's walked away scot-free. He *must* be brought to justice.'

Seeing the steely determination on Maudie's face, Bella winked at the Brig. 'She's not going to take no for an answer,' she said with a knowing smile.

The Brig smiled and relented. 'Well . . . if you insist.'

Maudie laughed for the first time in months. 'When do I start?' she asked eagerly.

'We'll get cracking first thing in the morning!' Bella replied.

The Brig looked relieved. 'Actually, an extra pair of hands right now will be a godsend,' he confessed. 'I've been feeling guilty about neglecting Miss Cox and the trainees.'

'You and your fancy woman!' Bella teased.

'And *you*, madam, can spend more time in the kitchen,' the Brig said.

'A woman's place is *not* always in the kitchen!' Bella briskly reminded him.

'My sentiments entirely,' the Brig agreed, 'but it's the only way we'll get a decent game pie in these parts!'

The next morning, before breakfast was served, Maudie joined Bella in the sewing room.

'Remember this?' Bella asked, waving the copied notebook in the air.

'How could I forget?' Maudie replied. 'I nearly had a heart attack copying it out!'

Over the next few days, Maudie's determination to bring Edward to justice spurred her on to such an extent she begged to do more hours.

'Pleeeeease,' she implored. 'It's not like I sleep these days. I just lie awake thinking of my Kit and cry all night long. Spying on Walsingham is much more productive!'

Bella and the Brig, grateful for a few hours' extra sleep, handed the night shift over to her.

'Ava will be annoyed with us for luring you out of the kitchen,' Bella said anxiously.

'I discussed my decision with Ava,' Maudie told her friend. 'She understands why I have to do this.' She gave a cheeky wink. 'In fact, she's a bit envious that I'm a part-time code girl and she's still stuck in the kitchen.'

'If you were all in here spying there wouldn't be any food for the trainees, and then there'd be a riot!' chuckled the Brig.

Maudie's excitement and drive paid off. A few days later, in the middle of the night, she intercepted a message from Edward that literally took her breath away. She ran into the bedroom she shared with Bella and shook her awake.

'Bella! Bella! Listen to this!'

Bella struggled to sit up. Rubbing her eyes, she mumbled, 'Go on, read it.'

'Meet Walsingham at the hut 2100 hours Thursday 21st.'

'The twenty-first!' Bella cried as she shot out of bed. 'That's tomorrow – today – tonight!' she gabbled.

Over an early breakfast in the kitchen, the Brig and the girls discussed which hut Edward might use for his clandestine rendezvous.

'It would be a disaster if we messed up by going to the wrong one,' Maudie sad anxiously.

The Brig fondly surveyed the brave girls he'd grown to love and depend on over the last couple of years.

'This could be our last chance to get Edward before he escapes to Germany –it has *got* to work,' he told them tensely.

'Then we must hedge our bets and cover *all* the huts we can think of,' Bella said firmly.

'Shouldn't we bring in the local police?' Maudie asked tensely. 'This could be too big for us to handle.'

All eyes turned to the Brig, who drummed his fingers edgily on the kitchen table. 'I am obliged to inform the police of the orders Kit and I received from Military Intelligence,' he answered quietly. 'The police, in fact, agree with me; if we have dozens of bobbies running around the place, giving the game away, Walsingham will immediately do a runner, and then we lose *everything*. How do you break the spy ring if the spy has gone?'

Maudie nodded and said, 'It's still a big risk.'

'It's a risk we've *got* to take,' Bella said staunchly.

Taking a deep, uneasy breath, the Brig returned to the subject in hand – the huts.

Ruby immediately suggested the beach hut in Holkham Woods. 'It's where the Walsinghams used to host their boozy beach parties before the war. The King and Queen were there one year,' she recalled.

Bella, who knew the estate better than anybody, listed some other possible venues. 'There's the lake hut, where we keep the rowing boats, and the gardener's hut, which is Peter's domain.'

'Any others?' asked the Brig.

'There are loads on the airfield,' Ruby replied. 'It would be impossible to patrol all of them, but Raf could alert his new superior officer and he could post extra security guards around them.'

'Good thinking, Ruby. Can you see to that?' asked the Brig.

'OK' he continued. 'We've got the beach hut, lake hut and gardener's hut. 'Any more?'

'One!' Ava cried. 'I've just remembered there's a hut in the paddock behind the stables. I'll check that.'

'Perhaps you should do the garden hut, darling. You know the area well,' the Brig suggested to Bella.

'I'll cover the beach hut,' said Maudie. 'I've walked that way lots of times.'

'That leaves me with the lake hut,' said the Brig.

'What should I do?' Ruby asked.

'Somebody's got to be in the house to pick up calls or pass on messages,' the Brig replied. Surveying the girls' tense faces, he added, 'He'll be armed. Take *no* chances.'

Later that day, he stayed glued to the transmitter while Maudie and Bella helped Ava and Ruby serve supper and clear away before changing into dark clothes and going their separate ways.

'Wish me luck!' Maudie said, and cycled off down the drive.

Ruby anxiously lit up a cigarette as she watched her dear friends disappear into the darkness.

'Oh, God,' she sighed. 'I've got a bad feeling about this.'

As Maudie cycled down Lady Anne's Drive, she could hear the wind soughing through the pine woods and, in the distance, she could hear waves breaking on the beach. Concealing her bike in some bushes, she made her way on foot through the dense forest, walking quickly along soft sandy trails which led in and out of the sand dunes. She knew the beach hut was set on a rise within a ring of stout pines that protected it from the harsh winter winds; in daylight, it was a good two-mile walk but, in the dark, tripping over rabbit holes and gnarled tree roots, she felt like she'd been stumbling around for hours. Shining the tiniest light from her torch, she checked her wristwatch. It was gone nine – God! What if she'd already missed Edward? Quickening her pace, she crept on, then stopped dead in her tracks as she heard a deep voice carried on the breeze. It was unquestionably Edward, she'd know his voice anywhere. Threading her way between tree trunks, she peeped out and saw a light glimmering up ahead. Taking a deep breath to control her ragged breathing, Maudie darted towards the light, a torch set down in the beach hut. Bending almost double so as not to be seen, she crept to the back of the building, where she crouched with her ear pressed to the clapperboard wall. The urgent three-way conversation was in German and English, and Edward was doing most of the talking.

'You need to arrange for me to disappear. I should have left immediately after the Holkham air raid, but Berlin screwed up,' he complained.

'Berlin are working on it,' one of the men answered.

'Working on it isn't bloody good enough!' Edward barked. 'For Christ's sake, I've been in hiding for a long time. I need to get out *now*!'

Maudie jumped as she heard a grunting noise that sounded like an angry Edward was physically threatening one of the men. 'I'll give you twenty-four hours, max. Do as I bloody well say, or I'll blow your cover.'

Grumbling, the men dispersed in opposite directions.

Left alone in total darkness, Maudie realized that she was trembling all over. Slumped against the back of the hut, she stayed a good half-hour, listening out for the sound of returning footsteps. When she thought the coast was clear, she hurried back through the woods. Clinging to the dark shadows of the tree trunks, she darted from one to the other till she reached the entrance to the drive, where, to her horror she found Edward waiting for her. Maudie cast about, frantic. Should she run back into the woods or jump into a nearby ditch?

As if reading her thoughts, Edward called out 'Don't even think about it.' As he walked towards her, he gave a harsh laugh. 'Shouldn't have left your bike in the bushes, little servant girl – bit of a giveaway,' he added, and grabbed her arm, twisting it behind her back. 'Can't leave me alone, eh, hot little vixen?' he whispered thickly in her ear.

'Don't flatter yourself,' she snapped.

'We'll leave our intimate chat till later,' he replied. He gagged her with his scarf, then dragged her by the hair back into the woods.

Though absolutely terrified, Maudie could have kicked herself. Her bike must have been poking out of the bushes – why hadn't she been more careful? But for the bike, she would be back at the hall, telling her friends what Edward was planning to do. Instead, she was his gagged prisoner, and being dragged deeper and deeper into the dark Holkham woods.

'God help me,' she sobbed behind the stifling gag.

A vision of Kit floated into her mind. What had her darling suffered before his Lancaster plummeted to earth, a burning ball of flames? He would have been unquestionably brave and so would she.

Bella was home safe and sound by eleven.

'Nothing to report,' she told Ruby, who was waiting tensely for the girls and the Brig to return.

Ava was next back. 'Nothing, apart from the Shetland pony nearly kicked the stable door down when I didn't go in to feed her!' she said.

The Brig got back before midnight. Looking quickly around the room, he asked, 'Where's Maudie?'

When it came to 3 a.m. and Maudie was still not back, everybody knew that something had gone wrong. A loud shout from Bella in the sewing room made them all jump sky-high.

'Walsingham's active – he's transmitting.'

Before dawn, they were joined by Tom and Raf. They split into pairs and set off at first light. Ava and Tom scoured every inch of the pine woods on horseback; Ruby and Raf drove the RAF jeep along the wide, sweeping beach from Wells to beyond Brancaster Staithe; Bella and the Brig combed the estate. The first place Tom and Ava searched was the beach hut, where they found no evidence of recent use. As they cantered back through the woods, though, Ava saw something green and shiny fluttering in a thorn bush.

'It's Maudie's scarf!' she cried, as she dismounted and snatched it up. Holding it to her face, she added with a catch in her voice, 'It smells of her favourite perfume, lily of the valley.'

Dismounting, too, Tom walked up and down the track, looking for further clues.

'Where is she?' Ava cried in anguish. 'What's happened to her?'

Not twenty feet away, in an old hide used for stalking deer and wildfowl, Maudie struggled and moaned as she lay gagged and trussed hand and foot on the floor.

'One word and I'll shoot,' Edward hissed in her ear.

Maudie sobbed in despair as the sound of Tom and Ava's voices receded; they'd been *so* close, but now they were leaving. Her only chance of escape had slipped away. As she rolled in despair on the damp earth floor, Edward leered, and ran his chubby hands up her bare thighs. Maudie gritted her teeth. He'd had all night to rape her, if he'd chosen to, would he do it now? Maudie sighed with relief as his radio transmitter bleeped into life, causing Edward to abandon his preoccupation with his hostage. She watched him with eyes as wary as a nervous hawk.

'Little do you realize, you heartless brute,' she thought to herself, 'that back at the home of your stately ancestors, your sister, my best friend, will be decrypting your goddamn cypher.'

Bella was indeed busy at work. That afternoon, she decoded two vital pieces of information; Maudie was Edward's prisoner, and he was planning his escape that very night.

'He'll be picked up by a getaway boat on Holkham beach at 2200 hours,' she told the group gathered tensely around the transmitter in the sewing room. 'He ceased communicating about an hour ago,' she concluded.

'Well, what are we waiting for?' Ruby cried. 'Let's go and rescue Maudie!'

30. Hostage

With icy calm, the Brig rallied everybody who could fire a gun: Peter, Tom, Raf and himself. They planned to wait until nightfall, then, wearing dark clothes, and with hands and faces blacked up, they would creep into the woods, where they hoped they'd be able to see where the rescue boat would land. They had agreed that each couple would cut through the woods at different points so that they could cover the mile-long stretch of sand dunes that gave on to the sea.

'I feel so frightened,' Bella admitted to the Brig. 'We're taking such a huge risk.'

The Brig held her close to his chest. 'Me, too, darling . . .' he said with a heavy sigh. 'Me, too.'

Meanwhile, Maudie, still gagged, had been dragged, struggling and groaning, out of the hide. Cursing and swearing, Edward pushed and shoved her along a track that led to one of the many block-houses that had been built to house gunners in case of a Nazi invasion from the sea. Smoking cigarettes, Edward and his collaborators, who had rejoined him, peered through the slitted holes in the block-house as they waited for the rescue boat to arrive.

'What about the girl?' one of the men asked.

'Shoot her!' the other barked.

'We can't do that,' the first man angrily retorted. 'She's done nothing.'

'She knows too much. She's seen our faces,' the second snarled. 'I say shoot the bitch now.'

Maudie's blood ran cold as she listened to them discussing her fate.

'Not yet,' Edward snapped. 'She might make a better hostage than a corpse.'

Hidden behind the dunes that fringed the beach, Bella, Ava and Ruby, along with their partners, and Peter, who watched alone, saw the boat approaching. It bounced in towards shore, then, with a light flashing, it cruised up and down as the skipper tried to locate his passengers. In a panic, Bella turned to the Brig. 'The light!' she cried. 'They'll see us.'

'They'll only see whoever is in range of the light. The rest will be in darkness,' the Brig replied calmly. 'Stay behind me, darling. Don't get in their line of fire.'

Maudie's rescue party left the cover of the sand dunes and sneaked, in the cloying darkness, through the high sand dunes, towards the vast expanse of beach. At the same time, Edward and his party left the block-house. Maudie was hauled, now gasping for breath behind the gag that had stifled her all day, towards the boat, which, once Edward had flashed a signal from his torch, the skipper powered up to the patch of headland they were making for. The boat's light was focused entirely on Edward, which gave his pursuers an opportunity to run forward under cover of darkness. Grasping Bella's hand in his, the Brig tore across the damp, squelchy sand. Peter, Ava and Tom ran, too, and they all converged close to the boat that was bobbing on the waves. Hearing splashing noises behind him, Edward whirled around to face his pursuers.

'Get back!' he called, as he saw them advancing. 'Come any closer and I'll shoot.'

By the light on the boat, Bella could see that her brother was using Maudie as a human shield.

'Please, Edward, I beg you – don't do this!' she implored.

Edward span around to snarl at his sister. 'Want to talk to me now, huh? Too late. I could as easily put a bullet through you as through this idiotic friend of yours.'

Behind his back, the skipper frantically beckoned to his passengers. 'Get a move on – be quick!' he bellowed, with a German accent.

Edward's collaborators rushed through the water and were hauled aboard by the irate skipper. Walking backwards with wide-eyed, gagged Maudie shielding his body, Edward also approached the boat. Bella swayed in the waves. Maudie was so tantalizingly close and yet so far away. Seeing his sister wavering, Edward fired off a warning shot.

'Any closer and she dies.'

Concentrating only on Bella and the Brig, who were directly in front of him, Edward failed to see Raf and Ruby, who, in total darkness, were to the left of him. Realizing that he could shoot Edward sideways on without putting Maudie in danger, Raf grabbed his opportunity. Pushing Ruby aside, he fired at Edward, who turned at the last minute. To Raf's dismay, the bullet whistled past him. As he moved quickly to take a second shot, the boat's skipper swivelled the light directly on to Raf. Ruby looked on in helpless horror as Edward aimed his gun at her beloved. Illuminated and blinded in the dazzling glare, Raf took a bullet to the head and fell face down into the sea.

'*Raf! Raf!*' a distraught Ruby screamed, trying to pull her husband's limp body out of the water. 'My love, my darling, stay with me,' she begged. She managed to drag his bleeding body on to the beach, where she desperately attempted to stem the flow of blood gushing from his head.

With his gun once again aimed at Bella and the Brig, Edward heaved himself and Maudie into the boat.

'Get the hell out of here!' he yelled to the skipper, who revved the engine hard and the boat bounced off over the glittering, dark sea.

Distraught at how disastrously wrong their rescue mission had gone, the Brig turned to run and help Ruby and Raf, but Bella grabbed him by the arm.

'*Maudie!*' she screamed in total despair. 'We can't just let her go.'

The sound of loud gunshots echoing out at sea almost made their hearts stop. The Brig and Bella ran back into the waves. They saw the boat swerve and, by the beam of its light, Bella thought she could make out Maudie throwing herself overboard. Bullets peppered the sea as her body sunk under the surface.

'Sweet Jesus!' cried the Brig. He flung off his jacket and started to swim towards her. Bella chased after him.

'Stay there!' he yelled over his shoulder. 'Shine your torch – see if she surfaces.'

Standing waist deep in the crashing North Sea, Bella, shivering more with terror and foreboding than cold, kept her torch firmly on the breaking waves. 'Maudie, Maudie, Maudie,' she prayed out loud. 'Live, please live.'

Holding her breath, she saw the Brig emerge from the water, staggering under the weight of Maudie's soaking-wet body, which he half carried, half dragged on to the beach. Bella ran to meet them.

'Is she OK?' she cried.

Too exhausted to speak, the Brig nodded grimly.

'*I'm going for the Land Rover!*' Tom yelled over the sound of the crashing waves.

'*Call an ambulance!*' the Brig shouted after him.
'*And the police, too!*' Bella cried.

Maudie and Raf were taken to Wells Cottage Hospital in the same ambulance. Raf was immediately surrounded by doctors and nurses, while Maudie was assessed nearby, in one of the treatment bays used to deal with the less seriously injured. Deemed to be suffering from shock, concussion and a with broken arm, she was transferred to the women's ward, and allowed no visitors apart from the police and the Brig, who desperately needed information from her.

'Five minutes, no more,' snapped the feisty ward sister.

Grateful, the Brig and a burly police sergeant nodded.

'Best not push her too much, sir,' the sergeant warned. 'The young lady's had a shocking fright, by all accounts.'

The Brig, whose thoughts were in total turmoil, nodded vaguely. 'Christ!' he thought. 'What have I done?'

As a plan, it could not have gone more wrong. And it was all under his instruction. He would have to live with this guilt for the rest of his life. He would have to ask himself over and over again whether it would have been different if he'd involved the authorities and moved things along the normal channels.

The sergeant interrupted his thoughts. 'This way, sir.'

Beautiful Maudie was almost unrecognizable. Her glorious red hair was slicked back off her face, which was beaten black and blue, her eyes were puffy and half closed, and her right arm was in a sling.

'Maudie,' he murmured, sitting in the chair close to the bed. He reached for her hand.

'Brig,' she whispered through bruised lips.

The policeman on the other side of the bed cleared his

throat and introduced himself. 'Sergeant Ditchling, ma'am, Wells Constabulary. I'm here to ask you a few questions.'

Keen not to waste a precious minute, the Brig gave Maudie's hand a soft squeeze.

'They were going to kill me,' she croaked, with great effort. 'Edward imprisoned me in the block-house by the beach.'

'Did he . . . ?' the Brig looked at the wary policeman. 'You know, touch you, like before?' he added discreetly.

Maudie shook her head 'He planned to . . . but he was kept busy . . . arranging his escape.' She spoke between ragged breaths. 'He was constantly sending messages to Berlin.'

'I was hoping the shot we heard was Edward being finished off by one of Germans,' the Brig said.

'No, sadly . . . other way round,' Maudie told him. 'One of the Germans pulled off my gag and untied me . . . Edward went mad. There was a struggle . . . Edward shot him in the head.'

The policeman seized his chance to ask a question. 'So that was when you took your chance to get away, ma'am?'

Maudie struggled to recollect the moment of her escape. 'Yes, there was a struggle . . . a lot of shouting . . . I threw myself overboard. Edward grabbed my arm.' She gazed down at her bandages. 'I wrenched away from him . . . jumped into the sea . . . I sank.' Seeing her struggling, the Brig offered her a glass of water, and she took a sip. 'Underwater . . . I tried to swim to shore.' Tears seeped out of the corner of Maudie's bruised eyelids. 'Walsingham got away,' she sobbed. 'After all our hard work, he got away!'

'Don't upset yourself. I think that's quite enough for now.'

The sergeant turned to the Brig. 'Let's leave her in peace and come back tomorrow.'

'The girls send all their love and long to see you,' the Brig said, as he rose to go.

'Give them my love back,' Maudie said sleepily.

On his way out of the hospital, the Brig spotted a wild and red-eyed Ruby in the waiting room with Ava.

'They won't let me see him,' she cried. 'I want to see my husband!'

Feeling helpless, the Brig sat down next to Ava, who whispered, 'They're trying to resuscitate him,' she shook her head, implying that it wasn't looking good. 'How's Maudie?' she whispered.

'Weak, exhausted, in pain,' he whispered back.

'You should get back to the hall,' Ava urged. 'Bella will be out of her mind, waiting for you.'

'I want to stay with Ruby for a while,' the Brig said sadly.

Hardly aware of him, Ruby stared blankly at the wall, rocking herself dementedly back and forth.

'Please God, please, let my Raf live. Please let my Raf live.'

An agonizing half an hour later, a doctor entered the waiting room. The Brig took one look at his grey, exhausted face and knew there was no hope. He watched him approach poor Ruby.

'I'm so sorry, Mrs Boskow,' he said gently. 'We did everything we could to save your husband.' He paused, and sighed heavily. 'He'd lost too much blood and . . .'

His words fell on deaf ears – before he'd finished his sentence, Ruby had crumpled to the ground in a dead faint.

When Ruby came to, the Brig drove her and Ava home, in a wretched silence. What a contrast to the excitement with which they had set off earlier – full of determination to put a stop to Edward and his collaborators' escape. The doctor had administered a sedative to Ruby before she left the cottage hospital, so she lay slumped in the back of the car in a deep, drugged sleep. Between them, the Brig and Ava half carried her to the bedroom the girls shared, then the Brig left Ava to undress Ruby and get her into bed. Racked with guilt, the Brig hurried to find Bella, who he clutched in his arms and wept.

'God Almighty! I blame myself for all this!' he cried.

'Brig, you took a calculated risk and –' she started to say, but he harshly interrupted her.

'Which has killed Raf!'

'You didn't do it rashly,' Bella insisted, as she wiped away his tears. 'Right from the beginning, you've taken advice from your superiors, and you decided against bringing in the police for all the right reasons. It's not your fault it went wrong,' she insisted.

His breathing becoming steadier, the Brig ran a hand through Bella's blonde curls and said bitterly, 'And none of it was to any purpose.' He groaned in despair. 'The man we wanted has got clean away, and a good, innocent man has died.'

Bella leant against his rapidly beating heart. The words he'd spoken were irrefutably true. For the rest of their lives, they would all have to live with the terrible consequences.

The next morning, having heard of the tragic drama on Holkham beach, the trainees assured Ava that they could get by on soup and sandwiches. Ava was touched by their thoughtfulness, and by their kind instinct to pull together in difficult times.

'They're good girls,' Ava said, with tears in her eyes, as she reported back to Bella, who was in the process of frying off onions for the start of a pea-and-mint soup. As the fumes from the onions made her cry even more, she mumbled, 'We'll make a stack of sandwiches twice a day.'

Ava nodded and swept a hand over her weary face. 'And we'll keep a big pan of soup permanently on the go.' Sighing, she lit up a Woodbine. 'We'll get by somehow . . . Christ, we'll have to,' she sobbed, tears now rolling down her cheeks, too.

Later that day, the Brig came to see Bella. 'The police have just gone upstairs to see your parents. I think you should join them.'

Bella went pale. 'I can't do it on my own. Please come with me?' she begged.

Hand in hand, they made their way to the Walsinghams' first-floor suite, where they found his lordship incandescent with fury.

'How bloody dare you, sir!' he bellowed at the detective inspector who had replaced the local Wells policeman.

'It is my duty to inform you of the facts, Lord Walsingham,' the inspector replied calmly.

Lady Walsingham laid a warning hand on her husband's arm. 'Are you seriously telling us that our son is a spy?'

The inspector answered curtly, 'He is. He's been spying for the Germans. If you have any doubts, you can check with the Brigadier here,' he said, nodding towards Bella and the Brig.

Ignoring Lady Diana's contemptuous snort, the Brig stepped forward. 'I'm afraid there's absolutely no doubt about it: your son's been working undercover for Abwehr, the German Military Intelligence in Berlin.'

His lordship's heavily jowled face turned livid with rage.

'I bloody well don't believe it!' he roared. 'It's just not possible that a Walsingham son would turn against his king and country.'

Bella took a step towards her father. 'It's true, Daddy. His brief was to spy on Holkham airbase. He's been feeding Berlin detailed information on the number of Lancasters on the base, and the dates and times of their scheduled bombing raids.'

'We have undeniable evidence of his activities,' the Brig continued. 'His treacherous actions have caused the death of nearly fifty RAF airmen. During his escape he murdered RAF Air Mechanic 1st Class Rafal Boskow in cold blood and he also shot his own comrade dead at point-blank range.'

Lady Walsingham swayed, then, pale-faced and shaking, she sank into a chair. 'It can't be true . . . ?' she said, in a terrified whisper.

Diana sprang to her feet. 'I don't believe a word of it!' she cried. 'It would be typical of Annabelle and her middle-aged boyfriend to come up with a cock-and-bull story to humiliate the Walsinghams,' she sneered.

Although he was red with indignation, the Brig replied calmly to Diana's impudent accusations. 'If you're in any doubt, there's documented evidence of your brother's escape at Wells police station. He has a German passport and goes under the name Heinrich Brun. Bella and I have been decrypting his messages in and out of Berlin for weeks, all of which are documented, too. The commanding officer at RAF Holkham will verify our reports, as will the War Office, for whom I work.'

'But you're just a scruffy teacher!' Diana scoffed.

'Training code girls is only part of my brief,' he answered, with icy control. Turning to Lord and Lady Walsingham, the Brig concluded, 'Lord Edward is a war criminal. If he ever returns to England he will be arrested, tried and hanged as a murderer and spy. It's our duty to inform you of the circumstances before the story's published in all the newspapers.'

With that, he turned and left the room. For the sake of her family, Bella hung back, but the hatred in their eyes told her she was unwelcome.

'You bloody little bitch!' screamed Diana, and threw her empty glass at the wall.

Closing the heavy door quietly behind her, Bella also left the room.

31. Requiem

Ruby managed to haul herself from her bed to make arrange-ments for her husband's funeral. The cheeky, laughing, giggling girl had died along with Raf. Her voice was flat and lifeless, her hair had lost its glossy sheen and her wonderful dark eyes no longer sparkled.

'I just want to die, too,' she cried, over and over again.

Her grief was so great nobody could reach her. She had been given medication, as she hadn't seemed able to cope, and walked about like a zombie, doing exactly what she was told. When she wasn't prostrate with grief, she washed up, cleared plates, served lunch like somebody in a trance, and she could often be found outside, standing in the back yard, smoking in the spot where Raf had always parked his jeep. United in their losses, Maudie and Ruby tried to help each other through the dark and painful early weeks of their grief. Though the RAF had informed Raf's parents in Poland of their son's tragic death, Maudie had offered to write a letter in Polish from the daughter-in-law they'd never met.

'You can tell them how happy you were together,' Maudie urged. 'How in love you were, how proud he was of his RAF uniform, how much he admired Captain Kit.'

Ruby stared vacantly at Maudie. 'I don't want to think of those things,' she sobbed, and tears rolled down her pale cheeks.

'But it would help them,' Maudie said softly. 'Imagine

their grief – they can't even come to their son's funeral because of the war in Europe.'

Ruby gave a reluctant nod. 'All right. If you think it will help them.'

Maudie squeezed her hand. 'It will, I'm sure.'

Ruby insisted on making all the funeral arrangements. Oddly enough, visiting the ancient Walsingham shrine every day gave her life some purpose. She loved the chapel where she and Raf had married; it would be there that his body would be taken before the requiem Mass, to rest in peace overnight. Consulting with the Catholic priest who had married them, Ruby took great care with the details: the flowers, the hymns and the readings. The one thing she had no interest in at all was the wake, so Ava, Bella and Maudie took control of the arrangements. With Peter's help, game was found, and Bella made one of her wonderful pies, Ava cooked cheese pasties and corn-beef fritters, while Maudie made Raf's absolute favourite pudding: deep-fried apple fritters with custard.

A vigil was kept the night before the funeral. Bella, Ava and Maudie joined Ruby in the tiny chapel, which was lit only by the glow of candles. Dressed in the blue RAF uniform he had been so proud of, Raf lay in his coffin, his head wound partly covered by his navy-blue cap. Ruby draped rosary beads across his chest and kissed his cold lips. As the poor, heartbroken girl wept herself dry, her friends gathered in a tight circle around her. Maudie's tears for her lost love flowed, too; her Kit had had neither coffin nor grave.

Ava said, 'Let's say some prayers.'

Doing so brought a strange peace to them all, and they stayed there, praying, till the Sisters of St Margaret, who cared for the shrine, came to lock up.

The next day, Dodds drove them back to the medieval shrine, which was packed to bursting point with Raf's RAF friends. A blaze of summer flowers – roses, lilies, sweet peas and carnations – graced the altar, their heady perfume blending with the incense the priest used throughout the hour-long Latin Mass. As the concluding hymn, 'I Vow to Thee, My Country', was sung, the Brig was surprised to see Lady Caroline Walsingham at the back of the chapel.

'Your mother's here,' he whispered to Bella.

Bella gazed in astonishment at her mother, dressed in an elegant silver-grey suit and a large hat adorned with black and silver feathers. As the organ played, several of Raf's closest friends lifted the coffin on to their shoulders and followed the priest, who was swinging the censer, that contained incense they left the chapel and walked slowly to the cemetery, passing golden barley fields speckled with bright red poppies on their way. When the coffin was lowered into the black earth, Ruby completely broke down. Almost unable to stand, she was supported by Bella, Maudie and Ava. As puffs of incense circled into the clear blue sky, where swallows swooped and swerved, the priest dropped heavy clods of earth on to the closed coffin.

'Dust thou art, and unto dust shalt thou return,' he intoned.

Ruby wailed in agony when the coffin was covered over and wreaths were laid.

'Oh, God!' she sobbed. 'Take me, too, let me be with him in heaven. Please, take me!'

Back at Walsingham Hall, Ava gave Ruby a sedative, and she fell into a deep, exhausted sleep.

Upstairs, Bella was talking to her mother. 'It was good of

you to come, Mummy,' she said, as she offered her mother a large glass of dry sherry.

'It was my duty to pay my respects,' her mother answered, in a tight, choked voice. 'After all, it was our son who killed poor Ruby's husband.'

Bella stared at her mother, who was visibly trembling. 'We indulged Edward right from the start,' Lady Caroline continued. 'He's brought eternal shame to the Walsingham name.'

With tears in her eyes, she left the room, leaving Bella staring sadly after her. She had never heard her mother say a word against Edward in all her life. She wondered if her father would say anything, or would he stay in denial, giving no comfort to his heartbroken wife?

About an hour later, the wake ended as the RAF servicemen from Holkham returned to their base for duty. Clearing away the empty dishes, Ava remarked, 'It's funny how folks are always starving after a funeral.'

'I suppose it's because the sadness of funerals makes the mourners happy to be alive,' Bella said with a wry smile.

Ruby made a worryingly slow recovery. She lost weight, grew pale and weak, and she was constantly sick.

'She looks like death warmed up,' Ava fretted. 'I think she should see a doctor.'

Tom drove Ruby and Bella to the Walsingham's family doctor in Fakenham. Bella stayed with the listless Ruby throughout her examination. When the GP started pressing Ruby's tummy, Bella grew alarmed: did she have some terrible disease brought on by shock and despair? Her anxieties doubled when the doctor drew the curtains around Ruby.

'I need to do an internal examination,' he said briefly.

After Ruby had dressed and the doctor had washed his

hands, he sat back in his chair and said with a gentle smile, 'My dear girl, you're pregnant.'

Something stirred in Ruby. For the first time in weeks, her dark eyes opened wide.

'*Me?* Expecting?'

'I'd say you're well over two months gone,' he replied.

Ruby turned to Ava. 'Raf's baby!' she exclaimed, as tears poured down her emaciated cheeks. 'Raf's little baby!'

Bella threw her arms around Ruby. She squeezed her tightly, then suddenly stopped. 'Sorry, mustn't squash the baby!' she said in delight.

Incredulous, a glowing Ruby laid a trembling hand on her tummy. 'My Raf's baby,' she whispered. 'Now I've got something to live for.'

There was great joy below stairs that night. A toast of strong, hot tea was served, which Ruby, the former champion brew girl, couldn't stomach.

'I wondered why I'd gone off fags,' she chuckled. 'Can you believe it?' she joyously asked her friends. 'Raf's not completely gone away, part of him is here, inside me, safe and sound.'

As the weeks passed, Ruby's morning sickness got even worse. Seeing her so pale and wan, Ava took control of the situation. 'You're staying in bed and only working when you're up to it,' she said, in her most authoritative voice.

'But . . .' Ruby protested.

'No buts, madam, your health comes first. You need to catch up on your sleep and get some meat on your bones. We want a strong, healthy, bouncing baby, not a sickly, mewling thing.'

Ava's strong words had the right effect on Ruby, who,

concerned for her baby's healthy development, ate and slept better than she had since Raf had died. When the sickness abated, she insisted on returning to work.

'I'm bored!' she declared, appearing in the kitchen, bristling with energy. 'Give me something to do.'

'All right,' said Ava, wagging a finger at Ruby. 'But no heavy lifting.'

'Stop treating me like cut crystal that'll shatter any minute,' Ruby protested.

'You're precious cut crystal to all of us, and we love you!' said Ava, and hugged her smiling friend.

As Ruby's tummy began to swell and her figure filled out, she had the glow only a pregnant woman possesses: a secret happiness that radiated out of her entire body. At night as she lay in her bed, she smiled to herself, as her fingers travelled over her baby bump.

'Look, Raf,' she whispered, 'our baby's growing. I promise I'll take care of him or her. Whether it's a boy or a girl, they'll know about their daddy – their beautiful, wonderful, darling daddy who I'll love till the day I die.'

In Stalag Luft VI, a German prisoner-of-war camp in Heydekrug, a far-flung town on the northernmost tip of the country, facing the freezing Baltic Sea, Kit yearned for Maudie. After being kicked out of the barn by the irate farmer's wife, he and Charlie had managed by an extraordinary stroke of luck to make contact with a member of the Polish resistance who led them to a safe house near Bremen. Unfortunately, one of the men, a double agent working for the Gestapo, had blown the whistle and, in a terrifying night raid, they had all been captured. The members of the resistance were shot and the rest were taken prisoner. In a filthy, stinking cattle truck the captives were driven halfway across the country to what Kit called, 'the coldest bloody place on earth!'

The prisoners in Stalag Luft VI were forced to work in a nearby slate quarry. Wearing their tattered POW uniforms, more holes than fabric, they hacked away at icy slabs of slate for twelve hours a day in sub-zero temperatures. Even though they had to do gruelling forced labour inflicted on them by the Gestapo, the emaciated men were barely fed and watered.

'To hell with this shit!' Kit swore, and fell on to his bunk bed, which was crawling with fleas. 'The bastards will either beat or starve us to death!' Furious, he jumped to his feet and stared out of the grimy window at the rows of wooden huts, all hung with long, pointed icicles and topped with a foot of snow. 'I'm not going to die here,' he said through gritted teeth. 'I'm going home to Maudie if it kills me!'

Galvanized, Kit joined the escape committee, which had recently learnt through a reliable agent that there were safe houses dotted along the Baltic coastline. Desperate to escape, dare-devil Kit would have considered anything, as long as it meant he could start making his way back to England.

'The escape route has always previously been inland,' a senior RAF officer on the committee explained to the group. 'But that way it's nearly fifty miles to the nearest safe house, which has had disastrous consequences. Escapees have frozen to death en route. If they don't freeze to death they get frostbite and collapse then the Gestapo pick them up and shoot them on the spot, poor sods,' he said, pausing to light a cigarette. 'The beauty of the Baltic safe houses is they're only a short distance apart – no more than ten miles, I'm told. The escapee is in less danger of dying of cold. He can travel incognito steadily along the coastline from safe house to safe house until he can board a neutral ship.'

'It's not one hundred per cent firmed up,' another officer commented. 'Our man overseeing the Baltic route, Captain Helsberg, says there are risks involved at this early stage.'

Reckless and desperate, Kit didn't care!

'Let me try?' he begged. 'If I get through, you and Captain Helsberg will know it's a viable escape route and you'll be able to send others after me.' Seeing the senior officers wary expressions, he added persuasively. 'If I pull it off and make contact with Helsberg, surely it would help you build up a safer Baltic network?'

The commanders exchanged cautious looks.

'Helsberg's Danish. He operates as a fisherman on board a fishing vessel which works its way up and down the Baltic coast, picking up escapees then dropping them off, moving them on. If Squadron Leader Halliday made it safely to Helsberg, it would certainly strengthen our links with the Danish resistance, maybe the Norwegians, too.'

Seeing the argument swaying in his favour, Kit quickly added, 'I could transmit vital information back to you, too. Come on,' he implored. 'I could just as easily die in the bloody slate quarry as I could on the run!'

The officers exchanged a long look.

'Well, if you don't mind the risk, why should we stop you?' the senior officer barked. 'That's if we can get you out, of course,' he declared, as he stood up to shake hands with Kit, who was grinning with excitement. 'Good luck, old chap. God go with you!'

After weeks of preparation, they managed to make arrangements with the driver of a horse wagon, a Pole, that

Kit should be taken out of the camp, hidden in the large inverted box which served as the driver's seat. It was tremendously risky, but Kit's nerve never failed – he was determined to try, whatever the cost.

'God, man, aren't you terrified?' Charlie asked Kit, the night before his escape.

'Of course!' Kit exclaimed. 'But I can't stay banged up here till the end of the bloody war!'

'You'll be tortured if you're caught, and they'll shoot anybody who's helped you,' Charlie warned.

'Then it's imperative I don't get caught,' Kit said determinedly. 'God! It's got to be worth the risk.'

Charlie clapped him hard on the shoulder.

'God speed – if you get back to Blighty, give my regards to that gorgeous girlfriend of yours!'

The following day, stuffed under the driver's seat and smothered in straw, Kit hardly dared to breathe as the driver set off and the horse clip-clopped towards the prison gates.

'Christ! Can you go any slower?' Kit thought, as his heart raced with fear.

The guard on duty checked the driver's papers, then, after giving the contents of the hay cart a random stab with his bayonet, he sent them on their way. So far so good.

The journey to the nearest town seemed to take forever, but it had its advantages, as Kit arrived at his first stopping point in the pitch dark. Slipping unseen into the safe house, he quickly burnt his POW clothes in a wood-burning stove, then changed into the fishermen's clothes that had been left for him. After donning a navy-blue corduroy sailor's cap, Kit looked quite the part with his thick, blond beard and wind-blasted, tanned skin. Travelling on foot, Kit made agonizingly slow progress as he moved along the coastline. But one day, bone-tired, weak from hunger and lack of sleep, he came to the outskirts of Rügen, from where he was able to make his way to the port, where he had instructions to seek out Helsberg's fishing vessel, *Mermaid*. Seeing German military police lounging around, smoking in the bars dotted around the port, Kit grabbed a fisherman's net, and flung it over his shoulder. Adrenalin coursing through his veins, he walked as casually as he could along the harbour until his keen eyes spotted the name *Mermaid* painted in blue on what looked like a decrepit old fishing boat.

Captian Helsberg welcomed him cautiously – nobody entirely trusted a stranger in the war years – but after a few weeks of working hard, hauling in fishing nets and taking his turn on the cooking rota, Helsberg started to talk more to Kit. He asked him about the safe houses he'd used along the Baltic coast.

'*Jah, jah, god god*,' he said, clearly pleased with Kit's reply.

'I can't thank you enough for helping me,' Kit said, sincerely. 'I'm longing to get back to England.'

The captain shook his head. 'You won't be going home any time soon,' he told a rather disappointed Kit. 'We lost our undercover radio operator and urgently need a replacement.'

Desperate not to be allocated a task that would detain him longer in mainland Europe, Kit prevaricated.

'I'm a pilot, Captain, that's my expertise – flying!'

Helsberg gave him a cynical look as he replied, 'And RAF pilots aren't trained to use radio transmitters?'

Feeling slightly ashamed of himself, Kit slumped in his chair and apologised.

'Sorry, Captain, of course I can use a transmitter. I'm grateful for your help. Now it's my turn to return the favour.'

The beaming captain poured out two glasses of schnapps. 'Welcome aboard, Englishman!'

Over the months, as *Mermaid* ploughed up and down the coast, apparently fishing for tuna but all the while picking up and dropping off prisoners of war on the run, Kit proved himself invaluable. Operating the ship's radio transmitter, he made s contact with resistance movements in Denmark, Norway and Sweden who were desperately seeking a safe passage for escapees. As soon as he was able to, Kit made contact with the escape committee he'd left behind in Stalag Luft VI, letting them know that he was with Captain Helsberg and was working undercover with him. And then he did what he really wanted to do: using the cypher he knew from experience that the Brig favoured, he sent a coded message home . . .

Back at Walsingham Hall, the radio transmitter, still in the sewing room, was always in operational mode and was manned throughout the day by either Maudie, Ava, the Brig or Bella.

'Even though he's flown the coop, we must keep listening in on Edward's frequency,' the Brig had insisted. 'He'd be a bloody fool to communicate with anybody, but given how arrogant and headstrong he is, he just might try.'

'What makes my blood boil is he got away,' Maudie said angrily.

The Brig nodded. 'It would have been a real coup to have handed him over to Military Intelligence.'

It was Bella who picked up Kit's message, late one autumn evening.

'Hey!' she called from the sewing room where she was

doing her shift with the radio transmitter. 'What do you make of this?'

Holding cups of cocoa, Maudie and the Brig hurried out of the kitchen to join her. The Brig smiled as he recognized the familiar cypher. 'It's the four-letter replacement pattern,' he said, nudging Bella off the chair. 'Budge over, sweetheart, while I decrypt it.'

Maudie watched in fascination as the Brig worked out the algorithm, then matched the coded letters. Suddenly, he stopped short.

'Sweet Jesus!' he yelped. Murmuring to himself, he tensely checked the message again.

'Is it Edward?' Bella cried.

'No,' the Brig answered, and turned to face Maudie. 'It's not Edward – it's Kit! He's alive – he's on the Baltic coast.'

Maudie cried out and dropped her mug of hot cocoa on to the stone floor. Terrified there'd been a mistake or that she'd misunderstood, she didn't dare believe it could be true. 'It can't be!'

'Check again, Brig,' Bella urged.

'I've double-checked already,' he declared.

'Send a message!' Maudie whispered.

'What message?' he asked.

'Something only Kit and his men will have known, something they shared the night of the raid,' Maudie answered slowly. After a brief pause, she said, 'Ask if there was a moon the night of the raid.'

The Brig sent off the coded message, then they sat in total silence and waited. A message quickly came back.

'Come on, Maudie, you can help me decode it,' the Brig

said, and put another chair beside the transmitter for her to sit on.

Maudie keenly watched the Brig matching the letters to his cypher. 'Bomber Moon!' she cried as the words appeared. 'Kit! Kit! Kit!' she chanted, hugging herself in ecstasy.

'You send a message, Maudie,' Bella said excitedly.

Helped by the Brig, Maudie tapped out the coded letters for Kit to read.

'COME HOME, MY LOVE.'

32. Knitting Bees

Maudie, who had barely slept with all the excitement, radiated joy the next day.

'He's alive, he's alive, he's alive!' she chanted like a mantra throughout the day.

Ecstatic as she was, Maudie was careful not to flaunt it when Ruby was around; she had her love back from the dead, but Ruby didn't. Wary of upsetting her friend, Maudie hugged her miracle to herself. Typically, it was straight-talking Ruby who broke the awkward, strained atmosphere. Sitting with her friends at the table, she looked them all firmly in the eye and said, 'I can see you're all walking on eggshells around me and I don't like it!'

Maudie, Bella and Ava exchanged guilty glances.

'It's wonderful news that your Kit's alive, sweetheart,' she said warmly to Maudie, who clutched Ruby's hand as tears filled her eyes. 'I know my darling can't ever come back, but it doesn't stop me from rejoicing with you.'

'Oh, Ruby!' Maudie cried, as she hugged her dear, sweet friend. 'I didn't want to upset you.'

'From the bottom of my heart, I'm happy for you, Maudie. So now,' she added with one of her contagious giggles, 'can you all stop pussy-footing around me, it's driving me mad! The sooner we get the atmosphere in this kitchen back to normal, the better.'

One golden autumn morning with fallen leaves crisp on

the ground, a letter addressed to Ruby arrived from Poland. Flustered and excited, Ruby ran to find Maudie.

'Look! Look! A letter from Raf's mum and dad!' she cried, brandishing the letter in the air. 'It's taken weeks to get here, and it's been opened,' she added breathlessly. 'Translate it for me, Maudie, tell me what they say,' she begged.

'Dear daughter-in-law,' Maudie dutifully translated. 'Though our hearts are broken, we are so very grateful for your letter from Norfolk, which Rafal loved so much. It gave us joy to know you were happy together. Maybe one day we will all meet, when this terrible war is over. We have nothing left now but memories of our beautiful son. We are quite alone in our endless grief.' Maudie stopped to wipe tears from her eyes. Ruby, stricken by their poignant words, also wept as her friend continued, 'We want to look after the woman our son loved so much. Please would you accept from us, with our respect and affection, this financial gift.' Maudie broke off to calculate the amount on her fingers. 'My God! That's nearly £1,500!'

Ruby, who'd been poor all her life and had lived in a tiny Walsingham tithe cottage along with her family since she was born, slumped in shock in one of the Windsor chairs beside the Aga.

'I'll be a rich woman!' she gasped. 'I'll be able to buy my own house! I won't have to move back in with my parents when the baby's born.' The tears came again as hitherto un-thought-of possibilities flooded into her head. Suddenly, Ruby's face dropped. 'We must tell them that I'm expecting Raf's baby, that's sure to give them something to live for,' she said, as, overcome with emotion, she wiped tears from her eyes. 'Maybe when this bloody rotten war is over I'll be able to visit them with their grandchild.'

Maudie squeezed her trembling hand. 'That would make them so happy,' she whispered.

Bella was delighted to lend Ruby some money until the funds arrived from Poland, and the joy of going shopping with the excited mother-to-be made the girls smile.

'I was going to get a second-hand pram,' Ruby confessed, 'but now I can splash out on a new Silver Cross. I ordered it in Holt this morning,' she said with an excited laugh. 'It's almost bigger than me! Nothing but the best for my Raf's child,' she added soberly.

'You'll be able to wheel the baby round town like a little prince or princess,' Ava chuckled.

'I bought some wool, too. I thought I'd knit the baby a little layette,' Ruby added.

'We could help you with the knitting,' said Ava. 'Start a knitting circle. Between us, we could knit four baby's layettes!'

'Good idea,' laughed Ruby. 'We'll knit for England!'

As the dark, gloomy autumn nights set in, the Walsingham knitting circle became a joy. After their work was done, Ava, Maudie, Bella and Ruby would sit around the kitchen table knitting, clicking their needles and winding wool as they drank cocoa and chatted. The baby's tiny layette grew night by night: little cardigans and tiny woollen leggings, bootees and a shawl. Then Maudie announced she was going to knit socks for Kit's pals at the airbase.

'I said we'd knit for England,' teased Ruby. 'I never thought we'd go as far as kitting out the RAF!'

Shortly before Christmas, with the year's second batch of trainees already receiving their postings in communication centres up and down the country, the girls sat knitting brightly coloured woollen squares that would eventually form a quilt for the baby. Uncomfortable with sitting too long, Ruby laid down her needles. Supporting her burgeoning tummy, she paced the room before announcing with a bright, triumphant smile, 'I bought a house today!'

Thunderstruck, Ava, Bella and Maudie gaped at her in disbelief.

'It's a cottage, actually, Angel Cottage in Burnham Thorpe,' she explained. 'I heard about it in the estate office last week, so I walked over there to take a look and it was love at first sight. It's right by the village green, opposite the Lord Nelson pub. Tiny, two up, two down, with a thatched roof and a pretty garden; it'll be perfect for me and the baby.'

Ava, who'd shared a bedroom with Maudie for a couple of years now and seen her through all her good times, and bad times, too, burst into tears. 'You're leaving?' she cried.

'Yes, lovie, I'm leaving the hall,' Ruby said incredulously. 'Imagine that!' she laughed. 'Raf's parents have given me the opportunity to set myself up as an independent woman.'

Bella laughed, too. 'I never imagined you'd dash out and buy a cottage!' she teased.

'When are you planning on going?' Ava asked, as she wiped away her tears.

'As soon as Angel Cottage is ready,' Ruby answered. 'I'll come into work when I can,' she added quickly. 'It's only a ten-minute cycle ride from here.'

Maudie rolled her eyes in disapproval. 'For God's sake woman, you're pregnant!'

'So?' Ruby giggled. 'That's not going to stop me from enjoying the pleasure of your company.'

'What will we do without our little ray of sunshine?' Ava asked.

'Get another housemaid!' Ruby joked.

Lighting up a cigarette, Ava apologized for her emotional outburst. 'Sorry about the tears, it's only 'cos I'll miss moaning to you when we're getting ready for bed!'

As Maudie resumed her knitting, she smiled thoughtfully. 'You're right to want your own home, Ruby. Nobody would want to bring up a baby below stairs!'

When Ruby took her friends to Angel Cottage, they could see why she'd fallen in love with it.

'It's charming!' cried Bella, as she skipped excitedly from room to room. 'We'll help you decorate.'

'I could make new curtains,' Ava volunteered.

'Everybody's been so kind,' Ruby said happily. 'Peter said he'd build me new kitchen cupboards and install a toilet. I thought I was going to have to manage with an outdoor privy, but Peter took pity on me!'

True to their word, the girls helped Ruby to paint the walls; there wasn't a wide variety of paint to be had in the local shops, but Ruby managed to track down a soft daffodil yellow for the baby's room, and Ava made thick, warm, cream-coloured curtains to keep out the winter draughts. Maudie found a chest of drawers in Wells, which she painted a light green, before adding little smiling garden gnomes on each of the drawers, in which the baby's clothes were lovingly laid, wrapped in tissue paper.

'All we need now is the baby!' Ruby giggled.

Bella found a stack of old bits and pieces for the house in the Walsingham attics, which the Brig drove over to Angel Cottage in Peter's Land Rover. There was a small sofa, a table and a couple of rickety chairs, a little dresser, a rag rug and a collection of surplus kitchen equipment: cutlery, crockery, a chopping board, two pans and, most important of all – a brown teapot!

'Time for a brew!' cried Ruby, as she christened the pot and made tea for her first guests, who sat around the wood-burning stove in the cosy sitting room toasting bread over the flickering flames. As Ruby handed round mugs of hot, strong tea, she smiled contentedly, and said, 'I can see that Baby and I are going to be as snug as two bugs in a rug here in Angel Cottage!'

33. A Quiet Christmas

There were no festive celebrations at Walsingham Hall that Christmas. Lord and Lady Walsingham stayed at home behind closed doors and Lady Diana went to London.

'They're too ashamed to show their faces to their snobby society friends,' Bella said.

'Fair-weather friends,' Ava retorted. 'Not there when they're really needed.'

It was the quietest Christmas the girls had ever known at the hall; there were no suppers, dances, dinners or shoots. Maudie took the opportunity to go home to the East End, Ava took her Tom north to meet her family, and heavily pregnant Ruby cycled in from her cottage in Burnham Thorpe whenever she was able, which left Bella and the Brig mostly alone in the empty, echoing hall, with the Walsinghams upstairs.

'I really don't feel like putting up a Christmas tree in the hall. It feels like the wrong thing to do this year,' Bella said to Ruby on one of her visits, as they prepared corn-beef hash and cabbage for lunch.

Ruby nodded. 'I'm certainly not in the mood for big celebrations. Let's just have a little tree below stairs to put our presents under.'

On Christmas morning, Ruby, who'd converted to the Catholic faith after Raf's death, called in at the hall on her way home from Mass and, to her surprise, found Lady Walsingham in the kitchen with Bella.

'Your Ladyship,' Ruby said, as she did her customary servant's curtsey.

'Merry Christmas, Ruby,' Lady Caroline said tentatively. 'I've brought you a present,' she added, handing her a small parcel wrapped in pretty paper and ribbons.

Ruby, who'd never received anything from the Walsinghams, apart from her wages, was shocked, but deeply touched. She carefully unwrapped the paper and gazed in wonder at the tiniest pair of lemon-coloured woollen bootees. Moved beyond words at the gift from someone so unexpected, Ruby cried, 'Oh, ma'am, they're lovely!' Holding the bootees in the air for Bella to see, she laughed with pleasure. 'Imagine my baby's little feet snug and warm in these!'

'They were Annabelle's,' said Lady Caroline quietly.

Bella turned to her mother in stunned amazement. 'You kept them all these years?' she asked.

Her mother nodded and smiled sadly. 'Along with your christening gown and a little wooden horse on wheels. You used to pull it around the garden for hours.'

Bella found herself strangely choked; she'd never sensed that her mother truly loved her, but the fact that she had chosen to treasure some of her possessions suggested that maybe she had been wrong. But before she could speak, her mother continued in her usual brisk tone. 'Your father's unwell. He's staying in bed. He says he feels faint and dizzy.' She took a deep breath. 'So, if you'll have me, I'd like to join you below stairs for Christmas dinner.'

Feeling intensely sorry for her mother, who had shed too much weight and turned grey with grief and shame, Bella smiled warmly and replied, 'You're very welcome, Mummy.'

'Thank you, Annabelle,' Lady Caroline answered, with

tears in her eyes. 'Given our ghastly circumstances, it would be too depressing for words to eat Christmas dinner alone.'

Peter, somehow, had managed to come up with something to grace the Christmas table: a squashed pheasant with one leg!

'It's roadkill,' he chuckled. 'But it'll be all right once it's plucked and stuffed.'

Only four sat down to dinner: Bella and the Brig, Ruby and her ladyship. It was an odd foursome, but in the cosy kitchen, pungent with the smell of the herbs and spices they'd managed to save, everybody enjoyed Bella's Christmas feast: delicious rabbit pâté, heavily embellished with fresh thyme, pepper and a shot of Lord Walsingham's best brandy; her famous rich gravy and sage-and-onion stuffing enhanced the flavour of Peter's roadkill pheasant. And because there was no dried fruit this year, they had jelly and a thin custard instead of Christmas pud.

As the Brig served coffee in the library, Bella took a tray of food up to her father. Tiptoeing into his room, she whispered, 'Daddy, Daddy, I've brought you some dinner.'

When there was no reply, Bella approached the silk-draped, high-canopied bed. which her father was slumped across.

'Daddy . . . ?' she whispered fearfully.

Laying her hand on his, she gasped in shock. His face was twisted in a rigid expression of pain, and he was stone cold.

'Oh God! Oh God!' she screamed, as she dropped the tray and ran out of the room and down the back stairs.

Hearing her cry, the Brig intercepted Bella halfway down the stairs.

'It's Daddy, I think he's dead!' she cried, flinging herself into his arms.

Hiding his shock, the Brig hugged her briefly before saying, 'Look after your mother. I'll go and check your father.'

The doctor arrived in sleeting rain and, after examining Lord Walsingham, he declared that the cause of death was a massive stroke. After the body had been removed by the undertaker, Bella sat alone with her mother in the upstairs drawing room. Midwinter darkness now shrouded the hall and there was a sharp chill in the air. As Bella lit a fire in the grate of the pink marble fireplace, her mother talked quietly as she sipped the brandy her daughter had poured for her.

'We must get word to Edward and Diana,' she said.

'I can tell Diana,' Bella said, 'but you must understand, Mummy, we have no means of contacting Edward.' Seeing her mother wipe away a tear, she added gently, 'We'll announce Daddy's death in the *Telegraph*. Maybe the news will filter through to him that way?'

'I've lost my husband as well as my son.' Her mother sobbed into her lace handkerchief.

Bella put a protective arm around Lady Caroline's bony shoulders. 'Mummy, I'll always take care of you.'

Weeping, her mother leant against her for support. 'Thank you, darling, I know you will.'

Bella smiled incredulously. She'd never thought the day would come when her mother actually needed her!

Ava and Maudie got back in time to help prepare for the funeral, which was the penultimate day of 1943, 30 December.

'I'm sorry for your loss, lovie,' Ava said, as she hugged Bella tightly.

'Thanks, Ava. I can't be a hypocrite. As you know, I've never got on with my father, but it was a huge shock seeing him lying dead in his bed. And whatever he'd done, he was my father. '

'Your poor mother must be devastated,' added Maudie, who looked stronger and happier after her stay with her doting parents.

Bella nodded grimly. 'She is,' she replied, 'but we're getting on a lot better these days,' she added with a shy smile.

'She appreciates you at last,' Maudie chuckled.

'Now, how can we help with the funeral?' asked Ava.

'Believe me, it won't be a big bash – my parents have hardly a friend in the world these days,' Bella replied sadly. 'Bloody Diana will come, and I'm sure some of the estate workers will want to pay their respects.'

'Don't forget Timms,' Ruby reminded her with a giggle. 'She's sure to come and gloat.'

The funeral party was larger than expected. Faithful estate workers turned up in their dusted-down black suits. At the last minute, Lady Diana screeched up in her expensive Daimler, and frowned in disapproval as she joined the small, sorrowful party making its way to the pretty little estate chapel.

'God, aren't any of Daddy's friends and colleagues here?' she asked, in an over-loud voice.

Bella groaned inwardly as she pointed out the blindingly obvious. 'They disowned the family after Edward's treachery was revealed. I actually think Daddy died as a result of it,' she added sadly.

'You'd think his little tart of a mistress would be here,' Diana added caustically. 'She couldn't get enough of him and his money when he was alive.'

'Shshh!' Bella hissed. 'Don't let Mummy hear you.'

'She knew all about it,' Diana replied. 'She's put up with Daddy's adultery for years.'

'Shut up!' Bella snapped. 'She doesn't need to be reminded of that today.'

After the simple service, Lord Walsingham's body was buried in the arctic-cold family crypt, which echoed to the sound of the mourners' clattering feet and whispered prayers. The shivering funeral party hurried back to the hall, where a welcome fire blazed in Lady Caroline's drawing room, which quickly filled up with mourners. The Brig passed between the guests with bottles of sherry and whisky, while Tom and Ava handed out beef-paste and cress sandwiches and slices of coconut cake.

'God! How the mighty have fallen,' Lady Diana moaned, at the sight of the simple rationed food.

Lady Walsingham, deep in conversation with Timms, ignored her cross daughter, who got steadily more and more drunk until, eventually, she fell asleep on the sofa. The guests drifted away, and Lady Caroline helped Tom, the Brig and the girls to clear away the dirty plates and glasses. As she laid an empty tray down on the kitchen table, she made an astonishing announcement.

'I've always felt guilty about doing nothing in terms of war work over the last three years. Now, I intend to make up for it. I want to do something substantial, something really useful – the problem is, I don't know exactly what.'

Tom was the one to break the stunned silence. 'You drive, don't you, Your Ladyship?'

Lady Caroline nodded. 'Of course – why?' she asked.

Handsome Tom grinned as he answered, 'Wells Cottage Hospital are desperately in need of an ambulance driver!'

34. Diana's Revenge

The day after her father's funeral, Lady Diana, bleary-eyed and hungover, gazed out of her bedroom window, which gave a good view of the paddocks, which were presently covered in a sparkling frost. She scowled as she saw Ava, whose dark hair had grown back quickly since her accident, grooming Lucas. Diana's fury grew as she watched her horse lovingly nuzzling Ava's chest as Ava, laughing, ran a comb through his golden-chestnut mane and tail.

'What the hell's she up to?' Diana snarled. She got up, dressed and headed towards the Walsinghams' small private dining room, where she found Lady Caroline clearing away the remains of her boiled-egg breakfast.

'Hell's teeth, Mother!' she exploded. 'We don't have to clear away our own bloody breakfast, do we?'

'It helps now that Ruby's gone,' her mother replied calmly.

Diana gazed at her mother in disbelief. 'You sound like you've crossed over – joined the other side.'

Ignoring her daughter's biting sarcasm, Lady Caroline said, 'I'm just popping over to the cottage hospital in Wells.'

'Why? Are you ill?' Diana enquired.

Lady Caroline shook her head. 'No,' she retorted. 'Their regular ambulance driver's been called up. so I'm taking over his job.'

If Lady Caroline had said she was about to orbit the moon

in a rocket. Diana could not have been more flabbergasted. 'You're *what*?'

'Becoming an ambulance driver, darling,' her mother replied briskly. 'You should think about doing your bit, too, Diana. Your behaviour is shamefully unpatriotic,' Lady Caroline said as she headed towards the door.

'For God's sake!' Diana seethed. 'Not you, too.'

Diana drank a cup of coffee, then, even more wound up, stormed over to the stable yard, where she found Peter mucking out.

'Where's my horse?' she demanded.

'Ava's taken him for a ride on Holkham beach, miss,' Peter replied.

'And exactly who gave her permission to do that?' Diana snapped.

'Tom Benson, the vet. Lucas needed exercising, so he asked Ava. She's an excellent rider,' he added approvingly.

Diana glared at him. 'So the bloody cook is exercising *my* horse!' she yelled. 'Outrageous!'

Busying himself with sweeping the yard, Peter turned his back on a seething Diana. 'Good day to you, miss.'

Out on the wide sweep of Holkham beach, Ava was walking Lucas back through the lapping, shallow waves. As the sea hissed in and out, scraping pebbles and shells on the sandy beach, she thought about the year that was about to end. How could any of them have imagined, as they danced at the New Year ball, how events would unfold? That Raf and Lord Walsingham would be dead, that Kit would be shot down over Germany and that Lord Edward, outed as a spy, would flee to Germany. Tossing his head and snorting, Lucas interrupted her melancholy line of thought.

'All right, darling,' she murmured, patting his golden flank. 'Shall we have one last blow-out on the way back?'

Giving Lucas his head, she sat low in the saddle as Lucas galloped full tilt across the beach. With her hair flying out behind her and Lucas's silky mane lifting on the cold easterly breeze, Ava smiled in delight as they swept past the pine woods, where Lucas, tired after exerting himself more than usual, slowed down to a steady walk.

'Good boy,' she said, laying her head on his warm neck. 'You're the best horse in the whole wide world!' She chuckled fondly. 'But I've worn you out. Let's get you home before you drop.'

Back at the yard, Ava tethered Lucas to a ring in the stable wall and left him saddled up near a brimming bucket of water to quench his thirst while she ran indoors to boil the kettle for his favourite meal, a hot bran mash. Minutes later, when she returned with a bucketful that smelt warm and yeasty, Lucas had gone.

'Where is he?' she called out to Peter.

'Miss Diana's just galloped off on him,' he replied.

Ava gasped in dismay. 'But he's already exhausted after our long ride on the beach,' she cried. 'He's in no state to go out a second time!'

'Sorry, miss, I tried to stop Miss Diana, but she was having none of it. She told me to mind my own bloody business,' he added disapprovingly. 'I was just coming to find you.'

In a flat spin, Ava ran to the bike shed, where she grabbed the first bike she could lay her hands on, then, pedalling furiously, cycled after Diana, praying as she went.

'God, please God, don't let her hurt him.'

Back in the Walsingham kitchen, Peter, out of breath from running across the yard, was hurriedly telling Bella what had just happened. Alarmed by the urgency in Peter's face, she immediately picked up the phone and phoned Tom at his surgery in Wells.

'I'll drive over right away,' he promised.

Meanwhile, Diana was galloping wildly along the track that fringed the woods. 'I'll show you what a real ride is,' she yelled, whacking Lucas's rump with a whip.

Though already weary, Lucas did what he'd done all his life: he tried his best. Sweating profusely, foam flecking his muzzle and bridle, he pushed himself into an even faster gallop. Racing along on her bike, Ava eventually caught up with the frenzied Diana.

'*Stop!* Please stop!' she begged. 'Lucas is exhausted – you'll kill him if you push him any harder.'

Pedalling at breakneck speed, Ava rode alongside Lucas, who was wide-eyed with fear. Reaching out, she tried to grab his reins. 'I beg you, stop!' she implored once more.

Diana raised her whip and slashed Ava across the face.

'*Bitch!*' she snarled. 'I'll do what the hell I choose with my bloody horse!' Kicking Lucas hard in the ribs, Diana headed straight for a high hedge that was looming up in front of them. 'Go! Go!' she screamed.

Ava gazed in complete horror at the high hedge; even if he wasn't exhausted, Lucas could never jump so high, he was just too old, but Diana had no such thought in her mind. Whipping him even harder, she urged the poor beast to do the physically impossible. Rising up like the hero he was, Lucas lifted his front legs as high as he could and hurled himself at the hedge. Clutching the reins, Diana screamed as she realized the impossibility of clearing the jump. Losing her balance, she rolled off Lucas's back and landed with a thud on the ground. Oblivious of Diana, Ava watched in horror as Lucas tumbled back down to the ground, where he rolled on his back, whinnying in pain. Horrified, Ava dashed towards him.

'Darling, darling boy,' she murmured, tears flooding down her face. Hearing her voice, Lucas turned his head towards her. The pain and fear in his eyes just about broke Ava's heart. 'Don't worry, boy, you'll be all right,' she soothed. 'We're going to get you better,' she added softly.

Her gentle, calm voice reassured Lucas, who neighed softly as she stroked her hand along the length of his neck, which was running with sweat. Ava barely noticed Tom arriving, but suddenly he was there beside her, examining Lucas, whose eyes were beginning to roll in his head.

'Tell me he'll be all right. Tell me he'll live,' she pleaded, as Tom ran his hands along the length of Lucas's front legs. As he did so, the poor beast groaned in pain.

Not daring to breathe, Ava waited.

'I'm sorry, darling,' Tom said. 'He's broken a leg.'

'No, no, no!' she wailed, and buried her face in her hands.

'Ava, he's in pain. You know what I need to do,' Tom said urgently.

Heartbroken, Ava lay down beside Lucas. She stroked and soothed him as Tom retrieved what he needed from his bag and prepared to inject a massive dose of sedative into the horse's neck. He acted quickly and, within a minute, Lucas's eyelids fluttered and he drifted into unconsciousness.

'Goodbye, my sweet love,' Ava whispered softly, as she stood up stoically in order for Tom to finish the grim task ahead – shooting a bullet into Lucas's forehead.

The loud shot brought Diana round. Bruised and dazed, she staggered to her knees, demanding 'What the hell's going on?'

Wild with anger, Tom turned on her. 'You stupid, selfish woman!' he raged.

'How dare you!' she yelled at him.

'Oh, I dare, all right,' Tom yelled back. 'Because of you and your idiocy, I've just put down one of God's best creatures.' He pointed at Lucas, beneath the hedge. 'Look what you have done – destroyed a perfectly beautiful animal.'

Ava, who had dropped back down to the ground to stroke Lucas, looked up at Diana. With tears coursing down her cheeks, she cried, 'You pushed him even when you knew he was too tired to make it – you did it on purpose.' Taking a deep, ragged breath, she added, 'I could strangle you with my own bare hands!'

'I'm not taking any more of this. I'm going home,' Diana stormed. Clutching her head, she wound her uneven way back down the track.

Peter brought the tractor and truck to winch up Lucas and take him away.

'Go home, darling,' Tom urged. 'You don't want to see this.'

Back at the stables, surrounded by all Lucas's tack, Ava started to cry all over again. Tara the Shetland snickered sadly. She'd spent all her life alongside Lucas, and she was bewildered that he hadn't come back home to her. Tom later found Ava weeping inconsolably beside her.

'She's lost without Lucas,' Ava sighed, as she rose to her feet and walked into Tom's open arms.

Seeing her lovely face muddy and tear-stained, Tom said tenderly. 'We'll have to find her a new friend to play with.'

Ava shook her head. 'No, Tom,' she said, as she filled up all over again. 'No horse will ever replace Lucas. He was the love of my life.'

Back in the Walsingham kitchen later that night, among her friends, Ava reached into a drawer for her packet of cigarettes.

'Diana did it out of sheer spite,' she told them, inhaling deeply. 'She killed Lucas just to prove a point – he was *her* horse and she could do whatever she wanted with him, regardless of the consequences.'

'Well, the good news is she's gone!' Ruby announced. 'She drove off half an hour ago with a bandage wrapped around her head.'

Ava exhaled cigarette smoke and said bitterly, 'I bloody well hope she dies en route!'

Ava urged Tom to return to his practice in Wells. Worried about leaving her, he stroked her face, where a livid bruise caused by Diana's whip was swelling up.

'You know, Tom,' she whispered, 'we had the best ride of our lives on Holkham beach today. Lucas was so happy, he just kept neighing with sheer excitement.'

'At least he had that – he had his last great ride with *you*.'

Tom reluctantly left, promising to return later for a New Year's kiss. Ruby, who was bone-tired, willingly accepted a lift home from Peter.

'I'll be glad to get my feet up – the little un's been doing a fandango inside me all day!' she joked. Kissing Ava, she said, 'I'll be fast asleep by midnight, so I'll say "Happy New Year" now, sweetheart.'

'Happy New 1944!' Ava said, kissing her back. 'Let's hope it's a better year than this one.'

As Ava soaked her weary body in a hot bath and Maudie mixed herb dumplings to go with the spinach soup she'd made earlier, a call from the sewing room made Maudie drop everything. Dashing into the sewing room, she saw a flushed and smiling Bella operating the radio transmitter.

'Is it him?' Maudie cried.

Bella nodded excitedly. 'He's made contact, but there's no message. It must be too risky,' she said.

Maudie threw up her arms and danced around the room. 'My Kit's alive, that's all that matters,' she said, and flung her arms around Bella's neck and kissed her on both cheeks. 'My love's alive and, one day soon, please God, he'll come home to me!'

PART FOUR

1944

35. The War Office

January 1944 was a time of simmering jubilation across the country.

'What with the Allies landing in Italy a few months back and the Soviets advancing into Poland, Jerry must be really starting to sweat,' Ava gloated as she lit up her after-lunch cigarette.

'Not used to being the underdog, eh?' Ruby added gleefully, as she stroked a hand over her burgeoning tummy.

'And what a victory for the Red Army!' Maudie exclaimed. 'Kicking the Germans away from Leningrad.'

'Oh, but the state of those poor souls who survived,' Bella sighed heavily. 'It's a wonder anybody's left alive after a nine-hundred-day siege.'

'I read in the paper that they were reduced to eating wallpaper and sawdust – cats, even,' Ruby said with a shudder.

'A million people died,' Maudie lamented. 'It's a crime against humanity!'

'Bloody Germans!' Ruby seethed. 'I wonder what God will have to say to them on their day of judgement?'

'Don't take too long over that question, ladies,' Ava chivvied, stubbing out her Woodbine. 'We've got meat-and-potato pies to make for thirty-two hungry mouths – let's get cracking!'

In the same week that the Leningrad siege was lifted, the Brig received a letter recalling him back to his desk job at the War Office. His heart sank. Much as he loved his communications work in London, the sudden recall meant leaving Norfolk and the lovely young woman he'd fallen head over heels in love with. At the age of thirty-seven, handsome Charles Rydal, with a first-class Oxford degree in Mathematics, had had a number of relationships with several women. The last one had lasted over two years but had been suddenly cut short when Gladys had been posted to Orkney. If the truth were known, he was actually quite relieved that the relationship had ended when it did. He preferred his bachelor status to any romantic entanglement; they generally got in the way of him doing what he wanted: playing chess, listening to Mozart on his gramophone, having a drink with his old chums in his club, or going to the Oval to watch a game of cricket.

And then along came his own sweet, adorable Bella, who had walked into his office. Pretty, so young and blushing, she'd embraced a new life working with code girls. He'd been intrigued by her right from the start, but he'd only really started falling in love with her when they met in the library to pursue her advanced training. When they kissed for the first time he realized he'd never, in all his thirty-seven years, felt like this before. Since then, their love had grown and grown, even through the terrible, hard times of Kit's prolonged absence and Raf's tragic death, which, for the rest of his life, the Brig would always hold himself responsible for.

And now he was about to tell the love of his life that he was leaving. After reading his instructions from the War Office, the Brig tucked the letter in his pocket, then went about arranging some urgent business in nearby King's Lynn. Later that evening, as he sat side by side with Bella in front of a cheerful fire in the library, he handed her the letter to read for herself. He watched her lovely, pale blue eyes scan the typescript, then she turned to him and burst into tears.

'You're leaving?' she whispered. 'You're going away!'

Close to tears himself, he hugged her tightly. 'Darling, darling,' he murmured, as he kissed her soft blonde curls and rocked her slowly back and forth. 'It's orders. They have to be obeyed.'

Bella drew away to wipe her eyes with her handkerchief. 'I'm sorry,' she hiccuped. 'This is pathetic behaviour.' Squaring her shoulders, she added, 'There are millions of women across Britain who said goodbye to their beloveds four years ago, when the war began. Here am I, moaning and weeping, when I've had you all to myself for so long.' Just thinking about the blissful happiness they'd shared together brought tears welling up in her eyes again. 'I'm being an utter baby,' she said, starting to cry once more. As she dabbed at her eyes, a shocking thought dawned. 'Oh, God! Who's going to train the girls now?' she gasped. 'Please tell me it won't be Miss Cox? I simply couldn't bear that. You leaving is bad enough, but if she takes charge, life will be a nightmare both upstairs and below stairs!'

'She won't be taking over from me,' the Brig assured her with a confident smile.

'Oh, do you know who will be?' Bella asked.

The Brig nodded. 'I was asked to find a suitable replacement.'

Looking puzzled, Bella picked up the Brig's letter, and peered at it closely. 'It says here you're to report for desk duty on Monday. That's only five days away. How on earth are you going to find somebody so quickly?'

'Luckily, I have just the right person in mind.'

'*Who?*' she cried in total frustration.

'*You!*'

Thunderstruck, Bella could only stare at him incredulously.

'You're the perfect candidate,' he told her calmly. 'You completed your training with distinction, then went on to study at a higher level. You're exactly the kind of person I'd be looking for to teach new code girls.'

When Bella's voice did return, it was high-pitched and squeaky. 'I can't possibly!'

'You can most definitely,' he assured her. 'You're unquestionably the cleverest student I've ever taught. You'll be an excellent tutor.'

As she opened and closed her mouth like a goldfish, the Brig added firmly, 'It's a done deal. I submitted your name to the War Office as my possible replacement, and they accepted immediately.'

'Oh, God!' she wailed.

'Stop worrying!' he laughed. 'If you have any problems, you can always phone me, and I can put you straight right away. You'll be fine,' he said, jumping her to her feet and kissing her full on the mouth. 'Now, my dearest, darling, lovely Bella, there's something else you have to do before I leave for London.'

With her head in a spin, Bella cried, 'What now, Brig?'

'Marry me.'

Once again, she stared at him incredulously. 'Really, *really*?'

'Really, *really*,' he laughed, and lifted her into the air and spun her round. 'I'm not leaving you alone in Norfolk for somebody else to snap up. You're my wonderful girl – will you marry me?'

When he had set her down on the ground, Bella laid her head against his shoulder. She'd never in all her life felt such a rush of ecstatic joy. Gazing up at the man she adored, she simply whispered, 'Yes!'

There was great celebration below stairs when Bella and the Brig broke the news to Ruby, Ava and Maudie, and Lady Caroline, too, who the Brig insisted on informing and involving. As they toasted the happy couple in vintage champagne provided by Lady Caroline from her late husband's cellar, Ruby hooted with laughter as she said, 'Oh, heck, Miss Cox won't take the news well. She's had her eye on the Brig right from the start.'

'Actually, as part of the rearrangement, she's been moved on to a training centre in Northampton.'

'Thank God for that,' said Bella gratefully. 'I don't think I could do the job with her breathing down my neck.'

As the Brig kissed his fiancée for the tenth time in less than an hour, Lady Caroline said warmly, 'Congratulations to you both. I've been longing to find the perfect husband for my youngest daughter for years, but I see now she is perfectly capable of doing that for herself.'

Bella blinked back tears – she really couldn't spend the whole evening weeping with happiness!

'Thank you, Mummy,' she said, and hugged her mother, who squeezed her tightly in return.

'At least one of my children has made a wise decision,' Lady Caroline said, with a sad smile.

The Brig approached to shake Lady Caroline's hand, but she offered him both cheeks to kiss. 'Do you mind if I call you Charles?' she asked politely. 'I really can't go around calling my son-in-law "Brig"!'

'It would be my pleasure, Lady –'

She stopped him short. 'Caroline.'

'Caroline,' he echoed, with a warm smile.

'Have you fixed a date?' Maudie asked.

'I drove over to King's Lynn this morning,' the Brig replied, producing a piece of paper from his pocket. 'I managed to get a special wedding licence. We're getting married on Saturday.'

'Saturday!' squeaked Bella. 'So soon!'

'I thought it might be nice to have at least one night for our honeymoon,' he said to a blushing Bella.

'One night!' Ruby sighed. 'Me and my Raf had a whole weekend in Hunstanton.'

'I hope you'll spend your short honeymoon here at the hall,' Lady Caroline said. 'We could prepare the Dower House so you have some privacy.'

'Granny's old house?' Bella asked, recalling her grandmother's pretty cottage, hidden away on the edge of the estate.

Lady Caroline nodded. 'I'll ask Ruby's mother if she can take everything in hand.'

'Thank you, Mummy, that would be lovely,' Bella, still blushing, replied.

'What're you going to wear?' Ava asked.

Bella burst out laughing. 'My black servant's dress and my white lace cap and pinafore!' she joked.

Her mother shook her head. 'I think I can find something a little more appropriate.'

'I suppose we'll have to invite Diana,' Bella said glumly.

Not wanting to take the shine off her daughter's happiness, Lady Caroline quickly said, 'I'll phone her later. It's probably too short notice for her to come, anyway.'

'What with her being so busy with her war work!' Bella couldn't help but mock.

Bella and the Brig couldn't bear to say goodnight. It was gone midnight before they finally tore themselves away from each other.

'Just think, my darling, tomorrow night, we'll spend together, and after that, it's for ever.'

'Apart from you leaving me, a young bride abandoned,' she groaned in mock-despair.

'It will make our time together all the sweeter,' he promised.

With only a day to go to her wedding day, Bella began to panic about the wedding breakfast.

'This is one meal you do *not* cook,' Maudie said firmly, as she, Ava and Bella began to clear away yet another breakfast of tea, toast and rhubarb jam.

'But . . .' spluttered Bella.

'I'm in charge!' Ava teased.

'We'll sort something out,' Maudie assured her. 'And Ruby's promised to cycle over this morning to lend a hand.'

Ava shook her head and chuckled. 'I swear to God, she'll give birth on that blasted bicycle!'

'The Brig's given the trainees sixpence each to go and buy lunch from the fish-and-chip shop in Wells,' Ava added. 'So we'll have plenty of time to prepare a small wedding breakfast.'

'You have to spend the day pampering yourself – book a hair appointment, buy a nightie,' Maudie giggled. 'You can't hop into bed with the Brig wearing that drab winceyette number. It's your wedding night – splash out!'

Bella nodded. She had twenty-four hours to prepare for her wedding day – the wedding breakfast could go hang!

'I'd start by visiting your mum,' Maudie said, with a knowing wink. 'She's got something to show you.'

*

Lady Caroline led Bella into her dressing room. Bella smiled as she recalled, as a little girl, hiding behind the heavy pink brocade curtains so she could watch her mother prepare for a glamorous night out. Her ladies maid, who allowed nobody in the boudoir but herself and her mistress, would towel-dry Lady Walsingham after she stepped out of her bubble bath, then dress her, starting with a silk suspender belt and French knickers and followed by a brassiere and a camisole in the same silk as the knickers. Over her expensive underwear the maid would drape her ladyship's evening dress, exquisitely designed in silk, toile, satin or velvet. In her secret hiding place, Bella would listen out for the soft sound of the gown slithering in heavy folds to the carpeted floor. Once dressed, Lady Caroline would sit before her gilt-edged dressing-table mirror, and her ladies maid would sweep her dark hair into an elegant chignon before applying make-up to her face. The last thing the maid would do was dab Chanel No. 5, from a cut-glass crystal bottle that stood on the dressing table, behind her ladyship's ears. After her mother had swanned out and the maid was busying emptying the bath, Bella would step out of her hiding place and inhale the heady perfume, which she forever after associated with her glamorous mother.

Lady Caroline broke her nostalgic train of thought. 'Have I ever shown you my wedding dress?'

Bella shook her head.

'It's nearly forty years old, but it's still rather beautiful,' Lady Caroline said, as she took the gown from the wardrobe that ran the length of the entire room and held it out for Bella to see.

Bella gazed in surprise at the dress, which was similar in design to the dress Queen Elizabeth – formerly the Duchess of York – had worn on her wedding day. A simple, straight-up-and-down flapper-style tunic made from deep ivory chiffon moiré, embroidered with pearls and silver thread, and with a strip of Brussels lace inserted into the bodice. Though old-fashioned, it was beautiful and it just about fitted Bella, who was a bit more fulsome around the hips and bust than her svelte mother.

'This should keep you warm on a cold January morning in draughty King's Lynn,' her mother said, as she draped a white fur cape over her daughter's shoulders, then offered her a pair of soft, white kid-leather gloves that reached beyond Bella's elbows.

Bella smiled in delight as she gazed at her radiant reflection in her mother's full-length mirror. 'It's a lovely dress, Mummy. Thank you so much.'

'I think a tiara would be a bit much,' her mother commented.

Bella nodded in agreement. 'I'll see what Peter has growing in his precious hot house.'

'Flowers would do nicely,' her mother said approvingly.

'And what about you, Mummy? What will you wear on my wedding day?' Bella asked excitedly.

'I'm in mourning, so I'll probably wear the black-and-grey outfit I wore for Raf's funeral,' she replied, then added, 'I've asked Dodds to drive us to the registry office and back home again.'

Twirling in front of the mirror, Bella laughed with happiness.

'One more day, then I'll be Mrs Charles Ryder!'

Lady Caroline was quite right: Bella would need the cape and the gloves. King's Lynn, the next day, was freezing cold, with showers of snow blowing in from the North Sea. But Bella was pretty and snug under her warm fur cape, and Peter had cut some hothouse white roses for the bride, which Maudie twisted around myrtle leaves to create a lovely winter coronet. It was a small but happy party inside the registry office: Lady Caroline, the Brig and Bella, Ava and Tom, Maudie and Ruby – and Peter and Dodds! Bella's friends wore their best suits, apart from Ruby, who wore a vast, ballooning maternity dress.

'I just hope my waters don't break while they're exchanging their vows,' an irrepressible Ruby giggled as they stood up for the service, which was led by a strict middle-aged woman, who relaxed slightly when she recognized Lady Walsingham.

Maudie was Bella's chief witness, and Tom was the Brig's best man. The service lasted under a quarter of an hour, then Dodds drove the newly married couple back home, followed by Tom, driving a packed Land Rover along the winding coastal road, which gave brief, tantalizing glimpses of the sand and the sea glittering steel bright and cold in the harsh January sunshine.

The wedding breakfast served in Lady Caroline's pretty drawing room simply wouldn't have been complete without the Brig's all-time favourite, game pie, which Maudie, copying Bella's famous recipe, had made as a surprise. There were hot jacket potatoes and meat pies, too, and a small amount of winter salad that Peter had grown in his greenhouse. For dessert, Ava had dug out a bottle of black cherries from the back of the larder and used them to make a fruity tart served with a dried milk custard. Good red wine, courtesy of Lady Caroline, topped the wedding breakfast off.

'Sorry there isn't a cake,' Ava said apologetically. 'There just wasn't enough time to cash in our ration coupons.'

'I doubt there's any dried fruit to be had in England at this stage of the war,' Bella replied. 'Anyway, who cares about cake? I've got everything I need,' she said, gazing adoringly at her new husband, who was settling uncomfortable Ruby on to the sofa.

'Do you think you should put your feet up?' he asked.

Ruby shook her head vehemently. 'Don't be daft, Brig,' she protested. 'I can't go making myself at home in her ladyship's posh drawing room.'

Hearing her remark, Lady Caroline went into professional ambulance-driver mode. Popping two pink silk cushions on to the sofa, she swung Ruby's legs into an upright position.

'There,' she said, smoothing the cushions for Ruby. 'We don't want you with swollen ankles, do we?'

Ruby blushed. 'Thank you, Your Ladyship,' she mumbled awkwardly.

After the toasts and the speeches, the bride and groom picked up their small suitcases, which they'd left ready in the entrance hall, and walked hand in hand out into the softly falling snow.

'Congratulations!' their friends called, as they showered them in confetti. 'Good luck!'

'Bye!' Bella laughed, blowing kisses in her wake.

Ruby's thoughts flew back to her own wedding night, when she and her young, gentle husband found ecstasy in each other's bodies. Smothering her sadness, she put on a bright smile. 'Don't do anything I wouldn't do!' she teased.

With his arm around his radiant bride, the Brig walked Bella through the snow to the Dower House. Fires crackled in the bedroom and the sitting room, Ava and Maudie had thoughtfully left food in the pantry, and, sitting chilling in an ice bucket, was another bottle of champagne, a gift from Lady Caroline from her swiftly depleting cellar. As Bella slipped out of her chiffon wedding gown, she held out her arms to her husband, who gently drew her down on to the bed. They didn't leave it for twenty-four hours!

36. Ruby's Baby

The Brig left Walsingham Hall on Sunday evening. After dragging themselves from their marriage bed, Bella helped her new husband pack a suitcase, which he loaded into the boot of his old Morris car, along with his obligatory gas mask. Standing in the still-falling snow, they clasped each other tightly. As she hugged her husband, Bella yet again marvelled at the selfless heroism of millions of women up and down the land, who, with a brave smile, a kiss and a cuddle, sent their men off to war. Thinking of them, Bella squared her shoulders and said with only a hint of emotion in her voice, 'Drive safely, my darling. Phone me when you arrive back at the flat.'

'My cold, lonely bachelor flat,' the Brig teased. 'Oh, how my life has changed for the better since I met you, Mrs Rydal!'

Bella's eyes twinkled as she recalled the rapture of their love-making, only hours ago.

'I'll have the Dower House ready and waiting for you as soon as you get leave.'

After giving his wife a last, long kiss, the Brig climbed into the driver's seat and started up the engine. 'If you hit any problems with the trainees, get in touch right away, and don't worry– they're going to love you.'

'Bye! Bye! Safe journey,' Bella cried, as the car pulled away and the Brig drove off into the dark night, with no headlights to guide him on his way.

Sighing, but smiling, Bella made her way into the hall, then to the bedroom she'd shared with Maudie for over three years.

When the door opened, Maudie looked up from the book she was reading. 'You all right?' she asked, with a knowing smile.

Bella fell on to her bed and rolled over on to her back.

'Oh, Maudie!' she laughed. 'I'm sad the Brig's had to go, of course. But even so, I've *never* been happier!'

Maudie giggled, she threw her book on to the floor, then hopped into Bella's bed.

'Did the earth move?' Maudie teased.

Bella sighed as she rolled over to cuddle her friend. 'It was pure bliss!'

As Bella took on her new role, Maudie and Ava had the lion's share of the work below stairs. Ruby, with less than a month to go till the birth of her baby, was essentially housebound, especially now, with the snow piled a foot high outside Angel Cottage. For all of Bella's nerves, she took to teaching like a duck to water. The Brig had been right; she was more than able to do the job. The new code girls were roughly the same age as Bella and they enjoyed her energy and humour; she communicated well, was always positive about their work and generous with praise. They particularly loved her challenging decrypting and encrypting classes, and her suggestions on creating a cypher intrigued her trainees.

'The cypher can be anything you and the person you're working with agree on,' Bella explained. 'A poem, a street name, a song, a film star.'

'Robert Mitchum!' a cheeky girl suggested.

'Don't make it too obvious, though,' Bella warned. 'For example, virtually everybody in the world knows who Errol Flynn is, so that would be a really easy cypher to decrypt.'

She would go on to explain carefully and patiently how to match up the letters of the cypher to the letters of the alphabet. Bella took great satisfaction in her trainees' progress, and she was proud to pass on the knowledge that her darling Brig had so skilfully passed on to her. At the end of every working day Bella never failed to assist Maudie and Ava in serving supper to the hungry code girls, who smiled at their tutor wearing a big, striped pinafore as she dished up corned-beef fritters and potato hash. Bella also made time to prepare game pasties and rabbit casserole for the trainees' table.

'I don't want Peter's precious game wasted just because you're too squeamish to skin a rabbit or pluck a duck!' she teased Ava and Maudie.

'All contributions gratefully accepted,' Ava said, wearily lighting a Woodbine while Maudie boiled up milk for bedtime cocoa.

'Any news from your husband?' Maudie asked with a wink.

'He's really busy,' Bella replied, then added with a giggle, 'He says he needs me to warm up his bed at night!'

Ava gave a heavy sigh. 'I envy you being married, Bella. I only wish Tom would pop the question. I fancy him more and more with every passing day.' Catching sight of Maudie's wistful expression, Ava quickly apologized. 'Sorry, Maudie, me and my big mouth.'

'I envy you both being able to see your loved ones,' Maudie freely admitted. 'You're very lucky.'

'We are!' Ava declared, then dropped her voice to a confidential whisper. 'But how do you stay chaste when your love grows stronger by the day? At least Bella's got a ring on her finger – if she falls pregnant, she won't be an outcast.'

Bella burst out laughing at the thought of being pregnant. Maudie cocked her head and gave her friend a quizzical look. 'Er, one thing does lead to the other,' she pointed out. 'You know . . . the birds and the bees?'

Bella blushed. 'Of course . . . I just can't imagine me as a mother.'

'The Brig would make a brilliant father,' Ava joked. 'He could teach your baby how to code-break in the cradle!'

Bella's eyes grew dreamy as she imagined the Brig holding their baby. 'You're right, Ava, he'd make a wonderful father.'

On Valentine's Day, as the Germans were preparing to counter-attack the Allies on the Anzio beachhead in Italy, Ruby went into labour, three weeks ahead of her due date. She'd gone outside to collect some logs for her woodburner, but she slipped on the icy path and fell flat on her back. As she struggled to her feet, her waters broke and amniotic fluid gushed between her legs. Frightened, Ruby started to cry; this wasn't how it should be, lying on her back in the snow – she should be upstairs, warm in bed with a confident, experienced midwife by her side. She managed to stagger to the back gate, where she waved to some children building a snowman on the village green.

'Help! Help!' she cried.

The children took a message to the Lord Nelson pub and, five minutes later, the agitated landlord came knocking on Ruby's door. Knowing that the pub was one of the few residencies that boasted a telephone, Ruby asked the landlord to phone Walsingham Hall and to notify her midwife in Wells, too. The call to the hall went straight through to Lady Caroline in the upstairs drawing room, who immediately ran down the back stairs to look for Bella, only to discover that her daughter was teaching. When she spotted Ava and Maudie clearing away the breakfast dishes, she hurried over to them to tell them the news.

Ava glanced outside. The snow had finally stopped, but it

was now piled up in high drifts. Looking panic-stricken, she murmured, 'Peter will never be able to drive us over there.'

'It's only three miles to Burnham Thorpe,' Maudie said. 'We'll have to walk. Come on, let's go now,' she added urgently.

As both girls set down the trays they were carrying, Lady Caroline exclaimed, 'It's freezing out there! You can borrow my winter coats,' she added, and dashed back upstairs. 'There are wellingtons in the garden room,' she called over her shoulder.

Five minutes later, wearing warm, and very expensive, fur coats and lined wellington boots that were used for shoots, Ava and Maudie set off through the snow.

'Tell Bella as soon as she finishes teaching,' Ava said, as they set off. 'And please phone Tom in Wells – we might need his help.'

'I will. Good luck!' Lady Caroline said as she waved them off.

As Maudie and Ava trudged the three miles through the snow, their anxiety for poor Ruby spurred them to run whenever they could. The drifts by the side of the tiny, narrow roads were high, but where the snow had been cleared, the lanes were slippery with sheet ice, which the girls skated along.

The journey, which would normally have taken an hour at most, took nearly two because of the hazardous conditions. When they finally arrived at Ruby's cottage, they found her leaning over the sofa, doubled up in pain.

'*Arghhhh!*' she howled, and held up one finger, then another and another and another. 'Every four minutes,' she gasped, as the contraction subsided.

Before another one kicked in, Ava said, 'Did the landlord of the Lord Nelson phone your midwife?'

Ruby nodded. 'She's on her way from Wells.'

Ava looked at Maudie, who shook her head; there was no way the local midwife, who cycled everywhere, would ever make it all the way out to Burnham Thorpe. Seeing Ruby's weary face, Maudie put a hand around her waist and helped her upstairs.

'Come on, my darling. Let's get you into bed, then I'll make you a nice cup of tea.'

As Maudie tended to Ruby, Ava dashed around the cottage, collecting up towels, sheets and newspaper, then she put the kettle on for tea. Upstairs, Ruby was in the grip of another contraction, which Maudie was monitoring.

'Still four minutes between them,' she said, as she checked her wristwatch.

'They've been going on for hours, but they're not speeding up like the midwife told me they would,' Ruby fretted, as Maudie wiped her brow with a cool flannel.

Before the next contraction, Ava and Maudie snatched a minute in private.

'I've no idea how to deliver a baby,' Ava panicked.

'Me neither,' Maudie whispered. 'But we mustn't let on we're out of our depth. Ruby's frightened enough as it is.'

By three o'clock in the afternoon, Ruby was in screaming agony, and both of her friends were at their wits' end.

Neither of them had noticed, through the long, hard hours of Ruby's labour, that a soft rain had started to fall, turning the snow that had piled up over the weeks into a grey slush. The sound of a horse's hooves clip-clopping outside made them both jump. Peering over the garden hedge, Ava saw Tom riding towards Angel Cottage on Drummer Boy.

'I don't think I've ever been so pleased to see you!' she cried, and virtually jumped over the hedge to run to him.

'Thank God! Oh, Tom! Thank God you're here.'

Tom leapt off Drummer and hugged her. 'I set off as soon as I heard the news from Lady Caroline,' he said. 'I knew I'd never get the Land Rover down the snowy lanes, so I came across country on horseback.' He smiled as he patted Drummer. 'Vets always travelled on horseback in the old days, so I thought I'd give it a go!'

Ava quickly withdrew from his embrace. 'Hurry!' she urged, as she helped Tom unfasten his medical bag, which he'd secured to Drummer's saddle.

'How is she?' he asked, tying Drummer's reins to a nearby fence.

'Bad,' a frightened Ava answered.

After examining Ruby, a grim-faced Tom took Ava and Maudie aside. 'The good news is she's well dilated. She'll probably want to push soon. The bad news is the baby's in the breech position.'

Ava and Maudie covered their mouths to smother their anxious cries.

'I've delivered breech calves and foals, but never a baby!' Tom admitted.

'Can you do it?' Ava asked.

'I'll just have to do my best,' he replied, with a small smile.

Tom washed and sterilized his hands before returning to his patient.

'You're doing brilliantly,' he assured the nervous mother-to-be, who clearly felt calmer now that Tom was in charge.

'Will it take long?' she asked.

Tom smiled, and said, 'You're well dilated, you'll probably feel the urge to push soon.'

Tom was right: Ruby very soon wanted to push. Though she was weary, she used every ounce of strength she had trying to push her baby into the world.

After an agonizing twenty minutes, just as they were all beginning to lose heart, Tom cried out, 'I can see it! Keep going, Ruby! One more big push and I think you'll have your baby,' he said, and as she pushed, with infinite care he turned the baby before easing it out.

When Ruby and Raf's baby lay mewling between Ruby's outspread legs, Tom neatly snipped the umbilical cord and announced joyfully, 'It's a girl!'

Delirious with relief, Maudie and Ava burst into tears. Tom removed mucus from the baby girl's lips and tapped her bottom to make her cry. The newborn's cry stirred Ruby, and Ava and Maudie settled her against the pillows.

'Say hello to your daughter,' Ava whispered, as Tom handed the child, now wrapped in a sheet and warm blanket, to Ruby.

'Raf's beautiful little girl,' Maudie said, as a radiant Ruby pressed her lips to her daughter's soft, warm cheek.

'Welcome to the world, my darling Rose,' murmured Ruby, as tears of sadness and joy rolled down her cheeks.

'Rose is a beautiful name,' Maudie said approvingly.

Ruby looked at Maudie, then at Ava, before adding with loving smile, 'Her full name is Rose Ava Maud Bella Boskow. She's named after all the people I love most in the world.'

As tears flowed once more, Tom chuckled. 'I think we need to put the kettle on!' he said.

As Ava brewed the tea in Ruby's small kitchen, she heard, above the sound of the steadily falling rain the shrill sound of a siren. Alarmed, Ava threw open the front door and there, standing before her, was Lady Caroline in her ambulance driver's uniform.

'I got here as soon as I could. It's taken a good part of the afternoon, what with all the melting snow and torrential rain,' she said robustly, as she stepped inside the house, followed by Bella, whose face was strained with anxiety.

'How's Ruby?' she asked.

Ava smiled as she gave her anxious friend a reassuring hug. 'She's fine. Worn out, but fine.'

Bella gave her a questioning look.

'A little girl!' Ava cried. 'Rose Ava Maud Bella Boskow!'

Bella clapped her hands in delight. 'It's probably the longest name in history, but it's beautiful!'

'She's beautiful, too,' Ava raved. 'Come and see for yourself.'

Lady Caroline wasted no time in getting mother and baby on to a hospital stretcher, then into her ambulance. Maudie stayed with Ruby and Rose, while Bella joined her mother in the cab. Before an exhausted Tom rode back home cross-country, Ava gave him a passionate kiss.

'You're my hero,' she laughed.

Lady Caroline briskly beeped the ambulance horn and waved impatiently out of the open window.

'Come along, Ava. All aboard!'

As Tom and Drummer set off at a brisk trot, Ava leapt into the back of the ambulance. Lady Caroline released the handbrake, then drove in the dark through the winding country lanes, now swimming in melted snow.

'Let's get mother and baby to hospital right away,' she said to Bella, who gazed at her mother with a new respect. She had never been more proud of Lady Caroline in her entire life!

37. New Life

Ruby and Rose spent a week in Wells Cottage Hospital, where both mother and baby were thoroughly examined and declared well and healthy by the obstetrician. Experienced midwives helped Ruby with breastfeeding. It was difficult to start with, as Rose had little appetite, and Ruby's nipples became painfully cracked. Everybody wanted to see Rose, who had her father's pale blue eyes and silver hair.

'It's like Raf's come back to me,' Ruby sighed, staring in rapture at her sleeping baby. 'I can't thank you enough for helping me give birth,' she told her friends when they visited her.

'You've thanked us enough by naming your baby after all of us!' Ava murmured, as she stroked Rose's soft downy hair.

'I wanted to put Tom's name in there, too,' Ruby admitted

'I think that would be taking things a bit too far!' Tom chuckled.

As a cold March set in, the girls heard on the radio of the first major daylight bombing raid on Berlin by the Allies, then, a few days later, another radio announcement told of the RAF's drop of three thousand tons of bombs during an air raid on Hamburg.

'Wow!' Maudie exclaimed. 'We're bombing the Germans hard these days.'

'Not before time,' Ruby said fiercely, as she hugged her baby close.

'We must have bombed Hamburg off the map,' Bella commented.

'No more than they tried bombing London off the map during the Blitz,' Ava reminded her.

Once Ruby got her strength back, the Silver Cross pram was put to good use: she walked the three miles to Walsingham Hall most days. If Rose was sleeping, she left her in the hall's back garden in the sunshine; if she was awake, she brought her below stairs, where everybody took it in turns to hold her.

Upstairs, Bella's code girls, halfway through their six-month course, were doing well. They were now familiar with creating cyphers and breaking codes but were being stretched even further by the rote learning of Morse code.

'You've got to get your speed up to twenty words a minute,' Bella told her boggle-eyed students.

'I'm working so hard I actually dream in Morse code,' one of the girls joked. 'I can hear the da-da-dip-dips in my sleep!'

'Good, that's the way it should be.' Bella laughed. 'The quicker the better, not just for the sake of getting the message across but also because the quicker you are, the less time you give the person on the other end to track your location.' Smiling at her suddenly serious students, Bella added, 'So work on your speed, girls. Keep dreaming those da-dad-dip-dips – you won't regret it!'

It was round about this time that Bella began to feel unwell. Usually the picture of good health and with an abundance of energy, Bella felt like she could hardly drag herself out of bed in the mornings.

'I think I'm coming down with flu,' she told Maudie, as she got dressed one morning, then, weak with exhaustion, fell back on to her bed.

'You should rest today,' Maudie advised.

'But what about the trainees?' Bella wailed.

'You can set them some work,' Maudie said firmly.

Bella stayed in bed for several days, weak and bored at one and the same time. She was thrilled when Ruby appeared one afternoon with baby Rose in her arms.

'We've come to cheer you up,' Ruby announced, and handed Rose over to Bella.

'I hope I've not got anything contagious,' Bella said, rocking the wide-eyed baby, who, day by day, looked more and more like her handsome father.

'I'll pop downstairs and make us a cuppa while the baby's quiet,' Ruby said, and got to her feet.

'Urgh! No tea for me,' Bella responded with a loud groan.

Ruby immediately sat back down on the bed. 'Say that again,' she said quietly.

'No tea for me, it turns my stomach.'

Ruby gave her a quizzical look. 'Maudie told me you were feeling sick?'

Bella nodded.

'Are your nipples sore and tender?'

Bella gave an experimental tweak. 'Ow! Yes,' she answered.

'Have you missed a period?'

Bella's eyes shot wide open.

'Have you?' Ruby asked again.

Bella tried to recall the number of weeks since her last period. 'I got in a muddle with my dates round about the time Rose was born,' she admitted.

'That was nearly a month ago,' Ruby said, and held Bella's gaze.

'Then I *have* missed a period,' Bella finally answered.

Ruby smiled, then burst out laughing. 'You're not ill, you silly sod. You're pregnant!'

Bella shook her head. 'I can't be!' she protested. 'We only had a night together.'

'That's all it takes,' Ruby giggled.

Though it was months now since Lucas had been put down, Ava desperately missed the beautiful golden-chestnut horse who she'd spent so many happy days with. She missed riding out with Tom, too.

'Why don't I borrow a horse for you, then we could go riding again?' he suggested.

Ava shook her head.

'Is it because you don't want to ride another horse?' Tom asked sensitively.

'Not entirely,' Ava answered honestly. 'What with Bella teaching and Ruby busy with Rose, it really wouldn't be fair to leave poor Maudie running the show while I go galloping across Holkham beach.'

'Fair enough, darling, but please can we spend a little time together soon?' Tom implored.

Later that week, when Maudie suggested that Ava took a couple of hours off, Ava shook her head. 'No, Maudie, it's just not fair.'

'*Please* don't feel guilty,' Maudie begged. 'If you take time off this week, maybe I can take a few hours off next week.'

Thinking this was a much fairer arrangement, Ava smiled. 'OK, it's a deal,' she conceded.

Tom picked her up on a lovely spring afternoon, and they drove along the narrow country lanes flanked by cherry trees, which were decked in fragrant pink-and-white blossom. Ava smiled, visibly relaxing.

'Oh, Tom, it's so good to get out into the fresh air.'

Birds whistled in the leafy treetops and, as they drove through the shallow waters of an unbridged ford, Ava laughed like an excited child as water flew up and splashed the car window.

'This is fun!' she giggled.

Enjoying the day, Ava didn't give a thought as to where they were going. She would have been perfectly happy to sit beside Tom and drive the length and breadth of Norfolk, so when Tom pulled over on to a farm track Ava was surprised.

'Where are we going?' she asked.

'Just got to drop off some antibiotics for a sick calf,' Tom explained, as they bounced their way over the rutted track that led to a traditional red-brick and flint Norfolk farmhouse surrounded by trim, green paddocks.

When Tom stopped the car, Ava stayed in her seat. 'I'll wait here for you,' she said, dreamily gazing into the bright blue sky.

Tom opened the passenger door and held out his hand. 'Come with me, darling. I want to show you something.'

Thinking they were going to see the sick calf, Ava was curious when Tom led her to one of the paddocks, where a stunning silver Arab mare was peacefully grazing.

'Hi, Hepzibah!' he called.

When the horse heard his familiar voice she raised her pretty head, then, with easy grace, she trotted towards the fence, where she nuzzled Tom's outstretched palm.

'She's beautiful,' sighed Ava, as she swept a hand along Hepzibah's fine, long neck, then tickled her small, pricked, silver ears. 'How old is she?'

'I delivered her three years ago, and broke her in, too. She's got a lovely nature, she's warm and trusting, and she rides like a dream,' he said, as he fed Hepzibah a carrot.

'Maybe the farmer will let me ride her out one day,' Ava said longingly.

Tom turned to her with a twinkle in his eye. 'You don't need to ask the farmer for his permission, Ava – Hepzibah is yours!'

Stunned, Ava gazed at Tom for several seconds before she finally blurted out, 'But I've *always* been the girl who rides other people's horses!'

Tom laughed as he pulled her into his arms. 'Not any more, my darling,' he whispered in her ear. 'I thought it was about time the local vet's future wife had a good mount of her own.' Before Ava could say a word, he smothered her lovely mouth in a deep kiss. 'Marry me, Ava Downham?'

'Tom! Tom!' she cried, as she struggled free of his embrace. 'Are you serious?'

'Absolutely!' he replied. 'My divorce came through last week.'

'Why didn't you tell me?' she asked.

'Because I wanted Hepzibah to witness my proposal!' he joked. 'Well – will you or won't you?'

Ava flung her arms around Tom's neck. *'Yes! Yes! Yes!'*

Radiant, an ecstatic Ava trotted back to Walsingham Hall on Hepzibah, leaving Tom to drive on ahead. Throughout the whole journey home, she had a smile on her face and stars in her eyes. Two wonderful things had occurred in the space of five minutes. At last, she had her very own horse, and a silver Arab at that! And she had gorgeous Tom Benson for the rest of her life! Things just couldn't get any better; all her dreams had come true in one glorious afternoon.

*

They met back up at the paddock, and after Tom had left, Ava, bursting with happiness, hurried into the kitchen. But when she saw Maudie chatting to Ruby, who was sitting in one of the old Windsor chairs cuddling Rose, her heart sank. How could she even think of announcing her engagement when she knew Maudie was worried sick about Kit?

'Had a good time?' Maudie asked, as Ava walked in and lit up a Woodbine.

'Fine,' Ava answered blankly.

Knowing her too well, Ruby wagged a finger at Ava. 'What're you not telling us?' she asked in a teasing voice.

Ava blew out a cloud of smoke before she replied. 'Tom's just given me a horse! A beautiful Arab mare.'

Ruby and Maudie gazed at her in delight.

'So why aren't you running round the kitchen screaming with joy?' Ruby persisted.

Ava sighed. She knew that tenacious Ruby wouldn't stop questioning her until she got to the truth. 'There's something else . . .' she said awkwardly. 'Tom proposed.'

Holding Rose, Ruby jumped up and ran to embrace Ava whose happy smile had returned. 'Congratulations!' she exclaimed.

Ava turned anxiously to Maudie, who hugged her, before saying, 'Were you trying to avoid telling us your good news?'

Ava nodded, and said, 'I know how worried you are about Kit, it felt like I was just rubbing salt in the wound.'

Maudie looked levelly at her dear friend and, as their blue and green eyes locked, Maudie spoke honestly. 'Some time soon, please God, my day will come, but until it does, I don't begrudge any of you your happiness.' Kissing Ava, she added, 'I hope you and Tom have a long and happy life together.'

'Amen to that!' cried Ruby.

38. The Baltic Connection

During his time working on the *Mermaid* fishing vessel, Kit had cautiously chosen his time to send several radio messages home. He was more than aware that his messages could be intercepted and the *Mermaid*'s position located, thus putting Captain Claus Helsberg at risk, and his undercover operations, too. Back at Walsingham Hall, the radio operators in the sewing room were equally cautious about returning messages to Kit but, between them, over several months, they'd had several exchanges, and it was in one of these messages that Kit had learnt the shocking news of Raf's tragic death. Devastated, Kit had gone up on deck, where he smoked several Capstans in rapid succession.

'God!' he'd murmured sadly, as he recalled Raf's eager, smiling face. Anger clawed at Kit's guts as he thought of Edward Walsingham and what he'd done. 'If I ever lay eyes on the bastard again,' Kit vowed, as he threw a cigarette stub into the dark sea below, 'I swear I'll tear him apart.'

During their time together Captain Helsberg and Kit had become both friends and allies. They developed a pleasant nightly habit of having schnapps together as they chatted through the events of the day. Helsberg had a great admiration for Squadron Leader Halliday, who had proved his worth as an undercover agent. So far, he'd not put a foot wrong, which is why Helsberg had been in secret negotiations about Kit's next posting. As the captain topped up their glasses one night, he said almost casually, 'Allied intelligence have reported that the Germans have ordered the production of "heavy water" at the hydro-plant in Norway.'

Kit looked up sharply. 'Deuterium oxide,' he said knowingly. 'A vital component in the production of nuclear energy.'

Claus nodded grimly. 'I'd guess the Germans are racing towards the development of an atomic bomb.'

'Jesus!' Kit exclaimed. 'That's all we need – an atomic bomb in the hands of Hitler, the maddest man in the world.'

Claus dropped his husky voice to a low whisper. 'Our Norwegian agents have received instructions from the Allies to destroy the hydro-plant.'

'Good!' Kit cried. 'Anything to deny Hitler the pleasure of blowing up Europe.'

'They're already putting together a crack team to take the target out,' Claus said, before pausing to add, 'I put your name forward for the operation.'

'Me!!' Kit was surprised. 'Why me?'

'I've seen you work: you have all the qualities for this mission – I know you're an excellent radio operator, and I'm told on good authority you can ski, shoot straight, fly a plane and lay charges.' He looked Kit straight in the eye. 'Would you be prepared to take on this highly dangerous mission?'

Kit considered his options for about ten seconds before replying, 'Yes . . . on condition that I get a safe passage back to England when the job's done.'

Claus grinned. 'That girlfriend won't leave you alone, eh?'

Kit shrugged, as he answered, 'Let's just say I made a promise I have to keep.'

'I'm sure there won't be a problem about getting you home.' Helsberg paused, before adding heavily, 'Once the job is done.'

*

Five days later Kit said goodbye to Captain Helsberg and his crew and set off on the next part of his journey home. After taking a train to Oslo, he was parachuted on to a desolate snow-covered plateau in central Norway. The noiseless glider which dropped him whispered through the sky without alerting the enemy to its presence. Once on the ground, Kit made his way through the icy terrain to a disused logger's hut. Here he met the men he'd be working with – Arne, Knut, and Jens, the team leader. With the temperature at well below zero, they impatiently awaited instructions, and when the message finally came through they skied across the mountains to the target area, which was built on the side of a steep, icy gorge.

'How do we get in?' Kit asked Jens, who had done several recces to the hydro-plant.

'We'll climb up the rockface to the railway line which runs directly into the plant,' Jens answered, pointing to a railway track, which Kit could just about make out through his binoculars. 'Safer to go under cover of the dark,' he added tensely.

Hidden in a pine forest with snow falling all around them, they waited for it to get dark, then Jens led the way to the sheer rockface, which they clambered up until they reached the ridge, along which ran the railway track.

'That's our way in,' Jens said in a low whisper.

They entered the factory by slicing through hefty padlocks on the factory gates with a pair of bolt cutters, then, dipping and diving through the icy darkness, they ran past a row of sheds and on towards a cellar door.

Jens pushed hard against it. 'Damn!' he muttered under his breath. 'Locked, of course.'

Looking tensely about, he added in a whisper, 'There's a

tunnel nearby that leads into the plant. If we can find the opening, we can use that to get in.'

It was Kit who found the entrance to the tunnel, by accidentally falling through a sheet of ice that cracked under his weight. Smothering a cry, he landed on all fours in front of the opening.

'This way,' he called softly to his friends.

After scrambling on their hands and knees about fifty feet along the tunnel, they came to another opening, through which they could see the rooms at the heart of the plant where the vast chemical tanks were stored.

Jens smiled and gave his comrades the thumbs-up. 'That's our target!'

Wasting no time Kit, Jens and Knut went on to autopilot, placing charges at strategic points around the tanks while Arne stood guard at the door, which they'd locked behind them on entry. Working swiftly and in silence, they laid all the charges, then turned to Jens for instruction.

'Light the fuses, then get the hell out of here!'

As the fuses started to fizz and spark, the four men dashed back down the tunnel, then out into the yard, where they ran past the sheds. They stopped dead in their tracks as they saw two German soldiers smoking cigarettes under the railway gate.

'Bugger!' Kit fumed. 'They're blocking our escape route.'

'Get behind the sheds before they see us,' Jens called softly.

'We can't hang about here,' Knut gasped. 'The whole bloody plant's going to blow in less than seven minutes!'

Adrenalin pumped through their veins, they waited for the soldiers to move on, which they did at a leisurely pace, after stubbing out their cigarettes.

'Go! Go! Go!' Jens urged his men, and they ran for their lives, down the railway line towards the rockface they'd climbed up. As they reached the end of the track, the first explosion went off and the light from the flames silhouetted the fleeing men.

'*Halte!*' the German soldiers they'd just evaded yelled, and fired their pistols.

Knut and Jens, already descending the ridge, were well out of range but Arne, bringing up the rear, was a clear target. Running, he stumbled as he was shot straight through the chest. Hearing his scream, Kit turned around, but Arne lay bleeding, sprawled full length across the tracks. As the guards advanced on him, Kit boldly held his position as he took aim with his pistol. Waiting until both guards were in range, Kit shot them one after the other in the head. A second and a third explosion lifted the roof of the plant, and flames combined with toxic chemicals to create a blazing inferno of smoke and heat. With the swirling smoke briefly obscuring him, Kit swung himself over the ridge, and quickly climbed down. After recovering their skis, the three men skied back in the dark to the logger's hut, where they quickly tuned into their transmitter.

'Mission accomplished,' Kit tapped out in rapid Morse code as the last charge they'd laid at the hydro-plant went off, turning the entire site into a massive bonfire. Knowing that any surviving Germans would soon be swarming the countryside looking for them, and that if they were captured they'd surely be tortured to death, they waited for their rescuers with their hearts in their mouths. When they heard the sound of a Lysander aircraft, they literally ran for their lives towards the prearranged landing site and pick-up point.

The Lysander took the three men to an obscure airfield

outside Oslo, where they briefly shook hands, then swiftly melted into the night in different directions. Kit's instructions were to go to the harbour, where he was to buy a beer in the Pelican café and wait for his contact, who turned out to be a drunken sailor. Almost falling on Kit, he swung an arm about him and dragged him to his feet. Then, in a totally sober voice, the seemingly drunken sailor whispered in English, 'Come with me.'

Swaying and bumping against each other, they staggered to a trawler that stank to high heaven. As the grinning sailor released Kit from his grip, he said, 'This stinking herring trawler is your ride back to Blighty, mate!'

Kit laughed out loud. 'Who cares what it is – just so long as it takes me home!'

39. Coming Home

By the time Bella visited the family doctor in Fakenham, she'd missed her second period and had absolutely no doubt at all that she was pregnant. Ablaze with happiness, she drove home, desperate to tell her mother and her friends, but the person she longed to tell most in the world was, obviously, her husband. She could imagine the joy on his face when he heard the news, the way his soft brown eyes would widen in surprise and his lips curl into an incredulous smile – which was exactly why she didn't want to tell him she was expecting his baby over the phone.

'I'll go to London at the weekend,' Bella told her mother and friends, as they took it in turns to hug and congratulate her.

'Is that safe?' queried Ruby, as she rocked Rose to sleep in her arms. 'You might stumble into a bomb crater and never be seen again,' she giggled.

'I'll make absolutely sure I don't do that,' Bella promised. 'And I'll avoid all falling bombs, too!'

The Brig was delighted that Bella was coming to visit him. 'We'll go out for dinner,' he said excitedly. 'Maybe go dancing afterwards?' he tentatively suggested.

Bella knew too well how much the Brig disliked dancing, and the fact that he was trying so hard to please her made her smile to herself. 'Let's not waste precious time dancing when we could be doing other things,' she said with a cheeky giggle.

*

A few days later, on a Saturday afternoon, Bella alighted at King's Cross station into a seething crowd rushing in all directions. Soldiers, sailors and young men in RAF uniforms, all bearing bulging kit bags, dashed across the station to catch departing trains. Evacuees clinging to their mothers' skirts were swooped away by nurses supervising their journey out of London, leaving desolate mothers weeping on the platform. In the chaos, Bella was relieved to see the Brig walking towards her.

'Darling!' she cried, and rushed into his arms.

Hugging her close, he inhaled the sweet smell of her soft, curling hair, which he stroked fondly. Standing back to look at her, he smiled at the sight of her radiant, glowing face.

'Darling, you look wonderful!' he cried. 'What have you done to yourself?' he asked.

Bella blushed, as she shrugged his question away.

'Come on,' he said, tucking her arm through his. 'Let's get you home.'

As they drove in a cab to the Brig's Pimlico flat, Bella was shocked at the sight of bomb-torn London. Barrage balloons floated high overhead. Five years into the war, the city had been crushed by relentless bombing raids. Bella gasped as they drove by block after block of shattered offices, factories, tenement buildings and centuries-old churches, former London landmarks, all reduced to piles of rubble and brick dust.

'Poor London!' she murmured sadly.

'Poor London, indeed,' the Brig agreed. 'She's taken quite a beating, but nothing kills her spirit. Londoners will never give up their city.'

'Bloody right there, guv!' the taxi driver chuckled through a smoking cigarette dangling from his lips. 'The bastard

Hun – begging you pardon, Miss – will never rule Britannia!'

When they got to his flat, which the Brig had tried to brighten up with a couple of bunches of spring flowers, he mixed them both a gin and tonic, which Bella firmly set aside. As the Brig sipped his drink he gazed admiringly at his wife.

'Well, you seem to have shaken off that bug that laid you low. I don't think I've ever seen you looking better, darling.'

'I don't think I've ever felt better,' Bella replied with a mysterious smile.

'Being away from your new husband obviously suits you,' he teased.

'I had something to remind me of you,' she answered coyly.

Completely unaware of the bombshell that she was about to drop, the Brig laughed. 'Oh! And what might that be?'

She took his hands in hers, before saying softly, 'I'm pregnant.'

The Brig gripped her hands so hard it hurt.

'But . . . we only had one night together!' he gasped.

Bella burst out laughing, as she repeated Ruby's wise words: 'That's all it takes!'

Pulling her into his arms, the Brig held her so tightly Bella could barely breathe. 'My love, my lovely girl,' he said on a sob.

As he loosened his hold on her, Bella was able to see what she'd travelled all the way from Norfolk for: the Brig's face suffused with joy, and his soft brown eyes brimming with emotion. Shaking his head and swallowing hard, the Brig murmured incredulously, 'We're going to be parents!'

Still stunned, he asked, 'When . . . ?'

'October.'

Anxious about her and the baby's health, the Brig frowned. 'Does that mean we can't make love till after the baby's born?'

Rising to her feet, smiling, Bella held out her hand and said boldly, 'I'm not waiting six months – take me to your bedroom, Brigadier Rydal!'

As Bella and the Brig were rejoicing in their good news, the smelly herring trawler bringing Kit home lumbered into King's Lynn port after ten days out on a stormy grey sea. Tears stung the back of Squadron Leader Halliday's sky-blue eyes. A year had passed since he'd flown out of Holkham air base that fateful night, and what a year it had been: he'd been captured, imprisoned and then been a POW on the run. Right now, all he wanted was Maudie in his arms. After he'd seen her, he planned to get straight back into a Lancaster and bomb the bloody hell out of the enemy. But his ultimate wish was to track down Edward Walsingham, wherever he was on God's earth, and have his revenge on a man who had murdered Raf and caused the death of so many other airmen.

On a bucolic spring evening, with cow parsley and bluebells knee-deep in the hedgerows, Kit stood by the side of the coastal road, where he hitched a lift from an army truck driver who dropped him right by the gates of Walsingham Hall. Filled with an emotion that completely overwhelmed him, Kit could only stand and stare at the long sweep of drive that led up to the house where the woman he loved was waiting for him. Dressed in scruffy fishermen's clothes and tanned by months at sea, bearded Kit was barely recognizable as the suave RAF officer from Holkham airbase.

Peter, driving his old jeep, would certainly have driven past Kit had he not flagged him down.

'Hey!' he called. 'It's me!'

Astonished, Peter screeched to an abrupt half. 'You're back, sir!' he cried.

Kit nodded and smiled, revealing teeth that gleamed white against his thick blond beard.

'I'm looking for Maudie.'

'You've missed her,' Peter told him.

Kit's face dropped in disappointment. 'Where is she? What's happened?' he asked anxiously.

Peter chuckled. 'Nothing serious, sir. She's just walked down to the beach for a breath of fresh air, she won't be long.'

Desperate to see her, Kit said impatiently, 'I'll go and find her.'

Knowing how big Holkham beach was, Peter leant over to open the passenger's door. 'Hop in, sir, I'll take you,' he said kindly.

Ten minutes later Kit was standing in the fading light on the vast, wide sweep of the beach, which was empty apart from one person walking along the water's edge. Scared that it would go dark and he would miss Maudie, Kit broke into a run, and as he did so some instinct made Maudie turn inland, where she saw the man she'd dreamed would somehow make it home safely running towards her.

Overwhelmed with joy, they covered the space between them as if they had wings on their feet, throwing themselves into each other's arms before – unable to stand – they fell to the ground, where they lay, their lips locked, lost in an ecstasy of love. It was only the hissing sound of the incoming tide that brought them to their senses.

'I'm all wet,' Maudie giggled.

'I don't care,' he replied, burying his lips in her glorious auburn hair. It tasted of sea water.

'We might drown,' she giggled again.

'I don't care,' he repeated, as his lips traced the seductive line from her chin to her shoulder and down to her breast. 'I'd happily die right here in your arms.'

Eventually, they managed to drag themselves to their feet and walked the two miles back to Walsingham Hall gripping each other tightly, stopping every five minutes to gaze at each other in wonder and kiss over and over again.

'You kept your promise,' she said. 'You came back to me.'

Kit pulled her close to whisper their motto, 'To the stars and back, my darling . . . To the stars and back!'

40. Double Bluff

One lovely late April morning, Bella was called from her class by Ava, who looked tense and anxious.

'You'd better go to your mother right away, Bella,' she said urgently. 'She's had some bad news.'

Hurrying up the elegant main staircase to her mother's suite, Bella wondered what could have happened. Was her mother sick? When she entered the drawing room she immediately saw from the stricken look on her mother's face that it was very bad news. Handing her daughter a letter to read, Lady Caroline burst into tears.

Bella sank on to the sofa next to her weeping mother and, with some trepidation, began to read the letter out loud.

Greenhalgh and Son, Family Solicitors
69 Long Meadow Lane,
Holt, Norfolk
April 20th 1944

Dear Lady Walsingham,
It is with deep regret that I write to inform you that your son, Lord Edward Walsingham, died in Berlin by his own hand on 4 April 1944.

Bella stopped short. 'Edward's dead!' she gasped. Shocked, she turned back to the letter: '"We learnt of this shocking news from his wife –" Oh, my God! He was married, too!'

'Why did he never tell us he had a wife?' her mother sobbed.

Bella squeezed Lady Caroline's hand. 'Mummy, face it: Edward told us very little.'

She continued to read: '"I enclose a letter sent to you, care of ourselves, from Lord Edward's widow, plus copies of a wedding certificate and Lord Edward's death certificate."'

Bella quickly turned the page to read the widow's letter to her mother.

Dear Lady Walsingham,
We met when you visited Edward in Cambridge. You may recall that we were close friends?

Bella stopped short again. 'My God! He married Geraldine!' she cried. 'Remember the posh dumpy girl he studied German with?'

Having had one too many shocks, her mother just gave a confused nod.

'"I enclose our wedding certificate to prove my official status as Edward's wife. We married in secret before Edward left to work in Europe while I remained in England,"' Bella read.

'Do you think it's true?' her mother asked.

Bella studied the two certificates, one in English, the other in German. 'They look authentic enough, but it's a damned weird set-up!' she exclaimed. '"I understand that, legally, because of the nature of Edward's work, I cannot inherit anything from the Walsingham estate."'

'Certainly not!' Lady Caroline cried indignantly.

'"Edward always said if anything were to happen to him, he would want me to rebuild my life with a new identity that had no association with him or his past. But without his financial support, I am virtually penniless! Edward assured me you would help me, which is why I have the confidence to write to you. He told me of the Walsingham family gold held by Coutts Bank. Would you consider helping his grieving widow by donating a sum of gold to the value of two thousand pounds to help her carry out your son's dying wishes?" The cheek!' Bella cried.

'She has a point,' Lady Caroline said thoughtfully. 'If the solicitor agrees that the certificates are authentic, then it would be the right thing to help Edward's widow establish a new life in a place where she's completely anonymous.'

'Mummy!' Bella cried. 'The woman could come cap in hand to us whenever she's broke.'

'Our solicitor would have to make it clear that this is a one-off payment for closure on the whole sad business,' her mother said, as tears welled up in her tired eyes.

'Two thousand pounds is a *lot* of money!' Bella protested.

'Darling, think about it. She could kick up a hell of a fuss and try to claim more. This could be a smart, tactical move and, if it is what Edward wanted . . . he is still my son, whatever he did . . .' Lady Caroline concluded bleakly.

Bella put her arm around her mother's shaking shoulders; she was shocked at how cold and removed from her brother's death she felt. She had ceased to have even a residual sisterly affection for Edward some time ago and was secretly relieved that he couldn't harm any more innocent people. But her heart ached for her poor mother. She had suffered two blows: first, her husband's sudden death at Christmas, and now her son's suicide.

'I'm so sorry, Mummy,' she said softly.

*

Standing on King's Parade in Cambridge, Edward Walsingham, two stone heavier than when he was last in England, his hair dyed black and sporting a goatee beard, examined his reflection in the large window of the Copper Kettle café.

After hearing of his father's death, Edward's first thought had been how he could lay his hands on some money. Given his circumstances, he would be denied any claim to his inheritance. A German spy couldn't possibly take on an ancestral title! But the family gold sitting in Coutts Bank in London was quite another matter. He wanted a part of that gold stash, but how to lay his hands on it? Then he had a brainwave: he would claim his money through Geraldine, his mistress, who was the nearest to a wife that Edward would ever get. He smiled as he imagined her hamming up the part of the grieving, penniless widow mourning the 'death' of her beloved husband.

Travelling with a false passport and identity papers, Edward had made his way from Berlin to Bremen by train, then crossed the North Sea in a decrepit passenger ship. He planned to stay with Geraldine, who was now a senior tutor in the German Department in Cambridge. She had pleasant set of rooms in King's College, where he could hole up until the business with his mother was wrapped up. Geraldine always welcomed him with open arms, particularly if he arrived armed with brandy, cigarettes and nylons. There was no doubt he had a soft spot for the old girl, they went back a long way, right to Freshers' Week, when she was at Girton and he was at King's. She'd been groomed for spy work along with him, but she had baulked at the eleventh hour.

'I don't fancy it,' she confessed. 'It always leads to some ghastly torture,' she joked. 'Far too messy, darling!'

Nevertheless, they'd remained lovers when he was in the

country, and she was the soul of discretion, plus, cunning Edward had kept a secret dossier of information on her, which he wouldn't hesitate to use if she tried any funny business.

Over a boozy, expensive dinner at the Ritz, followed by a very satisfactory night of sex in one of the hotel's most opulent bedrooms, Edward had had no problem persuading Geraldine to present herself as his desperate widow who wanted to flee the disgrace and shame of a treacherous dead husband.

'Darling, I'll weep convincing tears in my widow's black Hartnell suit and veil,' she had promised.

Back in Cambridge, in Geraldine's comfortable rooms, Edward paid out a considerable amount of money for a fake wedding and death certificate, then put them in an envelope with the callous letter he had concocted. After patting Geraldine's rather ample bottom, Edward asked her to address the letter to his mother for whom he showed not a jot of emotion.

'Now all we have to do is wait for the money to come rolling in,' he said, as he led smiling, eager Geraldine into her bedroom.

Back at Walsingham Hall, Maudie went about her work with a permanent smile on her face.

'You look like the cat that got all the cream,' Ava teased, as the two girls rolled pastry on the floured kitchen table for half a dozen meat-and- potato pies.

'I keep having to pinch myself to make sure I'm not dreaming,' Maudie admitted. 'Can you believe it's nearly a year ago since Kit was gunned down and Raf was murdered and everything looked so terribly bleak?'

Ava shook her head and said, 'A year! We'll never get over losing Raf, but his lovely daughter is nearly three months old, and Bella's expecting now.' Turning to Maudie, Ava winked mischievously. 'Soon be your turn, lovie!'

Maudie burst out laughing. 'Let me get married first!' she cried.

Their happy chatter was interrupted by Bella, who had hurried below stairs to tell her friends of Edward's death. Neither Maudie nor Ava could pretend to grieve over it.

'I feel very sorry for your poor mother,' Maudie said, with genuine sympathy.

'God! She must be in shock,' Ava said compassionately.

'She's in double shock,' Bella added grimly. 'His widow wants paying off.'

'Grasping cow!' cried Ava. 'You'd think she'd give Lady Caroline time to grieve before making a grab for her son's money.'

'They sound like the perfect couple,' Bella remarked bitterly. 'Both completely out for themselves!'

As Edward's complex plan to line his pockets swung into action, the RAF were preparing airbases around the country for a major raid on the German coastal batteries positioned along the Normandy beaches. A thousand aircraft would be involved in the D-Day landings, and the hope was that it would radically change the course of the war. The ground crews at Holkham airbase were working around the clock, making ready their Lancasters. A sense of tense expectancy ran through the airmen, who knew that, since Bomber Command's strategic bombing policy had been operational, Britain's battle in the air had grown in strength and power.

Knowing Maudie was terrified of him being gunned

down again, Kit, sworn to secrecy about any forthcoming raids, barely mentioned his work. But there was no hiding when a squadron took off: everybody in the area could hear the mighty Lancasters rumbling down the runway and taking to the air over the Norfolk turnip fields before flying out over the North Sea. The last thing Kit wanted to do to his beloved was inflict further fear and pain; like most of his comrades who were in love, he kept secrets to shield Maudie.

One night, when Maudie heard the deafening drone of Lancasters taking off, her blood ran cold. She didn't need Kit to tell her – she instinctively knew he was up there. She could even picture him, silent, stony-faced and determined at the controls of his beloved plane.

It was lucky that Maudie didn't know about Kit's raid on 5 June 1944. Five thousand tons of bombs were dropped on the Normandy beaches that night, the greatest amount in the war so far. D-Day, 6 June, dawned, the Germans were on the run, and the Normandy beachheads, where rocket launchers were permanently aimed at England and the Channel, toppled to the triumphant Allies.

41. King's College, Cambridge

Edward's plan might have worked but for his fatal mistake in sending a coded message to Berlin during the week of the D-Day landings. What drove him to behave so recklessly was the shock of what happened to the Germans; the superior Aryan power, under the leadership of Adolf Hitler, had been made fools of. They had been tricked by clouds of chaff – thin pieces of metallized glass fibre – which had been dropped from Stirling bombers to create an illusory false target on the enemy's radar screens. By the time the Germans discovered the smokescreen, it was too late. Fighter planes were upon them and they were being gunned down on the Normandy beaches.

While Geraldine was out giving a lecture, Edward tracked down her old radio transmitter, which she'd briefly used during her training period before abandoning the idea of spying. Edward set up the aerial and, using his code name, he logged in and started transmitting to Berlin.

Back at Walsingham Hall, Maudie, out of habit after months and months of checking the radio transmitter while Kit was away, still continued to tune in from time to time. Besides, she liked to keep up her Morse code. That afternoon, as she sat with earphones clamped around her head, her green eyes grew wide in amazement.

'Sweet Jesus!' she gasped, as she recognized Edward's code name, then – curbing her astonishment – she concentrated hard on writing out the coded message he was sending.

As soon as he'd signed off, Maudie ran into the kitchen, where she found Ava making tea.

'You're not going to believe this. Walsingham's transmitting!' she gasped.

Ava nearly dropped the teapot. 'But he's dead!'

'Then somebody's using his code name,' Maudie replied.

'Phone the Brig!' cried Ava.

When Maudie got through to him, he said, 'Read out the message, exactly as you wrote it down.'

Slowly and carefully, she repeated the message she'd written down in Morse code.

'I'll have a crack at decrypting it,' the Brig said. 'Can you let Kit have it, too? Between the two of us we might be able to get the location of the sender, which will give us a lead as to who it really is. Does Bella know?' he asked.

'No, she's teaching,' Maudie told him.

'Be careful not to mention this to Lady Caroline. She's upset enough about her son being dead, but imagine how devastated she'll be to find out it's a hoax. But then, it's exactly the kind of thing Walsingham is capable of.'

Maudie cycled faster than she ever had before through the lovely, winding lanes, barely noticing the birds singing their hearts out in the treetops in full summer leaf. She was surprised that she felt comfortable about being back at the airbase; she'd avoided it the whole time when she'd feared Kit was dead. Now here he was, suntanned and handsome in his RAF uniform, walking towards her with a wide smile on his face.

'Sweetheart!' he exclaimed, as he drew her into his arms and kissed her full of the mouth. 'This is an unexpected pleasure.'

Though Maudie longed to linger over his kiss, she pulled away to tell him the news.

Kit's arms fell from her shoulders. Stunned, he could only stare at her.

'It might be somebody using his code name,' Maudie added quickly. 'The Brig asked me to bring you a copy of the message I picked up this afternoon.'

Kit finally got his voice back. 'Could the bastard have faked his death?'

'Wouldn't put it past him,' Maudie answered, as she handed him a copy of the coded message. 'The Brig's trying to crack it to see if it really is Walsingham. He wants you to a have a go, too.'

'With pleasure!' Kit said eagerly.

'He said we might find the location of the sender by the strength of the signal,' she added.

Kit nodded. 'The louder and clearer the signal, the closer the sender,' he replied.

'I'll have to love you and leave you,' Maudie said, as she jumped back on her bike. 'I promised Ava I'd be back to help with supper.'

'I'll drive over later,' he promised. 'Especially if I have any news!'

As soon as Bella had finished teaching the code girls she skipped downstairs in order to help Ava carry the loaded supper trays up to the canteen. When she heard the news about her brother, she was shocked rigid.

'I need to talk to the Brig!' she cried.

'Best leave him to his work for the moment,' Ava advised. 'He's trying to crack the code,' she added.

Bella gave a brief smile. 'Point taken!' she said.

Maudie arrived back, and all three girls served cauliflower cheese, with barely a scraping of cheese, and Spam fritters.

As they worked, they had only one thought on their minds: was Walsingham alive? As soon as she was free, Bella also started to puzzle over the coded message Maudie had given her. When the phone in the hall shrilled out, she dashed to get it and, at almost the same time, Kit drove into the court-yard in his old MG.

'I can't be sure yet,' the Brig told Bella over the phone. 'I'm still trying to decrypt the code by using his old cyphers.'

Kit came bounding up to Bella. 'Sorry to be rude,' he said, 'but would you mind if I had a word with the Brig?'

Bella handed over the phone, and Kit spoke rapidly into it. 'It's Walsingham!'

'Sure?' the Brig asked sharply.

'Definitely. Who else always signs themselves out, *über Alles*? You know, the line from the German national anthem, *"Deutschland über Alles"*? Didn't you spot it at the end of the message?'

The Brig shook his head. 'Sorry, old man, I still haven't got to that bit. It's been a slow process,' he said apologetically.

'And there's more. I got my top signalling chaps to locate his whereabouts,' Kit added soberly. 'He's only in bloody Cambridge!'

There was a brief pause before the Brig, on the end of the phone, and Bella, standing beside Kit, said in unison, 'King's College, Cambridge!'

The Brig wasted no time in racing up from London and involving the local police constabulary in Cambridge. He and Kit met up with them the next day.

'We suspect he's at King's, his old college,' the Brig informed the detective in charge, who hastily outlined his plan.

'We'll surround the grounds, and position plain-clothes

policemen around the college, too. The sooner we move in on him, the better – if Walsingham is in the college, the last thing we want is to lose him.'

Edward was enjoying a quiet smoke while Geraldine was supervising her tutor group in the Gibbs Building. With no idea that he'd been rumbled, he rose and stretched, deciding to take a stroll by the river. As he opened the door on to a pretty quad where early roses were in bloom, Edward walked straight into a burly policeman who was standing guard by the door.

'Excuse me, sir –' the policeman began, but Edward delivered a swift right-handed punch which sent him reeling.

Edward dashed across the quad to the bridge, where he found another policeman on guard. Managing to dodge around him, Edward caught him off balance and pushed the poor man backwards into the river. Kit, who'd been standing with a police constable by the college chapel, saw Edward sprinting off.

'Bugger!' he yelled. 'He's getting away!'

The policeman broke into a run. 'I'll follow him, sir, you cut him off at Trinity!' he cried over his shoulder.

Luckily, Kit was familiar with the tiny paths and alleyways that linked the colleges. Tearing past Clare College and Trinity Hall, he ran across Trinity College Great Court then tore down the leafy back lane which led on to the Backs, where he intercepted Edward and knocked him to the ground. Winded but not hurt, Edward sprang to his feet and hit out at Kit, who retaliated with a savage right swing. Edward came at Kit with both fists clenched.

'You bastard!' he snarled.

Kit moved around him, keen to land another punch. *'Murderer! Bloody traitor!'* he swore, and threw himself on to

Edward. He would cheerfully have strangled him with his bare hands.

Fortunately, the Brig, the detective and his men had by now caught up with Kit, and dragged him away from Edward.

'Leave him!' the Brig cried.

Trembling and sweating, Kit stood over Edward. 'You filthy, rotten, stinking traitor, I hope you swing!'

The detective gave Kit, who was trembling in anger, a firm pat on the shoulder.

'Let's leave it to the law now, shall we, sir?'

It was left to the Brig to break the news to Lady Caroline: her son was not dead, but alive, and presently in police custody, charged with murder and treason.

'I had a long interview with Edward after he was arrested,' the Brig told Bella when they had some time alone. 'The bastard was only here to plot with his lover, his "widow", Geraldine. He was totally unrepentant – just said he had a right to the family gold, if nothing else.'

'Didn't he even think how much it would hurt Mummy?' she asked incredulously.

'Quite honestly, I don't think he thought about it,' the Brig replied.

'What will happen to Geraldine now?'

'She'll be questioned, she might go to prison for sheltering a traitor,' the Brig answered.

Bella gave a heavy sigh, 'God! This could kill poor Mummy.'

The Brig put an arm around her shoulders. 'He's behind bars now, my love,' he whispered reassuringly.

Bella looked up at her husband, as she replied, 'Thank Christ! It's the best place for him.'

42. Justice is Done

Just one week after the triumph of the D-Day landings, Hitler, in vengeful mood, rained V-1 bombs on London. Nicknamed Doodlebugs and Buzz Bombs, due to the distinctive sound made by the pulse-jet engines that powered them, the bombs fell every hour on London. Over an eighty-day period, more than six thousand innocent people were killed, over seventeen thousand injured and a million buildings wrecked or damaged. Londoners dreaded the deadly hush as the engine suddenly cut out before the bomb plunged towards the ground, followed by an ear-splitting explosion as the warhead hit its target. The indiscriminate bombing went on around the clock, in all types of weather, causing suspense and terror among the population of London, and in parts of Kent and Sussex, too.

After Hitler's revenge attack, the nation needed good news, and the month of August brought it. At the beginning of the month, the Polish army rose against the Nazis. By the middle of the month the Allies had invaded southern France and, on 25 August, Paris was liberated.

'The Nazi generals are so sick of Hitler they tried to bump him off themselves,' Ruby gloated.

'Pity their conspiracy failed,' Maudie sighed. 'As long as megalomaniac Adolf is alive and kicking, there'll always be suffering.'

August also brought news of Edward's trial date; it was set for the beginning of September. Bella begged her mother not to attend the trial, which would take place in the High Court.

'There can't possibly be a good outcome, Mummy.'

Lady Caroline shook her head. 'I have to be there right till the end,' she said sadly.

When Bella finally saw her brother, she felt like she'd been knocked sideways. He was no longer overweight, but thin and gaunt; his previously blond hair was heavily streaked with grey, and the bruising around his cheekbones suggested he had suffered some rough treatment while he was in prison. The trial lasted two days, and after it the jury found Edward guilty of murder and treason. When the judge placed the black cap, the ultimate symbol of doom for a condemned man, on his head, Bella's blood ran cold. After announcing the punishment – death by hanging – the judge closed the proceedings with the words, 'May the Lord have mercy on your soul.'

Though pale and trembling, Lady Walsingham sat dignified and erect as her son was taken back down to the cells.

'I think we all need a stiff drink!' the Brig announced, as he led his wife and mother-in-law from the courtroom.

A few weeks later, the day before Edward was due to hang, the Brig and Bella drove Lady Caroline to Wandsworth Prison, where she was allowed to see her son.

'I'd prefer it if you didn't come, darling,' she informed Bella. 'I'd like our final meeting to be between Edward and myself.'

Bella didn't argue. In fact, she was secretly relieved not to go. Rationally, she had no time for her disgraced brother, but in reality, every time she thought of the hideous death awaiting him in less than twenty-four hours she couldn't help but weep with sorrow.

'God! I'll be glad when this nightmare is over,' the Brig murmured, as he and Bella sat in the car waiting for Lady Caroline's return.

When she did emerge, after her hour-long visit, she looked like she'd aged a hundred years. The Brig leapt out of the car to help her into the passenger seat, where she sat staring vacantly at the rain falling softly on the windscreen.

'Thank God your father has been spared this,' she said, as tears rolled down her weary face. 'I had to know why Edward betrayed his country.' She paused to take a long, ragged breath. 'He said he'd always had the greatest admiration for Hitler and the Third Reich, that their vision for a new Aryan world inspired him.' Her voice dropped. She was worn out. 'He apologized to me, said he was sorry for the pain he'd put me through, but he was adamant that he had no regrets about his decision to turn his back on his country.' Straightening her shoulders, Lady Caroline inhaled deeply. 'Now, Charles, would you be so good as to take me home? The further away I get from this wretched place, the better!'

After the death of her son, Lady Caroline threw herself body and soul into her war work. Driving the ambulance and helping people in need gave her a reason to live. Something else which made her life worth living was her relationship with Bella. The daughter she'd previously despaired of had become, quite simply, the light of her life. She'd married a splendid man whose child she was carrying, she was an excellent teacher for the code girls, a magnificent cook, but most of all, she was the sweetest daughter a mother could ever hope for.

Lady Caroline spent more and more time below stairs with Ava and Maudie, sometimes with Ruby and Rose, and Bella, too, when she wasn't teaching. Laughter and easy conversation with people she trusted eased the pain and guilt that Lady Caroline would carry for the rest of her life.

43. Autumn Storm

The Brig arranged with his superiors at the War Office that he would take over teaching the code girls when his wife was no longer able to do so. He took the train down to Norfolk a few days before Bella's due date, in late October, and found her in blooming health.

'Shouldn't you be relaxing, darling?' he enquired after they'd warmly embraced.

Bella shook her head. 'I've never felt fitter,' she declared.

'You haven't got long to go,' he reminded her. 'I was hoping to find you knitting, with your feet up.'

Again, Bella shook her head. 'I'll rest after I've finised work this week,' she promised.

When she wasn't teaching the trainees, Bella could be found cooking up a storm in the kitchen.

'You've got the nesting instinct, all right,' Ruby teased, when she arrived with baby Rose to find Bella rolling pastry out on the kitchen table while soup simmered on the Aga and bread rolls baked in the oven.

'I'm doing as much as I can before I give birth.' Bella laughed happily.

Lady Caroline kept an anxious eye on the amount of petrol in her ambulance.

'With petrol rationed, I need to make sure there's enough in the tank to get Bella to the hospital when she goes into labour,' she told the Brig.

He rolled his eyes as he replied, 'She's nearly a week over-due, and bursting with energy.'

'First babies,' Lady Caroline said knowingly. 'Don't worry – it'll happen soon enough.'

She was right. The next day, just after lunch, Bella felt a sharp, stabbing pain in the small of her back.

'I think I'll go and lie down,' she told the Brig.

In the upstairs bedroom she now shared with the Brig, Bella sat on the bed, and waited to see what would happen next. When her waters broke all over her pretty pink silk eiderdown, Bella immediately phoned her mother at Wells Cottage Hospital.

'Mummy, I might need a lift soon,' she said nervously.

She heard her mother suppress a little gasp of excitement. 'Hold on tight, darling, I'll be with you as soon as I can.'

Hand in hand, Bella and the Brig stood in the magnifi-cent marble hall, waiting for the ambulance. As they did, so the sky darkened and rain began to fall. Lightning zigzagged across the horizon and thunder rolled ominously overhead.

'Just my luck to go into labour in a thunderstorm,' Bella joked, then let out a loud cry as another contraction kicked in.

By the time the ambulance arrived, Bella's contractions were coming every ten minutes. Lady Caroline jumped out of the driver's seat and ran through the belting rain towards her daughter. 'All right, darling?' she asked.

Bella nodded and smiled bravely.

'Righty ho, let's get you into the ambulance,' her mother said, as she and the Brig helped Bella into the cab. As Lady Caroline started up the engine, she said cheerily, 'Shouldn't take long.'

She couldn't have been more wrong. Five minutes down the road, the ambulance dragged to a shuddering halt.

'Damnation! What on earth . . . ?'

When she jumped out of the cab, Lady Caroline discovered that one of the back tyres was as flat as a pancake.

'Oh, God!' she cried.

Hearing his mother-in-law's cry, the Brig joined her in the pouring rain and stared in disbelief at the jagged hole in the tyre.

'What're we going to do?'

Lady Caroline made a snap decision. 'You're going to have to walk to the Cottage Hospital for help, while I get Bella into the back of the ambulance and make her more comfortable.'

Giving Bella a quick kiss, the Brig ran off in the direction of Wells, with only flashes of lightning to guide him on his way.

'Darling, I think you'll be more comfortable lying down in the back,' said Lady Caroline calmly.

Oblivious to anything but the growing pain, Bella allowed her mother to guide her on to the stretcher bed in the back of the ambulance.

'Oh, that's better . . .' she sighed, as she eased her aching body down. 'Argh!' she cried. 'There's another one coming.'

Lady Caroline helped her daughter breathe through the pain of the contraction, then carefully counted the minutes till the next one. Four minutes! They were speeding up fast. As a mother, Lady Caroline began to panic, but then her recent experience helping in medical emergencies kicked in and she went into professional mode.

'You're doing well, darling. Take a few minutes to relax, and breathe normally till the next contraction starts.'

Though frightened by the speed things were going, Bella gazed into her mother's dark eyes and nodded.

'You can take care of me, Mummy,' she said trustingly.

Tears stung the back of Lady Caroline's eyes. 'I most certainly can, my darling!'

As the Brig flagged down a lift to the hospital in the torrential rain, Lady Caroline was anxiously preparing for Bella's delivery in her ambulance. From her training, she knew in theory what to do but, nevertheless, she had to keep steadying her nerves. This was her precious daughter and her grandchild! She had to take the greatest care of them both.

When Bella started to push, her loud cries drowned out the sound of an approaching ambulance siren. Leaving the driver in the cab, the Brig and a local midwife ran through the rain.

'This way!' the Brig cried urgently.

As the need to push engulfed Bella's body, the Brig and the midwife stepped into the ambulance. The experienced midwife swiftly assessed Bella's progress.

'You sit up top, alongside your wife,' she said quietly to the Brig.

As Bella gripped her husband's hand, the midwife and Lady Caroline exchanged a brief, knowing nod.

'I can see everything's under control our end,' the midwife said with a confident smile.

Urged on by her excited husband, Bella gave one last almighty push and, seconds, later Lady Caroline brought her grandchild into the world.

Flopping back exhausted on to the stretcher, Bella closed her eyes and wept with happiness.

'Well done! I couldn't have done better myself!' the

midwife said to a smiling Lady Caroline, who tenderly cleaned the baby, then, after wrapping it in a sheet and a warm blanket, she handed the mewling bundle to her daughter.

'A boy!' the Brig whispered, as he embraced his wife and baby tenderly. 'We have a son, darling.'

'A son . . .' murmured Bella, as she stroked her baby's soft, downy hair. She looked up and smiled at her mother, who was weeping with joy, and added, 'A grandson, Mummy. A boy!'

44. A New Generation

Two months later, on New Year's Day 1945, William Charles Walsingham Rydal, heir to the ancient Walsingham estate, was christened in the same chapel where his ancestors were laid to rest. The service was attended by William's proud parents, his adoring grandmother, even his Aunt Diana (who kept a safe distance from Ava), as well as Ruby and Rose, Kit and Maudie, Ava, Tom and Oliver, who was staying with his father for part of the Christmas holidays. Little Rose, who was crawling everywhere, stole the show. Cooing and gurgling all through the service, she latched on to Oliver, who proudly lifted the adorable little girl into his arms so she could watch baby William being blessed with oil and water.

'*Splash!*' chortled Rose, as the startled baby, dressed in his mother's silk-and-lace christening robe, cried in protest, before sinking back to sleep.

'Ollie will make a sweet big brother when we have our children,' Tom whispered to Ava, who blushed with pleasure. The thought of bearing Tom's children and bringing them up with Oliver made her stomach lurch with excitement. Squeezing his hand, she whispered back, 'I just can't wait!'

The christening party laughed and chatted as they walked back to the hall, Oliver helping Ruby to push a giggling Rose in her pram, and the Brig proudly pushing his baby son in Bella's old pram. Back at the hall, they sat down to a delicious lunch which only Bella and Peter could have put together. Rationing, by the end of 1944, five years into the war, was more stringent than ever before, so Bella had turned to Peter to solve the problem. In the middle of the shooting season, Peter was able to find several pheasants from local gamekeepers, and Bella casseroled them with root vegetables, carrots, swedes, parsnips and turnips, enriched with Oxo and Lea and Perrins sauce. At the end of the celebration meal, the Brig charged everybody to refill their glasses with the wine supplied by Lady Caroline.

'A toast to my beautiful son and my wonderful wife,' he said, with an emotional catch in his voice. 'My dearest wish for William is that he will grow up in a country at peace.'

'Cheers to that!' cried the guests.

'Here's to 1945,' the Brig continued. 'May it bring us all peace at last.'

'To 1945!' cheered the guests, as they toasted the new Walsingham son, who was sleeping peacefully, cradled in his mother's arms.

Epilogue: 8 May 1945, VE Day

As the Soviets and the Allies raced towards Berlin, the nation seemed to be holding its breath. On tenterhooks, everybody listened to the radio news bulletins, desperate to hear that the war was *finally* over, Bella and her trainee code girls upstairs, and Maudie, Ruby and Ava downstairs. Ruby was kept busy minding both babies, William when Bella was teaching and his doting grandmother was busy driving her hospital ambulance, and her own little Rose who, at fifteen months old, was now walking and gabbling non-stop.

'I can't keep up with her!' Ruby laughed, as, holding William in her arms, she chased after Rose, who had become fixated by the dead hares and the pigeons hanging upside down in the cold larder.

'She's got nerves of steel, just like her mum!' Ava chuckled, as Ruby tugged her reluctant daughter back into the kitchen, where Maudie diverted her attention with some tiny tarts filled with Walsingham cherry jam.

'Well, I suppose we'll keep on cooking right till the bitter end,' Maudie sighed, as she set a large panful of water on the Aga and started peeling potatoes and onions for the beginnings of a soup. 'Can you imagine the day dawning when we don't have to cook four meals a day for thirty people?'

'Can you imagine cooking without rationing?' Ava said dreamily. 'Butter, cheese, meat, fish, white bread, bananas!' She laughed out loud. 'One day, that surely has to come.' she said, with yearning in her voice.

On 30 April they heard on the radio the best news imaginable, the news they never thought would come.

'Bloody Hitler's committed suicide!' Ruby cried, as she came tearing into the kitchen with Rose, after virtually running the three miles from Burnham Thorpe.

'We heard it, too,' Ava laughed. 'The end's in sight, girls!'

Bella came rushing down the stairs. 'Have you heard the –'

Ava, Maudie and Ruby all chorused back. *'Hitler's dead!'*

Unable to contain their joy, the girls rushed towards each other and, grasping hands, spontaneously danced around in an excited circle.

'Me, too, dance, mama,' Rose gurgled, as she grabbed the hem of her mother's skirt and jumped up and down.

Ruby bent down and lifted her rosy-cheeked, pale-haired daughter into her arms.

'We can all dance a happy dance today, sweetheart.'

After the unconditional surrender of all German forces to the Allies, everybody knew it was just a question of hours until there would be an announcement. It came at one minute after midnight on Tuesday, 8 May – Victory in Europe was officially confirmed. Nobody could quite believe it: after six long, long years of poverty, rationing, hardship, heartache and grief, the war was finally over. Stunned into silence, the girls stared at each other.

'What will we do now?' Ruby asked.

'Go back to normal . . . whatever that is,' Ava answered, gazing fondly at the ring which, barely a month ago, Tom had slipped on to her finger at their wedding in Wells, with Oliver taking pride of place as her cheeky, giggling page-boy.

'We can never go back to what we were,' Maudie pointed

out. 'You won't be going back home to Lancashire, Ava, not now that you're married – and I won't be working in my parents' East End bakery. After all we've been through, I never want to parted from Kit again! Our lives have been radically changed by this long war – nothing will ever be the same again.'

'Maudie's right,' Bella said. 'None of us is the same girl who walked into Walsingham Hall four years ago.' She smiled as she recalled their first tumultuous days together. 'But, my God, I wouldn't change a thing,' she added passionately. 'Well, of course there *are* a few things I'd change,' she added, glancing anxiously at Ruby. 'We'd all want Raf back.'

Ruby blinked back tears and nodded. 'I'd do anything to have my Raf back, even if it was only for five minutes, just to see his face and feel him close one more time.'

As Ruby brushed away her tears, her friends clustered around to comfort her, but Rose, more and more the living image of her Polish father, got there first and clutched her mother's hand.

'Mama, Mama,' she said sweetly, bringing the smile back to her mother's face.

Ava fell silent and lit up a Woodbine. What would they do, the millions of women who'd formed Churchill's Secret Army? They couldn't just resume a life of drab domesticity, washing and cleaning, shopping and cooking, not after they'd been a vital part of the drive to destroy Hitler. They'd forged new lives of their own – how could that be simply reversed? The war had, without doubt, turned the world upside down. Surely the customs and traditions of society would be changed for ever?

Bella interrupted Ava's line of thought. 'One thing's for

sure – today we're going to have a celebration like we've never had before!'

And, with that, the girls leapt to their feet, grinning. Bella was quite right, they needed to celebrate, and they didn't have a minute to lose if they were going to top their usual standards!

After Churchill's speech to the nation at three o'clock, the whole country was in victorious mood. Children had been let off school to enjoy VE Day and, dressed up in red-white-and-blue paper hats and costumes, they ran wild through the streets, waving Union Jack flags. At Walsingham, estate workers laid out rows of tables, draped with Union Jacks and decorated with jam jars brimming with buttercups and bluebells. On the sweeping lawn women and children quite spontaneously started to dance to the music that was jangling out from a loudspeaker somebody had fixed up.

When the girls heard from Kit that virtually every man and woman at Holkham airbase planned to join in the Walsingham festivities, Bella panicked.

'Much as I want them here, I've no idea what we're going to feed them.'

As strains of 'It's a Long Way to Tipperary' played out of the loudspeaker Ava grinned. 'Leave it with me,' she said as she dashed up the kitchen stairs.

'What's madam up to now?' chuckled Ruby, who was making a mountain of pastry with the help of Rose, whose face was covered in blobs of flour.

Suddenly, from outside, Ava's voice rung out, loud and clear through the loudspeaker system.

'If we're going to have a peacetime party, we need all your help!' she announced. 'Empty your cupboards and larders, dig up your spuds and veg, bring everything you've got to the hall and we'll cook up a storm for England!'

Half an hour later, when the Brig arrived from London to join in the VE Day activities, he found his son sitting up in the Silver Cross pram, gurgling at Rose, who was singing nursery rhymes to him. His wife was in the kitchen with the other cooks, who were being assisted by Tom and Kit. The table was heaped high with contributions from all over the estate, and from the RAF base, too.

'My God!' laughed the Brig. 'What's on the menu?'

Bella flew to him and, after kissing him warmly on the lips, handed him a pinafore.

'Here you are, darling,' she laughed excitedly. 'We need all the help we can get!'

By early evening, the tables on the lawn were groaning with every imaginable pie: bacon and mushroom, corned beef and onion, cheese and leek, sausage and tomato, mince and potato, cheese and potato – and that was only the savoury ones! The fruit pies, made from bottled and tinned fruit scavenged from all over the estate, consisted of damson, greengage, blackcurrant, apple, blackberry and spicy pear. There were piles of hot baked potatoes, salads from back gardens and allotments, Maudie's warm bread, and pickles and chutneys, too. Booze was supplied by the airmen, who rolled up with beer, stout, whisky, gin, and chocolate for the over-excited children.

'No more gas masks! No more black-outs! No more *war*!' the ecstatic children chanted.

Later that evening, after King George's awkward, stuttering voice faded away across the Walsingham lawns, which were fragrant with the perfume of stocks, peonies and lilacs there was hardly a dry eye in the crowd. Everyone gave a rousing rendition of 'God Save Our King' and the party started in earnest. Food was eagerly consumed by nearly two hundred hungry people, toasts were made, then, as night fell and the first stars came out, oil lamps were lit around the improvised dance area, where Glenn Miller's 'In the Mood' played out from a gramaphone and the dancing got underway.

Kit drew Maudie into his arms and, removing her cook's pinafore with a quick flourish, he swept her on to the dance floor, where, to the strains of Vera Lynn's 'We'll Meet Again', they waltzed with all the other couples, locked in each other's arms. As the song faded, and was to be replaced by a loud Joe Loss and his Orchestra number, Kit whispered in Maudie's ear, 'I've got a surprise for you.'

Taking her by the hand, he led an intrigued Maudie across the lawn to his MG, and they drove at top speed to Holkham airbase. Maudie laughed in delight when she saw his bright-yellow Tiger Moth sitting on the virtually empty runway.

'I think I've guessed your surprise!' she said, as she reached up to kiss him.

This time, Maudie knew where to sit. She hopped into the front seat, while Kit, in the pilot's seat behind her, settled the earphones over her head.

'We're connected, just like last time,' he explained, as he adjusted his own set. 'Now we can chat during our flight.'

Shaking with nervous excitement, Maudie adjusted her flying goggles.

'Fly me to the moon!' she cried, pointing at the sickle moon hanging low in the night sky.

Kit gave the thumbs-up sign to the air mechanic standing on the runway.

'Chocks away!' he called, as the mechanic swung the propeller and Kit opened the throttle.

Maudie gasped as the plane started to taxi down the runway; its light wood-and-wire frame bounced and rattled as it gathered speed, then, as it approached the turnip fields, which on her virgin flight Maudie had been convinced they'd crash headlong into, the Tiger Moth lifted like a great bird and, with graceful beauty, she took to the wide open skies. As the night air rippled through her hair and cooled her face, Maudie laughed out loud with joy and wild exhilaration.

It wasn't like her last flight. This time, it was inky dark, and the moonlit sky was brighter than the dark earth below.

As they drifted gently, gathering height, they heard the unexpected sound of church bells ringing out. From King's Lynn to Cromer and beyond, church bells pealed out a paean of victory. Tears stung Maudie's eyes, as she listened to the triumphant sound that gathered momentum as they flew over the coastal towns. Then, to her amazement, one by one, fires were lit along the beaches: Cley, Blakeney, Wells, Holkham, Brancaster, Hunstanton, King's Lynn. As one fire flared up, another followed, until the beautiful north Norfolk coastline was a string of burning beacons blazing out, shedding light into darkness. For the first time in six years, the night sky was lit up.

'Look, Maudie,' Kit called. 'Fireworks!'

Way, way down below, red, orange and yellow rockets fizzled up, then shot in a blazing arc before tumbling back to earth. Like a child, Maudie, enchanted, gazed down in wonder. Then, suddenly, her stomach lurched.

'Shall we loop the loop?' Kit chuckled, as he banked the Tiger Moth into the sky. 'Ooooh!' Maudie squeaked, as, on a breathtaking nose-dive, they dropped sharply, before Kit took the plane curling back up again. At the top of the dizzying spiral, Kit literally took Maudie's breath away.

'Maudie, beautiful woman, love of my life,' he said through the earphones. 'Will you marry me?'

Before she could answer, they were falling through the sky, looping the loop in a descending cycle during which Maudie could only squeal, slightly hysterically, '*Yesssssss!*'

Laughing, Kit swooped the Tiger Moth gently over the shoreline, which was speckled with victory beacons.

'Will you love me for ever?' he asked softly.

'For all eternity,' she answered, as tears of happiness streamed down her blushing cheeks.

'To the stars and back?' he asked, as he started to bank the plane up again.

Maudie threw out her arms as if to embrace the moon and stars and all the glorious universe. 'To the stars and back, my darling!' she sang out. 'To the stars – and back!'

Acknowledgements

Maxine Hitchcock at Penguin, who kickstarted, *The Code Girls* when she floated the idea of a stately home being requisitioned for wartime purposes, which completely fired my imagination. Clare Bowron, my wonderful editor at Penguin, for working so hard – even in the school holidays! Jon Styles, my very own spy and a mine of information on code-breaking and Morse code – sorry I nearly drove you bonkers! My friend Susie Stevenson, who came up with a brilliant double-bluff plotline; Chris Burton in Cambridge for always putting me straight about Second World War train stations which are no more; Clare and Roger Morton for their expertise on flying a Tiger Moth; Dee and Ellie Johnson in Oldham for being the first on my Daisy Styles Facebook page; my oldest friend, Ed Wrigley, for buying the entire stock of my books from W. H. Smith in Manchester! My children – Tamsin, Gabriel and Isabella – God only knows what I'd do without you!' Thank you, Norfolk! For your beaches and pine woods, shrines and chapels, pubs and chip shops, castles and towers, marshes and wetland – all wonderful places to set my story. And finally, thank you to the thousands of heroic code girls who worked tirelessly, breaking enemy code throughout the Second World War. They kept their secrets to the grave.

Books and Sources

Winifred Sullivan's private library of Second World War reference books, which were given to me after her death by her brother, Lawrence.

Russell Miller, *Behind Enemy Lines*

R. Douglas Brown, *East Anglia 1943*

IWM Duxford/ Imperial War Museum

North Creak Airfield and Museum, Norfolk

BBC Second World War Archives

The History Place